*Charm, devastating good looks & wealth
– these gorgeous, passionate Latin men
surely have everything a girl could want?*

MEDITERRANEAN
Men & Marriage

Take a romantic trip this summer with
three heart-warming, emotional novels
from Raye Morgan, Carol Grace
and Donna Alward

MEDITERRANEAN
Men & Marriage

RAYE MORGAN

CAROL GRACE

DONNA ALWARD

M&B™ and M&B™ with the Rose Device
are trademarks of the publisher.
Harlequin Mills & Boon Limited, Eton House,
18-24 Paradise Road, Richmond, Surrey TW9 1SR

MEDITERRANEAN MEN & MARRIAGE
© Harlequin Enterprises II B.V./S.à.r.l. 2010

The Italian's Forgotten Baby © Helen Conrad 2009
The Sicilian's Bride © Carol Culver 2009
Hired: The Italian's Bride © Donna Alward 2009

ISBN: 978 0 263 87398 6

025-0610

Harlequin Mills & Boon policy is to use papers that are natural, renewable and recyclable products and made from wood grown in sustainable forests. The logging and manufacturing processes conform to the legal environmental regulations of the country of origin.

Printed and bound in Spain
by Litografia Rosés S.A., Barcelona

THE ITALIAN'S
FORGOTTEN BABY
Raye Morgan

Dear Reader,

Living on a South Pacific island is different. Those of you who do it know this very well. You live with lush trade winds, elegantly swaying palm trees in the silver moonlight, the thunder of surf on the reef, dancing sunlight glinting on the ocean in the distance. It's all the background music of your life. I know – I grew up on an island.

Of course there's also the feeling of isolation, the heat and humidity, the mildew, the bugs and the coconut crabs and the huge snails – but never mind all that. We'll leave that part out and concentrate on the romantic side of island living.

There's also a nice earthy innocence to island life. That's what Shayna Pierce finds when she comes to Ranai to escape the media firestorm lifestyle she's been living in New York. She finds what she's searching for among the down-to-earth islanders, but she also finds love when Marco DiSanto appears in her lagoon. Will his presence ruin the idyllic life she's made for herself? Or will she find her own voice and make a stand for her choices?

So, are you ready to take a little vacation? Hop aboard. We're heading for an island where anything can happen!

Regards!

Raye Morgan

CHAPTER ONE

MARCO DISANTO lowered his long, elegantly lean body into the rickety bamboo chair and rested one elbow casually on the little round sidewalk café table. The heavy heat was offset a bit by the afternoon trade winds. Still, it was a good bet he was the only man on the island crazy enough to be wearing an Italian business suit in this climate.

Was he here on business, or was this a search for lost love? Maybe it was time he made up his mind and acted accordingly. With his free hand, he pulled a crumpled photo out of his pocket and flattened it on the surface of the table. Bracing himself, he glanced at it again.

No matter how often he looked at the picture, the shock of seeing those mesmerizing blue eyes gazing back at him sent a quiver of excitement through him. Eyes like that didn't belong in real life. He was pretty sure they only existed on the covers of science fiction books or on fantasy movie posters.

But the ticket agent at the Ranai airport had recognized her right away when he'd shown him the photo.

"Oh sure. That's Shayna. You can probably find her at Kimo's Café. She works there off and on."

So here he was, wondering why nothing looked familiar. Out of the corner of his vision, his attention was caught by crisp white shorts encasing a firmly rounded female bottom and set off by long and lovely tanned legs. He didn't want to make eye contact—not yet—but he turned enough to see a bit more, including a loose, gauzy top that fell provocatively off one lovely shoulder, giving a teasing glimpse of full breasts. Waves of blond curls cascaded almost to her shoulders and framed a pretty face that was alive with laughter. He drew his breath in sharply, muttered something slightly obscene in Italian and looked down at the picture.

Yes, he had the right woman. But he'd never seen her before in his life. Not in the flesh, at any rate.

Who the hell could she be? The man at the airport had called her Shayna, so he supposed that must be her name. Other than that, he knew nothing about her.

He slid the picture into the pocket of his suit coat and sat back at the remote table on the patio of the fashionably shabby waterside café. He would wait. She would have to get to him eventually.

Funny that he couldn't remember her. Funny that he couldn't remember anything from the recent two weeks he'd spent here, on vacation in the Traechelle Islands. He'd tried. It just wouldn't come. Something about the accident—or maybe something about what had happened while he was here—had caused his brain to block it out. The psychiatrist who'd been assigned to him during his recovery had a name for this kind of thing: selective amnesia.

"It will probably begin coming back to you bit by bit," he'd said, frowning at Marco as though he were a specimen in an experiment. "Interesting case. I hope you'll keep me apprised as to your progress."

That was doubtful. If modern science had no answer for him, he would have to deal with this on his own. In the meantime, it was damn annoying. Those two weeks loomed like a black hole in his life. He found it very difficult to try to move on when he had this empty place that needed filling. He knew he'd come to this island resort, but he didn't know what he'd done while he was here—or whom he'd done it with.

An added problem—he was missing some very important designs he'd been working on. Had he left them here? He needed to know, and he needed to find them, quickly. And so he'd come back to see if he could reconstruct just exactly what had happened to his missing two weeks.

She came out of the café carrying a tray bristling with tropical drinks, all pastel colors and tiny exotic umbrellas. He watched as she set it down on a table crowded with tourists and began to pass the drinks out. Someone said something to her and she laughed, throwing her head back so that her thick blond curls caught the breeze and flew around her face. He could hear her laughter, hear her voice, though she was too far away for him to understand just what she was saying. He stared at her, hard, even pulling off his dark aviator's glasses for a moment to get a better look. Surely this should strike a chord with him if anything would.

But no. There was nothing.

He pulled the photo out again and looked at it. Yes, it was definitely the same woman. There she was, laughing the same way, and there he was, his arm around her shoulders in a manner that spoke of intimacy. One look said it loud and clear—at the time the picture had been taken, the two of them had been lovers. Just knowing that sent a hot current of interest through his pertinent regions. How could he have wiped his memory clean of something like that?

She picked up the empty tray, throwing a comment back to the table which made those around it erupt with laughter, and he braced himself for the moment her gaze would meet his. What would she do? Would she recognize him? Would she smile and come quickly toward him, reaching out for a hug, a kiss? Would she open up the floodgates to his lost two weeks?

But she turned to another table and began to take their order. He wasn't going to find out yet. He relaxed. He had another few moments to watch her.

And she was definitely good to look at. She moved with style and grace, and a certain languor that evoked sensuality. She seemed to belong to these islands, like a natural part of the landscape of paradise. Just watching her move made his male instincts sizzle.

But there was no recognition triggered. None at all.

He'd thought just coming back might remove the roadblocks and trigger his memories. So far, that hadn't happened. Once he'd found the picture, he'd been certain, that if he could find the woman again, that would do it. There was no getting around the fact that this woman was not the sort a man would easily forget.

He watched her weave her way among the tables in the outdoor café. She was coming closer. In another moment, she would see him. The moment of truth.

There was a smile on her lips as she turned. It froze as she caught sight of him. Those blue eyes were even more hypnotic in person, but right now they were filled with shock and then went cold as ice. Turning on her heel, she fled.

It took him another beat to realize she really was running from him. He hadn't expected that. Rising, he started after her, but a table full of young people had just begun to leave and they filled the aisle, talking and laughing back and forth and blocking his path. By the time he'd made it around the corner she'd taken, he'd lost her. He looked up and down the rutted street, but she was nowhere to be seen.

"Damn," he swore softly, frowning. Now what?

Shayna Pierce stopped herself short, gulping in air, and looked at her little Vespa. Her impulse had been to hop on and head for the hills. The only trouble was, there were no real hills—not that kind, anyway. What the heck was she doing? It was a small island. She couldn't hide from him if she tried.

She could always wait for dark and take her motor boat out into the ocean, heading for the even smaller island of

Coco where she'd been hanging out for the last month or so, just in case. But in the meantime, what was she going to do? Stay concealed in this dusty lean-to? Hardly.

She sighed, wheeling out her little Vespa. She was pretty sure he would be in the road, looking for her. She was surprised he hadn't followed her right into the shed. He knew where she parked it when she worked at Kimo's Café. Stopping, she took a deep breath before stepping out into the sunlight again.

Why was he back? Her emotions buzzed like a swarm of angry bees, making her dizzy. She had to admit just seeing him made her heart stutter and her stomach feel as if she'd just started off on a roller-coaster ride. What could you do when your feelings turned traitor like that?

Fight them. That was all that was left to do. But running wasn't going to change all that. She had to face him and have it out. There was no other way, now that he was here. With a soft groan of regret, she pushed the double doors open and wheeled her Vespa out into the road.

There he was, facing out of town, hand shading his eyes, looking in the wrong direction. She kick-started the engine on her scooter and he whipped around, staring at her. With as haughty a look as she could manage, she settled into the seat and drove forward, pulling up next to him.

"Hop on," she said. "We need to talk."

Pulling off his sunglasses, he looked directly into her eyes. He seemed to be searching for something he didn't find. There was no warmth in his gaze, no evidence of shared memories, of past intimacy. Her heart sank. He really did despise her now, didn't he? Probably had from the beginning. Well, in many ways, the feeling was mutual.

Oh, brother—whom was she trying to kid? Just looking at him made her heart thump like a bass drum and the rest of her innards go all warm and gooey inside. He was such a beautiful man with his Roman profile, his huge dark eyes shaded by eyelashes thicker than any male should be allowed to have. And then there was that long, gorgeous body and those wonderful hands….

No! She looked away. She had to stop before she fell off the Vespa in an old-fashioned fainting spell.

"Come on," she said impatiently. "We'll go to my place. We can talk there." She threw him a quick glare, just to keep her spirits up. "Unless you're too busy," she added, ready to be defensive if he gave her reason to be.

He didn't say a word. Instead, he swung his leg over the seat behind her, grabbed the edge for balance, and held on as she started off.

Her heart thumped hard and her mind was in chaos. She'd really thought she would never see him again, and now, here he was. There were a hundred reasons why she wished he hadn't come back. And there was one very clear reason why she was holding off a big, embarrassing swoon. She was crazy about him.

Or at least, she had been before she realized they had a connection she hadn't known about. An ugly, painful connection that made a relationship between the two of them impossible.

Still, here he was, and what had been between them, and what had destroyed that, had to be dealt with. They were both reasonable people. They had to come to terms with things.

She raced down the dirt road at full speed, the wind in her hair. She had a lot of questions. Was he going to answer any of them? First, she wanted to know if he'd ever really cared for her at all, but that was one she was never actually going to ask. All signs pointed toward a negative.

Then she wanted to know how much her father had paid him to come find her. And last—and the most puzzling one—why hadn't her father contacted her yet? She'd been so sure, once she realized Marco was working for her father, that someone would show up to drag her back to New York. That was why she'd gone to hide out on Coco Island for the last month.

But no one had appeared. There had been no word of anyone coming. So what had happened? Had Marco decided not to tell her father where she was after all? Had he had second thoughts? If so, his demeanor didn't show it.

Still, she was hoping, deep in her heart, that his return meant…. No, she wouldn't put it into words. She couldn't let herself get her hopes up. She wasn't that naive.

Pulling the scooter to a stop in the little clearing near her tiny house, she turned off the engine. Marco got off and she followed, looking at him, trying to be as cool as he was acting.

But then a funny thing happened. He stopped and scanned the area, as though he'd never been there before. That was odd. Ordinarily, he would be striding toward her house by now.

"Go on," she said, gesturing with a jerk of her head, but he turned to eye her warily.

"You go first," he said.

She frowned. There was something way off center about all this. Was he sick? Was something seriously wrong? Suddenly filled with a wave of worry and compassion, she stepped toward him.

"What is it, Marco?" she asked. "Is something the matter? Do you feel all right?"

The panes of his dark glasses flashed at her mockingly, as though he were sneering at what he perceived as her attempt to get closer. "I'm fine," he said shortly. "Let's go. You lead the way."

She hesitated. He sounded the same. He looked the same, except for that coldness she'd seen in his eyes. But something wasn't right. He didn't seem like the same person at all.

She remembered the first time she'd seen him, not two months ago. She'd just come back hot and tired from a hike along the far side of the island and she'd been going into her cabin when she heard the shout from out in the water. Shading her eyes, she'd seen someone struggling just inside the reef. Teenage lifeguard training kicked into gear and she dashed toward her little outboard motor-equipped dinghy.

Shayna to the rescue! She'd felt like a real contributing member of society—she was going to save a life.

Cranking on her motor, she'd raced out to where she'd

seen the man struggling. He was still thrashing around in the water. But it didn't take long to realize this wasn't quite a life-threatening situation. The water inside the reef was crystal clear and turquoise blue from a distance. But as she stopped the boat and stood up to survey the scene, she saw one tired man and an array of floating blue bubbles that spread out like a little navy fleet. The poor guy had got himself caught up in a mass attack of Portuguese men-of-war and he'd tried to fight back.

"Ouch," she'd said, wincing as she looked down and shaking her head as she noted the large red welts on his neck and shoulders—and even his face. "Didn't you see them coming?"

The look he cast was full of fury. He said something mean and menacing in Italian and she'd grinned. "It's not going to kill you unless you're allergic," she told him sensibly.

"*Certo*," he said back through gritted teeth. "I'll just wish I was dead, that's all."

She shrugged. "I know it's painful." She tried to hold back her grin, knowing any signs of amusement would infuriate him. And she couldn't really blame him. "Just remember, it's only temporary."

She shook her head, looking at him now. If only she'd known who he really was at the time. But would it have made a difference? She really didn't know.

She remembered how her gaze had hovered over what she could see of his beautifully molded body. As she recalled it now, he'd been wearing swim trunks, but the rest was out there for anyone to stare at, and it was worth the look. She'd felt her eyes sparkle with appreciation. Who didn't like a nicely formed male figure? Still, there were other concerns to consider.

"Come on into the boat," she'd told him. "I'll help you."

He was still splashing around in the water as though he felt it his manly duty to battle these little attackers and she lost patience.

"Look, do you want a ride in to shore or not? I've got things to do."

He didn't wait for another invitation. In seconds he was hauling himself up over the side of the boat.

"Water," he'd grunted, writhing and grimacing.

She knew he wasn't talking about being thirsty. Looking like a man on the edge, he'd pointed at her canteen but she reached for a cup.

"Not fresh water," she'd told him crisply. "Salt water will help wash off the tentacles better and it acts to sort of neutralize the sting."

He gave her the sort of skeptical look strong-willed men often used when they didn't think you knew what you were talking about, but he grudgingly submitted to the salt water she poured over his welts, wincing and biting his lip.

"I'm going to rub your skin," she'd said, trying to maintain a clinical facade. She knew she wasn't going to be able to ignore the fact that this man had a body created to make grown women weep with gratitude and she was going to have to let herself react to it eventually. He was trying to take care of the sea creature remnant stinging his skin, and she'd stopped him.

"You'll just get it all over your hands," she said, as he groaned at the pain.

She searched the bottom of the boat and found a rag that was relatively clean. Turning back toward him quickly, she began working on the gelatinous blobs that littered his back, pouring out salt water, then rubbing away the residue.

"How's that?" she asked after a quick scrub.

Turning, he gave her a look and then took the rag from her, working on his chest himself.

"Thanks," he said shortly. "I may not sound like it, but I really do appreciate this."

"You're welcome," she answered sweetly, then hid a smile as she watched him taking care of the last of the mess. Filling the cup with sea water again, she threw a splash over his shoulders, then another on his neck, and he gasped as the cool water hit his skin, then went back to work with the rag.

She watched him, bemused. He was certainly gorgeous. There didn't seem to be an ounce of anything extra on him. He looked fit and muscular, about thirty years old.

Just right for me, she'd thought at the time with a silent chuckle. Getting to know a man like this was exactly what she'd been trying to avoid, but she had to admit, she tossed that idea away with a sense of regret.

"I never want to go through that again," he'd said once he'd removed most of the tentacles. "I felt like something was yanking a thousand hairs out of my flesh, one by one. I've never felt anything that seemed so simple to be so damn painful." He frowned. "It was horrible," he said, as though he was afraid he hadn't convinced her.

"So I've heard," she said.

He turned to look at her, and as she thought of it now, she realized he'd really been seeing her for the first time. His head went back and his gaze skimmed over her, lingering on her bare, tanned legs. "You've never been stung?"

"Not me. I pay attention to what is going on around me." She knew she sounded smug, but she couldn't resist teasing him a little.

"I was just…" He stopped himself, obviously realizing he was beginning to sound defensive. He narrowed his eyes. "This is new territory for me. It won't happen again."

She'd smiled. She'd believed him then and she believed him now. He had the look of a man who didn't usually do much daydreaming on the job.

"They looked so pretty, like little blue balloons sailing toward me in the water. I didn't realize they were even alive until they began to sting."

She nodded wisely. "Many of the most beautiful plants and animals in paradise hide a deadly poison," she noted, talking more philosophy than biology.

To her surprise, he'd laughed. "Is that meant as a warning?" he asked her, and she laughed, too, realizing how it could be interpreted that way. She liked the cast of his dark eyes as they warmed with amusement. And she thought—maybe he wasn't such an aloof character, after all—once he wasn't in pain.

"Sit tight," she said, moving to position herself to use the outboard motor. "I'll take you back to shore."

She'd sensed him studying her again as they raced over the blue water. To her surprise, she found she rather liked it. She'd come to these islands almost a year before and in all that time, she had very carefully avoided inviting any male interest.

She wasn't here for romance. She was here for sanity. It was her intention to live modestly and attract very little notice from the locals. The tourists were a necessary nuisance, since she worked at Kimo's, but she'd managed to make herself friendly in a reserved sort of way that seemed to work. She'd only had a few incidents where she'd had trouble getting rid of an over-zealous male.

All in all, living here had worked out great. No one seemed to question her presence. No one had actually accused her of being in hiding. Maybe that was because so many of the drifters who had made their way here were just like her, avoiding life somewhere else. No one asked too many questions. She'd hoped he wasn't going to change that trend. She still had hopes along those lines, but if that were the case, why had he come back?

She glanced at what she could see of the skin along his neck. There was no lingering evidence of weeks before when the men-of-war had stung him so badly. She remembered how, on that day, she'd brought him in to shore and tied her dinghy up to the little pier she used. Her small house was a bit back from the water, but it was visible between the coconut palm trunks, its bright yellow exterior and the riotous red hibiscus bushes around it standing out from everything else along the beach.

"Are you staying at the hotel?" she'd asked him then, toying with the idea of offering him a ride back to town on her Vespa and then shrugging it aside. She didn't want to give him ideas, and anyway, she'd figured a nice long walk would be good for him.

"Is there really only one?" he'd asked, seeming to be amused by that thought.

"Hotel?" She nodded. "We're pretty remote," she noted. "We don't really get a lot of tourists. Most of the passers through are here for the fishing or for the seasonal yacht regattas."

"I see."

"So….which are you?"

"Which am I?" he'd repeated, as though wondering himself. "Neither, actually," he said cryptically. "I guess you could say I'm here for repairs. A little recuperation."

He'd had the tone of someone who didn't welcome too much delving into his affairs, so she'd let it drop.

And she knew now that had probably been her big mistake. She found out soon after that he'd only come to the island because he was looking for her. Well, he'd found her. And then he'd left without her.

And here he was, back again.

But that had all happened then, four weeks before. She looked at him sharply. This was now. Why was he back?

It had only been a few minutes since they'd arrived on the Vespa. He was still standing in the clearing, looking a bit lost, and all she was doing was remembering—thinking about the old Marco who had been here before. This new Marco seemed somewhat annoying in contrast and not half as appealing. But maybe the fact that she knew things about him now that she didn't know then had something to do with that.

If only she'd given him the third degree at that point on that day four weeks ago when she'd found him in the water, she might have saved herself a lot of trouble.

CHAPTER TWO

MARCO COULD TELL she was wondering what to do with him and maybe mulling over things from their shared past, so he waited, letting her stew. He needed some time himself. He was having trouble dealing with all this. A beautiful woman, a forgotten past—it all seemed so outlandish. He could certainly understand Shayna's appeal. He had no doubt his vacation on Ranai had been pretty spectacular, if she had been his companion in the way all evidence suggested. But that only made it even more crazy that he couldn't remember her.

And there was another thing. Why had she run from him?

That was the question he needed to hear answered. He'd seen the look of fear in her eyes. Her first reaction had been surprise, but fear had followed quickly, and she'd turned and dashed off as though…what? He'd never been known as a pushover where ladies were concerned, but he'd certainly never been a Blackbeard, either. What had she expected him to do? Whatever it was, she'd thought better of it soon enough, and decided to be reasonable.

But he couldn't rid himself of that nagging question. Why had she run? It had shocked him and shaken his confidence in a strange way he wasn't used to. Maybe this situational amnesia had more facets than he'd thought. Maybe his subconscious really wanted to shield him. Maybe there was something about himself he wasn't going to like finding out.

He would have been less surprised if she'd acted casually unconcerned about his existence, or if she'd walked up, gazed at him with no recognition at all and asked if he wanted a menu. But she hadn't done that. She'd taken one look, known him immediately, and turned and ran.

What had he done to her? He had a small shiver of unease deep inside. What could he possibly have done to bring on a reaction like that?

He looked at her and tried to read her thoughts by the look in those exceptional blue eyes. She was hesitating, expecting him to start for her house. And that presented a problem. He didn't know which house was hers. There were two little houses, one on either side of the clearing. He stood back, pretending to be polite, waiting for her to take the lead.

He'd planned to tell her right away about losing his memory. Now he wasn't so sure. He hesitated. As he stood in the clearing, island life seemed to blossom around him. The sound of the surf on the reef provided background music to parrots calling to each other in the trees and someone in a distant house singing a catchy island song. The heat was a physical presence, and the sunlight seemed to slant into his eyes. If he wasn't careful, the island magic was going to eat away at his sanity. And that made him think that it might be the wiser course of action to let things cruise for a while as he tried to figure out what upset Shayna. He might as well give it a bit of time to see what he could glean from her conversation before she knew the truth.

And if neither of them was going to make a move, at least he had to say something.

"How long have you lived here?" he asked without thinking.

She turned to stare at him. "What are you trying to do, stir up some small talk?" she asked tartly as he realized his mistake.

This was something a friend would know. He was going to have to take care not to sound like a stranger.

"Why not?" he responded lightly.

Why not, indeed.

She bristled, one hand on her hip. He was still looking around as if he didn't recognize the place. She would like to think that he was opening his eyes to what he'd lost when he'd destroyed their relationship. That he was re-evaluating some of his actions. Unfortunately, she couldn't quite buy it.

"We're a little beyond that, don't you think?" she muttered, shaking her head. "Come on," she added, starting off down her path at last. "Let's go inside. I'm dying for some iced tea."

"Sounds good to me," he agreed, following her. His gazed dropped to her cute bottom and he quickly looked away. Until he found out what the problem was between them, he wasn't going there.

Her house was tiny, set on stilts and surrounded by riotously flowering plants. It was exactly what a beautiful young woman who lived in the tropics should have for a house, he decided, but that was just what made him wary. It was all too perfect, too lush, too sensual—like a trap. Was that what had happened before? He'd probably fallen for her like a ton of bricks, right from the start. He was going to be more careful this time.

He followed her up the wooden steps and across the wide lanai, pulling off his dark glasses as he did so. Inside, she had an open floor plan tastefully decorated in pastels and rattan furniture. He glanced around the room but didn't see any sign of anything personal that would tell him anything. There was one framed photograph high on a shelf, but not much else, no mementoes of trips or triumphs. She didn't seem to reveal much easily.

She went into the little kitchenette and opened a small refrigerator, pulling out a pitcher of iced tea and reaching into a cupboard for two tall glasses. He took his gratefully and drank most of it down. It was a hot day.

"So," she said, leaning on the counter between them and gazing at him levelly, "you're back. I assume there's a reason?"

He leaned on the counter, too, just to keep things even. "I came back to find you."

Something flashed in her eyes. It wasn't particularly friendly, but there was a wary question behind the guardedness. She was angry and resentful about something, but she was ready to be coaxed back into friend-liness. If he could just figure out what that would take, he would do it.

"Well, here I am," she said, trying to be flip. "Though I didn't know I was missing."

Their gazes met and held. There was a hesitant question in her beautiful eyes, along with that touch of resentment. He frowned. This was a mystery he was going to have to get to the bottom of.

"Look, Shayna, I don't know why you're so angry with me," he said, putting his glass down on the counter. "I don't know what I did." And he leaned back a little, expecting a vigorous response.

And that was pretty much what he got.

"You don't know?" She stared at him as though flab-bergasted. "Marco Smith—" She stopped. "Oops, I forgot. It's really Marco DiSanto, isn't it?" Her start-lingly blue eyes were glaring at him now. "What are you doing, having memory lapses now? Don't know what you did! Please."

Whatever his mistake had been, she didn't like it. That much was evident. He watched her anger, wishing he knew how to quench it.

"But I guess you *are* forgetting things," she said crisply, waving a hand at him. "Look, you've only been gone a few weeks and already you've forgotten how we live in the tropics." She shook her head. "Don't you feel overdressed in that suit?"

"I had a meeting with a client in Singapore just before I caught the plane out here," he explained, looking down.

She shrugged.

"At least get rid of that suit coat."

"I'd like to," he admitted, shrugging out of it. "With your kind permission," he added, exaggerating his manners.

She hesitated and he could tell she had the impulse to come around the counter and take it from him in order to hang it up somewhere. But she was reminding herself that she was angry and an angry woman didn't do things like that for the object of her anger. So she stayed put, but it was obviously an effort.

"Just hang it on the back of that stool," she muttered, and her cheeks reddened a bit.

Marco's instincts were right on the money. Shayna was a mass of conflicting emotions right now and that made life more uncomfortable than she was used to. She watched him take care of his jacket and loosen the knot in his tie. He tugged open the top three buttons on his silky white shirt, unbuttoned his cuffs, and shoved one sleeve up to his elbow. She was fascinated as he began a transformation. With each adjustment, he seemed to lose a bit of his reserve. He was sloughing away a more formal civilization and sinking into island life and, for some crazy reason, that made her heart beat faster.

"Stop it!" she said aloud before she realized what she was doing.

"What?" he said, looking up in surprise, the second sleeve only beginning to be pushed up.

"N...nothing," she said quickly, flushing. "I wasn't

talking to you, I was just…" Her voice trailed off. There was no way to explain.

But she could take this as a warning. She was still vulnerable to his charms and she had to beware.

All she had to do was remember how easily she'd fallen under his spell a few weeks ago. He'd looked very different that first day. There had been no business suit then. In fact, there had been very little covering his beautiful body after she'd rescued him from the little blue men-of-war.

Once back on the shore, she'd gone against her better instincts and invited him in for iced tea that day, too.

"My name is Shayna Pierce," she'd said once they'd settled at this same counter that day.

There was just the slightest hesitation before he'd answered. She should have paid more attention to that.

"Marco," he said at last. "Marco Smith."

She'd gaped at him. He was so obviously Italian, from his dashing dark looks to his very sexy accent. The name seemed like a fake from the start.

"Smith! Are you serious?"

"Yes."

His dark eyes had gazed at her levelly, just a touch of humor in their cloudy recesses.

"You doubt me?"

She'd flushed. Doubt him? Not at all. Here in the islands, everyone was entitled to whatever name they wanted to use. Who was she to judge him? Her own name was as phony as…well, as a three-dollar bill. She'd made it up and now that she was used to it, she found that the name she was hiding under suited her much better than her old name. "No, of course not."

But he'd been so gorgeous that day. As she remembered it, after a few minutes of sipping and conversation, she'd found her gaze straying to his muscular chest once too often.

"Where exactly did you leave your clothes?" she'd asked him a bit fretfully.

He was feeling much better by that time. The red welts had mostly melted away.

"What do I need with clothes?" he'd responded, half-teasing. "Isn't this the tropics? I thought you all walked around like children in the Garden of Eden."

She'd laughed, teasing right back. "Even Adam was embarrassed when he realized Eve was looking at him cross-eyed."

"I don't embarrass that easily," he said, and at the same moment, his gaze caught hers and held and she felt a rush of sensual excitement in a way she'd never experienced before. There was a knowing glint in his eyes, which told her he had thoughts of exploring things between them, things that would come too close to intimacy. Things she couldn't allow. She didn't think she'd ever read the signals in a man's eyes quite so clearly as she did at that moment. She'd been uncharacteristically tongue-tied for a good twenty seconds.

He'd broken the spell by smiling and speaking casually, as though none of that had happened at all.

"As for my clothes, they are back on the beach somewhere. Closer to town. The water was so clear and the fish were so beautiful, I guess I got caught up in the moment and swam pretty far from where I started."

She'd sighed, looking at him and biting her lip. It was one thing to pal around with a half-naked man on the beach. Somehow it seemed very different here in her home. It had made her uncomfortable.

He'd noticed. "I'd ask to borrow one of your shirts, but I have a feeling that would be a tight squeeze," he said lightly.

"I'll find you something," she'd said, jumping up and then afraid she'd sounded a bit too eager. "Uh, I'll be right back."

She took her time, rummaging through her closet shelves and waiting for her cheeks to cool down. And then she remembered the Hawaiian shirts a previous tenant had left and pulled them out, choosing a bright yellow one with a red parrot on the front.

"Here you go," she said as she came out into the living room again, expecting to find him still at the counter. But he wasn't there. Instead, he was across the room where he had obviously been studying the things on her display shelves. As she came into the room he'd turned and stared at her, a completely new look on his face.

"Didn't you say your name was Shayna Pierce?" he'd asked, at the same time studying her closely.

She remembered blinking and feeling a tiny thread of alarm slithering down her spine. What had he seen on her display shelves?

"That's right."

He'd frowned, staring at her face. "Are you sure?"

She gave him a sideways glance of annoyance. "Last time I looked," she said tartly.

He shook his head and gazed at her narrowly. "There's something familiar about you," he'd said softly.

Her mouth had gone dry but she rolled her eyes and said, "Oh, I hope not."

"Why would you say that?"

She'd searched his eyes. He was smiling again and she felt a sense of relief. Whatever he'd thought he saw, he'd already forgotten about it.

"No reason." She smiled back a bit warily. "It's just that we like our privacy out here in the islands. It's pretty much a 'don't ask, don't tell' situation. You're playing with fire if you delve too much into others' lives." She shrugged. "You have your life and I have mine. We tend to let sleeping dogs lie."

He'd given a snort of amusement. "You're just an encyclopedia of useful sayings," he noted, teasing her again. "I'm sure I'll be improving my English if I'm around you long enough."

She'd laughed and teased him back, but his recent reaction stayed with her for a while. She certainly had her reasons for avoiding his curiosity. There was nothing she was prepared to share with him. As she remembered it now, she'd shaken his question away at the time and held the shirt out for him and he slipped into it, leaving the buttons undone so that the shirt hung open. There was still a lot of gorgeous flesh on display, but it was a big improvement, and she'd thought that she could relax a little.

What a fool she'd been. Relax! She'd invited a viper into her life, a spy into her home, and she was thinking she could relax.

At the time, she'd been somewhat concerned that he might recognize her face, but she'd thought that wasn't very likely. Only a year before, her face had dominated the tabloids, but she'd taken steps to make herself look very different from that girl who'd been considered a media sensation. Her hair had been shorter, straighter, redder, and she'd faced the world with a permanent pout.

Attitude, they called it. Spoiled selfish brat behavior, she called it now. To the tabloid-reading public, she'd been considered a "bad girl" who always went right to the edge of trouble, but didn't quite slip over that cliff. Few had understood how tempting that fall would have been to her. Anything to save her from the life she'd been leading.

She'd been born Summer Hudson, daughter of Glendenning Hudson, one of the richest real estate moguls in Manhattan—a man who partied with film stars and raced yachts for recreation—always firmly in front of the cameras. As a child, her birthday parties had been covered on the evening news, her first ride on a pony documented, her first prom night celebrated. She'd grown up in the public eye.

She knew most people would choke with laughter if she told them it wasn't easy being rich and famous. But the truth was, it wasn't. Living life on a constant high of attention was exciting at times, but it quickly became a numbing sort of hell. That public ordeal might have been tolerable if only her private life had given her the support she needed—the support anyone needed. But her father's insatiable appetite for publicity and acclaim left her with no safe haven.

In fact, she sometimes thought it had driven her a little insane. She did things, said things, ended up with people, who were obviously all wrong for her. Life was a mad, speeding carousel with clown faces coming at her out of the dark, and as it began to turn faster and faster, she knew she had to jump off or it would destroy her.

She'd tried often enough, and each time, her father had found a way to pull her back into the spotlight. Finally, she'd escaped secretly and on her own, using a lawyer friend as her only contact to let people know she was okay, and she'd made her way, with a new identity, to this most remote of tropical islands.

When she'd first arrived she had been exhausted and heartbroken, as damaged as a broken butterfly. She'd thought she would stay for six months or so, heal herself, take a deep breath and go back into the fray a stronger contender.

But it had been so different living here—being a real person, not a media creation; living by her own rules instead of serving as the center of other people's emotional attachments and needs. Being able to understand that people were dealing with her as a normal person, not as some kind of sick icon.

She'd grown. She'd expanded. She felt as though her heart were bigger now. Her life was bigger. She knew what real joy was. And most important, she knew she would never voluntarily go back.

No, she hadn't been concerned about him recognizing her, and that was just as well, since it seemed he'd already figured out who she was long before. It might have been nice if he'd let her in on that little secret that first day. Then she might have avoided the opportunity to fall for someone so wrong.

But she had fallen. And then she'd found out who he really was, why he really was there, and her heart had broken in two. Seemingly heedless, he'd left the island. She'd tried to get over him. She'd been stern with herself and attempted a quick recovery. And now she'd realized he'd left her with more than memories. Her world had tilted on its axis. That changed everything. And yet....

Well, now he was back. What next?

As she pulled herself back to the present, she found him leaning forward and looking at her with a strange, intense light in his lush dark eyes. She had the feeling he was looking for something in her he just wasn't finding and he was losing patience with the search.

"Would you like something to eat?" she asked as a quick distraction.

"I'm not hungry," he said, and it was lucky. Just the passing thought of food made her queasy at the moment. The last thing she wanted to do was let him see her current condition. That was something she was going to keep from him at all costs.

"Tell me, Shayna," he said abruptly, "what is it that you want from me?"

She drew back, surprised. His tone was just…unacceptable. That was the word. Who the heck did he think he was, anyway? She stared at him, sending daggers his way. He was, after all, the one who had come back. She hadn't asked him to.

"Oh, I don't know," she said, a bit of sarcasm showing. "An apology would be nice."

One dark eyebrow rose and he looked a little startled. "An apology for what?"

Her eyes flashed. "Well, that's the crux of the matter isn't it? If you don't feel there's anything to apologize for, forget it."

She knew as the words left her mouth that she was falling into the usual female trap of expecting a man to understand how his actions had affected her. You had to explain these things to them. Saying "forget it" just gave them an out to do exactly that. She bit her lip. Was he going to try, at least?

He started to say something, then changed his mind, as though he was reining in what he'd really like to tell her. She waited, simmering. Of all the arrogant men in the world, she had to choose this one.

But she still reacted to him. When she thought of his kiss, her body warmed with memories. Looking at him now, she could hardly believe it hadn't been a dream. He seemed cold and somewhat angry. At first she had thought he appeared very much the same, but she'd been wrong. He was like a different person. She put a hand over her mouth, holding back that queasy feeling again, a feeling that was beginning to be a regular around here. Closing her eyes, she swayed, waiting for it to ease. There was no denying the signs. It was only waiting to be confirmed by the doctor.

Finally, he shook his head and gave a short laugh. "Okay, Shayna, here's the deal. You know who I am, don't you?" He said it, as though that still surprised him.

"Of course I know who you are." She frowned, beginning to find this conversation eerily convoluted. But that didn't mean she wasn't up for the challenge in his tone. She leaned toward him. "In fact, I know both of who you are."

His wide mouth was like a slash against his handsome face and it turned up at the corners.

"Both, huh? Are you referring to my well-known split personality?"

He sounded as if he was teasing, but he had to know what she was talking about.

"Is that your alibi?" she tossed back.

He blinked, and then his eyes narrowed. "Do I need one?"

"You tell me. You're the one with two names." She winced. There she went again, talking before thinking. After all, she had two names herself, and he knew it very well.

But, strangely, he didn't seem to have caught her very obvious mistake. Instead, he just looked puzzled.

"This is fascinating," he said lightly. "Why don't you give me a full explanation. What are my two names?"

"Well, first there's Marco Smith, the man I got to know for two weeks."

His dark eyes looked bewildered by that name. "Smith?" he repeated, giving it an Italian accent that made it seem all the more phony.

She sniffed, assuming he was just covering his tracks.

"And then there's Marco DiSanto, the man I only met that last day, before he bid me a careless adieu and flew off into the clouds, never to be seen again."

"That doesn't make any sense," he told her, shaking his head and frowning. "And anyway, I'm here, aren't I? Marco DiSanto, in the flesh."

She cocked her head to the side, pretending to consider the dilemma.

"Where do you want to go with this? Shall we discuss which one I liked better?" She shrugged. "That's easy. I liked the liar, of course. He was funny and sexy and great to be with."

His puzzlement was growing, but she'd gone too far to stop now.

"But you see, that's the paradox. He was the lie. Bye-bye Marco Smith." She pretended to wave a fond farewell toward the doorway. "Marco DiSanto, on the other hand, was not very nice to me. He told the truth, but it was a truth I didn't want to hear."

She stared into his eyes, looking for any tiny sign of regret he might be willing to bestow. Just a hint. It might have made her feel better.

For just a moment, she remembered how he used to laugh with her, his white teeth flashing against his tan skin. She would give almost anything to see that laughter now, that warmth. Instead, she saw amusement, but she couldn't tell if he was smiling with her or against her. He had a sense of reserve in his face as he looked at her. She wanted passion and he was giving her polite appreciation instead. A little passion, a bit of memory, would have cancelled out a lot of her resentment.

But instead, he asked her a question she wasn't expecting.

"Do you always tell the truth, Shayna?"

That startled her. She turned away. He knew the answer to that. He knew she'd lied to him about who she was for two weeks, just like she lied to everyone. She supposed it was only fair that he bring it up, since she'd brought up his lies. But still…

He went on, speaking softly.

"Truth can be a slippery thing. You know what they say. One man's truth is another man's fairy tale."

She sighed. It seemed he did want to make her suffer. Well, she could give as good as she got. She gave him a direct look.

"Telling stories did seem to be a talent of yours when you were here before," she noted.

He barely acknowledged her dig, waving it away as though he had larger things on his mind.

"Okay, here's some truth for you, Shayna." He paused, took a deep breath, and let it out. "I don't know you."

Her head whipped around and she stared at him. For a few seconds, she went back over his words in her head. Had she really heard what she'd thought she heard?

"What are you talking about?"

He met her gaze firmly. "I don't have any idea who you are. I feel like I've never seen you before in my life."

For a second or two, she felt sick. The room seemed to sway. She closed her eyes and steadied herself, then looked him in the eye again, searching hard. The man she'd spent all that time with just a few weeks ago had to be in there somewhere, but she couldn't find any sign of him at the moment.

"Is this some kind of game, Marco?"

"No. It's not." He shook his head, holding her gaze. "I'm serious as a midnight clock."

She pulled her arms in close around her. It was a steamy tropical day, but she was shivering. Something in his words, something in his attitude, had chilled her to the core.

"I do not know who you are. I can't remember a thing."

CHAPTER THREE

"I KNOW THIS IS HARD to believe," Marco said, running a hand distractedly through his thick dark hair. "I can hardly accept it myself."

Shayna drew her breath in softly, then let it out again. "Accept what, exactly?" she asked, surprised that her voice wasn't trembling. "Please explain."

He stared at her for a long moment, then laughed shortly. "You see, that's the problem. How can I explain what I can't remember?"

"Marco…"

"Okay, I'll try." He grimaced. "When I left here, on my way back to Rome, I must have taken a regular flight, since that's all that comes through here. But somewhere along the way, I transferred to a small plane, a commuter flight, and we went down in the Mediterranean off Sicily."

She gasped. "Oh, Marco!"

"The pilot and another passenger were killed, but somehow I was rescued. I woke up in a hospital in Napoli. I couldn't even remember who I was, much less where I'd been."

She had to hold herself back. Every instinct cried out to go to him, to touch him, to convey her feelings as best she could. Despite everything, she cared about him more than she'd ever cared for any other man. Whatever it was she felt for him was pretty darn close to love. You couldn't just throw that away at will. It tended to linger.

"Were you hurt? Are you all right?"

He looked at her and managed a slight smile. "I'm fine, Shayna. Physically. And over a few days, most of my memory came back."

She nodded slowly, feeling very much at sea. These were circumstances she'd never dealt with before. It was hard to imagine how this could be true.

"But not all."

"No, not all. I seem to have totally lost those two weeks I spent here on Ranai. I can't remember a thing about them."

She shook her head, trying to wrap her mind around this weirdness. And at the same time she had to decide whether or not she believed him. Could this really be true? Was there any reason he might want her to think this in order to gain some sort of advantage—though she couldn't say what that might be. Just the thought of that made her feel a bit guilty. After all, didn't she trust him?

Hell, no! The man had lied to her from the beginning. Marco Smith indeed.

She didn't say it aloud, but her eyes flashed and she wondered if he realized this whole story was a bit hard to swallow. Memory loss. Amnesia. She'd never known anyone to have it before. Why him? Why now? What did he want?

"How odd," she said softly.

"Yes. Odd and awkward."

Her brow furrowed as she purposely tried to harden her heart toward him. She had to stay objective if she had any hope of finding out the truth. There were certain questions that came up about this. Her eyes narrowed as she studied his face. Time to see if he had answers.

"If you couldn't remember anything about those weeks, how did you know where you'd been?" she asked.

He didn't seem surprised that she had questions. "I had a copy of my plane tickets, and records of my reservations at home in my office."

"In Naples?"

He nodded. "Yes. That is where I live most of the year."

She nodded. That seemed reasonable enough.

"Do you know why you came?"

He hesitated. "I was probably looking for a vacation of sorts. A getaway. A place to work in peace on…some ideas and problems I had."

Hah. That wasn't the half of it. But maybe he didn't remember that part. It hadn't been until that last day that she'd even known he was a world-famous racing yacht designer—and worked with her father. Glendenning Hudson loved competitive sailing and had the money to hire the best. Marco DiSanto was his designer, his ace in the hole when he competed in some of the biggest offshore races. And Marco had very carefully kept all that from her for those two weeks and probably wouldn't have told her at all if she hadn't walked in on him in his hotel room and seen the evidence with her own eyes.

"Why did you come here in the first place?" she challenged. "To Ranai, I mean."

He frowned, shaking his head. "Damned if I know," he muttered. "That's part of the mystery."

"Uh-huh." Okay, she could either buy that he didn't remember or she could suspect him of all kinds of nefarious things. It was up to her. Which way was she going to bend?

And finally, the *pièce de résistance*.

"So tell me this," she began slowly and carefully. "If you don't remember anything about your time here, how is it that you knew to come and find me?"

A slow smile began to spread over his handsome face. He knew what she was doing and it obviously amused him. Reaching into his pocket, he pulled out a crumpled photograph and flattened it on the surface of the counter before her.

"When they recovered my luggage from the wreck, I searched it as soon as I could get to it. I was looking for souvenirs, mementoes, pictures, anything to jog my memory." His dark eyes sparkled as he smiled at her. "And this was all I found."

She stared down at the image of pure joy the photo had captured. Her heart beat faster. She remembered that day. Kimo had taken the picture. It was the day before Marco left, the day she had decided she just might be in love. The day before she'd realized that Marco was not who he pretended to be.

"So you came to find out who this overly friendly female might be," she managed to say lightly.

"The clerk at the airport pointed me in the right direction and gave me your name." He shrugged with Mediterranean charm. "And you know the rest."

She could hardly stand to look at her face in the picture—or his, either. She had been so happy. She'd been so sure....

Rising from the bar stool, she walked across the room and went out onto the lanai, folding her arms across her chest and staring out at the ocean in the distance. She wanted to go for a swim. A long, cleansing swim. The water looked cool and clear and refreshing.

He'd come up beside her and was looking out at the horizon, as well.

He hesitated, then said, "I'm sorry."

She looked at him quickly. "Sorry? But surely you didn't do this on purpose. It's not your fault."

He shrugged. "The result is the same." He grimaced, obviously loath to go on. But he seemed to think it was necessary.

"You see, to you, I'm a man you think you know well. Very well." He winced slightly and glanced at her, then away again. "To me, you're a stranger."

She stared at him. Yes, she did see. And what she saw was about as disturbing as it could get. If what he was telling her was true, he didn't feel any ties to her at all. No passion. No friendship. No memories of the good times they created together. No memory of that one enchanted night they spent together. For him, all that never happened.

If a tree fell in an empty forest and there was no one to hear it, did it make a sound? Was it real? If she was the only one with the memories, would they fade away, like old photographs left out in the sun? Had they ever really happened? Or would they become misty dreams that only she knew anything about?

Despite her shock and her surprise, she very quickly understood a number of things about this situation. First, any feelings he might have had for her didn't exist. All her dreams were in ashes. There was hardly any point in going on with this.

Second, she now realized he had never gone back and told her father where she was because he didn't remember that he was supposed to do that. Right now, he didn't even seem to remember who she was. And that was why her father hadn't shown up yet. He still didn't know she was here.

That was the good, she supposed. But it hardly compensated for all the rest.

"So in the end, you came back here," she said softly. "Why?"

He thought for a moment before he responded. "To recreate a personal narrative," he responded carefully. "I need to find the pieces of the puzzle and put them into the picture so that I can feel whole and go on with my life."

"Oh." So it was all about him, was it? But she really couldn't criticize him for that. After all, how could he care about people he didn't remember he knew?

"And there's one more thing," he said, looking around the room as though he'd lost something. "I was working on some plans. New designs. They weren't in my luggage when it was recovered. I was hoping to find someone who might know what I did with them."

"Plans?" She looked at him expectantly. She hadn't seen any evidence of him working on any plans until the last day when she'd gone to his hotel room. That was when she'd first seen the large, detailed papers, spread out all over the floor. And that was when she'd seen the logo for her father's company on one of them and realized Marco was not who he was pretending to be. "What sort of plans?"

She held her breath, waiting to see if he would tell the truth this time, but he didn't hesitate.

"Shipbuilding blueprints. And some experimental designs. Some ideas I was working on."

"Designs?" she asked, as if she had no idea what he was talking about.

"I design open class monohulls. Racing yachts."

"Ah." Yes, she knew that now. "Are they important? Something you can't replicate easily?"

He gave a short laugh. "Something I probably can't replicate at all. It's very important I find out what happened to them."

Shayna had a sad epiphany. She'd found the answer to one of her main questions. His plans—that was why he'd come back. It had nothing to do with her. She should be happy about that. He was a liar and a sneak, and she didn't want any part of him.

No, Marco hadn't come back to find her. Maybe he had come back to fill in the blanks in his memory—if there really were any. But that was also beside the point. What he'd really come back for were his plans.

"Is it very important to find them?" she asked.

He gave her the most candid look he'd allowed so far. "It's the only important thing," he said firmly. "It's my legacy, my life."

At least he was honest about it, but unease churned inside her as she considered the facts. The plans were all that mattered to him. As far as he was concerned, she didn't exist except as a means of finding his precious plans. She sighed. It was almost a relief to know the truth. This way, there was no question. She had to push him out of her life and she had to do it right away. He'd already done enough damage.

"I'm sorry, Marco," she said shortly, turning away. "I don't know anything about your plans."

He frowned, watching her progress back into the house, then followed her inside and studied her face. "But if we spent a lot of time together…"

She looked up. "I'm sorry. I'm afraid I can't really help you." She met his gaze with a cool determination. He wasn't going to manipulate her. "We spent some time together. We had some laughs. But that was about it. You didn't exactly let me into your life in any meaningful way."

As she said the words, she realized, with a sinking heart, how close to true they had to be.

He picked the photo up off the counter. "This picture gives a different impression. I'd say more than a few laughs were sparking between these two people." His gaze held hers. "You and me."

She didn't let him see her involuntary wince. "Photography tells lies."

"Not this one."

"How could you know that? You don't remember anything. Isn't that right?" She looked at it. "This picture is fiction, pure and simple."

He frowned, not accepting her judgment at all. "But we did spend time together."

She drew in a sharp breath. "Yes."

"And you have some idea of what I did while I was here, where I went, whom I saw."

She hesitated. If she wasn't careful, he was going to draw her in again. "Well, I noticed a bit, here and there," she said, sounding rather defensive but not sure how to avoid that. "I wasn't exactly following your every move, you know."

"But you could help me map out a sense of what I did and where I did it."

No, she could not. She had to nip this idea in the bud. "Are you serious? I'm a waitress. I was working at Kimo's during that time. You came in for breakfast every day. We said hello."

He stared deep into her eyes for a moment, then turned away, groaning. "Shayna, don't try to snow me with this 'I was too busy to pay any attention to you' nonsense."

"What do you mean?" She coughed nervously, then tried again. "We had a laugh or two together. We went on a couple of jaunts around the island. And that's about it." She shook her head emphatically, her hair slapping her on the cheek. "I can't help you."

He stared at her. "Then who can?"

She avoided his gaze. "I really don't know." She made a show of glancing at her watch. "Sorry, but I'm going to have to cut this short. I've got some things I need to do. I'll get you a ride back to the hotel."

"Shayna…"

She looked up at him and attempted candor—or at least the appearance of it. "I can't help you," she said again.

He held the picture up, not saying a word.

She flushed. "We weren't that close," she insisted. "Nothing happened."

His eyes narrowed and his mouth tightened. "That's not really true. Something happened."

"What are you talking about?"

He stared into her eyes for a moment longer, then shrugged and turned away. "I guess I'll ask around at the hotel," he said. "Maybe someone there knows something."

"Good idea." She could hardly wait to get him out of her house. A flash of color from outside caught her eye and she saw a couple of neighbors passing by. "Oh, there's Jilly," she said, moving quickly back onto the lanai. "Hi there," she called out.

A young girl of about fourteen turned and waved. "Hi, Aunty Shayna," she said, her short dark curls bobbing about a pretty, tomboyish face. She had the mixed-race look of someone with the strains of almost every continent and culture creating the young, coltish beauty of her appearance. Walking with her was her constant shadow, Kali, a boy of about twelve who lived nearby.

"Jilly, do you remember Marco?" She gestured toward the man as he came out to stand beside her.

"Howdy, Mr. Smith." Jilly gave him a grin and a sort of salute. "You're back. Great. Wait until I tell Eddie."

"Who's Eddie?" Marco asked out of the side of his mouth.

"Her little brother," she responded softly. "He took a special liking to you when you were here before."

Marco gave her a skeptical look. "Really? I usually don't get along with little kids all that well."

She gave him a tight smile. "I know," she said, then more loudly, to the young girl, "Do you and Kali have time to give Mr. Smith a ride back to the hotel? You can take my dinghy."

"Yahoo!" Jilly celebrated with a whoop. "I will be so careful, Aunty Shayna, honest I will."

Shayna had to laugh at her enthusiasm. Jilly was as expert a boat handler as anyone else on the island. Her father had taught her well before he'd disappeared on a fishing trip. Now he was gone and there was no boat for Jilly, so she cherished every chance she got to take out Shayna's dinghy.

"Okay. Just as long as you two stay inside the reef and bring it right back and don't go joyriding with your friends."

Jilly's face became very serious. "I no longer have any friends. I've given all that up. Those kids in town are just too childish for me."

Shayna stifled the laugh that threatened to reveal

how seriously she took that statement. "Good. That's fine, then."

"Okay. I'm good with boats, Mr. Smith," Jilly professed earnestly. "I'll keep you dry. Honest."

Shayna laughed softly, then turned to Marco while the two youngsters ran down to the pier to prepare for shipping out.

"Mr. Smith?" he asked her questioningly.

"You might as well face it. Even if you don't remember doing it, you told everyone your name was Smith. That's how they know you."

"Smith," he muttered disparagingly. "Not very creative."

He went back in to grab his suit coat, then paused on his way down to the shore to catch his ride to the hotel.

"We're not done, Shayna," he said, his gaze traveling over her face in a way that seemed to be seeing things she didn't really want to reveal. "I don't give up so easily."

She started to turn away and he reached out, fingers curling around her upper arm, and pulled her back to face him. "You haven't even begun to tell me all you know about this," he said softly.

She gazed back with a touch of defiance in her eyes.

Looking down into her face, he hesitated. Why not? Why not kiss her? He wanted to. Evidence suggested that they had the background for it, even if he couldn't remember. But no, he couldn't make a move like that until he found out just what had torn them apart at the end of his stay. And until he saw a little less of that fierce resistance in her eyes. So instead, he gave her a crooked smile.

"I'll be back," he said.

Then he was on his way down to the pier where Jilly and Kali were waiting with the dinghy. Shayna watched him go, rubbing her arm where he'd touched her, feeling a little shaken. She saw the hardness in him, the power that would let him sweep away all her inhibitions and take over if she wasn't careful. That was what made him so dangerous. That was why she needed him off the island as quickly as possible.

But now that he was giving her a bit of space, she allowed herself to enjoy the look of him, just a little bit. He moved with an easy athletic grace and she felt a catch in her breathing. If only things hadn't gotten so complicated. If only…

Shayna was busy until evening, cleaning up and then working on a new set of kitchen window curtains out of some dyed burlap material she'd picked up at the island's one general store. She welcomed Jilly back when she returned the dinghy, then tried to get her mind back on the curtains, but her thoughts wouldn't stay away from what had happened that afternoon.

And what had happened was all about Marco. He was here and he wasn't going away any time soon. It was all very well to decide to ignore him, but if he really had come back to find his missing plans, he wasn't leaving until he knew where they were. If he really didn't remember anything about his visit, he wasn't going to have a clue as to where to look. He couldn't remember what he'd done or where he'd been. If he really was telling the truth. Which she doubted at times.

How could he have forgotten? The memories were so vivid in her mind. But the brain was a weird and scary place—and it contained all sorts of things its owner knew nothing about.

"Ugh." She made a face. This was getting a bit thick, wasn't it? Better to stick to the world she saw before her eyes. At least there, she knew what she was doing.

She fixed herself a simple meal of cheese toast and a green salad, and then found herself staring down into it, unable to eat a bite. She kept wondering what he was doing. Was he still at the hotel? Had he found someone else to talk to? He was determined to find his missing design plans. She thought for a moment, trying to remember what she could about them and how they'd looked that morning, all spread over the hotel room floor.

She'd seen her father's company logo on a few of them—and the name Marco DiSanto right next to it From then on, she'd been on a white-hot tear, unable to process any other information. Once she'd realized who he really was she'd been sure she knew why he was here. Her father had sent him, of course—sent him to find his daughter and drag her back to New York. And hadn't that been what he'd been trying to do by urging her to come back with him? She'd almost fallen for it.

That last night had been magic, all star-filled and moonlit. They had toasted the time they'd had together with sparkling wine, regretting that he was to leave in the morning, and when he began to whisper in her ear about going with him, she'd really been tempted. Her heart had cracked painfully as she'd tried to explain to him why that was impossible. He didn't want to listen, and they had parted just this side of angry with each other for the first time. That was why she had gone to his hotel room so early the next morning, eager to make peace. And instead, the pretend world she'd been living in had broken wide open and she'd come face-to-face with reality.

Did she love him? Maybe. But it hardly mattered. There was no hope, and she knew it only too well. Besides, he wasn't the man she'd fallen for. That was all a great big hoax.

And now she was committed to getting him out of here as quickly as possible, and if that meant helping him find those plans, she'd better get with it. She would have to be proactive.

As long as he really didn't remember anything about his stay here, if she helped him find his plans, he'd go back where he came from and she'd be home free. The only complicating factor was the little hitchhiker she'd acquired along the way. She sighed and flattened her hands over her stomach. There was nothing showing yet, but she knew the truth, even though she hadn't seen a doctor. The fact that she was probably pregnant wasn't quite real to her yet. She hadn't thought through all the implications. She was planning to do exactly that—just as soon as she got Marco out of her hair and on an airplane for Italy. Or a slow boat to China. Whichever came first.

So she'd better get prepared. And what did that mean? A shower, of course. Washing her hair. Putting on something pretty and trekking on over to his hotel to tell him she'd changed her mind. Heaving a big, long sigh, she squared her shoulders and got on with it.

A bit over an hour later, she was on her way. First, she stopped in at Kimo's Café to apologize for having run off earlier. He waved her regrets away. The large Hawaiian was so laid back, nothing ever seemed to bother him much.

"No worries," he told her. "Lunch was about done by then anyway. We didn't have any trouble taking up the slack."

She gratefully kissed his cheek and promised to be in early for the breakfast crowd in the morning, then slipped off to cross the road and made her way to the Ranai Hotel. Climbing the wide steps to the entry, she hesitated at the double doors. Was she really ready to do this?

"Get a grip, Shayna," her inner strength said firmly. "If you don't guide your own destiny, someone else will do it for you."

She nodded. Her inner strength had the answer, as usual.

"Okay," she said aloud and she reached out to swing open the door. "Here I go."

CHAPTER FOUR

MARCO SAT IN THE HOTEL BAR at a beautiful old mahogany table overlooking a wide veranda. He was nursing a whiskey and brooding over the stunning sunset that was spreading its orange and gold effects over the peaceful ocean. The place itself had strongly nostalgic vibes. It gave off the sense of a time fifty years past when men really could get lost and start their lives over in the South Seas.

He wasn't having a lot of luck in igniting his own memories. He'd looked through the old-fashioned hotel register for past entries and, sure enough, there was the name Marco Smith, clear as day. What had he been thinking? The counter attendant didn't know anything about it. When he'd asked him, all he'd gotten in return was a smile and a shrug.

He'd had a bit more luck with the waiter here in the bar. A young, rakish sort, he looked like a college kid making a little money with a summer job in the tropics.

"Do you remember me?" he'd asked him curiously.

"Sure. I remember you. You were here a few weeks

ago. You asked me some stuff about sailing conditions around here."

"Sounds about right," Marco murmured softly. Then his gaze sharpened. "Did I hang around here a lot? In the bar, I mean."

"You don't remember?" He grinned. "Dude, why would you? You were mostly heading out for picnics with Shayna. That's the way I remember it. And the rest of us were feeling a little envious, I must admit. She usually doesn't fraternize, if you know what I mean."

He knew exactly what the young man meant, but that wasn't the point. It was more confirmation that he really had been here, and that he had been with Shayna a lot of the time. No matter how she tried to shade it now, he knew she could help him if she wanted to. But the waiter was treating it like a joke and he knew he wasn't going to get anything else relevant out of him.

No one took anything very seriously here on the island, and everyone took everything very slowly. He supposed it had something to do with the humidity and the heat, but it was going to drive him mad in short order if he didn't learn to ignore it.

He liked things to happen fast. He needed to find his plans and he needed to find them now. Looking down, he saw that his fingers had tightened on his glass until the knuckles were white. Carefully, deliberately, he made them relax.

And then he thought about Shayna. It had been a long time since he'd felt this sort of tug toward a woman. Over the past few years, he'd thrown all his passion into designing, into making racing yachts as beautiful and as fast as possible. And it had paid off for him. He was at the top of his game. Or at least he had been before the accident. And in his world, competition was everything. If you weren't at the top, you were falling behind someone else. He was determined not to let that happen to him.

Women usually didn't come into the picture. They only complicated things. As soon as they got your attention, they wanted to dominate it, and suddenly there was no room for anything but them. He'd been there. He wasn't going there again. Life was too short.

But Shayna…

Not only was she a beautiful young woman, there was something strangely compelling about her. It was difficult to know how to treat her. He wasn't sure what sort of relationship they'd had. He didn't know what they'd done together, what sort of interplay they had worked out between them—what they'd decided, what they'd left for later, what they'd agreed to leave out completely. It was very odd having this chunk of his life missing. It was hard to go on without knowing where those two weeks had left him. The worst was knowing what to say to Shayna. He felt as if he were walking on quicksand there.

One thing was sure, as far as his relationship with her was concerned. He was going to have to find out what the fight on the last day of his stay had been about— just exactly what she thought he should apologize for. And she was probably the only one who could tell him.

A sense of movement made him glance up into the long mirror over the bottle-filled counter, and there she was, coming down the steps behind him into the bar area. He sat watching her with pleasure as she hesitated, looked around the room, caught sight of him and started his way. She had her hair swept up in an old-fashioned do from the World War II era. She looked stunning in a halter dress accented by a lacy throw balanced artfully at her shoulders and a wide skirt that danced around her knees as she walked. And those legs! There was no getting around it—the woman was a knockout. He could feel a slow grin starting as he met her gaze in the mirror and he had no intention of dousing it. She was playing right into his current sentimental fantasy.

She stopped right behind him, placed one hand on her hip and struck a pose as he kept watching in the mirror.

"Of all the wine spritzer bars in all the South Pacific," she said while he turned slowly to face her, "why did you have to turn up in mine?"

He looked up and smiled, then swallowed quickly and tried to go into Humphrey Bogart mode to fit in with her scenario, putting on a world-weary attitude.

"I make it a habit to turn up in all the worst places."

She shrugged one shoulder, looking down at him in what she obviously hoped was a sassy 1940s' manner and flipped her hair back flirtatiously. "What's a girl have to do to get a drink around here?"

He shrugged. "You could try a whistle." A devilish light was gleaming from his dark eyes. "You know how to whistle, don't you?"

Her own eyes flashed and he wasn't sure at first if it was from annoyance or amusement.

"Spare me the mercy lessons," she said, sinking into the chair across from him. Now he could see that her eyes were sparkling with laughter, but she was doing an admirable job of keeping a straight face. "And get me a Shirley Temple, will ya?"

"For a classy dame like you? Anything." He signaled the waiter.

"Anything?" she responded with a quick smile. "Wow. If I'd known it would be this easy, I'd have tried this years ago."

"It's never too late," he said smoothly.

Their gazes met and they both grinned, and suddenly there was a bond between them that hadn't been there before. She glanced at his mouth, remembered how sweet and silky his kiss had been, and felt herself flushing. Just thinking of it made her ache with a dusky longing that she knew she had to suppress as quickly as possible.

"So you've decided to come clean, have you?" he said, not noticing her discomfort. "I have to admire your courage."

"Admire away, big boy," she said tartly. "I deserve it."

"You most certainly do," he agreed.

She laughed softly, abandoning the playacting at last. "Don't you sometimes wish you'd lived in the first half of the last century?" she said. "They seemed to have so much more heart in those days."

"It only looks that way from a distance," he responded cynically. "They had the same problems then that we do now."

The waiter appeared to take their order.

"Hey, Shayna," he whispered, giving her the eye as he presented himself. "Lookin' good, girl."

"Thanks, Bobby," she said casually.

Marco narrowly avoided rolling his eyes before ordering her a soft drink and himself another whiskey. His natural male flare for competition kicked in without delay.

"An admirer of yours?" he asked once Bobby had withdrawn.

Shayna looked up, surprised. "Not really. He's just a kid."

"Have you ever dated him?" he asked, watching her reaction.

She gave him a look he might have considered scathing under other circumstances. "I don't date any-one," she said coolly.

But Marco knew she'd time to spend with *him* when he was here before; at least, that was the picture he got from what others told him. A strong sense of possession rose in him. He fought it back. Where in hell had he got the idea that she was supposed to be his?

An image formed in his head. A memory? Soft skin that smelled of orange blossoms, a pristine sculptured hairline, a whisper that lingered, his lips on the long curve of a neck, a warm hand sliding inside his shirt. Just as quickly as it came to him, it faded again, but it left behind a tingle of excitement. He drew in a sharp breath and steadied himself. He had to avoid this sort of thing. He was here to find his plans, not to reignite what he assumed must have been a romance.

"I take it you've decided to help me after all?" he noted, looking at her.

"I've decided to try," she said. "I figure two heads are better than one."

He nodded. "Thanks. I really appreciate it."

She smiled, glancing at him and then away again. If he knew her motivation for changing her mind, would he still appreciate it? Maybe not. But that didn't really matter. She was only here to make sure he left the island as soon as possible—and before he remembered who she was or why he'd been here in the first place.

"Okay Mr. Marco Smith," she said with a quick smirk. "What do we do first?"

"The first thing I want you to do," Marco said, gazing at her levelly, "is to tell me who you really are."

Shayna looked up, her eyes wide and startled. "Wh-what do you mean?" she asked quickly.

Her overreaction surprised him and made him wonder, for just a moment, what she was expecting. But he went on and very soon forgot about it.

"I've been sitting here enjoying the sunset and musing over this strange situation."

Bobby brought the drinks and she reached for hers as though it were a lifeline.

"What strange situation?" she murmured, wishing he would change the subject.

"*Your* strange situation."

"Oh." She took a sip of her drink put it down again, back in control. "Why don't you explain what you mean?" she asked him, using a steady look to cover up her unease.

He sat back and studied her from under lowered lashes. "I want to know why a woman like you would be here on her own in these islands, so far from the hope of finding…oh, say a high-end department store or a five-star restaurant. It occurred to me that it just doesn't make any sense." He raised one dark eyebrow cynically. "What's the story, Shayna?"

Funny, but he'd never asked her that question before. But then, he'd known who she was then—and probably guessed why she was here. He hadn't felt the need to probe for information. Far be it from her to help him out with his personal questions. She met his gaze steadily and answered with calm deliberation.

"Here in the islands it's okay to ask a question like that. Some people are happy to tell you all about their background. But if someone doesn't respond, well, right away, you leave them alone. You don't push."

His face changed as he realized she was challenging him. "You're telling me to back off."

She blinked at him calmly. "Exactly."

He set his jaw. "I don't want to."

They stared at each other for a long moment, gazes locked. She knew she couldn't do this for long. Her own feelings were going to show.

Breaking away from his hard dark eyes, she made an elaborate show of sighing. "I can understand that you might feel that way, Marco. However, I came here to talk about you and your missing plans. My unusual choices in life aren't under consideration at the moment. Let's just leave me out of it."

He stared at her for a few more beats before he shrugged. "As you wish," he said, but his gaze sharpened as he looked at her and she could tell that her avoidance only increased his interest.

"Okay," she countered. "Here's what I want to know from you." She leaned forward. "What's so special about these design plans? Why can't you just re-create what you did before?"

He half laughed, scoffing at the question. "If I can't remember what I did, how can I re-create anything?"

She threw out her hands. "But if you can't remember that, how do you know you produced something of genius in the first place?"

He stared at her for a moment, said something rude in Italian, then gave an extravagant shrug. "I just know."

She shook her head, as though despairing of him, and his face lost some of its hardness as he smiled at her. "And anyway, if I could remember what was on those plans, I wouldn't need them so badly, now would I?"

"You are maddening," she pronounced, taking a long sip of her drink and giving him a mock glare over the rim of the glass. "But then, they do say genius is a form of insanity, don't they?"

He shook his head as though she were a trial, but a cute one. "All right, Shayna, I'll try to explain to you. I've been designing sailing ships all my life. It *is* my life.

But I've only been getting major international recognition over the last few years."

She nodded. "I'm sure you deserve it," she murmured.

"I do," he said boldly. "I've made some important innovations. The people I work for are very rich and they don't throw their money away on useless developments. They want to win races. They hire me to help them do that."

"I understand."

"But I'm not the only one. There are a hundred designers who would like to take my place. Many of them work night and day, trying to beat me to the punch on new ideas, trying to win. You understand?"

"Of course."

"And some even cheat."

She waved a hand in the air. "That goes without saying."

He nodded. "Lately there is a man who is following closely in my footsteps. Salvo Ricktorre is very good, and he's always just one step behind me." He made a very Italian gesture with his hands. "I can feel his breath on my neck. He seems to come up with ideas very similar to mine very soon after I have them. I've developed the habit of keeping my sketches and blueprints in very secure places, just to be sure he isn't seeing them."

She nodded approvingly. "That sounds like a wise thing to do."

"Yes. So when my plans go missing, I can't help but wonder if he has something to do with it."

That garnered a small frown, but she still said, "Understandable."

He sat back and looked pleased that she concurred. "Of course."

She nodded slowly. He was leaving something out. Should she bring it up? Should she mention her father? It might be a good way to smoke him out—if he was giving her a snow job. And if he was on the level—well, that would be obvious, wouldn't it?

She bit her lip nervously. It was a risk. If he was on the level, and he really had forgotten everything from those two weeks, bringing up her father's name and then looking him straight in the eye might just jog his memory in ways she wasn't going to be happy with. Still she almost felt it had to be done. Taking in a deep breath, she prepared to do it.

"Who are you working for right now?" she asked, her heart in her throat as she said the words.

"Right now?" He hesitated, then shrugged and went on. "My most important client is a man named Glendenning Hudson. You may have heard of him."

She nodded. Her mouth was so dry, she wasn't sure if she could form words. She forced herself to meet his gaze and then she waited, wondering. Would he remember now?

"He's crazy, of course," Marco went on blandly. "Most of these superwealthy people are. But they want the best and if you don't give it to them, they go to someone who will."

She nodded again. She certainly agreed that he was "crazy." That was the whole point.

"Glendenning Hudson," she said slowly, turning her

head but watching him out of the corner of her eye. "Didn't...didn't he have a daughter?"

She turned back to face him, her heart beating so hard she was sure he must hear it. It took all her strength to keep from letting him hear how rapid her breathing was now.

He frowned, as though trying to remember. "I think so. Some little party girl who's the apple of his eye, as I remember. One of those rich girls who grow up too fast and crash and burn too early."

"Just one of many, huh?" she said a bit breathlessly. "Not particularly memorable."

"No." He made a face and shook his head. "I think I saw her once. Someone pointed her out at a restaurant. But I can't recall anything much about her, actually."

"Not your type?"

"My type?" He laughed as though it were not even worth considering. "Not at all. I'm not a teenager anymore. I have other things on my mind."

Despite everything, that stung.

"So only immature boys would be interested in a girl like..." She paused for a moment, then forced herself to say the name she used to use. "Summer Hudson."

She searched his eyes quickly, but there was nothing to indicate that he had any idea what she was talking about.

"No," he said casually, leaning back and stretching. "Girls like that spend too much time in rehab to be interesting," he added.

His words cut into her soul, leaving scars, and she knew that was crazy. What was the matter with her? Of course he despised Summer Hudson. *She* despised that girl she used to be. She didn't want to be her anymore. That was exactly why she was here. But it still hurt to know that he didn't think any more of her than that— that he hadn't had some magic epiphany when he'd seen her, hadn't been able to see past the nonsense down to the worthy core.

But then, no one else had, either. It was a good thing she'd escaped all that and come here. At least she had a chance of being a decent person. As long as she stayed.

"Anyway, to get back to my missing plans, you do understand why it is important that I find them?"

She raised her gaze to meet his and she nodded. "Yes. What I don't understand is exactly what is missing and where they might be." She challenged him brightly. "And why you are so sure they even exist."

"Oh, they exist, all right. I couldn't possibly have gone two weeks without working on something."

She shrugged. "Then where are they?"

"Good question. That's what I'm asking you."

"I haven't got a clue. I wouldn't even know for sure what I'm looking for." She hesitated, knowing there was no hope in dissuading him from this search, but thinking it was worth a meager try at the very least.

"I think you ought to go back home and look in your recovered luggage again. After all, if they are gone, how do you really prove they were ever there if you can't remember what you did?"

He shook his head, frowning at her. "This is beginning to sound like a fractured version of 'Who's on first?' Just listen for a moment. Don't talk."

Ah, yes, she had to admit, this sounded like the Marco Smith she'd known and loved. All that Italian brashness and arrogance came out in flashes now and then, and this was one of them. Lucky she had a sense of humor, she decided, and then she pretended to zip her lips together and looked at him mockingly while she folded her hands in her lap.

He gave her a fretful look, then went on. "When I'm working, I'm always jotting down specifications, looking for new combinations, figuring the math, checking the statistics on temperatures, wind, tides and so on. And I'm always sketching. Then, when my ideas begin to gel, I draft out more formal blueprints. And as I work, I constantly make copies of everything I do. In the end, I'll always have two sets of plans."

He looked at her and she nodded helpfully, her lips still zipped. He rolled his eyes and went on.

"I usually carry the originals with me in a portfolio and mail the copies to myself in a cardboard mailing tube. Just in case. This time, I ended up without either copy." He looked at her expectantly and she smiled, her lips still pressed together.

"Shayna, speak," he ordered impatiently. "I didn't mean it. I only wanted you to give me a chance to explain."

"Ahhh," she said, as though she'd just been released from holding her breath. "Thank you." She couldn't resist a grin.

"Okay, here's all I know. I only went up to your room in the hotel once, and that was on the morning of the day you were to leave. And when I walked into your room, I saw the floor covered with blueprints and other design papers."

He nodded, narrowing his eyes. "Yes, that is how I usually organize them, and put them in order, especially if there are a lot of them. I was obviously preparing for the trip." He frowned. "And you never saw me working on any of them before that?"

She paused to think. Was it going to be giving anything away to tell him the truth? Wouldn't he begin to wonder why he had kept this from her? But there was no way to hide what actually happened. "No. I'd never seen any of them before."

"I never talked to you about them?"

"No." She thought back for a moment. "You were obviously interested in yachts and sailing, but you never told me why."

He shook his head. "Strange. I can't imagine why not."

Because you didn't want me to realize who you were, she could have told him, but she held her tongue.

"What was the room like? How did it seem to you?"

She closed her eyes, trying to remember what the room had looked like. She had walked in, full of anticipation. She was going to tell Marco that she would find a way to go with him. He'd been sitting at the small hotel room desk, working on something, and he'd looked up at her and grimaced. He knew what was coming next—just as soon as she looked down and saw the logo of her father's company on many of the papers. She knew in an instant that this was a major betrayal— that Marco was not who he had pretended to be, that he was not really the person she'd fallen in love with. The pain of that realization still tortured her. You didn't forget a moment like that easily.

Opening her eyes again, she looked at the man who had engineered that dishonesty. "It was just a normal room," she told him crisply. "There were papers all over the floor. That's all I know."

She began to gather her things together. He watched, puzzled. There it was again, that moment in the hotel room. Something had happened, something that had ruined their relationship. Why didn't she just come out with it and stop wasting time?

He grabbed her wrist, fingers circling it, to get her full attention.

"Shayna, tell me what happened that day."

She glanced at him and then away. "Nothing happened," she said shortly, pulling away from his touch. "It's getting late. I'm going to have to go."

He rose. "I'll see you back to the house."

"No need. I've got my Vespa." She threw him the briefest of smiles. "I do this all the time. The island is safe. You don't have to worry about me."

Her lacy wrap fell down onto the chair as she rose and he picked it up, reaching out to put it back around her shoulders. As he did so, his hands lingered on her upper arms. Her bare skin felt smooth and firm and fabulous, and for a long moment, he couldn't pull his hands away.

And then she turned and looked at him and he winced, realizing he was reacting to her like a lover, not a new acquaintance. And that made him wonder—just how close had they been? He knew what the photograph he carried with him presented. He knew what his instincts told him. But she hadn't said a word. And she was avoiding the issue, even now.

"Tell you what," she said, pointedly moving away from him. "I've got to work the breakfast shift tomorrow. If you can be ready at about ten-thirty, we'll go hunting for your plans."

That sounded promising. "Where do you propose to go?"

She eyed him coolly. "Everywhere you went when you were here before. We can retrace your steps and check it all out. You'll touch base at every point of the past you've forgotten." She shrugged. "At least, every point I know about. I'll give you a chronological tour in one day."

"That would be terrific."

"I'll be at Kimo's Café in the morning," she said over her shoulder as she walked toward the door. "Meet me there at ten. I'll help you retrace your steps from your visit. Who knows? Maybe we'll figure out what happened to your plans."

He wanted to thank her. He thought he should say something. But she didn't give him a chance. She sailed down the wide staircase and out into the parking lot before he realized what she was doing, and by the time he reached her, she'd started the Vespa and was backing out of the parking space. With a cheery wave, she was off, and all he could do was stand there and watch her go.

CHAPTER FIVE

MARCO SAT drinking black coffee and trying to stop staring at Shayna as she made her rounds of the tables, smiling and laughing with the customers. Today she was dressed in a brightly colored pareau, a Tahitian wrap skirt and a matching halter top, leaving a beautiful expanse of silky bare skin between the two. As he watched her, he had a twinge of unease. She was always lovely to look at, but today there was the hint of something more. Hadn't he seen her somewhere before?

Well, of course, there was yesterday, and then there was the time his mind had stolen from him. Those were givens. But something else, something older and longer ago teased at him. He wished he could think of what it was. But even more, he wished he could get back his two missing weeks.

Maybe if his brain were clearer. He'd had a horrible night, tossing and turning, and it had nothing to do with drinking too much. Dreams had slithered in and out of his sleep and then he'd woken and tried to capture the fleeting images his dreams had left him with. He had a feeling the dreams were built out of those missing memories, and if he just woke up in time, he could pin the facts to the wall and then he would be able to unravel the truth.

Pulling out his sketchbook, he tried to concentrate on what he did best, dig into problems of sailing design. But as he put pencil to paper, he realized his doodling was turning out to be a woman's face instead of the hull of a sailing craft. He stared at it. He hadn't done any figure drawing since his days at university, but here he was, making a pretty decent stab at getting Shayna right.

She came toward him with a coffeepot and he quickly flipped the page on the sketchbook. There was no point in being blatant about the fact that she fascinated him.

"Have you had any sudden revelations this morning?" she asked as she freshened his coffee.

He had a hard time focusing on her words. Something about that beautiful expanse of tan and creamy skin, revealing a neat little belly button and a lovely curving waistline made him feel like a stammering schoolboy. He couldn't seem to rip his gaze away from her midriff. So near and yet so far. He had a sudden fantasy of his lips against that gorgeous flesh, his tongue exploring that belly button, and he had a hard time keeping down the groan of pleasure that threatened to come out of his chest.

Wow. He hadn't realized he could be caught out like that at his age.

"What?" he said vaguely, forcing himself to look up at her eyes but completely unable to remember what she'd asked him.

She frowned disapprovingly. "Revelations," she repeated. "New ideas. Light bulbs going off over your head."

"Huh?" he said, then began to regain control. "Oh. You mean about where the plans might be?" He took a quick, cleansing breath. "Not yet. How about you?"

"Me?" She looked startled. "What do you expect from me?"

"Memory. You still have yours."

She frowned. "Yours has got to be in there somewhere. Try harder."

He shrugged. "I have tried harder. And I've done relaxation therapy. And I've gone to hypnotists. You can't get blood from a stone." Shaking his head, he swore softly. "My Roman ancestors conquered the world, you would think I could conquer this one stupid thing."

His frustration was mirrored in his dark eyes and she regretted being impatient with him. After all, he was the one who actually wanted his memory to come back—as far as she was concerned, it could stay lost.

"That's very true," she said more sympathetically. "But you are hardly a stone." She smiled at him. "Don't worry. It's bound to come back to you eventually. Patience is a virtue."

"And I am nothing if not virtuous," he said wryly.

That made her smile. She couldn't resist a quick, admiring glance at how he looked today. He wore chinos, deck shoes and a pale blue polo shirt that molded itself to the muscles of his upper body like cling wrap. It was all good. Too good.

She'd spent most of the late evening making phone calls. From the station chief at the airport to the manager of the hotel, she'd contacted anyone she could think of who might have an idea where the plans had gone. She'd even come in to work early to search the back rooms here in the café, just in case he'd stopped in for a snack before heading to his flight back on that fateful day. Perhaps he had left the portfolio at his table and someone had stuck it in a cupboard somewhere and forgotten about it. So she'd searched, but so far, no luck. Maybe their trip today would bear fruit, though she didn't have a lot of hope. Somehow she had a feeling that anything left behind two weeks before would have shown up by now.

Biting her lip and shaking her head, she turned away. "Hang in there. I've got two more tables and then I'll be ready to go."

He watched her head for a table full of young couples and he flipped back to the portrait he'd been drawing. He stared at it for a long moment. What was it about this woman that kept tangling with his emotions? His mouth twisted and he ripped the page out of the book, crumpled it in his hand, and aimed at a nearby trash can. It was a decent attempt, but it had missed all her special magic, and he wasn't going to accept anything less.

A half hour later, she finished up and they headed for the shed where she kept her Vespa. She kick-started it and he climbed on behind, but this time his hands didn't go to the edge railing to hold on. With no hesitation, his large hands clamped down on either side of her waist, practically spanning the distance and holding her completely in his control.

She felt as though she'd just taken a sudden drop off the edge of a tall cliff, and it took a second or two to get her equilibrium back. Then she turned to look at him. He looked right back at her, not smiling, almost daring her to complain. She stared at him for a moment and then gave a small, almost imperceptible shrug.

"So I guess you don't feel like such a stranger anymore, is that it?" she noted dryly.

A slow smile tilted the corners of his wide mouth. "Just drive," he said.

Shayna drove, but she took note of Marco's move toward a new level of intimacy. They were going to have to get this task done quickly. It was obvious he was beginning to feel he could take over for the old Marco, in more ways than one. That just couldn't be allowed to happen. She was highly susceptible to male influence. She knew that. It was the reason she was here, as far from her father as she could get. Did she have to stay away from Marco, too?

Maybe so.

They swung by her house so that she could change, and there was Jilly waiting on the front stairs, a small boy of about three in her arms.

"Hi Auntie Shayna," she called out as they left the Vespa and started for the house. "I brought Eddie over. He really wants to see Mr. Smith."

Marco recoiled for a moment, glanced at Shayna, then at the children.

Jilly looked up at him, so young and bright-eyed and innocent. He almost grunted aloud, but stopped himself in time.

"Marco," he reminded her carefully. "The name is Marco."

She blinked like a young owl. "Okay, Mr. Marco," she said. "Here's Eddie."

She released the little boy and Marco stared down at him. His thumb was planted firmly in his mouth, but the huge, almond-shaped eyes were filled with some sort of earnest hope that took him by surprise. Marco almost took a step backward. No one should depend on him this much.

"Hi, Eddie," he said, putting on a slightly forced smile.

Eddie didn't say a word. Never taking his eyes off Marco's, he took a few steps forward, and then his free hand reached out and took hold of Marco's slacks, the grubby little fingers curling tightly into the fabric as though he would never let go again.

"Hey, little guy," Marco said, half laughing, but somewhat startled as he patted the boy's head a bit awkwardly.

"He missed you lots and lots," Jilly told him in her matter-of-fact manner. "When I told him you were back, he smiled."

It was heartwarming to be missed, and the child seemed pretty darn adorable, but Marco didn't have any memory of ever having seen him before in his life. It would seem the two of them had developed some sort of relationship. That was unusual for him. He usually avoided getting too close to little ones. You never knew how long they were going to be around. He'd had enough experience losing contact with a cherished child to make him wary of repeating the situation.

He patted the boy's head again, hoping to be friendly but detached, then looked to Shayna for help. "Don't you have a cookie or something Eddie might like?" he asked, trying not to sound too desperate.

"Coming right up," Shayna said with a reassuring wink. "Let's all go in and see about it."

Eddie didn't want to let go of Marco's slacks, which made walking a bit awkward, but once inside, Shayna was able to coax him away with a huge chocolate chip cookie and a cartoon DVD in the player. She served milk with the cookies and they left the youngsters in the front room with the entertainment.

"He's such a duck," she whispered to Marco as he followed her into the kitchen. "But he hasn't said a word since his father went missing last month. I think he must be transferring the attachment to you."

"Pop psychology," he muttered, glancing back into the room where the kids were. "What happened to his father?"

"Went overboard on a fishing trip." She shrugged, then added as an aside, "Though rumor has it he's AWOL on purpose. Who knows?"

Marco looked at the little guy with a larger measure of sympathy after hearing that. A moment later, as he lowered his long body to sit on the rattan couch in the front room, Eddie shot up beside him and sat very close, little legs out straight, as though trying to copy whatever he did.

Shayna watched, touched at the scene. Marco hadn't

gone out of his way to cultivate Eddie when he'd been here before, but the boy had been fascinated by him from the first. She was glad to see that Marco wasn't trying to fend him off. Poor Eddie was having a rough time of it with his father missing and his mother gone trying to get work wherever she could.

And so was Jilly. She had a lot of sympathy for the girl and what she was going through. Losing a parent when one was just beginning to learn what life as an adult was all about was rough. She knew from experience, though for her it had been a little different. Her mother and brother had died in a car accident when she was about Jilly's age. Instead of having to take over the family chores and baby-sitting responsibilities, she'd been drafted into providing emotional support for her father. If her mother had lived, would she have gone down that glittery yellow brick road she took into her twenties? She hardly thought so. If her brother had been there to help deflect some of the intense influence from her father, would she have been a more normal adult? She had no doubt of it. She'd missed them both so much; they still haunted her dreams.

"Is your mom working at the hotel today?" Shayna asked Jilly.

Jilly looked up and nodded. "She's going in after lunch. She likes to work there. Sometimes people give her tips." A look of alarm came over her face. "Oh! We better go back. She's probably looking for us now."

As she turned toward her little brother, Eddie's little hand shot out and curled around the seam of Marco's slacks again, fingers digging in.

"Eddie! We have to go home." She tried to pry his fingers off the fabric, but the little boy's face was set with determination. "Oh, Eddie!" she wailed.

"Here." Marco put his hand out, palm up, in front of the boy. He looked down at him and smiled, this time with genuine warmth. "We'll make a deal," he said.

Eddie looked at him, then at his hand, but didn't take the bait. His dark eyes were watchful, but unforgiving.

"Come on," Marco said gently. "We have to shake on it."

Eddie's questioning gaze looked at Shayna, then back at Marco. Tentatively, he put out his left hand.

"Nope," Marco said firmly. "The other hand. Come on."

Eddie's little face was pained. Slowly, almost undetectably, his fingers began to loosen their hold on the pants.

"I'm going to promise you something," Marco told him. "Shayna and I have to go on a trip around the island, but we'll be back tonight."

His hand finally slid off the fabric and landed in Marco's, looking small and vulnerable there. Marco turned his own hand and enveloped the little one so that they were shaking.

"We'll be back," he said, looking earnestly into Eddie's face.

Alarm bells rang in his head the moment the words were out of his mouth. It was so easy to make promises to little kids. And so easy to break them. He knew that from his own childhood. How many times had he waited at the tall windows in his mother's house, hoping and praying that his father would show up for his visitation day? And how often had his prayers been answered?

No, if he made this promise to this boy, he had to keep it. No matter what.

"We'll be back," he said firmly, "and I'll bring you a red licorice whip. Okay?"

Eddie's face lit up and for a second, it almost looked as though he were going to say something. But the moment faded as quickly as it had begun, and there was no sound from the child. Still, he pumped hands with Marco. They had a deal.

Shayna watched this whole scene, entranced. Not matter what, Marco was great with little kids. She smiled at the handshake gimmick, but the smile froze when he mentioned the licorice whip.

Wait a minute. How had he remembered that Eddie was a fool for red licorice? He couldn't have just plucked that out of the air…could he?

Who knew? Maybe he had. But she kept thinking about the day, a few weeks ago, when they'd stopped in at the little general store for supplies, and Marco had casually picked up a package of red licorice for Eddie. His gift had been received with a rapture that had surprised and pleased him. Could he be starting to remember things? Could that reaction from Eddie have stayed with him when nothing else had? It didn't seem logical.

They waved goodbye to the children from the front porch, and then Shayna gave him a sideways smile. "You were sweet to Eddie. He needs a good male role model."

"Whoa," Marco said quickly. "I'm not a role model."

"Maybe not," she said with a sigh. "But poor Leila can't do it all by herself. She tries to get all the work she can, especially at the hotel, and Jilly tries hard to be a good babysitter. But she gets distracted and Eddie takes off on his chubby little legs. The next thing we know, there's Eddie showing up at the hotel or wherever Leila is working that day. They have to watch him like a hawk."

Marco tilted his head, considering that little story and taking it to heart. "Well, you can't blame him, poor little guy. After all, with his father missing, I'm sure he's scared he'll lose his mom, too. So he takes off after her, just to be sure she comes home."

She shrugged. "I suppose so."

He sighed and turned to her.

"Where the hell am I going to find red licorice?" he asked distractedly. "Do you suppose anyone has it here?"

She smiled, feeling a small flutter of relief. It didn't seem that his memory was coming back after all. "Don't worry, we'll find some. I'll help."

They went back into the house and she headed for her bedroom to change for the island trip. She took off the pareau with regret. She probably wouldn't get to wear that again for another year at least. Any moment now, she would start expanding at the waistline.

"How come you're Aunty Shayna and I'm Mr. Marco?" Marco called from the living room. He'd slipped onto a bar stool and leaned against her counter with both elbows.

"They know me better," she called from her room. "It's sort of a tradition here in the islands. To the children, close family friends are called Aunty." She chuckled. "You want to be an uncle?"

"That's not necessary," he said. "Mr. Marco is better than Mr. Smith, though." He groaned, rubbing his face as though trying to wake from a bad dream. "Are you seriously trying to convince me that I was using a phony name when I was here before?"

"Yes, Marco. We all knew you as Marco Smith, and probably no one over twelve bought it for a minute. But that's the way things are here. If you wanted to be a Smith, everyone was okay with that. We're easy."

He grunted. "It must be confusing to a little guy like Eddie," he noted more to himself than to her.

"Maybe." She sighed. "Poor Leila—their mom. She's having a hard time of it since her husband went missing. And Jilly has pretty much become the nanny for the babies."

"There are more of them?" he said, then winced at the horror he'd allowed to show in his tone.

"Besides Jilly and Eddie?" she responded. "Two more. Jamu is eight months and Ali is about ten." She poked her head out and grinned at him. "Here in the islands, we consider children a blessing, not a burden. It does change your outlook."

"I suppose so," he murmured, but he wasn't really listening. Memories of another little boy came tumbling back into his heart and he turned away, fighting it. A little boy named Carlo who had been the child of a woman he was pretty seriously dating at one time. When she'd decided to move on to other relationships, he'd lost his connection to the boy, and it had hurt more than he'd ever thought possible. That was a painful chapter in his past, a chapter he didn't want to revisit. If he had to lose a period of his life to amnesia, why couldn't it have been that one?

He glanced at Shayna as she came out of the bedroom. She didn't know about little Carlo, of course. No matter how close they had become before, he knew he wouldn't have told her about Carlo. Setting his jaw, he pushed thoughts of the little boy he'd cared so much about away and turned his mind to the woman in front of him.

She'd changed into denim capris and a bright Hawaiian shirt and he had a moment of regret that the naked stomach was gone. But she'd pulled her hair back into a ponytail and she looked downright adorable anyway. Good enough to kiss. Only she didn't have that "Hey, why don't you kiss me?" look in her eyes that a man liked to see before he made that move. So he let the moment pass.

"I'll bet you were a tomboy," he remarked, looking her over. "All you lack are the freckles on the nose." His eyebrows rose as he surveyed her feet. "But I hope you're not planning on hiking or climbing any trees today," he said.

She lifted her chin. "Why not?"

"Flip-flops?" he said, looking askance. "You really want to drive around on your Vespa in those?"

He glanced pointedly at her feet and she flashed her sandals proudly.

"You call them flip-flops. Some people call them

thongs. Here in the islands, we call them zoris and everybody wears them."

"Not me," he said stoutly.

She grinned. "Not yet," she amended for him.

He couldn't resist grinning back, then shook his head. There was so much about her he didn't know. "Where are you from, Shayna?"

Something flashed in the depths of her blue eyes. He sharpened his own gaze, trying harder to read them, but whatever it was he'd noticed for just those few seconds proved elusive.

"What makes you think I wasn't born right here on this island?" she challenged, her gaze clear as glass.

He shook his head slowly, taking in her various assets one by one. "I don't buy it. You give off cosmopolitan vibes. You've been around. Haven't you?"

"Have I?" she shot back, though a veil seemed to draw a shadow over her eyes. "That's pure speculation and a pretty subjective evaluation."

He shrugged. "It's mine and I'm sticking to it." He turned as she walked around him, as though keeping her pinned with his steely gaze and planning to reel her in eventually. "The question is, where?"

She sighed, avoiding him.

"The U.S., I'd say. East Coast. Maybe even New York. Hmm. Let me think...."

A look close to alarm swept across her face and she glanced up, pressed her lips together, and then shrugged in a sort of mini-surrender. "Okay. You're right. I wasn't born here." She flashed him a stern look and grabbed her keys before she started out the door. "But I mean to die here. And that's what counts."

He followed, frowning. He didn't get her at all. Why was she still avoiding every personal issue? "Just hold off on that for a while, okay?" he said wryly. "At least until we find my plans."

"Don't worry," she said back over her shoulder. "You've got me for the duration."

He didn't bother to react. Anything he might have said would gain him nothing but scorn from her and he knew it. Still, he had to chuckle, deep inside. He had her, did he? Funny, it didn't feel that way. It seemed more likely that *she* had *him*—over a barrel.

Fifteen minutes later, they were cruising down a winding road that threaded a trail between two jungle-like thickets of tall, slender trees and opened out onto an endless white sand beach, rimmed with multiple coconut palms. The trees looked as though they would be reaching for the sky if it weren't for those darned old trade winds bending them toward the ground.

"This is Tanachi Beach," she told him as he dismounted from the scooter. "What do you think?"

He didn't say anything for a moment. Slowly, he turned, taking it all in—the gleaming sand, the black rock formations, the crystal blue sea, the white foam of the waves pounding out on the reef.

"Wow," he said softly, shaking his head.

She came up beside him, pleased with his reaction.

"We came here, you know. The second day you were

on the island. We set a blanket down right over there and had a picnic lunch we'd brought from home."

"Really." He turned to look at her, bemused. "Why didn't we bring along a picnic lunch this time?"

She met his gaze with a touch of defiance and decided to tell him the truth. "Because we're not playing around with the idea of beginning a romance today," she said firmly.

That set him back on his heels for a second, but he didn't waver. "We aren't?" he countered with a gleam of humor in his eyes. "Speak for yourself."

She managed a simple glare before starting off toward the rocks. He followed her through the sand, and then they stood side by side and watched the water lap against the shore.

"So you're telling me we did play around with that very idea when I was here before, aren't you?"

"More or less," she allowed.

He searched her brilliant blue eyes. "So what happened, Shayna? What came between us? What ruined everything?"

She stared at him for a long moment, then looked away. "It was a short-term thing," she said. "We both knew it was just for fun, just for the moment. Neither one of us expected anything long-term from it."

It was easy to say those words and it didn't even hurt too much to say them. But once they were out there, they wouldn't fade. They hung in the air, mocking her, and she couldn't get them to move on out of the way. Mainly because they were lies. She'd expected a lot more than a bit of fun. She'd thought she'd found a man like no other, the sort of man she'd been waiting for all her life. Knowing Marco, seeing the sort of man he was—at any rate, the sort of man she'd thought he was—had thrilled her at the time.

Her eyes stung for a moment and she had to turn away from him. She'd had dreams. Oh, yes, how did the song go? Clouds in her coffee. That was the way it felt now. No one much liked dreams gone bad, did they?

"When people talk about tropical beaches, this is what they have in mind, isn't it?" he was saying, still reacting to the scenery.

She nodded, swallowing her regrets and forcing herself to get back to normal. "I think so. It is so beautiful here."

"Yes." He looked around again. "Inspirational, even." He raked fingers through his thick dark hair. "And you're telling me I didn't do any sketches while I was here with you?"

"No. Not a one."

"Strange."

She shrugged. "Maybe you had other things on your mind."

He felt a smile forming and gave in to it. "You mean, like that romance thing you were talking about?" he teased her.

She gave him a look and didn't answer that. Instead, she tried to get back to business.

"Okay, take a good look. Doesn't anything ring a bell? Tickle your memory? Bring on a feeling of déjà vu?"

Slowly, he shook his head. "No. Not a thing."

She shaded her eyes and looked at the ocean. It seemed to go on forever. Sometimes being on an island could feel lonely. Everything she'd grown up with was so far away. She didn't often get that feeling, but right now, she had a little hint of it. And it chilled her a bit. There was reality to face here.

She was going to have a baby. Marco's baby. Just the thought made her catch her breath and feel ill, so she pushed it away. She would think about that and all its implications once they found his plans and got him safely off the island. Then she would decide what she was going to do. Until then, she had to pretend everything was normal.

Looking up and down the beach, she felt a quiver of nostalgia.

"You really don't remember this?" She waved her arm in an arc as though indicating the whole panorama before them. "Not even a little tiny bit?"

He shoved his hands down into the pockets of his slacks and hunched over, looking uncomfortable. "That's right. I don't get any memory vibes at all."

She shook her head, looking at him as though she had a hard time believing what he'd said.

"How could you have forgotten?"

She said it softly, more to herself than to him. She remembered. She bit her lower lip and let recollection flow. Their first kiss had happened right there by the jagged outcropping of volcanic rocks. She'd been showing him how the waves had broken through that part of the reef and came rushing in to the shore, depleting as they came but still carrying enough force to make a great display of sea foam against the rocks. As she turned to see if he was impressed, she'd found he was studying her instead of the ocean.

"I love when you get so excited about something," he had said softly, reaching out to push back a strand of hair that had come loose and was falling across her face. "Your eyes sparkle and your face lights up with a glow, like rose petals."

She'd blushed, right there on the beach. There was something so sweet and simple about his words and yet they conveyed a warmth she wasn't used to in men she'd dated. Maybe it was the slight Italian accent, maybe it was the honesty in his tone, the earnest pleasure in his face, but something had struck a spark in her and she'd lifted her face and reached for him.

His arms had come around her and his mouth had found hers, warm and hungry in the coolness of the ocean spray. She'd loved his kiss from the first, and his hard body excited her in ways she didn't expect. Despite the reputation she'd had over the years, she didn't usually feel passion with the men she knew. What she did feel was a sort of desperation, a need to blot out loneliness, a hunger for something she never did find. So the sense of sweet desire he conjured up surprised her and took her breath away.

Embarrassed, unsure of how to deal with the new feelings, she'd had to pull away quickly, laughing. Then she ran away and he'd followed her, chasing across the beach until he'd caught her, tackled her from behind and they both went down into the sand.

She treasured that day. She was pretty sure she'd never feel another like it. But that was then. This was now. She glanced at him sideways. How could he be that same person and yet not have that experience in his memory? It was like dating a twin or something.

Suddenly, she wanted him to kiss her again. The feeling swept over her like a wave and she could hardly breathe. She knew how dangerous this was, and that she had to fight it. She was being tossed around by a current of emotion, and she had to remember to keep her head above water.

This isn't really the man you thought he was, she told herself silently. *He turned out to be a deceiver. It wouldn't be the same.*

She knew that. But she still wanted his kiss, ached for it. Turning away, she ran again, just as she had the other day, but this time she wasn't laughing. Just like before, he followed her. Had she known he would? Had she done this because she was sure of it? She really didn't know, but when he caught her, when he pulled her around to face him and took her face between his hands and touched his lips to hers, she heard a soft cry and realized, to her horror, that it was hers.

But she forgot that soon enough. His mouth on hers was hard and soft at the same time, cool and hot, rough and smooth. Her arms slipped into a circle around his neck, and she arched her body into his. It felt right and natural, and she wanted him so badly.

The wind tossed her hair and the sun was hot on her

shoulders, but all she knew was the smooth warmth of his mouth, the hard excitement of his body, the thrill as his hands began to move up under her shirt.

No. She had to stop this. If she didn't, she would just be repeating her last mistakes, doing it all over again, falling for a man who wasn't what he pretended to be. Surely she couldn't be this stupid. Could she?

CHAPTER SIX

GATHERING ALL HER STRENGTH, Shayna pulled away.

"Shayna…" Marco tried to pull her back again.

"No, don't say anything," she said, backing away, her eyes huge with remorse as she fooled with her hair, pulling it back into the ponytail band. "That was a mistake. A big, big mistake. I didn't mean to do it and…"

His face changed. If she didn't know better, she would have thought that was pain in his dark eyes.

"Don't say you wish it hadn't happened," he told her roughly. "Just don't tell me that."

His tone caught her by surprise. He seemed to feel strongly about it. But what the heck, so did she. Her chin rose. "All right. I won't tell you. But that doesn't mean it isn't true."

He looked at her for a moment, then the anger slipped away and he relaxed until he had a soft laugh for her. Shaking his head, he said, "Shayna, you can twist things around so that they mean exactly the opposite of what they are supposed to mean. You drive me nuts."

"The feeling is mutual," she said, trying to maintain

a huffy exterior but failing on all counts. She shook her head, exasperated but somewhat amused at the same time. "This is too much. You're doing just exactly what you did before."

His face was a picture of innocence. "What I did before? What did I do?"

She threw out her hands. "These patterns must be ingrained in you somewhere. Even if your mind doesn't remember, your body does." She gave a short, humorless laugh. "Your body doesn't have amnesia, Marco. Isn't that remarkable?"

He frowned, trying to understand her. "Will you tell me what you're talking about?"

She heaved a sigh and shrugged. "You're re-creating what happened when I brought you here the first time."

He made a face. "Because I kissed you?"

"Yes."

His brow furrowed over that one. "Shayna, any man worth his salt is going to want to kiss you, anytime, anywhere. He doesn't need to have his body especially trained for it."

"Oh!" He was being frustratingly dense and she gave up, turning away. "Never mind." She looked toward the sea, then back at him. "So that's over now. Don't feel this changes anything. We're back to being wary adversaries."

"We are?" He looked adorably bewildered. "I mean…I didn't realize that was what we were in the first place."

"You don't pay attention." She studied him, the set of his jaw, the way his eyelashes made lacy shadows across his cheeks in the sunlight, the slight stubble of his beard that was beginning to show, his mouth—oh how she wanted to kiss that mouth again. Against her will, her own smile surfaced.

"Oh, just forget it," she said in semidespair. "What just happened never happened. Okay? Come on, I'll show you some caves."

She started off across the sand, only looking back to see if he was following. He was, though more slowly than she would like. He was obviously thinking over what had happened, even after she'd told him not to. That made her smile, but she turned so he wouldn't see.

"Here they are," she said, stopping before an area that looked like an ordinary landslide of rocks.

"Where?" he asked, coming up behind her.

"Look closely," she said, pointing out the opening.

"Not bad," he told her admiringly. "I never would have noticed them on my own."

They had to lower themselves over the slide and then wedge themselves between a couple of large rocks, but finally they were inside, and it was breathtaking. The air was cool, the light was filtered and the ceilings were ten feet high.

"It's like being in a natural cathedral," Marco said, speaking softly as though in respect.

"Isn't it?" She nodded. "I love this place. Come here." She showed him where they could lie on their stomachs in the cool sand and look out through an opening at the waves on the reef.

"This is like a World War II pillbox," he told her. "I've been in some up in the Marianas Islands."

"But this isn't man-made," she noted.

He turned to look at her, lying so close beside him and yet untouchable—at least if they played by her rules. This wasn't going to work. Everything she did today was turning him on. If she only knew the thoughts that were going through his head—no body memories needed.

"This is interesting," he said a bit impatiently, "but you're getting us off the track. We're looking for my plans."

"I know."

He shrugged and glanced around the edges of the cave. "Have I been here before?"

"I don't think so. I didn't bring you here."

"Then why are we here?"

She settled back into a comfortable position, propped by an elbow. "I thought it was a good place to use to go over your memories and try to figure out how and when they stopped."

"Sounds reasonable. But we've got to stay focused or we'll never find anything."

"Agreed."

He met her gaze and winced, as though her eyes were too bright for him. Frowning slightly, he turned his head. "Okay. I'm ready. Ask me anything."

"I'm not going to ask. You're going to tell."

He looked back warily. "Tell what?"

She'd hoped he would be spontaneous about it, but if he needed prompting, she was ready to do that, as well.

"Okay, here's my idea. Why don't we backtrack?

Try to take your memory up as far as it goes. Maybe that will trigger something."

He shrugged. Lying here in the cool sand on the floor of a sea cave seemed a strange setting for this, but you never did know what might set off recollections. Actually, her suggestion sounded better than anything he'd received from the psychiatrist.

"Okay. I remember…." He closed his eyes and threw his head back, leaning into the sand. "I remember about a month ago, I was considering three or four different places for my vacation. I wanted a place that was off the beaten path. I needed to rest. I'd just had a big career setback and I needed space and time to use to recover and regroup."

"A career setback? What do you mean?"

He opened his eyes and looked at her. "I told you about the designer who has been dogging my steps. He actually did steal some plans from me at one point." He grimaced. "At least, I think he did. The plans he submitted were so close…." He shook his head and grimaced, remembering when Glendenning Hudson had shown him what his rival was offering for sale. "Anyway, just knowing that such unique thinking so close to mine was out there shook me at first. I couldn't prove they were actually stolen from me, but I wanted to take some time to evaluate the matter and figure out how I was going to get inspiration back. I needed to get away, get my head straight and come up with some new ideas for racing design. I wanted to get back my momentum."

She nodded. All perfectly understandable. "So you

were trying to decide where to go. What were the possible places?"

"Tahiti. The Caribbean. I was also thinking about going back home to Italy, just to lick my wounds."

She smiled at the picture that conjured up. But her smile quickly faded as she realized the next logical step in this journey. She was going to have to ask him the question that might restore his memory of why he'd come here in the first place. Would he suddenly snap his fingers and say, "*Oh, right. It was your father who sent me here and he wanted me to bring you back. How could I forget that?*"

That was the question, wasn't it? Carefully positioning herself so that she watch him closely, she asked, "How did you happen to think of coming here?"

His eyes narrowed as he considered the question. She waited, holding her breath. But when he started talking, she let it out again. It was obvious he didn't remember what she'd feared at all.

"That was a bit odd. Not like my usual decisions. But I'd seen pictures of these islands in the office of my most important client. Glendenning Hudson, in fact. We were talking about him last night. Every time I visited his office, I couldn't take my eyes off those pictures. They haunted me. The geography was so unique, so beautiful, so peaceful and calm. I just felt I had to go there."

She looked away, relief mixed with a sense of eerie coincidence. She knew exactly what he meant. She'd sat in that same office and been mesmerized by those same pictures. She could visualize it now, the large pictures that covered the walls, the huge models of racing yachts on pedestals beneath the pictures. It was quite a scene, and one she'd grown up with. When she'd decided to hide herself away from her old life, these islands had been the first place she'd thought of. The only thing that had made her hesitate was fear that it would be the first place her father would look for her, as well.

But she'd risked it. She knew her father's visits to the islands were from twenty years before. He hadn't been there since and probably didn't think of them as relevant to her in any way. And for a long time, it had looked as though she'd guessed right. She kept in touch with her old life through her lawyer. He sent reports and called once a month to check on how she was doing. He also let her father know she was okay, though he did it anonymously so as not to suffer the wrath of Glendenning Hudson. She knew her father was searching for her, but he was one of the main reasons she'd had to run from her old life, and she couldn't risk seeing him until she was sure she was strong enough to tell him she wasn't going to be his tagalong ever again. It was only now that she'd had time and space to sit back and look at her life that she realized how much he had used her to enhance his own image. And how he would just use her again if she went back.

"Never going back." That was what she said to herself every morning after she'd washed her face and looked up into the mirror. "Never, ever going back."

But she knew he thought he needed her. He was just too big a personality to let her find her own way. He loved it when she trailed along in his orbit.

She'd been nervous when she'd first arrived, jumpy, always sure her father or one of his assistants would show up and ruin everything. But as the weeks passed and that didn't happen, she'd begun to relax.

And then Marco had arrived.

He talked about her father's office and the work he'd done for her father without hesitation, making her think his memory loss must include what she assumed was that original assignment to come after her. She only hoped he didn't remember it until she got him back off the island. Of course, that all presupposed that this was all on the up-and-up—that he was telling her the truth. That this wasn't just a ruse to get her to let her guard down.

She looked at him strangely. She wanted to believe him. She was ready to believe him. Yes, she'd pretty much accepted that he really didn't remember that she was the daughter of the man whose pictures he'd been so taken by.

"I went to bed that night determined to make my decision in the morning," he was saying. "And the next thing I knew, I was waking up in the hospital. Almost three weeks had gone by. At that point, I couldn't even remember who I was."

She felt a pang of guilt. Sometimes she forgot that he had been in a very bad accident and that he was still suffering. "But most of it came back to you?"

"Yes, little by little. It was some time before I realized no more was coming and I'd just lost two weeks of my life." He sighed. "Now I want to recapture those weeks."

"What if they don't come back to you?"

"Then at least I'll have your memories to use." He raised one sleek dark eyebrow her way. "You're going to tell me everything."

She stared at him. That wasn't likely, was it? Did he really think that?

Reaching out, he touched her cheek with the flat of his hand. "You are going to help me remember, aren't you?" he asked her softly.

Her breath caught in her throat at his touch. "No," she said quickly, pushing his hand away. "But I will try to help you find the plans you think you've lost. I've already been doing that. In case you hadn't noticed."

He gave her a bittersweet smile. "Here's an idea. Maybe we should try out more kissing for a while. That might break the logjam."

She rolled her eyes. "In your dreams."

"Why not?" Reaching out again, he took a strand of her hair this time and curled it with his fingers. "The evidence suggests you and I were pretty close a few weeks ago."

She hesitated, then took a deep breath. "We were close at one point. However, by the time you left, we weren't."

He frowned, studying her. "The picture…"

"The picture depicts a time before I knew who you really were." The words were out before she could stop them and she waited, heart beating, for what he would have to say.

His frown had deepened and he obviously thought this whole situation curiouser and curiouser. "So you found out I design fast sailboats. Was that so horrifying you felt you had to drop me like a bad penny?"

She closed her eyes. He still didn't remember. "Yes."

"Why?"

She opened her eyes and stared straight into his. "You really don't remember, do you? Don't worry. At some point it will come to you."

Jumping to her feet, she began to brush off the sand. "We'd better get out of here before the tide comes up," she noted. "Come on. I'm going to take you to visit with an odd friend of mine."

He straightened reluctantly. "Did you say an odd friend or an old friend?"

She grinned. "Gigi is very definitely odd," she explained. "And though she's probably in her forties, she wouldn't appreciate being called old at all. And doesn't act it, either."

They squeezed out through the opening and soon were back on solid sand, marching along toward where they had left the Vespa.

"I take it I've met this lady before?" he asked.

"Oh, yes." She stifled a knowing grin. "Maybe seeing her again will be the shock that starts you on the road to recovery."

"Sounds good."

Did it? Shayna sighed. Maybe so. She was certainly getting tired of hiding things from him and waiting to see if he were hiding things from her. She yearned to be free and open with him, to hear his explanation for what he'd done, to tell her side. He was actually a great guy. Wasn't he? All evidence seemed to support that. There was only that original flaw—the fact that he'd lied to her. But maybe they could fix that. It wasn't likely, actually, but if they didn't try....

Did she dare start that conversation off? Maybe. Maybe soon. If she couldn't get him to leave, at least she could help him wake up to the reasons he should go.

"Shayna, I hate to look a gift horse in the mouth." He stopped himself and almost laughed. "Let me start that over," he said smoothly. "Shayna, I appreciate all you're doing to help me," he amended quickly. "But I need to know one thing. How is all this running around the island going to help me find my plans?"

She struck a pose before him. "We're re-creating your stay. I'm taking you around to see all the places you visited while you were here."

He looked pained. "But I didn't carry my portfolio along with me, did I? After all, you saw all my papers right there in the hotel room that last day."

"Good point," she agreed breezily, turning on her heel and starting off again. "But you're overlooking one thing. The people I'm taking you to see were people who came in to see you off that day. There's a chance they might have seen something, or you might even have given them your papers for safekeeping. Plus, you told me that you always made two sets of papers. I only saw one. You said you often mailed them ahead in a cardboard tube."

"True."

"And, bottom line," she said with a carefree shrug, sashaying in front of him toward the scooter, "seeing these places and people again might just jog your memory."

Funny how he was finding her more and more appealing. He smiled at her, as indulgent as a lover. "Okay. I'm sold."

They'd reached the Vespa. Marco turned back for one last look at the gorgeous beach line, but Shayna was still mulling over the possible hiding places for finding his plans. She turned to him.

"Marco, about your portfolio. You carried it separately from your main luggage?"

He nodded. "Sometimes. Sometimes I was able to get it all put into one bag. I just can't remember what I did that day."

She frowned. "But the second set…. I wonder where it was. I don't remember seeing it at all."

He took hold of her shoulders, staring down into her face. "Okay, think back. Try to remember everything you can about the plans, from the first to the last."

She shook her head. "I didn't see you working on any plans until that last day. You didn't do it when I was around. Maybe you did it in your hotel room, probably when I was at work at Kimo's Café. But whenever we were together, you weren't talking about any plans."

"Okay, so you came into the room and what did you see?"

She gazed up at him. He was serious about this. When he talked about the missing designs, she saw an intensity he didn't seem to have about anything else.

"I've told you. Your papers were spread out all over the floor where you were organizing them."

"And that was the first you knew about me design-ing yachts."

"Yes."

His hands dropped from her shoulders and he turned to stare at the horizon. That was odd and didn't seem like him at all. He hadn't thought about this much, but it was a mystery why he wouldn't have told her from the beginning. And this calling himself "Smith" was just another puzzle in the game. He must have had some ra-tionale, but what in the world could it have been?

The only thing he could think of was that he'd decided to stay on Ranai under an assumed name so that Salvo Ricktorre couldn't find him and send his spies out. That was probably it. But why carry the pretense to such lengths that he wouldn't have told Shayna the truth? That he actively hid it from her? He really couldn't fathom that one.

He frowned, kicking the toe of his shoe into the sand. "What's your theory on that?" he asked her, looking up from under his brows.

That startled her. "What do you mean?"

He shrugged. "Why do you think I didn't tell you I was a yacht designer?"

Oh, that. She knew the answer to that, but she wasn't going to tell him. Quickly, she batted the question away. "Why do *you* think?"

He frowned, seriously considering this. "I have no idea. Do you really think I deliberately didn't want you to know?"

She drew in a long breath before she answered that

one. "Yes, I do think that." She bit her lip with regret. She shouldn't have admitted that. But still, it was hard not to be honest with him. Something in her just wanted to be open with him, to tell him everything, and all that she was thinking. She had to fight it every minute.

He nodded, a bit troubled by that. But then he looked at her pretty face and changed his mind. "Here's my theory." His own face softened a bit and his warm gaze caressed her. "I fell crazy in love with you the moment we met."

That one made her blush, she couldn't help it. She turned away as warmth flooded her. Oh, if only she could count on something so clean, so pure, so candid. But it had been her experience that life just wasn't like that at all.

"Oh, please."

"No, hear me out." He moved closer and she could tell he had the urge to touch her, but he was fighting it, at least for now.

"I think maybe I saw you and I fell so hard, all ideas and thoughts about sailing went out of my head. All I could think about was you." He shrugged. "It's a simple straightforward sort of explanation. I find the simplest is usually the best."

She shook her head, trying not to smile. He was saying pretty much the opposite of what she'd been thinking. Who was closer to the mark? She wished she could believe it was him.

"I don't think so."

"I believe it." He reached out and touched her shoulder, and she jerked away. But he didn't back off. Instead, he took her more firmly, his hand at her neck, and let his fingers slide along her collarbone. "I can imagine wanting nothing more than to be with you, to hold you, to kiss you." He moved even closer and his voice was husky when he said, "To make sweet love to you."

"Marco!" She pulled away from his touch and turned toward the scooter.

"I think I wanted you more than I wanted to design yachts," he said simply.

She got onto the Vespa and searched for her key. Her fingers were trembling, and she didn't think they should be. His words were lovely, in a way, but not realistic, especially considering the real reason, which only she seemed to remember at this point. "You live in a dream world, don't you?" she muttered.

He raised an eyebrow. "It wasn't like that?"

She glared at him. "No it wasn't like that. Not a bit like that."

He tilted his head to the side, considering, as his gaze slowly traveled over her face. "But we did kiss."

"Yes," she admitted reluctantly.

He got onto the scooter, sliding in behind her and putting his hands at her waist.

"And I did hold you, sort of like this." He leaned forward and began to nuzzle the crook of her neck. "Now about the lovemaking…" he murmured, and that was when she kick-started the Vespa and took off with a jerk that practically had him flying off into the jungle.

He laughed, she bit her lip and bent forward. She would be a speed racer if that was what it took to get him to stop teasing her.

But once they were out on the main road, she pulled over and turned off the engine, remembering that she hadn't called Gigi to warn her of their impending visit. Pulling out her cell, she poked in the number and hoped for the best. Phone service was hit-or-miss on the islands. Luckily, she got a connection.

"Hello?" a deep but very feminine voice answered.

"Hi, Gigi. It's Shayna."

"Hi, doll. What's up?"

She glanced at where Marco was pacing along the side of the road near the Vespa, listening in on every word. "Remember Marco Smith?"

"Of course I remember Marco Smith. Delightful man. Knew his sailing. I'll tell you this—he taught me a few tricks when we went out on the water."

"No kidding." She fought back the inevitable jealous pangs that threatened to reassert themselves after hearing that little boast. "Well, he's back."

"Wonderful. Bring him by."

"I'd like to. Right now, in fact. But I must warn you. He's not Marco Smith anymore."

"You don't say." She laughed. "Since I can't imagine a man that masculine having a sex change, what's the deal?"

Shayna gave a spurt of laughter she couldn't contain after that image flashed into her mind. "No, it's not a sex change," she assured the older woman, laughing again when she saw the look of horror on Marco's face. "Just a change of identity. You see, his real name is Marco DiSanto."

"No! The yacht designer?"

"That's the one."

She laughed again. "I should have known. Why didn't I think of that at the time? I knew he was some sort of professional. He just knew too much. But somehow I didn't connect the name. Hah! Get that little rascal over here so I can give him a piece of my mind, will you?"

"Uh, one more thing, Gigi. He's got amnesia."

"What?"

She flashed a questioning look Marco's way and he shrugged his permission for her to go into it.

"He doesn't remember a thing about his previous visit here. So be kind."

"Kind? I'll shake some sense into him, more likely. Amnesia indeed!"

Shayna laughed. He could use a little shaking, she was thinking. "We'll be there in minutes."

"Good."

She clicked off and grinned at Marco, still gnashing his teeth over the sex change reference. "Come on," she said cheerfully.

"Let's go see Gigi."

CHAPTER SEVEN

HE CLIMBED BACK ABOARD, being careful to stay away from her neck this time, and asked, "So tell me about this woman you're taking me to."

"Gigi knows sailing. You spent a lot of time with her when you were here before."

Funny that she could mention that so calmly now. At the time, she'd been jealous. It had seemed that every time she had to work, he would suddenly be off with Gigi, testing out her new yacht in the open waters. She'd never been invited along and she'd just assumed that Gigi, a tall, beautiful older woman, was the draw. It was only later that she realized there really had been another motivation at work—the opportunity for sailing. He'd been working on ideas of his own.

Gigi had a huge estate right along the waterfront. They rode down the long driveway, rimmed with tall coconut palms, and stopped before a huge white mansion that looked like something from the nineteenth century, wraparound porch and all.

Before they had time to disentangle themselves from

the scooter, a long, lanky woman walked out in a bright red bikini, accented by huge dark glasses and one of the flimsiest cover-ups she'd ever seen. Shayna suppressed a grin. Despite everything, including her periodic fits of jealousy, she liked Gigi. Men tended to react with quick interest when they first met her, not realizing that her lack of modesty showcased a woman who was just natural and unaffected and totally unconscious of how she came across to others. She wore that dangerous swimsuit for comfort, nothing more, and she was slightly built and sinewy enough to get away with it. She didn't have a provocative bone in her body. This was Gigi and she meant no harm to anyone.

Stalking toward them like a hunter with a blunderbuss, she ripped off her dark glasses and stared penetratingly into Marco's eyes. "So you don't remember me, huh?" she accused.

"I'm sorry," he said with a friendly grin. He obviously liked her on sight. "And you have a very memorable face, so it's not that."

"Memorable?" That got her to straighten, her green eyes narrowing. "In what way?"

"It's lovely," he said quickly. "Really beautiful."

Gigi shrugged her unconcern. "Of course." She reached out a hand to help him off the scooter. "Come on down to my dock. You'll remember everything once you see the *True Yar* again."

Marco joined her willingly, glancing back at Shayna with a rueful shrug. "Maybe that will work. Let's take a look."

The yacht was gorgeous. As he walked down the boardwalk to the pier, he filled his senses with it, with the sight of it, the smell of the sea, the sound of the water. It suddenly occurred to him that he looked at women the same way he looked at beautiful sailing ships. No, he had to correct that. Lately he was looking at Shayna the way he looked at beautiful sailing ships, and other women the way he looked at ordinary sailing ships. She was special. There was no denying it.

Once aboard, he ran his hands over the wood and shook his head. "Wonderful ship," he said reverently. "Where do you get men to crew her?"

Gigi's smile was radiant. "My estate workers are part-time crew. I hire them for their sailing abilities and then teach them how to garden and paint and all the rest."

He was impressed. "Good plan." He noticed the sails as they flapped in the wind. "Did I go out on her with you?"

Gigi nodded. "I took you out into deep water for a half-day trip. Twice."

He nodded, knowing he wouldn't have passed that up for anything. "Was I working on designs?"

"Oh, yeah. You were sketching things and jotting down numbers the whole time. Doing measurements with your wind and weather instruments and using mine and jotting things down constantly." She shook her head. "I don't know why I didn't figure out who you were at the time."

He frowned, wondering why it had been easy for him to let Gigi in on what he did with his life while he'd obviously felt he had to hide that information from Shayna. Strange. He just didn't get that at all.

He filled her in on the missing plans, about which she claimed to know nothing. She had come in to see him off that last day, but just for a moment, and she hadn't noticed anything about his portfolio. They went over the times they'd been together and tried to analyze what could have happened, but all their noodling didn't get them anywhere.

Finally the housekeeper brought them out iced tea and sandwiches and as they ate, Gigi went on about her wonderful husband, Jimmy, who had brought her here to the islands ten years before.

"Where is he?" Marco asked guilelessly.

She waved a hand in the air as though that were an inconsequential matter. "Jimmy went to the mainland to get supplies. He'll be back one of these days."

"Oh." Marco looked at Shayna. Shayna looked at her sandwich.

"In the meantime," Gigi said cheerfully, "aren't I doing a good job of maintaining this place? Come on, admit it. I've got my own private paradise here."

There was no denying that. Her place had to be the envy of the island. They made plans for Marco to come back the next day for another trip out to deep water, and then Shayna began to prepare him for their next stop.

"I'm going to take him to Naliki Falls, the short way," she told their hostess.

"Uh-oh." Gigi grinned. "That's quite a hike."

Shayna nodded, her eyes sparkling with laughter. "I've been looking him over. I think he can handle it."

They both gazed at him critically, studying every part until he began to turn a little red under all this scrutiny.

"Hey, don't worry about me," he said, flexing his wide shoulders in a manly manner. "I can hold my own. Just give me a chance."

Shayna looked at Gigi and shrugged. "He wants a chance."

Gigi frowned and twisted her mouth to the side. "Gosh, I just don't know."

"Very cute," he muttered, pretending resentment, but actually enjoying the give-and-take. He didn't think he'd ever felt more comfortable with a woman than he did with Shayna. Somehow their personalities seemed to fit together in ways that pleased him. It was frustrating to feel that there was an obstacle between them, something he couldn't deal with because he didn't know what the hell it was. He sighed, rubbing his head. Today they were looking for his lost plans. Tomorrow he was going to dedicate to finding out what he'd done to hurt Shayna, and figuring out how to make it up to her.

"Don't forget, Elmo's having a luau today," Gigi reminded Shayna as they were leaving. "You should take Marco by. Didn't he and Elmo go out on a fishing trip together while he was here before? Maybe Elmo remembers something."

"Good idea," Shayna responded. She'd forgotten all about the luau and she'd planned to attend from the first time she'd heard about it. Half the island should be there. "It'll be a good way to pick up an evening meal while we're at it."

Marco appraised her—her lovely coloring, her brilliant blue eyes, the wonderful velvety texture of her skin—and wanted to hold her. "Will there be dancing?" he asked hopefully.

"Hula dancers," she responded brightly.

Gigi laughed, seeing the way his mind was working. "I don't think that is what he has in mind," she said. "Don't worry. I'm sure there will be a band."

"Good." He patted his stomach. "I've got to work off some of this great food I've been wolfing down."

"Don't worry about that," Shayna told him with a laugh as they waved goodbye to Gigi. "That's what the hike is for."

"What's Gigi's husband like?" Marco asked as they made their way back to the Vespa.

Shayna smiled and stretched out her arms, enjoying a cool breeze that was coming through. "You got me. I've never met him."

That seemed strange. "How long has he been gone?"

"That's just it. I don't know." Shayna pulled the scooter around to get into position for starting off. "He's been on the mainland getting supplies for as long as I've known her."

Marco grunted cynically. "Does the guy actually exist?"

"That is the question, isn't it?" Shayna waited to feel him settle in behind her and prepared to turn on the engine. "I don't know if she really believes he's coming back, or if she uses it as a way of keeping overeager suitors at bay."

"Whatever," he said with sigh. "She knows how to manage beautiful sailing ships. The *True Yar* is in perfect condition. She must work on it night and day."

"It's her obsession," Shayna agreed. "At least until Jimmy comes home."

He thought about that as they raced on down the road. He was obsessed with ship design, Gigi was obsessed with her yacht. Were they both letting things get in the way of caring for people? He'd been down this path before, wondering why he didn't find a woman and fall in love. Was the career too important to him? Were the yachts? Was he letting gorgeous objects blind him to the need for human contact—and love and tenderness? He hadn't had time to find an answer to that question when Shayna turned off the main thoroughfare and started them bumping down a rutted side road.

"Here we are," she said, pulling the scooter into a small clearing. "This is the hike to the falls."

He got off the scooter and walked to where he could get beyond the brush, then looked at the sheer cliff she was pointing to.

"What?" he said, reacting with shock. "No way. We're not climbing up that, are we? That's impossible."

"What's the matter, big boy?" she said, giving him a little sock in the chest with her fist. "Too tough for you?"

"I don't know about tough," he said, scratching his head as he surveyed the terrain. "I'm not an experienced climber, by any means. But I would say this climb is beyond the realm of an amateur. So if you think…"

His voice faded away. She'd already begun the climb…and she was doing it barefoot, her zoris stuck in her pockets. He gaped at her. She was climbing like a monkey. This was nuts. He had no problem braving the high seas on a tiny sailboat, clinging to the rigging in high winds when the sails needed tending, sweeping out over rough waters in shark-infested areas. He'd done that sort of thing all his life. But climbing around on slippery rocks in a bug-ridden jungle? This was not his idea of fun.

Still, he couldn't stand here on the ground while she shimmied up into the clouds, could he? Grumbling in annoyance, he started up after her, only to find himself sliding back down on every other hold. It was definitely a case of two steps forward, one step back—when he was lucky.

A bird swooped down and almost took a hunk out of his hair.

"Hey," he called up to her after he fended it off. "At least tell me what to look out for in the way of animal life."

She glanced back down and grinned, obviously tickled that she was beating him. Finding a small ridge, she sat down and waited for him to catch up.

"Snakes," she said at last as he sat down, too, panting. "Look out for snakes and silver lizards that bite."

"Great," he said, giving her a baleful look. "I'll do that."

"When I first got here," she went on, "I was told there were no snakes, but that turned out to be a lie."

She realized the admission she'd made as soon as the words were out of her mouth and she groaned silently, hoping he wouldn't pick up on it.

But he did.

"When *did* you get here, Shayna?" he asked right away. "How long have you lived here?" Reaching out, he gave her a little playful pretend punch in the arm. "Come on. Time to spill the beans."

The sparkle went out of her eyes. Slowly, she shook her head. "I told you my life was not up for discussion."

He stared at her for a long moment, then shrugged. "Okay. Let's get this thing over with." He frowned toward the jungle that surrounded them. He could hear animal calls in the distance. He would hold off on getting worried until they started to come closer. Maybe.

"What is the purpose of this hike again?" he asked, the tiniest thread of resentment in his tone.

"To see the falls," she said, and started off confidently. "They're wonderful. Come on."

But by now he'd gotten the knack and she soon found that her lead had dwindled to nothing. They hiked through a stream and past a nest of brilliantly feathered birds who scrambled and squawked at being interrupted, and finally, the summit was reached.

"Look at that. It's magic, isn't it? It just overwhelms me every time."

He looked. He had to admit it was okay. They had a panoramic view of the jungle, right on down to where it met the blue ocean. Beautiful. Thrilling, in its own way. But was it worth what they'd gone through to get here? Maybe he was being a wimp, but he didn't really think so. He was hot and sweaty and sore, and he'd cut his hand. He didn't love it.

"So tell me, Shayna, what does this hike have to do with finding my plans?" He pinned her with a hard look that was almost a glare.

Her smile was sunny and completely innocent. "Nothing."

He gaped at her uncomprehendingly. "What?" he said.

"I just thought we needed a little exercise," she said.

He was about to answer her sharply when he noticed something. Sounds. He climbed a little higher and looked over the top, down to where the waterfall hit bottom. There were people down by the waterfall's edge. Lots of people. Family groups. Little children. Mothers with strollers.

"Wait a minute. There are cars over here." Standing, he waved a finger at them and looked back at Shayna. "Those people down there drove to see the falls. Didn't they?"

She climbed up to where she could see what he was seeing. "Sure," she said simply. "You can get to it off the highway from the other side of the island."

Outrage wasn't a word strong enough for what he felt. He'd made the hike, but he hadn't liked it much. And now he saw that it was all for naught. "We could have driven here. We wouldn't have had to go through all the misery."

She shrugged, her sparkle back as she looked at him, mischievous as a kitten. "Sure, but where's the fun in that?"

He made a strangling sound, and she replied sunnily, "This amnesia thing is great." She grinned. "I got to do this to you twice."

"What? You dragged me here before?"

"Sure." Her grin widened. "Maybe you'll get a new round of amnesia and I can do it again."

He stared at her for a moment. Her smile was a little too cocky and her eyes gleamed just a little too brightly. He lunged.

"You're going to pay!"

She tried to run, but this time he was too fast for her, so she squealed instead. He held her close and growled at her. "You were just trying to torture me, were you?" he teased. "Well, turnabout is fair play. So let's see. What could I do to torture you?"

He pretended to think, and she tried to squirm out of his arms and shrieked again. But not for long. He dropped small, hot kisses along her neckline and in an instant, all resistance melted away. She sighed, arching her neck for him, closing her eyes as his mouth covered hers. He kissed her, sinking into her intoxicating warmth and she kissed him back, opening to him, accepting him with a passion she'd never felt for any other man. Every part of her sizzled with excitement at his touch. She began to need him with a deep, dark current of desire. For just a moment, she was his, and he was hers, and that was all that mattered.

A shout from below was a wake-up call, and though it wasn't aimed at them, it was enough to remind them they weren't alone. She drew back and looked into his dark, limitless eyes, but he didn't let her out of his arms. He held her close, pulling her up against his chest so that she could hear the wild beating of his heart. She sighed, happier than she'd ever been.

She gazed down at the falls. He might not appreciate them but she certainly did. They were gorgeous from here—the jungle dripping flowers, the smooth flow of water over the edge, the drops spraying out and catching the sunlight in diamond sparkles, the crash as the water hit the rocks, the red and green parrots squawking in the trees, the white lacy butterflies like living flowers against the cliff. This place, along with the beach, epitomized the island to her. She loved the peace, she loved the excitement, she even loved the danger. She loved everything about Ranai. It had saved her life. She was more determined than ever that she would never leave.

Pulling back, she looked into his handsome face. "I've got to admit that this, more than anything else, has convinced me that you really have had a memory loss," she told him.

He smiled, his gaze tracing the outline of her face as though he were memorizing it. "Why?"

"If you had remembered this hike, you wouldn't have made it a second time, would you?"

He almost laughed. "You've got that right." Then he finally let her go, shaking his head. "They invented cars for a reason, Shayna."

She laughed, still carrying the happiness he'd given to her. "Come on," she said, preparing to climb back down again. "Let's go to the luau."

Darkness hadn't fallen yet but the torches were already lit, lining the long, winding driveway as they made their way to the top of the hill. They could hear the music before they shut the engine off.

"How do you want to play this?" she asked him.

"Shall we tell people you've lost your memory? Or will you just go around with a smile on your face and pretend to know everyone?"

He nodded. "Let's go for the latter at this point, unless we have to resort to the good old-fashioned truth. You can point out people I need to remember for sure and I'll play it by ear from there."

There were people spread all over the grounds of the beautiful glass and wood house that jutted out over the valley. At this point, alcohol seemed to be flowing more freely than food, though the delicious aroma from the cooking pit filled the air, as did the Hawaiian style music. A group of very large men, most of them Polynesians, played ukuleles and sang in high falsetto voices, while a line of hula dancers swayed. The beginnings of a gorgeous sunset was making amazing watercolors across the surface of the sea. The ambience was perfect. Another wonderful island evening was in store.

Marco talked to a lot of people in the next half hour, not one of whom he remembered at all. But the conversation was engaging and no one seemed to notice when his answers seemed a bit disengaged. Still, the only meeting that really stuck with him was the one he had with Eddie's mom.

"Mr. Smith, hi. I heard you were back."

Marco turned to find himself talking to a beautiful young woman with huge, haunted eyes. She held a tray of appetizers and he took a stuffed mushroom automatically, even though it was the last thing he wanted.

"Hello," he said, stammering slightly. He had no idea who this was. "Uh…nice to see you again."

She smiled and offered him a cracker with a shrimp on it. "Here," she said in a husky whisper. "Better fill up on these. The Kalua pig is nowhere near done. It'll be hours before you'll get any real food."

"Oh. Of course." He took the cracker and began a balancing act that included his drink.

She smiled, watching him, but made no move to help until the shrimp began to slide off the cracker. Finally, she reached out and caught it just before it hit the deck. Calmly and without a word, she popped it into his mouth, just as though that were the most natural thing in the world to do.

"Want another?" she asked.

He shook his head, trying to chew as fast as he could. "Why don't you have one?" he suggested once his mouth was clear.

She shook her head. "I can't. I'm a server." But there was a sad, hungry expression in her eye and she said it so regretfully that he couldn't help himself. He turned the tables on her, taking a shrimp from the tray and tucking it into her mouth before she could stop him.

"Oh!" she said, laughing, but she chewed and swallowed quickly, after a few surreptitious looks around to see who might be watching. "There's dinner," she said happily.

Marco grinned. She was adorable, but who the heck was she?

As she waved and strolled off to serve appetizers to the others, Shayna appeared at his elbow.

"So you've seen Leila," she noted. "She's working every single job she can come up with to keep those kids fed."

"Leila!" Of course. Why hadn't he realized it? "That's who that was."

"You didn't know?" She gave him a look.

"No. She's gorgeous, isn't she?"

"Yes, she is." Shayna felt her jaw tightening, stopped, and laughed at herself. That reaction was so typically female. *Every time another woman got a compliment didn't mean that she was suddenly in competition with you*, she reminded herself. In many ways, that seemed like a holdover from her old life that she had to get rid of.

They strolled over toward the entertainment and watched the beautiful Tahitian dancers churning their hips. The action was fun and the music was wild, and everyone seemed to be having a heck of a time. But Marco wasn't getting anywhere. He wanted to get back to the reason they were here.

"Is there anyone I should be talking to that I haven't?" he asked Shayna, getting a little impatient with it all.

"Elmo," she said. "He's the one giving the party, after all."

"Okay. And how is he connected? What might he have seen?"

She twisted her mouth, thinking back. "He took you out fishing one day while you were here before. You came back fairly inebriated but without any fish at all." She fixed him with a schoolmarmish look. "But you seemed to have had a good time."

"So I guess his boat was of the inboard motor variety?" Marco noted.

"Yes. All rigged up for deep sea fishing. But I had the impression you two mainly sat around drinking beer and telling each other stories about fishing glories of the past. Though I could be wrong." She put her nose in the air, teasing him. "You never know."

He wanted to kiss her when she teased him like that. But he had to keep his focus. "Lead me to him," he said instead, feeling a bit regretful but doing what was necessary. "Let's see what the man knows."

Elmo was a big, gruff Danish bear of a man who'd come to the islands as a teenager and stayed for good. He'd done well as a home builder for the high end trade that had developed over the last ten years or so, wiping out his previous image as a beach bum. And he loved to give parties.

He remembered Marco fondly and there was a lot of backslapping and loud joking about beer and large fish that got away. But when Marco tried to pin him down on remembering anything about his portfolio, he drew a blank.

"I remember you jotting down information now and then," he admitted. "But I never really paid much attention."

Another dead end. Elmo was called away, and Marco found Leila at his side again with a new plate of appetizers.

"Pigs in blankets," she whispered to him. "I bet they're your favorites."

They were. He took two.

"I hope Jilly and Eddie haven't been driving you crazy," she said before heading off. "I haven't been home much in the last few days so I haven't been able to keep as close an eye on them as I usually would."

"They're fine," he said. "They're beautiful children."

"Oh, thank you," she said, and seemed to mean it. "They're so good, too. They're home right now and Jilly is fixing them tacos for dinner." She had a faraway look in her eyes, as though she wished she were there with them. "I hope this party doesn't last too long," she murmured, more to herself than to Marco.

There was a veil of secret sorrow about this woman and he couldn't help but be intrigued. She looked so spunky, yet vulnerable, that it made him want to do something for her.

"Leila, I was sorry to hear about your husband."

"Yes." Her dark eyes flashed his way. "He disappeared out by Sangria Island."

"No sign of him?"

She hesitated. "Well, they searched Sangria and those two little islands right close. Then I told them about the island where he used to go with his dad as a kid, Grigos, and they said they searched it, but…" She scrunched her face tightly for a second or two. "You know, I don't think they searched enough. That's why I'm trying to make some extra money so I can charter a boat and go out there and look for myself."

Yes, she certainly did have spunk. He nodded approvingly.

"Hey, Leila, good for you. Even if you don't find anything, you'll feel better because you'll be sure."

She nodded. "You know, Mr. Smith—"

"Call me Marco."

Her smile was a little shaky. "Okay. Marco." She sighed, her gaze wandering nervously. "I know people have probably told you that Tony had a girlfriend and he might have jumped ship to...to go be with her," she said, her voice breaking. "But that's not true. Yes, he is very handsome, and yes, he has always had an eye for the ladies." She turned her eyes back to meet his, and he could see that they were shimmering with unshed tears. "But what people don't understand is, he loves me and he loves the kids, and there is no way he would leave us. Not ever."

She gazed up into his face beseechingly, as though he could do something about this, and he was at a loss.

"I...I'm sure he'll turn up," he said unconvincingly.

She gave him a tight smile and turned her attention away as she melted into the crowd again. He watched her go, his heart breaking for her. He knew his answer hadn't done anything to satisfy her or make her feel better in any way. He'd never felt more inadequate. If only he could think of something....

Evening turned into night. The sunset had come and gone. And suddenly, he remembered Eddie. He went looking for Shayna and finally found her near the koi pond.

Shayna had been mixing freely, talking to so many people that it took her aback to realize how many friends she'd made in the little less than a year she'd lived here. Everyone treated her like an old-timer. The cliques and backbiting she'd known in her milieu at home weren't apparent here. She felt good about that. She felt a part of things. Best of all, she didn't get the sense that she had to do something to excite the crowd and justify her existence as she'd felt for most of her life before she came here. People accepted her for who she was. No circus tricks.

Of course, things weren't perfect. There was the occasional jealous woman who acted as if she had to protect her man from cheating bait such as Shayna. And there was the occasional lecherous man who thought he could talk his way into gaining a few sexual favors. But she'd learned how to deal with problem people over the years and that sort of thing had pretty much died down since the first six months she'd been here.

She was happy here on Ranai. She was whole. The only thing missing was a man of her own. And a child. But she was pretty sure she'd taken care of that last request—thanks to the original Marco, the one she'd fallen for weeks ago. The trouble was, she was getting the two Marcos mixed up. They were blending together in her mind. And that was just too dangerous.

The reality was, she adored both of them. And even more reality—she was pregnant. If only she could tell him. If only he would be happy about it, as a father should be. She could close her eyes and pretend, but fantasy did not become her. She was going to have a baby, and she was going to have this baby alone. Had she really faced this yet? She was afraid the truth would overwhelm her if she let herself think about the gravity of the situation.

She was walking out toward the terrace when Marco caught up to her. She'd been still thinking about how she had to beware of him and how hard it was to do that. Somehow that fear, that wariness, translated into seeing her only refuge as being in his arms. Before she knew what she was doing, she found herself clinging to him, pressed tightly against his chest.

"*Cara mia*, what is it?" he said, lifting her chin so that he could look into her eyes. "What's the matter?"

She shook her head, unable to speak without letting him know how close she was to crying. He dropped a soft kiss on her lips, she made a tiny sound, like a kitten, like a sigh, and his arms tightened around her. She felt safe, protected. How could that be when the one she feared was the one holding her? It didn't make any sense.

"I'm sorry," she said, pulling away. "I'm being a big baby. I'm…I'm really sorry, Marco."

"What is it, Shayna?" he asked, catching hold of her hand. "What has frightened you?"

"Nothing." She managed a fairly good smile and congratulated herself on it. "Nothing at all. Now what was it you were coming to tell me?"

He frowned, wishing he understood what had upset her. He was glad she'd turned to him instead of away, but he didn't understand it. And he'd been shocked by the deep, fierce emotional response he'd had—as though he would do anything he had to do to make her smile again.

"Shayna—"

"Hush," she said, shaking her head. "It's nothing. But I was just thinking. What about Eddie?"

He nodded quickly. "That was exactly what I was coming to tell you. We've got to go. We forgot all about Eddie. I made a promise. I've got to keep it."

CHAPTER EIGHT

"OH, MY GOSH!" Shayna said, alarmed as she looked at her watch. "I hadn't realized it was so late."

"That's the problem," Marco agreed. "I don't know what time he goes to bed, but we still have to find a place that sells red licorice."

"Uh-oh." It dawned on her that this was serious. She could tell by the look in his dark eyes that he was going to find a way to keep his promise no matter what it took. "The little general store in town sells it, but they are probably closed by now." She frowned, pursing her lips.

"What are you doing?" he asked impatiently.

She held up a hand. "I'm trying to think if there is any other place where we could buy the licorice."

"There must be another store. A general store, a grocery, a candy store."

"Not with that sort of red licorice." She shook her head, genuinely worried now. "We can stop by Howe's Market on the coast, but I doubt it."

"Well, let's go. If we hurry, maybe we can catch the store at the marina before they close."

She was glad he'd remembered his commitment to the boy. Not many men she'd dated would have done it. Or, once they'd realized it was going to be an imposition to get the candy, they would have decided the promise could wait until the next day. No problem. Just a little boy who would learn how easy it was for adults to lie to him.

Luckily, Marco didn't seem to be one of that type. A woman always liked to see a man keep his word. It was pretty important to the stability of a relationship.

Relationship! Who was she trying to kid? She had no real relationship with Marco and never would. How could she let herself get this close to a man who had been hired to spy on her by her father?

They raced back over a darkened road. Howe's Market along the coast was already closed. Marco was kicking himself for having forgotten until so late. When he thought of Eddie with his bright brown eyes looking at him so earnestly, sure that he would do what he'd promised, it made him sick to think he might disappoint him. Poor little guy. His father was missing and his mother was suddenly gone all the time. He thought of how she was working so hard for her kids and he felt even worse. How could he have forgotten such a simple thing?

A scene flashed into his mind, a moment in his own childhood. His father had been a busy man, director of a huge international shipping enterprise and after his parents had divorced, he'd become more and more remote. To Marco, he'd been a distant sort of god to be worshiped from afar—hardly a warm, fatherly figure.

As a boy, he'd yearned to be closer to him, to get some of his attention. There had been so many lonely days when promises made were broken.

There had been the time, when he was about ten, that his father had sworn he was going to make up for all those missed dates. He would take Marco overnight to attend a sailing competition being held off the Isle of Capri. He could still remember the feeling in the pit of his stomach as he leaned on the balcony railing, staring out into the darkness, waiting to see the headlights of his father's car coming up the long driveway. They never came. He found out later that his father had gone without him, had forgotten all about taking him, in fact. He'd laughed. He'd pretended it was no big deal. But that was the day his trust in fathers died.

But what did he care, really? He barely knew this little boy. He wasn't the boy's father. He wasn't the boy's anything. They had no real tie to each other. No, it was something more than that. There was a certain empathy he felt. The boy had lost his father. He himself had lost a father, even if only emotionally. But he knew how much that loss had hurt, how it devastated his life for a time.

They arrived at the little town, turned at the marina and swung around the corner. There stood the general store, silent and closed, with only one neon sign flashing, an advertisement for beer.

Marco jumped off the scooter and bounded to the front door. "Hello," he called, pounding on the door. "Anyone in there?"

No one responded and he went quickly to the back, trying the same thing. Nothing. He came back to where Shayna sat.

"Quick, we need the store keeper's phone number," he said.

Shayna gaped at him. "Sorry, that's not something I keep on me for emergency grocery requests."

"Well, you should," he said distractedly. Searching the signs on the front of the store, he found a phone number and decided to try it. The ring sounded over and over again in his ears. No one answered. He swore softly.

He stared at the store, set his shoulders, and then he turned and walked back to Shayna, who was still on the Vespa. He looked troubled. Raking his hair with his fingers, he grimaced.

"Okay, I'm going to have to break in."

She felt as though she'd been hit by lightning, flattened to the pavement. "You're kidding," she gasped.

He shook his head, his eyes cold as ice. "No. I have to get that licorice. I don't see any other way." He began rummaging in the saddlebag.

"You're crazy," she said, hardly able to process what he was planning to do. "You're out of your mind."

"Maybe." He found an oily rag and began to wind it around his hand and then grinned at her, wiggling his eyebrows. "But what if I'm the lunatic you're looking for?"

He was enjoying this. She couldn't believe it.

"I don't want a lunatic," she snapped. "I want someone with a cool, clear mind and common sense."

"No." He shook his head. "That won't help us. We're thinking outside of the box here." He put his hand up to the light from the scooter, testing how well the cloth had wrapped. "Lunatics are better for that."

He was really planning to break into the general store. She couldn't fully process that. She grabbed his arm. "Marco, you can't do this. Don't you see? You'll get arrested."

He barely looked at her. "Think so?"

"You'll get thrown in jail."

His grin was fleeting this time. "Will you bring me a file in a cake?"

"No."

He looked at her, one eyebrow raised. "Snob. What have you got against jailbirds?"

She threw her hands down, exasperated with him. "Oh, I don't know. Maybe the fact that they tend to be crooks!"

He thought for a moment, then heaved a heavy sigh. "Eddie's bedtime must be fast approaching, if it's not already come and gone." He looked back at her. "I can't help it, Shayna. I've got to get him that licorice."

She jumped off the scooter and came to him, putting a hand on his arm, trying to think of ways to soothe his conscience. "I know but, there's got to be another way. Maybe if we just thought this through…"

He held his rag-covered fist up for her to admire, then looked into her eyes. "Are you with me?"

"No," she moaned. "You can't do this."

He shook his head. "Oh, but I can." His jaw was set.

"If you can't bring yourself to do a little burgling for a good cause, stay here."

He turned and started toward the window set just above a drink cooler where he planned to break in. She gave a cry of exasperation and ran after him.

"Stop!" she ordered firmly. "Don't you dare break that window. You'll probably slash an artery or something."

"I'll be careful," he said without looking back at her.

"Stop, Marco. I mean it." She grabbed his arm and pulled him around to face her, looking up into his face and feeling a little wild about it. "I'll help you, but not like this."

His frown was suspicious. "How, then?"

She almost had to laugh at his resistance. He looked like a boy threatened with an extra school day.

"Believe it or not, I've got a trick or two of my own up my sleeve," she told him. "Give me a minute to see if this works."

Running back to the scooter, she pulled her purse out of the saddlebag and dug for a credit card, then went toward the front door of the store. A car went past slowly and she paused in the shadows, trying not to look guilty and not succeeding very well. But the car didn't stop. Meanwhile, Marco was unimpressed.

"The old credit card in the door lock trick?" he scoffed. "That went out with high button shoes. Modern locks are made to resist that one."

She waved the card at him. "Modern locks, sure. But you forget. We're on island time now. 'Modern' is a concept, not a reality here."

He shrugged. "Even if you get the main lock, surely there will be bolts inside."

"Marco, the thing you don't understand," she said as she set up to try her idea, "is that there is virtually no crime on Ranai. So no one takes all those extra precautions you need to take in the city. We just don't need to."

She tried the credit card against the edge of the door, then used it to pry a little.

He grunted, looking over her shoulder with growing interest. "So where did you learn how to do this, anyway?"

She gave him an arch smile. "I went to boarding school. We always needed someone to let in the girls who got back late at night." She set the card just right and wiggled it a little. There was a click and the door swung open. She beamed at him. "Voilà," she said with a flourish.

He grinned his admiration for her lock-picking abilities, then walked right past her into the store. "Good work," he said shortly, seeming to forget all his dire warnings. "Now let's find that licorice."

Luckily there was a big box of the whips right by the cash register. Marco picked three, looked at the price, pulled coins out of his pocket and slapped them down on the counter.

"There we go," he said, then hesitated. "I'd better write the store owner a note. Got a pen?" He grinned. "Or better yet, got a lipstick on you?"

She rolled her eyes. "What do you think I am, some kind of gun moll?"

"That was the part you were playacting last night, wasn't it?"

She held up a finger. "Note the operative word—playacting."

"Okay. I guess I'm going to have to steal a pen, as well."

"Wait a minute," she said, caught by the ridiculousness of it all. "You're going to steal a pen so you can write the man you're stealing from a note? Don't you think that's overdoing it a bit?"

He frowned, thinking it over. "It does seem a bit convoluted, doesn't it?"

"Well, never mind. Here's a pen." She produced it out of her purse, along with a tiny notepad of violet-colored paper. "But hurry. We really don't want anyone finding us here."

He hurried. The note was apologetic. He even signed his name. In minutes they were back on the scooter, racing toward home and Eddie next door.

The house looked quiet, but lights were on. Shayna and Marco approached the front door with trepidation. Jilly pulled it open right after their knock.

"Hi, Mr. Marco," she said brightly.

"Hi, Jilly." He shifted his weight, feeling awkward. "Is Eddie home?"

Jilly looked surprised. "He went to bed already."

"Oh." More shifting of weight. Shayna gave him a little shove from behind and he grunted. "I...uh...I brought him the licorice I promised."

"Oh. Great." She smiled. "But he already brushed his teeth."

Shayna smiled at her. "Wow, Jilly, you're such a

good babysitter. You take good care of the little ones. You've already got them all to bed and everything. Your mom is lucky."

Jilly looked pleased. "I'm trying to help her."

A movement caught Shayna's eye, and there was Eddie peeking around the corner. She poked Marco again and gestured in Eddie's direction with her head.

"Eddie!" Jilly cried in dismay.

"Oh, Jilly," Shayna said quickly. "I know it's not fair to put you in this position, but Marco promised him red licorice and he promised he would bring it tonight. Would it be okay if he just gave him the candy and Eddie could save it for tomorrow?"

Jilly looked from Eddie, to Shayna, to Marco and back to Eddie. She shrugged. "Sure," she said sunnily. "Okay, Eddie, come on out."

Marco grinned at him and he came out, hesitated a moment, then ran to Marco, who enveloped him in a big bear hug.

"Hi, Eddie," he said, holding the little boy close. "I told you I'd bring you some red licorice, didn't I? Here it is. You'd better not eat it until tomorrow, okay?"

He nodded, taking the long red whips, his dark eyes shining.

"Okay, kiddo. See you tomorrow. You be good for Jilly, okay?"

Eddie nodded again, and Shayna and Marco gave Jilly a wave and, in Marco's case, a wink, and they left the little house.

"You know, it really feels good to do the right thing,

doesn't it?" Marco said, his chest puffed out as they made their way back to the scooter.

"Absolutely," she responded, hiding her grin.

She drove him back toward his hotel. As they turned the corner toward the two-story building, she jammed on the brakes.

"Hey," he cried.

"Look at that," she said, pointing toward the parking lot.

"Uh-oh." He looked. Two black-and-white cars were parked along the side, their lights swirling. "Looks like the cops are here."

"Oh, goodness," Shayna agreed. "Both cars. This must be something serious."

He gave her a sideways glance. "Like, breaking into the general store, maybe?"

She gasped. "Oh, gosh." She put a hand to her mouth and her eyes got very wide. "Do you think…?"

He nodded. "Yup." He groaned. "I probably shouldn't have signed that note."

She turned and stared at him. "What shall we do?"

He shrugged. "I could walk in and give myself up."

"Or?"

"Or go home with you and wait until tomorrow."

"They might check my place."

"You think so?"

She thought it over. "Not tonight," she said, shaking her head. "Their investigations tend to last a long, long time, because they get to do so few of them. So they savor the moment, so to speak. I bet they won't come out until tomorrow."

"Well, then…"

"Oh, why not just go on in there and tell them what happened? Get it over with. Sheriff Joe's a good guy. I could explain to him. I'm sure he'd understand."

Marco considered that for a moment, his head to the side and his eyes narrowed. "If you were the one on the hot seat, I have no doubt he'd listen to reason. Something tells me he won't be so accommodating for me."

"No, Joe's okay, really."

He raised an eyebrow. "How do you know this?"

She shrugged. "Joe's been trying to date me since I got to the island, and…"

"And you've turned him down?"

"Yes."

He threw up his hands. "There you go. Now we've added jealousy to the mix. I'm out of here."

"Marco…"

"Let's go. I can't risk being tied up in jail for too long. I'm going sailing early with Gigi. I got things I want to get done tomorrow."

She frowned. "Maybe you'd better not go on that."

"No." He shook his head. "I have to go. This isn't just for fun, Shayna. I've got something I really need to accomplish."

She looked at him, perplexed and not sure what he was talking about. Something to do with re-creating his plans, she supposed. "Well, I didn't sign that note, but they will probably find out we're connected at some point and be pounding on my door in the morning."

He nodded. "And in the meantime, we might as well go there and get some sleep."

She sighed. "I suppose so. Everyone is still at the luau. I'm surprised the cops weren't there, too."

"So we should have this side of the island to ourselves," he said lightly. "We'll have a sleepover."

"You," she said pointedly, "can sleep on the couch."

He grinned and put his hand over his heart. "You wouldn't be so cold to a lonely soul about to be sent off to jail."

"I would," she countered. "And gladly."

She turned the scooter toward her home, and they were off.

They were hungry. It had been a long day filled with strange experiences and they needed a little food, a little drink, to help them unwind. Shayna made a shrimp salad and garlic toast and then poured golden liquid into two wine glasses—Chardonnay for Marco, sparkling cider for herself. They ate on the lanai with a candle as their only light until the moon came out. They could hear the surf in the distance. The air was cool and fresh and full of promise. The scent of plumerias wafted in the air.

They sat without speaking for a few minutes, then Marco turned and looked at her. "You know what we didn't remember to do?"

She turned and smiled at him, enjoying the slight lilt to his language. "What's that?"

"Dance." He looked at her with a strange, sensual longing in his eyes. "I want to dance with you."

Her heart beat quickened. There was something in that look of his…. She shivered. *Don't do it, Shayna*, her better counsel warned. *If you do it, you know very well what might happen.*

She shouldn't do it. She should be stern and cool and keep control of the situation. She took a deep breath and prepared to tell him so.

"Hold on, I'll turn on some music" came out of her mouth instead but she didn't regret it.

Moments later, she was in his arms and they were swaying to soft sounds and dancing across the lanai in the moonlight, floating on blissfulness. And it was even better than she'd hoped it would be. There was something so lovely about being held close by a large, strong man that you were crazy about, and yet not in the throes of passion, but in the structure of music. So near and yet so far. Temptation balanced with form.

"How did you get to be such a good dancer?" she asked him dreamily.

"I was a child prodigy," he teased, then relented. "Actually, I had a sister who needed someone to practice with. And I found I liked it."

"You're a natural," she said with a sigh, thinking of her own brother. He would have preferred a dirt sandwich to a day of dancing. Her smile was bittersweet. It was at odd times like this that she missed him most.

She sighed and leaned a little closer against his shoulder. He buried his face in her hair, taking in her scent.

"Where did you come from, Shayna?" he asked her softly. "What are you doing here on this island?"

She sighed, closing her eyes. "Why do you want to know?" she murmured.

"At first, looking at you, I thought you were a natural-born child of the tropics. You seemed to be part of the exotic beauty of the place." He dropped a soft kiss on her forehead. "But now that I know you better, I know that's a posture of sorts. You're no more a native than I am."

"Oh, yeah?" she said groggily in a pathetic challenge.

"You're a transplant. But where from? What for? What made you come hide away on this island?"

Her head snapped around at the phrase *hide away*. He'd finally gotten her goat and she pulled back to give herself a little space from him.

"What are you talking about?" she said crossly. "What makes you think I'm hiding something?"

"We're all hiding, Shayna." They were barely swaying together now, not really dancing, and he had grown philosophical on her, a trend she wasn't sure she liked.

"You know, I think if you want to be analytical about all this, I'm probably hiding things, too. I've been thinking about my memory loss and what could have caused it. I probably let myself go those two weeks while I was originally here. I'll bet I became free and natural in ways I hadn't done in years. Maybe like I'd never been before. And perhaps my psyche couldn't take it. Maybe my more rigid self had to blot it out. Maybe I just had to come back to it slowly and digest it and assimilate it with the rest of me."

She stared at him for a long moment, then rolled her eyes as she pulled herself out of his embrace.

"Oh, brother," she said, turning toward the table. "I think I need another glass of sparkling cider."

He followed her and took over filling both their glasses with the shiny golden liquid. Each caught the moonlight and seemed to glow with its own light.

"To islands," he said, raising his glass for a toast.

"To islands," she echoed. "And the people who hide away on them."

He laughed, enjoying her again, and she bent forward to kiss his lips.

It was a simple gesture, and she'd meant it to be a quick salute, an expression of light affection, but once her lips touched his, a fire that had been smoldering seemed to burst into flames. She meant to pull away, to back off, and go back to her drink. Somehow the kiss lingered and then his hand came up, cupping the back of her head and holding her there. Her mouth softened, opening to his tongue, and her arms came up and circled his neck.

"Oh," she gasped, coming up for air, but he didn't give her a chance to retreat. He kissed her again, and again, and their kisses became deeper and more urgent. Now her fingers were digging into his hair and his hands were sliding up under her shirt, leaving a trail of fire as they found her breasts. Her nipples were erect and so sensitive that she cried out when he touched them. Her hips began to press against his as she melted into his body. The fog of passion clouded their minds and smoothed the way toward an appetite for love. They both knew it. But the sensation was so intoxicating, they didn't want it to stop.

And then Shayna knocked over her glass of cider.

She pulled away, panting, and stared at the spilled liquid. Then she looked up at Marco. "Wow, that was close," she said, and he laughed. Giving him a look, she went to the kitchen to get a cleaning rag. He watched her with regret, but he knew better than to try to resume the activity.

Meanwhile, he poured her a fresh glass of cider.

"Shayna, you've been quite wonderful to me," he said. "You didn't have to be so accommodating this second time around. As I understand it, the first time ended in acrimony. So I want you to know I appreciate the way you've tried to help me this time."

She caught her breath and glanced away, feeling a little guilty. After all, she had her motives that he knew nothing about. It wasn't as though she'd done it all out of the goodness of her heart.

"Why not?" she said lightly. "We'd been pretty friendly the first time, for the most part."

He nodded, looking at her searchingly. "We did seem to spend a lot of time together, you and I."

She nodded. "We did."

He gazed at her for a long moment, then reached out and took a handful of her hair, letting his fingers sift through the shiny strands. "We did some kissing."

She drew in her breath. Where was he going with this? "Yes," she admitted. "Yes we did."

"And?"

She blinked at him. "And what?"

His shrug managed to be incredibly sensual, but she supposed that was the Italian in him.

"Did we do more than that?" he asked, his voice low and husky in a way that sent her pulse racing. His hand cupped her cheek, and he leaned closer.

She had to put some steel in her spine or be forever lost. So that was exactly what she did. Stiffening, she pulled back from him.

"They have a way to say this in Hawaiian," she told him, eyes flashing fire. "*Kapu.* Forbidden. We won't go there."

As he watched her, he so wanted to remember. He ached to remember. He wanted as much of her to carry with him as he could possibly gather, and memories were all a part of that. Sweet memory—he needed it back.

He wanted to find his plans, of course, but more than that, he wanted to find her.

"Shayna," he asked softly. "Did we fall in love when I was here before?"

She gasped, shocked by the nerve of the man. "How can I answer a question like that for you?"

"Forget about me. Did you?"

"Did I what? Fall in love?"

"Yes."

She glared at him. "That's not fair. Don't ask me." She turned and went back into the house, effectively closing off that topic.

His eyes narrowed as he gazed at her, and then he followed her in. He supposed that was answer enough. There had been something special growing between them, something that had been destroyed by what happened at the end of his stay. Once he found out what that was, maybe they could move ahead. But he had a feeling that would be dependent on getting his memory back. And finding his plans.

And as he had that thought, another came to him.

"You know one place we haven't searched for my design plans," he said, glancing around the room. "How about right here?"

"Right here?" Alarms went off in her head and she shook it, hoping he didn't see it. "Don't you think I would have noticed?"

"Who knows?" He gave her a penetrating look. "Sometimes things in plain sight are more hidden than anything else."

She hesitated. The last thing she wanted was to have him looking over her shoulder while she went rummaging through her things.

"That doesn't make any sense," she protested. "I never even saw your plans except in your hotel room. Why would they be here?"

He shrugged. "You're right. It's completely illogical. And that's why we should do it."

She stared at him and couldn't avoid melting a bit, her smile of reluctant affection taking over. It was a ridiculous idea. But maybe that wasn't fair. After all, she wanted to find the darn thing as badly as he did. Why not give her house a good search?

"Okay, we will search my place." She threw her hands out in surrender. "Just so you know, just so you are reassured. Come on." She began to open cupboards and look behind appliances. "There's nothing you can see that's going to discomfort me."

At the same time she was feverishly going over each room in her mind, wondering if there was something that would trigger his memories or fill in some gaps. Was there anything she really needed to hide before she let him do this? The pregnancy test that she'd ordered? She had it in her smallest bathroom cabinet—surely he wouldn't look there. But just in case, maybe she ought to be the one to search her bathroom.

She steered him toward her library and bookshelves, chattering cheerfully the whole time, and she went on into her bedroom to explore her closets and under the bed. Marco was left behind to finish up the main part of the house.

After searching behind doors and under tables, he looked around the room for ideas. Could there be a secret compartment? A gap in the wall? It was hardly likely.

For some reason he felt himself inescapably drawn to the items on her shelves. There was no room to hide a big portfolio there, but maybe some items had been stuck in books, or left between knickknacks. It seemed natural to head right for them. He rifled through a book or two, to no avail. And somehow his eye was drawn to a framed photograph in the middle of the highest shelf. Something about it drew him in.

He stared at the photo. It was an old one of a woman of about thirty and a little girl of maybe five or six. He knew right away it was Shayna and her mother. Nothing was written on the front of the photo, but he recognized the little girl immediately. And there was something eerily familiar about the mother, as well. Reaching high, he picked the picture up, and right away he felt a frisson of excitement. Turning it, he noted the faded writing on the paper on the back. It was so pale, he could hardly decipher the words, but even so, he knew, suddenly, that this was going to change everything.

CHAPTER NINE

MARCO READ THE WORDS on the back of the picture and he stood there for a moment, incredulous. Then it was as though the sky had opened and light was shining through. Those words pretty much explained everything, but more than that, they opened the portal. He knew instinctively that his memory was no longer blocked. It might take a while to get it all back, but it was on its way. The fog was lifting and the light was beginning to shine.

Staring at the picture, he had a flashback of sorts. He winced, wondering if he'd dreamed it. But there it was again. He saw himself just a bit over four weeks before, standing right here, holding this same picture, reading the note on the back, flipping it over to look at the little girl in the picture again and realizing, with astonishment, just exactly who Shayna really was.

The memory of that day filled his mind. He'd heard her coming back and he'd put the picture back up on the highest shelf, then turned to see her coming toward him with a bright yellow Hawaiian shirt in her hands. There was a large red parrot on the front, and she was handing it to him, telling him to put it on to cover the half-naked state he'd been in since she'd pulled him out of the ocean. The knowledge of who this was and what a co-incidence he'd stumbled into had gone through him like an electric shock. It was astounding. Her father was his biggest client.

There had been rumors about her but he hadn't paid any attention to them. He remembered trying to keep up with conversation as he searched his memory for just exactly what he'd heard about her, but it wasn't until later when he'd called a contact in New York who was socially in the know that he'd learned she was really missing.

"Why do you want to know?" the contact had asked. "And hey, where are you, anyway?"

He hadn't answered either question. He'd known in-stinctively that she was hiding here. And if she didn't want him to know who she really was, he wasn't going to push the issue.

The circumstances he'd found himself in amazed him, but he'd been sure that the quickest way to turn her off would be to let her know his connection with her father. And right from the beginning, turning her off was the last thing he wanted to do. She'd appealed to him in a way no woman had in years. He wasn't going to do anything to mess that up.

Besides, he was here incognito himself. He didn't want anyone to know who he was, either. So it all fit together, he'd thought at the time, quite nicely.

Now he knew that it hadn't been nice and convenient

at all. He'd very nearly destroyed everything by keeping things from her. It was something he vowed never to do again.

He put the picture back on the shelf, just as he had done before, and he stood frozen. What should he do now? He'd had a memory breakthrough and he wanted to tell her about it, but what would it mean for the two of them and their relationship? She was still in the bedroom, searching for his missing work.

Suddenly he realized that his portfolio was the last thing he was concerned about anymore. His mind, his emotions, everything was wrapped up in his feelings for Shayna and how she was going to take it when he told her he had his memory back.

She came out of the room with a sigh, apologizing for being unable to help him once again, despairing of ever finding anything. He thought fast. Should he tell her? Would that drive her away? Should he hold off and see what else happened before he let her know?

Sure. Good idea, Marco. Go right back to keeping things from her. Way to build a solid relationship. No, whatever the cost, it was going to be honesty and openness from now on.

She was still talking, but her words died in her throat as she saw his face. "What?" she asked him.

Wordlessly, he reached up for the photograph and handed it to her. All the blood seemed to drain from her face as she took it.

She stared at the photograph. It was almost twenty-five years old. There was no way he could have known who this was. Slowly she turned the picture. There was writing on the back. She'd forgotten about that. Barely visible, it was in her mother's graceful handwriting.

"Mrs. Glendenning Hudson and daughter Summer at five years—ain't we cute? Love, Doris."

Her mother had written that to her aunt Veronica who had given the picture to Summer after her mother's death. There should have been tear stains on the paper, as well. There had been a period of time when she'd cried over it almost every night. Just looking at it still brought a lump to her throat.

She looked up into Marco's eyes and all hope that he had been unable to read the inscription died. He knew. And more than that, he was remembering things.

"Shayna," he said, reaching for her.

She backed away, keeping just out of his extended area. "So you know," she said roughly, her eyes full of regret.

He took a step toward her, not sure what she thought he knew.

"I do know who you are," he said. "I know your real name is Summer Hudson."

She turned her face away so fast, her hair whipped her cheeks. "No," she said fiercely. "You don't know who I am at all." She looked back at him. "That's not my real name anymore. It hasn't been for almost a year. And it never will be again."

To him, that was hardly the point, but he was beginning to realize it meant everything to her. "Shayna," he began again.

"You don't know me at all," she said firmly, just to

make sure he got it. "You still don't remember what you did here two weeks ago, and…"

"I think I'm finally getting some of my memory back," he said gently.

"Ah." A lot of the steam seemed to escape her anger as she took that in, leaving her a bit deflated. "Well, that's interesting."

He wanted to hold her while he said these things, but her body language was still too hostile so he held back. "I think I finally understand what happened between us that last day."

"Do you?"

"I remember how angry you were when you saw my papers and realized my tie to your father. I remember some of the charges you made."

She nodded slowly, her eyes hooded, emotionless. "I remember them, too," she noted dryly. "And they still stand."

He clenched his fists at his sides. "Shayna, your father did not send me here. He had nothing to do with me coming. I didn't discuss any of this with him. He didn't know where I was going or even that I was coming here at all."

"Really." She was obviously unconvinced.

He shook his head. "What gave you the idea that he'd sent me?" he asked.

"It was a little transparent, don't you think? You arrive here and where is the first place you show up? In my bay. What are the odds? And then you get chummy very quickly."

He groaned. "Shayna, Shayna, what man in his right mind wouldn't want to get close to you?"

"You gave me a phony name right from the first. You kept things from me like what you do for a living, just so I wouldn't draw any conclusions." She shrugged, her face sad and distant. "When I realized you worked for my father, I could only conclude one thing—my father had sent you here to bring me back to New York. Or at the very least, to spy on me."

He shook his head. "I came here on my own. It had nothing to do with your father. I remember distinctly how I decided to come here. It had everything to do with those huge photos of the islands I would see every time I went to his office. The images just haunted me. The opportunities for sailing here are so fantastic. But it had nothing to do with him, personally."

She frowned, puzzled and still suspicious. "Then why the phony name?"

"I wanted to work here in peace, without anyone knowing I was here." He gave her a crooked grin. "I'm a little bit famous too, you know."

She digested that for a moment, then added, "But you knew who I was, didn't you?"

"Not at first." He nodded toward the framed photo she was still holding. "Not until I picked up that picture and looked on the back. Don't you remember? It was that first day. You'd gone to find me a shirt and while you were gone, I was browsing your shelves."

She thought about that. "So when I came back with the shirt…"

"By then, I knew you were Summer. It threw me for a loop at first. I thought it was an awfully strange coincidence, too. I called a friend in New York to find out what the deal was and he informed me that you'd been rumored to be missing for quite some time."

Her eyes widened with alarm. "Did you tell him…?"

"I didn't tell him anything, not even where I was staying."

"Oh."

"Shayna…" He stepped toward her again, and again she backed away.

"No," she said, her eyes still dark with trouble. "Leave me alone, Marco. I have to think this through."

He dropped his hands to his sides and nodded. "Tell you what," he said. "I'll go for a walk down along the tide line. I've got some things to think about, too."

"Okay." She turned and went into her bedroom. He stared after her for a moment, then he headed for the shore.

Shayna threw herself down on her bed and waited for tears to come. But her eyes were dry. What if he was telling the truth? What if everything had been coincidental and innocent, just like he said they were? Did that mean that she could let herself be in love with him?

That was only one of the dilemmas that tortured her as she lay on her bed and tried to be sensible. There were so many, the most painful being what she would do if she did let love take over—and then he left. And always in the background, there was the specter of her father hovering over everything. He could so easily swoop in, like a giant, evil bird, and destroy her life again.

Finally she'd had enough wallowing in her own torment. She went into the bathroom and cleaned herself up, freshened her makeup, and headed down to the water's edge to find Marco. He was half a mile down the beach, skipping stones into the water in the moonlight.

"Hi," she said as she came up behind him.

He turned and looked at her, judging if she was touchable. She smiled, and so did he as he took her into his arms. She raised her face for his kiss and his lips touched hers gently and sweetly.

"What are you thinking about?" she asked him as they began to walk together along the water line.

"A lot of things. I'm beginning to remember, Shayna."

"I wasn't sure I wanted you to."

"I know."

"But it's good. You had to remember sometime."

He pulled her closer with an arm around her shoulders. "I should never have left you," he said, a ragged hint of emotion in his voice. "When I realized the suspicions you had, I should have stayed and dealt with them. I thought I would go back to Italy and take care of some business and then come back and all would be well. But the accident happened, the amnesia."

She looked up into his face. "What do you remember?"

He nuzzled her ear. "How good you smell and how good you feel."

She laughed, pushing him away. "Tell me," she ordered him. "I want to know what you're finding out."

He put his head to the side, trying to think of a way to explain it. "Actually, the process is pretty low key. It doesn't happen all at once, it doesn't come to me in a rush. It's more like…like opening the tiny doors on an Advent calendar, one incident at a time. Each time I go to a new door, there's new information, and bit by bit, it's fitting together to make a complete picture."

"And it all got started by reading my old name on the back of that picture?"

He nodded. "Though I've been having a few other flashbacks all day. Just nothing obvious."

She sighed. "I thought you knowing Eddie loved red licorice was a pretty interesting piece of the past," she said. "Though you didn't seem to connect it to anything else."

"Ah, yes." He grinned. Little Eddie. Now he could remember the incident that had cemented their friendship. He had a feeling even Shayna didn't know about it.

"I think it was good the way you cared about Eddie today," she said slowly. "I…I liked it."

He turned to her. He wasn't as sure as she was, but he knew one thing. Eddie was a boy worth making an effort for.

Over the years, he'd thought he didn't like children much. They just weren't a part of his repertoire. And then, wham—little Eddie. He remembered now the first time he'd seen the little boy and felt that tug on his heartstrings. It was the morning of his second day on the island and he'd been walking toward Shayna's house, wanting to see her again and thank her for rescuing him from the Portuguese men-of-war the day before. At least, that was his excuse. He'd been walking through a stand of coconut palms and just as he came out on the other side, he heard boys yelling, "Jump, Eddie! Come on, jump!"

He turned in toward the noise, curious to see why they wanted Eddie to jump. Nearby he found a scrum of nine- and ten-year-old boys surrounding a tin hut with a little three- or four-year-old boy hanging from the roof, holding on to the edge for dear life. He wasn't crying, but his teeth were clenched together so hard, it made his face look square. His little chubby hands were holding on as tight as he could manage, but it was obvious it wasn't going to last for much longer.

"All right, boys. Out of the way."

The boys fell back, startled that an adult had arrived.

"Okay, Eddie," Marco said calmly. "You can let go. I'll catch you."

There was no response from the young one. He just held on tighter, barely glancing down.

"Eddie, I've got you. Trust me."

Finally the boy looked down and met Marco's eyes. He blinked. Something signaled between them, and he let go. He fell right into Marco's arms and he gave him a hug.

"There you go. What were you doing up there, anyway?" he asked as he set him on the ground.

Eddie wobbled for a moment, then got his balance and glanced up. "Nothing," he said. He blinked again, then began to back away. "I think I hear Jilly calling," he said, and then he turned and ran for home. Marco laughed, watching him go.

And that, it seemed, was the beginning of a beautiful friendship.

That seemed to happen quickly here on the island. Too bad he couldn't spend more time collecting friends and less looking for that damn portfolio.

And that reminded him.

"Funny, but I still don't know what happened to my designs."

"Really?" They sat on an old log and gazed out at the surf, glowing white on the reef. "You can't remember what happened after I left your hotel room?"

"Sure, I remember that. I packed the originals in my portfolio and headed for the airport."

"How about the copies in the cardboard tube?"

He stretched, getting the kinks out of his long body. "That's what I can't remember. I'm pretty sure the portfolio lies at the bottom of the sea in Italy. But that tube…" He shook his head, frowning. "I don't remember going to the post office with it as I usually would."

"That's not a surprise. Our post office is only open on Wednesdays and Fridays. You were leaving on a Sunday."

"Ah. So…did I mail it on Friday or did I give it to someone else to mail for me?"

She shook her head and they both sat silent for a moment, trying to remember.

"Nothing?" she asked at last, and he shook his head.

"Nope."

She sighed. "Well, you're closer than you've been. So maybe it will come." Rising, she shook off the sand. "Let's go back and have a bowl of ice cream and get some sleep. You've got to get up early to get to Gigi's in the morning."

He looked up hopefully. "What kind of ice cream?"

She smiled. "Chocolate mint."

He rose, too. "My favorite. Lead the way."

They marched back, arm in arm, saying silly things and laughing. Shayna glowed with happiness. This was what she loved. Having someone who fit her moods and made her laugh….someone who liked ice cream and made her sizzle with passion, too. What could be better?

They sat at the counter in her little house, eating their ice cream and talking softly. Finally, Marco brought up an uncomfortable subject.

"Tell me this, Shayna. Why are you so afraid of your father showing up and finding you?"

She shivered before she could stop herself. "Be… because he'll try to take me back to New York."

He frowned, not fully understanding. "You don't have to go. You're a grown woman. You're on your own. He doesn't have any power over you now."

She turned her huge eyes on him and he could see right away that she was fearful of the very concept of facing her father. "You're wrong," she said. "You don't know what he's like."

A feeling welled up in him, a sense of shared danger, a sense of shared response. He knew what she was feeling and he knew he could help her deal with it. Reaching out, he touched her cheek.

"Ah, but I do. And I know exactly what you mean. He's strong. He's got charisma like no one else I've ever met. He can make people do things they know they shouldn't just by the force of his personality. I know. I've done some of those things."

She regarded at him with pure, unalloyed gratitude. He understood. So few did. Everyone thought it would be neat to have a father like that. They didn't know, didn't understand. Sure, her father had a magnetic personality. He had wealth and power. And because of that, he could have shielded her from some of the worst that the paparazzi had to dish out if he'd wanted to. The trouble was, he didn't want to. He was proud of having a daughter who appeared regularly in the tabloids. He loved the notoriety, the pictures in the paper, the family name appearing in the gossip columns. He would get the paper and chortle over it.

"Look here, Summer. Look how they caught you with your dress half off your shoulder. I can't believe they would print something like that in the paper."

He loved it. She didn't.

"But here's something I don't understand," Marco was saying. "Isn't it kind of crazy to come here to hide and to be working in a tourist trap café if you don't want to be noticed?"

She sighed and leaned across the counter, feeling sleepy. "Not really. I dyed my hair and did some things that make me look real different from Summer. And also, I had to think this through from the beginning. I needed some sort of cover here on the island, and I also needed to do something to make some money." She gave him a mischievous smile. "I didn't think fishing would bring in enough."

"You don't have any money?" He was astounded. After all, her family was rolling in it.

She shook her head. "I only brought a limited amount with me." She looked into his eyes earnestly. "Don't you see? The whole point was to be a normal, regular person. How could I do that if I brought along enough to buy anything I wanted?"

That made sense, he supposed. And he looked at her with new respect, knowing she was so dedicated to this project, so determined to make herself whole.

"Anyway, I figured anyone who saw me and noticed the resemblance would just say, 'Gee, she looks like that face that was all over the tabloids a while ago, doesn't she? How funny to think of Summer Hudson with blond hair and waiting on tables in a place like this. The real Summer Hudson would be dancing on the tables, don't you think?'"

The bitterness in her tone startled him.

"Was that really your image?"

"Sure." She lifted her chin. "It was an image I...I hated." Her voice broke and she cleared her throat.

Reaching across the counter, he took her hand in his.

"I never actually did most of those things," she told him earnestly. "But once the public gets that picture into their heads, there is just no way to turn it around again."

He saw the haunted clouds in her eyes, heard the anguish in her voice, and his heart went out to her. He didn't want her to have to face that sort of life again, not when it caused her so much pain. He wanted to be her protector, to hold her in his arms and watch over her from now on. At least, that was the impulse he was feeling. Was it realistic? He couldn't tell right now, not while she was so close and he was feeling such deep emotion at the sight of her.

"And that's why you're so afraid of your father finding out where you are." He shook his head. "Shayna, you still see him through the eyes of a little girl. Stop doing that. Look him square in the face and tell him exactly what you think, what you want, what you're willing to do. You're a grown woman. You can do it."

She shook her head. She was incredibly sleepy. It was way past time for bed. "No, Marco. When he tells me what to do, I do it. That's the way it's always been. I can't help it. I guess it's just a Pavlovian thing. I have to stay away from him at all costs. At least, I have to do that if I want to maintain my sanity. He's just too scary."

Reaching out, he pulled her closer and dropped a kiss on her warm lips. "In case you haven't noticed, Shayna, I'm scarier than he is. And you've certainly faced me down."

She giggled, curling into his embrace. This was the way life could be if only… Oh, well, it didn't bear thinking about.

They dragged themselves out of their respective beds and to the counter for breakfast early the next morning, groaning and complaining. Then Marco took her scooter and raced off into the dawn. She yawned and went back to bed. She was sure the day would bring some challenges, and she wanted to be as rested as she could be. She slept the sleep of the innocent and woke about nine.

It was around ten in the morning before she got the expected visit from Sheriff Joe. He announced himself by knocking on her door, then slouching against the doorjamb in what he obviously considered was an impressive tough-guy pose.

"Hey, Shayna," he said, giving her the eye as she opened the door to let him in. "I think you've got some explaining to do."

"Who, me?" she responded innocently, all big-eyed. "I don't know what you're talking about."

He shouldered his way in with just the hint of a swagger. "It is my understanding that you have been friendly with a certain person suspected of perpetrating a crime in our community."

She blinked at him. "Huh?"

He frowned, obviously irked that she didn't pick up on his lingo quickly enough. "You were seen yesterday in the company of one Marco DiSanto, sometimes known to be traveling under the alias of Marco Smith. Is that correct?"

She smiled. "Yes, Joe. I do know him very well."

He shook his head, as though this information saddened him. "Just what kind of a con man is this jerk, anyway?" he asked her, dropping the semiofficial tone and talking friend to friend.

"He's not a con man." She laughed. "Oh Joe, sit down, I'll pour you a cup of coffee and tell you all about it."

And she tried. She charmed him. She gave him cookies to have with the coffee. She explained the whys and the wheres and the how-comes. She opened up her heart. But Sheriff Joe was adamant.

"The perpetrator, Marco DiSanto, alias Marco Smith, is the sort of felonious assaulter who needs a little jail time to let him think through his life of crime," he stated categorically. "Do you know where he is right now?"

Shayna realized she could be perfectly honest about that. "No, actually. I have no idea where the winds of chance have taken him right now."

He eyed her suspiciously, but she just smiled.

"Well, you might as well let him know that he'd better contact me soon or I'll be coming after him."

"I'll be sure he understands the gravity of his situation," she promised.

He lingered at her doorway, looking her up and down again. "Say, you know, there's a film festival of funky old movies at the Bijou Saturday. How about you and me…?"

She was already shaking her head. "Sorry Joe," she said. "I'm going to be busy."

His shrug was good-natured. "Can't blame a man for trying," he said as she waved him off.

"See you later, Joe."

She wasn't working today but she thought she'd go into the village to see what was going on. And then she had an idea. Leila was working at the hotel. What if she slipped in there and got Leila to open the Lost and Found room so that she could check around for Marco's lost cardboard tube herself? They had supposedly checked when she called, but she really didn't trust them.

With that in mind, she walked into town. The air was breezy and the coconut palms were swaying all along the beach. As she walked past the marina, she noticed a few new yachts had arrived. And then she did a double take. There was a sleek beauty turning heads—and flying her father's colors from its mast. There was no doubt. Just what she'd been dreading all along had finally happened. Glendenning Hudson had come to town. Her heart froze in her chest.

She walked home with all the speed she could muster, breathing quickly. Coconut crabs in borrowed shells skittered out of her way. Her father was here. What now?

CHAPTER TEN

SHAYNA'S PANIC WAS REAL and for a few minutes, over-whelming. Her worst nightmare had come true. Her father was here and her life was probably in ruins. This island had been her refuge, her paradise. And now he was here. Would he try to take her back home? Of course he would. What else was he here for?

Her impulse was to make a run for it, but there was really nowhere to run. Marco had told her to stand up to him. Should she try that? It didn't seem likely. It had never worked before.

Her father had an ego as big as the oceans he sailed on, a very hungry ego that needed constant feeding. Most people around him got exhausted with the effort. He was insatiable.

It had been one thing when her brother was alive. The two of them had conspired together. Kenneth was much better at standing up to their father, and the two of them would laugh about his encounters with the big man. But once Kenneth had died along with her mother in a car accident…she closed her eyes, pushing back against the pain that always rose in her when she thought of those deaths. They had damaged her life in so many ways and left her a wounded person.

Her father had manipulated that, used it. And she had ended up a hollow husk of a woman, not worth knowing or listening to. But that was then and this was now. Today, she knew she was worth something. She was a real and vibrant person. And she was happy. She couldn't let him take that away from her. No matter what, she had to fight back.

In the meantime, what could she do? She paced the floors, then decided to go on a hike. After all, if her father came looking for her here, she would have no escape plan.

It was later that afternoon, as she was on her way back toward home, when her phone chimed. She was surprised. Her phone didn't ring that often; phone service was spotty at best. Sometimes it seemed as though you had to wait for a beam up to a satellite and back again before a call went through, and it all depended on if that satellite was in the right position at the right time. But this time it was coming through loud and clear, and it was Marco.

"Hello?" she said breathlessly.

"Hi. Shayna?"

"Yes! What is it? Are you okay?"

"We're okay." The call was breaking up and she held her breath, trying hard to hear every word. "We're coming in, but we're not going to Gigi's dock. We're heading for the main marina."

That was a surprise. "The main marina? How come?"

"We've got a special person on board."

"What?" She couldn't imagine why they would have added someone from the middle of the ocean. How did that work exactly?

"Shayna, we found Tony."

Shock sizzled through her system. "Leila's Tony?" she practically shrieked.

"That's the one."

"What! Where! When!"

"We found him on an island. Grigos, actually. He's basically okay but a bit feverish—undernourished and suffering from sunstroke, and he got hurt recently, trying to capture a wild boar. Could you have medical help there to meet us?"

"Of course."

"And Shayna, get Leila and the kids, too."

She felt like dancing on air. "Marco, what on earth have you done?"

"Nothing."

"Oh, it's something all right." She laughed aloud. "Something pretty wonderful."

"Just get a medic to the scene, okay?"

She could hear the happy grin in his voice.

"Will do."

Her heart was thumping hard as she snapped her phone shut and put it away. This was huge. This was bigger than her petty little problem with her father. This was so much more important. Marco had found Tony. What a miracle. What a man he was.

But she had her own part to play and she had to get moving. She knew where the doctor was right now. He was always in the same place in the late afternoon—the hotel lounge. After a hard day of medical healing, he liked to toss back a few tall ones. And who else was probably there, holding court with whomever he could get to be his makeshift audience? Her father. She didn't have to be told. She knew he was there. It fit his pattern.

Well…that didn't matter anymore. She was going to brave facing the lion in his lair. Changing into silk pants and a light shirt, she headed for the village at a brisk clip.

It didn't take long to get to the hotel, and she bounded up the wide stairway, heading straight for the bar. She looked around the lounge as she entered. Her father was sitting in the middle of the action, as usual, but her gaze only lingered on him for a moment. The doctor was there, as always, and he seemed to be enjoying things more than usual. There was Bobby, leaning on a chair. Kim, the hotel manager was sitting next to her father at the table. Various tourists and fishermen had pulled up chairs nearby, gathering around as her father held them all spellbound with his jokes and his stories and his oversized personality. He was at the center of attention, just where he loved to be. And then he glanced up and saw her.

Their gazes met and held. There was so much emotion there. She loved her father, deep down, and he was all she had left in the world. But he was no good for her and they both knew it. He was willing to go with it, she was not. He would ruin her with hardly a backward glance, and she knew that, too. But that didn't mean she didn't have feelings for the man. In some ways, she adored him. Everybody did.

He stood up. She stood still. And now, just what kind of drama did he want to make out of this encounter with his wayward daughter?

"It's good to see you," she said loud and clear, and suddenly realized just how true it was. A surge of emotion seemed to burst inside her. This was her father, her only living relative. She hadn't seen him for almost a year and she hadn't realized how much she'd missed him until this very moment. Without a second thought, she stepped up and threw her arms around him as tears filled her eyes. He pulled her into a big bear hug and she laughed, holding on to her father, her life.

"I've come to take you home, honey," he said, his voice choked.

She felt the pull. She loved him and she wanted to please him. He was her daddy and he'd just told her what he expected of her. How could she turn from him? How could she tell him that she wasn't going to live the way he wanted her to anymore?

Closing her eyes, she heard Marco's voice. "You're a strong woman, Shayna. You're not a little girl anymore. You have to live the way you know is right for you."

Opening her eyes again, she faced her father. Her heart was beating so hard, she thought she would faint. Reaching out, she took hold of the back of a chair to keep from falling. But she looked him right in the eye and lifted her chin.

"I'm not going with you, Daddy. My home is right here."

There was pandemonium at the marina. By the time the *True Yar* slipped into the waterway, all the hotel's inhabitants and customers had come pouring out of the building, along with Leila and all her kids, and all her friends, and all her relatives, and everyone else within earshot. People were running up the beach to get there in time to see the great arrival.

Shayna had the doctor in tow, ready to scramble aboard once the *Yar* had been moored in tight. She could see Marco at the wheel, and her heart swelled with pride. There was a lot of shouting and calling back and forth as the yacht was secured and a gangplank raised. Leila and the kids poured onboard and gathered around where Tony was lying on a small mattress. Semidressed in a neon green bikini, Gigi regaled the crowd with the story of the rescue, and Shayna noticed that even her father was quiet for a moment or two, listening.

"Well, it seems that Marco talked to Leila at the luau last night and she told him that she just couldn't shake the feeling that Tony was out there somewhere, maybe on Grigos Island, and she was saving up to pay for an expedition to see what she could find on her own. So Marco says to me, 'Hey, why don't we head on over there and take a look?' And I say, 'I'm up for it.' And we set sail for Grigos."

"I thought that island had already been searched," someone called from the crowd.

"Maybe so," Gigi said with a wide-armed shrug. "Maybe he was unconscious under a bush at the time and they didn't see him. Maybe he didn't actually get washed ashore until the next day. We didn't see him at first. It took us a good hour and a half, and then, just when we were about to give up, we found him in a cave, sound asleep, staying out of the noonday sun, just like you have to do to survive these things."

"But how did he get there?" someone else called in.

Gigi made a face. "He's not real clear on that. We'll have to wait until the doctor patches him up. He's pretty close to delirious at times, with the fever and all. But he did remember being washed overboard when they were going through the Sangria Channel. He grabbed on to a big driftwood log and hoped for the best, as he saw his boat heading on without him. He must have hung on a long time, but thank God, he made it to land. So I'm sure we'll get the rest of the story when he's well enough to tell it."

The buzz from the crowd grew louder as everyone had to have his say on this amazing story, but Shayna wasn't really paying attention. Marco had found her among the onlookers and was coming her way. She turned to meet him. He gave her a crooked grin and a questioning look, and she ran to him. There was no hesitation. He took her into his arms, and then she was inside his embrace, where she wanted to be forever.

"Hey, Mr. Superhero," she said, laughing up at him.

He tried to look modest. "It was nothing," he said.

Then he grinned, his eyes shining happily. "Actually, it's about the coolest thing I've ever done."

"I know."

He kissed her. It was a public kiss, so it wasn't as intimate as it could have been. But it was full of life and fire and the thrill of victory, and Shayna thought she'd never been kissed with so much conviction before.

I love you, she thought, but even now, she didn't dare say it aloud.

The celebration went on late into the evening. People set off bonfires all up and down the beach near the area where Shayna had her little house and Leila was raising her big family. There was singing and dancing and people just kept bringing food. Shayna and Marco sat with others around the biggest bonfire while Jilly's friend Kali was trying to teach Marco how to play a ukulele.

"I can play a mean guitar," he claimed. "And I've tried the mandolin. How hard can ukulele be?"

Hard enough to keep the whole gang in stitches over his efforts. He'd finally begun to sound as if he knew what he was doing on a nice Hawaiian tune, when suddenly Jilly stood up and pointed.

"Oh, Mr. Marco, look at Eddie!"

They all turned to see what she was talking about. And there was Eddie, struggling to drag a big long white cardboard tube through the sand. A hush fell over them. Marco stood up and waited as Eddie came toward him. When he got close enough, he stopped and looked up into Marco's eyes.

"Hi, Mr. Marco," he said in a high childish voice. "I saved this for you." And he plunked the tube down at Marco's feet.

Marco and Shayna gaped at each other. Then Marco reached down and lifted the tube, breaking it open and looking inside. There were the copies of his plans, the ones he'd been looking for all over the island.

"Eddie." He looked at the boy. "Eddie."

Leila came running up, breathing heavily. "Oh, Marco, I'm so sorry," she said. "Eddie has been hiding this under the house all this time. I didn't know. I'm just so…"

"Eddie," Marco said in wonder. "Where did you get this?"

He pointed at his mother. "I got it at Mama's work," he lisped.

Leila shook her head. "I think he means he found it at the hotel," she said.

Shayna rose to stand beside Marco. "You mean one of those times he followed you to work?" she asked, but Leila shook her head.

"No, I remember what happened. I took him to work with me one day last month. The day Mr. Smith…well, he's Marco now, but you know what I mean. It was the day he left for Italy. Jilly had a piano lesson, so I had to take Eddie with me. Of course, I wasn't supposed to, so I had to hide him from the manager so I could work. But he got loose in the hotel and I had to send him home with one of the other girls. She just told me he had a white tube with him when she took him. He says now that he got it—"

"From the mail room," Marco said, smacking himself on the forehead with the flat of his hand. "I remember now. I put it there to be taken to the post office as soon as it opened." He groaned, laughing into Shayna's shocked expression. "*Dio santo*, how did I forget that?"

Leila still looked stricken by the whole affair. "Eddie, you tell Mr. Marco how sorry you are."

Eddie had to say it around the thumb in his mouth. "Sorry." he muttered.

Marco went down on one knee. "Eddie, you shouldn't take things without telling people. But in this case, you did me a favor. You kept my papers safe for me. And I appreciate that." He opened his arms and the boy allowed himself to be hugged, but only for a moment.

The others went on celebrating, but Marco and Shayna went up to the house and he showed her what the plans entailed. The drawings were beautiful, and they were both enjoying the showing until her father appeared at the door.

"So this is home for my little girl," he said, looking around as though he couldn't believe she lived in such a hovel. "And you're really happy here?"

She watched him as he and Marco made small talk. Her feelings for him were so mixed, she felt a touch of nausea and wasn't sure if it came from that, or from the tiny treasure she carried inside her.

"What luck to find you here," her father told her, his handsome face craggy in the artificial light. "I'm on my way to a regatta in New Zealand and just stopped off here by chance."

"Really?" She found that hard to believe. It seemed one too many coincidences. "So you'll be on your way in the morning?" she asked hopefully.

"Yes," he said. Then he clapped Marco on the shoulder with his big hand. "And I want this young man to come with me." Seeing Marco's face, he added, "In fact, I'm going to insist on it. And since you are still under contract, I think I've got the upper hand on this one." He said it with charming good nature, but there was steel behind his words.

Shayna felt as though she were standing on quicksand and her father was making the earth shake. Why had he come? No matter what else happened, her father being here had ruined everything. Even if he didn't take her back to New York, everyone would know that she was really Summer Hudson and they all would expect her to live up to that reputation. Was she going to have to go find another island to live on?

"Here's the bottom line," he was saying to them both. "I want my daughter back home in New York and I want my designer back working on my yacht. Now let's start working toward those goals, shall we?"

Marco stared back. Up until this very evening the whole focus of his being had been to find his plans and get back to working for this man. To regain his status and his career. But now that he was face-to-face with what that really meant, it didn't seem to matter so much anymore. The only thing that really mattered was Shayna and finding a way to have a life with her. His career was great and all his success had been wonderful, but it hadn't brought the sort of happiness an afternoon hike to a waterfall had brought him. More of that was possible here with her, and he was going to reach for it.

At the same time, he was bound by his contract. He had to fulfill the agreements he made there. He owed Hudson some work, and he was going to do what was expected of him. But he would be back. He was sure of that.

"Of course you'll come back with me, Summer," her father was saying. "Marco will be coming, as well. You understand that, don't you?" He put an arm around the younger man's shoulders. "We have big plans, Marco and I. He knows where he needs to be. He can't stay here with you, even if he really wanted to." His smile was deceptively benign. "If you want to be with him, you're going to have to come along, sweetheart."

Shayna stood up and swayed a bit. But she wasn't feeling shaky any longer. She understood what was going on here. She was losing Marco. He had to go. Of course he had to go. He'd never promised her anything else, had he? She'd known ever since that day in his hotel room that it would end like this. And he could make all the promises he wanted, once he was gone, his allegiance to her would begin to fade rapidly. He would put off coming back. Time would pass. She would be like that sad lady in *Madama Butterfly*, waiting for a man who was never coming back.

Her father knew that she understood this. That was why he was pulling Marco away. Marco was his bait, his inducement. Well, for once it wasn't going to work.

She wasn't sure why she felt so strong this time.

Maybe all Marco's pep talks had worked. Or maybe it was the fact that she was carrying her baby and she wasn't alone. She had a new focus for her life. It would break her heart to see Marco go, but she still had her child.

"I'm not leaving," she said, her voice clear as a bell. "I told you, Daddy, I belong here now. This is where I'll stay."

And she turned on her heel, heading into her bedroom and leaving the two men behind to make their plans. She was done with them both.

It had been almost a month since she'd seen Marco. He'd left that next morning on her father's yacht and they hadn't stopped by the island on their way back from New Zealand. He'd called twice. And that was that.

She didn't cry anymore. She'd done enough crying. She was moving on, planning for her baby and learning more and more about standing up for herself. She had to stand up for herself. There was no one else to stand up for her. And that was good.

So here she was, about to become a single mother.

Ah, the irony. All those years of being the wild child among the glitterati and she'd come through scot-free. Now she was on an island, living like a normal person, falling for a real, solid man, and she messed up like she never had when she was being the party girl. But that was no way to think of it anymore. She was a mother. Despite everything, it brought her such joy.

She was still conflicted about Marco. She loved him, she knew that. He'd never said he loved her. She'd just assumed it. She'd been so sure he was about to tell her so. He acted as though he loved her. She'd been waiting, just trembling there on the brink, for him to say the words that would seal the deal. But he never did and then, suddenly, he was gone.

He had left her with something, though. And he'd taught her a lot. Still, he could say he would stand up to her father all he wanted, but when it came right down to it, she'd been the one who'd stood fast. Of course, she could hardly blame him. On the one hand, there was Glendenning Hudson with his power and his money and his charisma, and his ability to give Marco everything he'd worked for all his life, to make him center of the yacht racing universe, to give him contracts and contacts that would put him at the pinnacle of success. On the other hand, there was poor little pathetic Summer Hudson, playacting at being Shayna Pierce, island girl. What kind of choice was that? He'd taken the only path he could, the only one that made any sense. Unfortunately, she wasn't on it.

Even so, she would have given anything to have him back. And every night, she turned out the light with this silent prayer.

"Please, Marco, remember me."

She'd gone to bed with a good book, but it wasn't holding her interest. She was jumpy tonight. Still, she had to get some sleep. She turned out the light, said her usual prayer and closed her eyes.

They popped open ten seconds later. There was the

strangest sound. She was used to the night sounds here—parrots arguing late at night, flies buzzing in after a breadfruit had dropped with a plunk in the yard or the sharp crash of a coconut hitting the roof. But this was unusual. She strained her ears. Someone was playing a ukulele, and playing it badly. And the funny things was, he was starting to sing.

"La donne è mobile..."

Italian opera on a ukulele? Her heart nearly leapt out of her chest. That could be only one person in this world and it sounded as if he was on her front lanai. Jumping from bed, she skidded in the hallway and ran for the front door, flinging it open.

"Marco?"

He didn't say a word, but he erased the distance between them in two long strides. She was in his arms and he was kissing her hungrily. A few fleeting thoughts skimmed through her mind—like maybe she should check if he was just visiting or back for good before she handed him her heart on a silver platter. But the doubts didn't linger. He tasted too good to be denied.

"You'd better come in," she said at last, panting a bit. "Oh, Marco, I've missed you."

"I came back as quickly as I could," he told her as they walked in together, his arm still around her as though he couldn't bear to let her go for an instant. "I wanted to get everything done and cleared up. I sold my apartment in New York and leased out my house in Italy."

She turned and searched his dark eyes. "And my father?"

He smiled, his beautiful white teeth flashing against his tan skin. "I completed all my obligations to your father. I'm free of him, just like you are."

"Oh, Marco!" She kissed him again and again and they fell together onto the couch, still holding on, needing to feel body on body.

He sat back, stroking her hair, devouring the sight of her like a starving man. "Shayna, you're so beautiful. When shall we get married?"

She pulled back, shocked. "Married? Who says we're getting married?"

He looked surprised. "Don't you want to get married?"

"Of course I do." She pouted. "But nobody's asked me yet."

"Oh. Here, wait a minute." He fumbled in his pocket. "How's this?" Gracefully, he slid off the couch and went on one knee, then held out a velvet box and opened it. A huge diamond sent lightning bolts of sparkle all around the room.

She gasped, then started laughing.

"Shayna Pierce, will you marry me?" he asked dutifully.

"Marco DiSanto, my answer is yes!"

Slipping the ring onto her finger, she held it up to the light and swooned. Meanwhile, Marco was frowning. He'd just noticed a pile of baby magazines on her coffee table.

"What's this?" he said, lifting one and gazing at the happy babies pictured on the cover. "What's all this?"

"Babies," she told him. "Don't you want a baby?"

He looked at her, enchanted with the idea, as though it were the first time he'd ever given it a thought. "Yes. We should have babies." Pulling her closer, he nuzzled her neck and dropped kisses on her chin line. "Why don't we get started on that right away?" he suggested in a sultry fashion.

"Sorry," she said. "You're too late."

He pulled back and stared at her. "Too late?"

Pulling her sleep shirt up, she grabbed his hand and put it over her belly. "Do you feel that?" she demanded.

He waited a moment, then frowned and shook his head. "I don't feel anything," he said.

She nodded confidently. "You will very soon. Our baby will wake up and let you know she's there. Just give her a few more weeks."

He turned and looked at her with disbelief. "We're pregnant?" he said in astonishment. "Why didn't you tell me?"

"I'm telling you now. Are you happy about it?"

He put his hands on either side of her face and gazed lovingly down into her eyes. "Shayna, I didn't know what happiness was until I fell in love with you. And making little copies of our love will only make that happiness expand."

And that was the last word on that subject.

THE SICILIAN'S BRIDE
Carol Grace

Dear Reader,

Can you tell that I love Sicily, with its mysterious inland mountains, its trendy cities, its rumbling volcano and its wonderful beach resorts? If you have any doubt, you'll be convinced of my love affair with this island when you read *The Sicilian's Bride*. I've tried to capture a newcomer's fascination with the scenery and the people by giving an American woman a Sicilian vineyard, which she inherits from an uncle she never knew. Then I've put an obstacle in her path to achieving her dream of finally finding a home of her own. That obstacle is a wealthy and hard-working winemaker who thinks he deserves to have her vineyard – not her.

When my family and I vacationed in Sicily a few years ago I said to myself, "I must set a book here." Thanks to Mills & Boon for giving me the chance to share my passion for the delicious and spicy pasta dishes eaten in charming coastside restaurants, for visits to cathedrals and palazzos and best of all for the people of Sicily – warm-hearted, opinionated and incredibly generous to foreigners like me.

Best wishes

Carol

Carol Grace has always been interested in travel and living abroad. She spent her junior year in college at the Sorbonne and later toured the world on the hospital ship *Hope*. She and her husband have lived and worked in Iran and Algeria. Carol says writing is another way of making her life exciting. Her office is her mountain-top home overlooking the Pacific Ocean, which she shares with her inventor husband. Her daughter is a lawyer and her son is an actor/writer. She's written more than thirty books and she also writes single titles. She's thrilled to be writing for Mills & Boon® Romance. Check out her website – carolgracebooks.com – to find out more about Carol's books. Come and blog with her fun-loving fellow authors at fogcitydivas.com

CHAPTER ONE

ISABEL MORRISON was lost. She'd been driving around on dirt roads for hours looking for the Monte Verde Vineyards. There were no signs at all out here in the country. The small rented Fiat was not equipped with GPS or air conditioning and she was sweltering in the September heat. She'd known it would be hot in Sicily, but not this hot.

No wonder there was no one around to ask directions. Only mad dogs and Englishmen were out in the noonday sun. And one American looking for her piece of the American dream, far far from home. All she wanted, all she'd ever wanted, was a home of her own.

The home she was looking for, if she ever found it, would be a place to start over. A place to put down roots at last. A place where no one knew what mistakes she'd made in the past. A place to earn a living growing grapes in a vineyard she'd inherited from an uncle she'd never known.

As an orphan, she'd been left on the doorstep of the home for foundlings with nothing but a basket and a blanket and a note asking the good sisters to take care of her. Which they had done, as best they could. She'd known nothing of an uncle. Least of all what he was doing in Sicily and why he'd left her a vineyard. All that mattered was that someone cared enough to leave her an inheritance—and what an inheritance! A home of her own. Not only that, but vineyards too.

She'd done everything she could before she'd left home: read a dozen guide books, taken Italian lessons and a short course in viticulture. She believed in being prepared and self-reliant. Being naive and too trusting had gotten her heart broken. Never again.

Now if only she could find the old villa—the Azienda—and the supposedly neglected vineyards on the Monte Verde Estate, she'd be in business. The business of settling in, growing grapes and producing the great little dessert wine, Amarado, that the place had once been known for.

According to the map the solicitor, Signore Delfino, had given her it should be right...over...there.

"I can have someone take you out there next week," he'd said.

"Thank you, but I can't wait until next week," she'd answered. Next week? She'd been waiting all her life for a place she could call her own and now she couldn't wait another day. She'd wondered if he was stalling. He'd tried to talk her into selling the place before she'd even seen it.

"I must advise you," he'd said, "the property is in some dis-repair from neglect. If you want my advice…" He cleared his throat. "You should sell it to a local family who are prepared to make you a generous offer. I can handle the details for you." The way he'd said it indicated she'd be crazy to turn the offer down.

"Please tell the family I appreciate their interest, but the property is not for sale." No matter how much they offered, she wouldn't sell, and she'd find it on her own, thank you very much.

On one side of the road was a rushing stream lined with eucalyptus trees, and on the other side, golden wheat fields lay next to vines heavy with fruit. The air was heavy with the spicy smell of the trees and the scent of wheat drying in the sun. But she couldn't figure out how to get to where she wanted to go.

Yes, it was hot and the air was dry. Yes, she was lost. But she was also nervous and scared at the prospect of actually turning grapes into wine that was good enough to sell in the upscale market. One thing at a time, she told herself. Maybe there would be a kindly old caretaker who would take her under his wing and show her how it's done. He'd say, *Your uncle talked about leaving the place to you. How you'd carry on the family tradition...Let me help you get started.*

She smiled to herself, picturing the scene. One way she'd dealt with rejection in the past was to lose herself in an imaginary world, to the dismay of her teachers and foster parents who accused her of being a dreamer. It was her way of escaping the hard edges of reality.

As a graduate of the School of Hard Knocks, she'd learned early on in life to have an escape route when life's problems got too overwhelming. Another coping mechanism that had come in handy to was to act in a confident and self-assured manner, especially when feeling the opposite.

Just when she thought she'd have to turn around and go back to the little town of Villarmosa and get more directions, she spotted a man picking grapes. Exactly the kind of man she would need to hire to work in her fields. Even if there was a kindly mentor on the premises, she'd still need laborers. The man in sight was strong, tall and muscular and obviously used to hard work. Being a local, surely he'd know where her vineyard was.

She was so excited she slammed on the brakes, and skidded to an abrupt halt.

He looked up. She grabbed the map, got out of the car and

walked toward the field where he stood staring at her as if he'd never seen a stranger here before. Which made her feel better about staring at him. She stared at his blunt nose that looked like it might have been broken a few times. She stared into his eyes, impossibly blue in a sun-tanned face.

Then her gaze moved down. He was shirtless, and his jeans rode low on his hips. Very sensible in this kind of weather. And very sexy too. She swallowed hard and tried to tear her eyes away from his broad chest covered with a light dusting of dark hair, but couldn't. Perspiration broke out on her forehead. She couldn't seem to take a deep breath. Maybe *this* was her property. Maybe he worked for her already and she'd be making wine this fall with his help. No, she couldn't get that lucky.

"Hello," she called when she finally caught her breath. *"Ciao, signore. Per favore, dove e la Villa Monte Verde."* A whole sentence. Maybe the grammar wasn't perfect, maybe her accent shouted out that she was a tourist, but she was proud of herself for trying. When she had tried to talk to the lawyer in Italian yesterday, he'd switched to English.

Not a chance with this rugged type. She wondered if all the hired hands were this gorgeous. It didn't matter. One reason she'd jumped at the chance to move to Sicily was for a fresh start and to avoid relationships, no matter how attractive the men were. In a new environment, with a brick wall around her heart and a system of warning bells in place, she was ready to take on a new challenge. She was willing to make mistakes along the way, just as long as they weren't the same mistakes she'd made in the past.

The man frowned and gave her a long scrutinizing look that made her pulse quicken and her heart race. From what she'd seen in the airport, Italian women were so chic, so effortlessly stylish, she must look positively shabby to him in her wrinkled shirt and the plain wash-and-wear skirt she'd pulled out of her suitcase. If he even noticed.

His gaze moved to her rental car across the road. She was close enough, just across an old wooden fence, to see a hostile look appear in those incredible blue eyes. She'd imagined people would be friendly here. Maybe she was wrong.

He didn't say a word. Hadn't he understood her Italian? Or did the place go by another name? "La Azienda Agricola Spendora?" she said hopefully.

"You must be the American who arrived yesterday," he said in almost perfect English. His deep voice with a slightly seductive accent sent shivers up her spine. A simple laborer he was not.

She let out a breath she didn't even know she was holding. "How did you guess?" she said lightly. "I suppose my Italian needs some more practice."

He shrugged as if he really didn't care if she was an alien from another universe or if she spoke grammatically perfect Italian. "What can I do for you, miss?" The words were polite, but his tone was cool, with a sardonic edge.

Never mind. She didn't have to make friends with everyone she met. For all she knew he was overworked and underpaid despite his ease in speaking English, and probably tired and thirsty. It was still possible she could hire him, even if he had a chip on his shoulder. She could use someone who spoke English and was a hard worker.

"My name is Isabel Morrison and I'm looking for my vineyard, the Azienda Spendora." She couldn't help the note of pride that crept into her voice. The words *my vineyard* had such a nice ring to them.

"I'll give you a ride. You'll never find it on your own," he said. He reached for a shirt hanging from the branch of a tree and put it on before she could protest. How many times had it been drummed into her not to take rides from strangers? This was the kind of stranger who set off flashing detour lights in front of her. Too well-spoken, too sure of himself, too eager to take her heaven knew where.

"Really, it's okay, I can find it. I've got a map," she said, hating the hint of nervousness in her voice.

"Are you afraid of me?" he asked, looming over her with all his six-feet-something and broad shoulders, shirt half-unbuttoned, blue eyes challenging her either to admit or forget her fears.

"No," she said a little too quickly. While a voice inside her murmured, *Well, maybe just a little.*

"I'm Dario Montessori and I live nearby. In fact, these are my vines." He waved an arm in the direction of the fields behind him. "I know everyone for miles around and everyone knows me. Come along. You might meet some neighbors."

"Now?"

"Why not? *Nussun tempo gradisce il presente,* as we say in Italian. Wait here. I'll bring my car and pick you up."

This was an order there was no resisting. Besides, she did want to meet her new neighbors. It would be silly to pass up an opportunity like this. After all, she wanted to fit into the local village life. What better way than to be taken around by a native? So she waited there until he pulled up in a red-and-black convertible with leather seats. No ordinary farmhand could touch this car with under a hundred thousand. Who was he really? Why was he going out of his way for her?

"If you're planning to kidnap me," she said with a touch of bravado, "don't bother, because I don't have any rich relatives you could hit up for the ransom."

He slanted a glance in her direction. The look on his face

told her she'd just spouted the most absurd thing he'd ever heard. "I've lived here all my life and I don't believe there's been a kidnapping around here in one hundred years. Relax, you're in Sicily now. As for the Azienda, I'm warning you, when you see it and the condition it's in, I am certain you'll be willing to sell it to me."

"It's funny," she said thoughtfully, "you're the second person I've heard of who wants to buy it from me. Just yesterday…"

"That was also me," he said, turning up a bumpy, dirt road. "Your solicitor was representing my family."

"The family that owns most of the land around here? The family that makes prize-winning Marsala and exports Cabernet all over the world?"

He nodded.

"Then you already know I'm not going to sell it."

"You haven't seen it," he said flatly.

"I saw a picture of it on-line. It looks charming."

"Hah," he said and shook his head at her ignorance.

So he too was trying to discourage her. In the photograph the house appeared to be small, and it was located on rugged terrain at a fourteen-hundred-foot elevation. But it looked snug and was situated in a picturesque grove of olive trees and grape vines.

"That picture was taken some years ago when our family owned it. Antonio let it fall apart."

Isabel bristled at the criticism of her uncle, although he might have deserved it. As a family member she was surely entitled to criticize him for allowing the place to disintegrate, but this man was not. At least not in front of her. "Perhaps he had reason," she suggested.

Dario gave her a steely look that told her more than words that there was no good reason.

"Did you know him well?" she asked.

"He kept to himself. But it's a small town. Everyone knows everyone."

"I see," she said. But she didn't see. What was her uncle doing in Italy?

"He left the place in a mess," Dario said.

"I'll clean it up," she insisted. "I don't mind hard work. I know how to paint and make repairs. I've done it before." She'd even done it in her San Francisco rental unit when her landlord had refused to pitch in. Here she'd have the incentive of improving her own property.

He raised his eyebrows, probably surprised by her determination. He hadn't seen anything yet. She'd been criticized for years for being strong-willed after she left the orphanage.

"Isabel's a very headstrong girl," the social-service workers had agreed. She'd been moved from house to house, from foster family to foster family. No wonder no one wanted her with her bright-red hair and her stubborn disposition. No wonder she was passed over for younger, sweeter, more obedient little children. No one wanted to adopt a child with "inflexible" or "rigid" written on her reports.

It hurt to be overlooked, standing there, tall and gawky, enduring being examined and finally rejected time after time. But she got over it. Even when she was officially declared unadoptable because of her age, it had just made her more eager to grow up and set out on her own. This was her chance. She'd show them.

"Do you know anything about growing grapes?" he asked.

"Some, but I know I need to learn more," she admitted.

"Do you know how to prime a pump, irrigate fields, fight off frost? Do you know how hard it is to fertilize volcanic soil, are you prepared to wait for years to harvest your grapes?"

he demanded. He was almost enjoying this inquisition, she realized. She could tell by the way he looked at her, the way he raised his voice to be sure she caught every word.

What really annoyed her was the way he assumed she was far over her head and had no business even trying to break into *his* field.

"Or are you in love with the *idea* of growing grapes," he continued, "and of bottling your own wine?"

She bounced out of her seat as they hit a dip in the road. "Years?" she said. "I can't wait years. I need to make wine and make a living from it. Surely it's possible. I'll hire help. If it's so hard to produce wine on the property, why do you want to buy it?"

"It is hard, even for us. But we have experience. Historically, it's our land. Has been for centuries. For hundreds of years most Sicilian wine was shipped off the island, to be blended into other wines. But now we're getting the attention from the world markets we deserve. Twenty-six generations of Montessoris grew grapes there before we were forced to sell it to your uncle a few years ago."

"Forced?"

"It's a long story and it doesn't concern you. We had a sales slump, followed by financial problems which induced us to give it up, but we've recovered and now we want the land back where it belongs. To us. What difference does it make to you? You've never seen it, you've never lived on it or farmed it. You didn't have picnics there, eat the grapes off the vines or swim in the pond. It means nothing to you."

A pond? She had a pond? She'd stock it with fish, swim in it and watch the birds drink from it. Now she was sure she'd never give it up. She sat up straight in the leather bucket seat. "You're wrong. It means a lot to me. A chance for me to do something different, to earn a living from the land my uncle left me."

"Your uncle never grew a single grape there."

"That doesn't mean I can't. I haven't seen the property, but it's mine and I plan to live there and make it my home. It's my right to settle there, my chance to make a fresh start. Surely everyone deserves that."

He shook his head as if she was naive and stupid. She'd been called worse. "I don't know what you've been doing," he said, "but if you want a fresh start, why don't you buy a hotel, start a newspaper or open a café? All of those would be easier for a newcomer than making wine. Take my word for it. Viticulture takes time and patience and a feeling for the land."

"I appreciate your advice," she said with all the manners she could muster in the face of his blatant cynicism. "But you have to believe me when I say I'm prepared to do whatever it takes to succeed."

He continued to steamroll over her plans for the future as if she hadn't spoken. "Want some more advice?"

Before she could politely say no, he went on. "Get a job. It's an easier way to make a living than making wine. Make someplace else your home. You know I could be taking you to a totally different property and you wouldn't know the difference."

Startled, she asked, "Are you?"

He turned to look at her as if she'd accused him of cold-blooded murder. Wordlessly he pointed to a crooked hand-carved wooden sign on the side of the road, and said "Azienda Spendora."

She let out a sigh of relief. He wasn't kidnapping her. He wasn't trying to fool her by taking her to another property. She was here. This was all hers. It was a dream come true. Or a nightmare. As soon as they pulled up in front of the house she saw what he meant.

There were tiles missing from the roof and cracks in the stained cement walls. She got out of the car and stifled a wave of disappointment. Whatever she felt, she couldn't let him see her frustration at the house's failings. He'd interpret it as a sign of weakness and just renew his futile efforts to buy it from her.

"You don't have to stay," she said. "I'll just look around and catch a ride back."

"Catch a ride?" he asked incredulously. "This is a private road. No one's been on it for months, not since your uncle died."

"Was there a funeral?"

"Of course. What do you take us for, savages? The whole town was there."

The implication was that she was the only one missing. Obviously he thought she had no sense of family obligation. Maybe he thought *she* was a savage.

"I didn't know he existed until I got a letter from the lawyer." She took a deep breath. "Don't worry about me. I'll walk back."

He skimmed her body with a cool, disdainful assessing gaze as if wondering whether to believe she hadn't known her uncle. He took in her short skirt, her white shirt and the strappy sandals she'd thought perfect for a hot Sicilian summer day, but which were hardly sturdy enough to walk miles down that rutted dirt road. Okay, so she was dressed all wrong. She wasn't Italian and she was out of her element. Why couldn't he give her a break, cut her some slack?

"I'll stick around," he said. "It won't take you long to realize this is not the place for you."

The man was maddening with his dark pessimism. She wished he'd leave. She'd rather walk barefoot over hot coals than know he was waiting for her to cave in and give up her inheritance.

She turned to look at him. Puzzled, she said, "Stick around? Where did you learn English?"

"From a tutor," he said in his incredibly sexily accented English. "Being in the wine business, my father had all six of us learn English, the universal language of trade. Bernard taught us all the slang and swear words he knew. They've been quite useful."

"I can imagine," she murmured, surprised that he'd deigned to favor her with such a long response. How long would it take her to learn Italian with all the slang and the swear words she'd need to live here? The difference between his privileged background with tutors and a large family and the way she'd been brought up was mind-boggling. She wondered if he knew how lucky he was. He probably took his family for granted. Most people did.

Instead of waiting, he followed her onto the veranda, stepping carefully over rotten boards and through the front door that swung open and creaked on rusty hinges. When a giant spiderweb brushed against her face, she stifled a scream and lurched back so fast she bumped into him. He put his large hands on her shoulders to steady her or more likely to keep her at a distance, and she fought off the temptation to let him prop her up for a moment while she caught her breath. But Isabel Morrison would never rely on anyone but herself again. Not even for a moment. Instead she straightened her shoulders and forged ahead.

"It was just a spider," she said, more to herself than to him. If she didn't talk to him, maybe he'd go away. Or at least wait outside and let her explore on her own. With his imposing build, the brooding expression in his blue eyes, his way of speaking English that gave a new meaning to everything he said, he was impossible to ignore. She couldn't concentrate on the house. Not when he filled the place with his tall, masculine presence and his overwhelming confidence. All she knew was that no matter what its flaws, no matter how much he offered her for it, this house was hers and she was holding on to it.

Behind the house was the small pond dotted with water lilies. She leaned down and dangled her arm in the cool water.

"For irrigation," he said.

"Or swimming," she said. She pictured lawn furniture, a striped awning, and herself cooling off in the fresh water on a hot summer day in her very own pond.

He braced his arm against the stone wall and surveyed the scene. Was he resentful of her enjoying her own pond? Or was he simply remembering summer days when he had swum with his siblings here and feeling sorry that he never would again? From the look on his face she doubted he had any happy memories at all. What was his problem? Was it really only her and her ownership of this place?

His dark hair was brushed back from his face making his strong features stand out like those on a stone carving. He might have first looked like a farmhand, but now she could see him for what he was, the aristocratic lord of the manor, totally accustomed to having his way. To acquiring whatever land he wanted. And full of resentment at knowing this land was hers now.

"I'd avoid the pond," he said curtly, "unless you're not afraid of water snakes."

She pulled her arm out of the water and dried her hands on her skirt. Spiders, snakes, what else?

"You can see it hasn't been used for years," he said. "Your uncle…"

"I know. He neglected it. I know why you sold it, but why did he buy it from you?"

"Probably thought he'd cash in and make a fortune from the grapes. A lot of people have the idea it's easy and profitable to grow grapes and make wine." He pointedly looked right at her, leaving no doubt about who he meant. "It's an illusion. Outsiders often can't tell the difference between a burgundy and our local grecanicoa, let alone how or when to harvest an Amarado grape. It's hard work."

"I don't doubt it, but…"

"I know, you don't mind hard work. Believe me, you have plenty of it ahead of you."

She wanted to say he had no idea of how much this place meant to her no matter what condition it was in. She also wanted to ask him how and when to harvest these special dessert-wine grapes, but that would just confirm his suspicions that she was no different from her uncle, both ignorant dreamers. Maybe she was worse, since she hadn't even paid for the place. She didn't even know what she was getting.

"The first spring frost he let the vines freeze and came roaring down the mountain to take refuge in the valley and never went back." He shook his head with disgust.

"He was out of his element. What did you expect?"

"I expected him to sell it back to us before he died. But he was just as stubborn as you. All I want is the land back," he said. "Back in the hands of someone who appreciates the *terroir*, the soil, the land where these grapes are grown. Is that so hard to understand?"

She straightened and put her hands on her hips. "Give me a little credit. I didn't just take the next plane over here. I did my homework. I am prepared to appreciate the *terroir* as much as anyone. Even you. And I haven't insulted *your* relatives, you know, as you have my uncle."

"Go ahead. If you met them, you'd see my younger brother

is immature. My mother is domineering. My grandmother hopelessly old-fashioned. My grandfather is stubborn and opinionated but hard-working. Years ago he planted some of these vines, nurtured them, picked the grapes and bottled them. I take responsibility for their loss. Now I owe him and the whole family to get them back."

She didn't understand why he took responsibility or why he owed them when it was a family operation, but she couldn't mistake the hard edge to his voice. He was not only determined, but he had his whole family to back him up. She was outnumbered. It didn't matter. She had the deed to the land. They didn't. Sure she felt bad for his grandfather, but for once she was going to put herself first.

They couldn't force her to sell—unless she couldn't sell her wine because it wasn't good enough or because what he said about waiting years to see any profit was true. Or unless something else unexpected happened. Even in the heat of the midday sun, a cold chill ran up and down her arms. Had she made a huge mistake by coming here? Thinking back, all the surprises in her life had been unhappy ones except for this inheritance, which she took as a sign her luck had finally changed.

She noticed Dario hadn't mentioned a wife in his list of relatives. Which didn't mean he didn't have one. Anyone who looked like him was bound to have a woman in his life. But who would put up with that bitterness she heard in his voice or that single-purpose determination that left no room for anything else? Were those the same traits he saw in her? Surely she wasn't bitter, although she was certainly determined. He shouldn't begrudge her a small piece of land if he owned half the valley.

She'd like to meet his family, just because they were her neighbors and she wanted to fit into the local society, but they probably already hated her as he did for refusing to sell her land to them. Nonetheless, she envied him. What wouldn't she give for a big family she could tease and criticize and love despite their failings?

"What does your family think of you?" she asked. Maybe she was the only one who saw him as a difficult person to deal with. She doubted it. Not with that iron jaw, ice-cold blue eyes and stubborn chin. Or did he suddenly turn into a devoted grandson and lovable sibling when he was home? That was hard to imagine.

"Cold, ruthless and heartless. They say I'm different because I'm not relaxed and easygoing like a true Sicilian. I'm too determined, too driven, even obsessed. When things go wrong I don't shrug and say tomorrow will be better. I *make* it better. That's why…" He stopped in mid sentence, with his gaze fixed on her, as if he could make her see she had no chance against a formidable foe like him. She could imagine what he was going to say…*that's why I will take possession of this land and you won't.*

"But they love you anyway," she suggested. She hoped she didn't sound as skeptical as she felt.

He didn't answer. After a moment she filled in the silence. "You're very lucky. I never knew my parents. I never knew any family at all. No grandparents, no home, no family. I was an orphan." She kept her voice light, as if being an orphan was no more important than being brown-eyed or left-handed. She hated being on the receiving end of pity. But how she'd envied the kids with a home and a family, especially those with grandmothers. The kind who baked in kitchens that smelled like fresh bread, wore aprons and had laps to curl up in. How did she even know they existed? From picture books and from other kids. Certainly not from experience.

"I grew up in foster care," she explained.

He looked puzzled but he didn't say anything. She began to feel foolish for going on about her background when who cared, really? Maybe it was that he had no idea what she was talking about.

"Never mind, it's not important. You say my uncle never made any wine while he was here?"

"He wasn't here that long. Breezed into town from America or God knows where, bought the vineyard, walked away from the vineyard and soon afterward he died. No one knew much about him. Where he really came from, why he was here at all. Some people said he was on the run from the law in California. Who knows? It was clear he had no idea what it took to run a demanding operation like this. All those wasted grapes. Whatever wine there is was made by my family and it would be in the cellar."

Dario led the way to the kitchen where stone steps led to the wine cellar. In the kitchen they passed an ancient cooktop tilted to one side. The place reeked of cold and loneliness. It would be a job making it livable, but she could do it. There was an old wooden icebox and an oven with its door hanging open. It wasn't quite her dream kitchen, but it could be.

It was as if someone had been in a big hurry to get out of here. If Dario hadn't been right on her heels, Isabel might have allowed herself a moment of respect for the man who'd left her this place, but with Dario around, she pretended she wasn't affected by the depressing sight.

"Needs a little cleaning up," she said matter-of-factly. After all, no house was exactly the way you wanted it. There were always improvements to be made.

"It needs more than that," he said. "You haven't got running water or electricity or heat."

"I don't need heat, not in this climate."

"You will. If you stay."

"I will stay," she assured him.

As if he'd orchestrated it, a huge rat ran out from under the sink. She screamed, slammed the ice box door shut and jumped up onto an old wobbly wooden kitchen chair.

He shook his head, as if the skittish behavior of women was no surprise to him at all. To him she was just another woman over her head and unable to cope with hardship. Was it so strange she was frightened of rats? It didn't mean she was a defective person.

After a pause he said, "I thought you wanted to see the cellar." He held out a hand to help her off the chair. He might despise her and dismiss her as unfit to live here, but she had to admit he had manners.

Isabel took a deep breath. "Of course." No rat would keep her from her goal. No single-minded Italian would either, no matter how gorgeous he was, how blue his eyes were or how irresistible his accent was. He had no idea how many people had told her she was crazy to quit her job and go to Italy. Everyone she knew advised her to sell the place sight unseen, buy a house in California with the money and keep her job.

That was the sensible thing to do, but for once in her life Isabel didn't do the sensible thing. She needed to make a move. Get away from everyone who knew what a fool she'd been. A big move that would force her to be more self-reliant, to face new challenges with a new strength of purpose. To turn her back on her past and friends who treated her with concern and the sympathy she didn't want. She'd come five thousand miles and nothing would keep her from doing what she'd set out to do. And finally, she'd never give her heart away again, not when it was finally healed and whole.

This man had no idea how humiliating it would be to give up, to go home and admit she'd made another mistake. If she had a home, which she didn't. It would take more than a rat in the kitchen, more than a hole in the roof, more than a hostile neighbor. Much more.

She took his hand and gingerly got down off the chair, then walked with all the dignity she could summon down the stairs to the damp, cool basement. Again he was right behind her, his warm breath on her neck, though she would have preferred to explore alone, to find some hidden treasure like an old bottle of some fabulous vintage on her own.

The walls were lined with racks and racks of wine in dusty bottles. Some were empty, their corks lying on the floor, but others looked well-aged but possibly still good. How would she know? He pulled a bottle off the wall and held it up so she could see it from the light that filtered through the small dusty windows. "Nineteen ninety-two," he said. "My grandfather's Bianco Soave. Sealed with wax. That was a good year, a gold-medal year." He pointed to the seal affixed to the label.

"I guess some years are not so good?"

"With grapes as well as life," he said, as a cloud passed across his handsome features. "Some years are best forgotten." He wasn't looking at her. For all she knew he was talking to himself. Even in the dank semi-dark cellar she could tell from his expression he wasn't just being philosophical. He meant something had happened to him, and whatever it was, he had not forgotten it. She wanted to ask him how someone like him, surrounded by a big supportive family and acres of productive grapes would have even one bad year? How bad could it be? Bad enough to sell the place to her uncle, but it couldn't have been as bad as last year was for her.

"Was it a drought or a fungus?" She'd read either could devastate a vineyard.

"Yes," he said, but he didn't elaborate.

She could understand if they'd had losses due to a disaster out of his control. But maybe it was something more personal. If it was, she'd never find out any more. Not from him.

She could understand his not wanting to talk about it. Last year had been a nightmare for her, the worst of her life, and she'd done her best to hide her shame and embarrassment from the world.

Then she'd got the letter from the lawyer and her life had turned around. Coming to Sicily to claim her inheritance was the easiest decision she'd ever made. This would be her good year. She would make it happen. And one of these days she too would win a prize for her wine. Her lips curved in a half smile as she pictured the gold labels on the bottles, labels she would design herself.

She sent a sideways glance in his direction. His hand was wrapped around the wine bottle and he was watching her as if he knew she was dreaming a dream that wouldn't come true. But it would. As if he was waiting for her to give up. Give up? On her first day? He didn't know her.

After a long pause he broke the silence. "Not discouraged?"

She shook her head. "Of course not. The wine is yours," she said waving her arm at the racks that lined the stone walls. "All of it. Take the bottles with you."

"Legally it's yours," he said coolly. "But I'm curious to see how this one has held up."

He scraped away the wax with a knife hanging on the wall and popped the cork with a rusty opener, then he tilted his head back and held the bottle to his mouth. Fascinated, she watched the muscles in his throat move while he drank it. Her mouth was dry. He handed the bottle to her. His fingers brushed her hand and goose bumps broke out on her bare arms. It was the cool damp basement that made her shiver, not this tall, dark Sicilian stranger.

"Try it," he ordered. "Tell me what you think of it." She knew what he thought. She could have no educated opinion. So why did he even ask?

She put her lips where his had been and tasted the wine and him at the same time. She felt a quiver of excitement. Maybe it was second-hand contact with his lips, maybe it was the old fermented wine. It wasn't fair to put her on the spot this way, testing her to see if she knew anything about wine.

Unnerved by the way he stood there, arms crossed, way too close in that small space, his eyes glittering in the dim light and brimming over with self-confidence, she couldn't think of a single original thing to say.

"Ciao," came a voice from somewhere above them. *"Chiunque nel paese?"*

"My brother," he muttered. Then he swore in Italian. At least it sounded like swearing.

So much for the bonds of Italian brotherhood, she thought as he brushed by her on his way up the stairs.

CHAPTER TWO

DARIO took the stone steps two at a time leaving the American heiress behind. That's all he needed—his brother interfering just when he was finally making progress. At least he thought he was. It was hard to tell when she kept insisting she wasn't discouraged. But no woman in her right mind would take on a run-down operation like this. Most women he knew wanted a beautiful house, land, money, excitement and more.

Naturally the woman he compared all others to was his ex-fiancée, Magdalena, who'd made it clear the life he'd offered her was not enough. Surely this woman would have to agree, sooner rather than later, that this run-down dump of a place was not enough for her, no matter what the long-term possibilities were, and run back to where she came from, which was where she belonged.

"What are you doing here?" he asked Cosmo, who was standing in the stone patio, his car parked in front of the house.

"I heard from Delfino the American woman might be on the property. I wanted to say hello and welcome her on behalf of the family."

"Are you out of your mind?" Dario demanded, struck by his younger brother's immaturity and lack of common sense. "Welcome the woman who has already refused to sell the property back to us? The woman who's keeping Nonno from realizing his dream before he dies?"

"Nonno's dream or yours?" Cosmo asked.

Dario ignored the question. He knew what his brother thought. He knew what the whole family thought of him. They thought he was obsessed with trying to recover this land they'd written off long ago. Maybe he was. But maybe he should be. Because it was his fault they'd had to sell the land, and now it was his responsibility to get it back. It was so obvious. Why couldn't they understand that?

"What were you going to do, bring her flowers and roll out the red carpet?" Dario asked.

"Of course not, but be honest, Dario, you're the one who cares more than anyone about getting the place back. Give it up."

It was true. No one in his family had any idea how important it was for him. How much he blamed himself for what had happened—and would continue to blame himself until he'd got the property back and their wine won the gold medal. Then and only then could he put the past where it belonged. Until then…

"It's gone," Cosmo said. "Get over it. Stop blaming yourself."

"Easy for you to say," Dario said. "It's my fault we had to sell. You know it's true."

"Forget it," Cosmo said. "It's over. We have vineyards enough. Let this one go. I came by to see for myself if the new owner is as beautiful as I heard," Cosmo said.

Dario shook his head. "You heard wrong. How do those rumors get started? She's not beautiful at all." It was true. Her mouth was too large, her nose too small. Her hair was the color of copper in the sunlight, but that was definitely her best feature.

"So she's not beautiful. What is she like?"

"Just offhand, I'd say she's stubborn, proud, determined

and naive. And overconfident. No idea what it takes to make wine. As soon as she realizes this place isn't for her, she'll be on her way. But right now she's wavering." Unfortunately that was just wishful thinking. He didn't detect any sign of wavering in this woman. "If you don't leave now you might say the wrong thing and she'll be here forever. It's not fair to her to encourage her."

"Encourage her?" Cosmos teetered on the edge of indecision. "I just want to meet her and say hello."

"Not today."

His brother wasn't happy about it, but after a few more exchanges, he finally left and Dario breathed a sigh of relief. It didn't matter what the new owner looked like, she was new, she was a challenge, and he didn't trust his brother to stand up to her. He'd feel sorry for her when he heard she was an orphan and forget the goal, which was to convince her to sell by pointing out the obvious: this was not a place for a novice, a woman on her own, a foreigner who knew nothing about viticulture. It was in her own interests either to find another house in Sicily or go back where she came from. He only wanted what was best for her—and for his family of course.

Though feeling sorry for an heiress didn't make sense, his little brother was a flirt and a playboy and loved to have a good time. In other words, a typical Sicilian. He was easily swayed by a new girl in town with a fresh face as well as a few curves in the right places. He had charm and affection, yes, but those were traits not needed today.

Dario knew from painful experience what his brother ignored or wouldn't believe. That women are masters of deceit. They were seldom what they seemed. Beautiful or not, they could look innocent and act vulnerable, but they were hard as polished marble and equally strong-willed, self-centered and capable of lies and deception.

When Isabel emerged from the kitchen, a bottle of wine under her arm and a smudge of dirt on her cheek, Dario knew his brother would have stood there, mouth open, gaping at the American heiress, taken in by her apparent lack of pretense and that dazzling red hair and pale skin. No, she wasn't beautiful, but she was striking in a way Dario had never seen before. She had a certain freshness and large helping of pride of ownership in her new acquisition—the Azienda.

Good thing his brother had left. He could just see Cosmo falling all over her, offering Italian lessons, sightseeing and God knew what else. Just what he himself might have done before he'd met Magdalena. And had his eyes opened and a knife stuck in his back.

The American was the new girl in town, with something undeniably seductive about her mouth and her body. Dario would have to be blind not to notice her long shapely legs. She had soft brown eyes that widened in surprise, and a rare smile that tugged at the corners of her full lips. Yes, his brother would have been smitten at first sight and would have rolled out the red carpet for the intruder.

Dario knew better than to be swayed by a pretty face framed with hair the color of autumn leaves, no matter how innocent she seemed. He'd been burned once. Never again. Even after more than a year had passed, his mistake in trusting Magdalena rankled like the sting of a wasp.

His approach, the correct one, was to keep his distance from the heiress, show her the worst of her property and then pounce with a generous offer. It would be kinder in the long run than sitting by and watching her struggle but ultimately fail.

"My brother just stopped by."

"I'm sorry I didn't have a chance to meet him," she said. "Why didn't he stay?"

"Another appointment," Dario said. "Maybe some other time."

"I found another bottle of wine I'd like to try." Isabel held up two glasses. "Would you like some?"

She was offering him his own wine? He clamped his jaw tight to keep from erupting in pent-up frustration. Yes, it belonged to her now, but still. He wanted to pound the wall to relieve his irritation at watching her play the hostess role. Even with the smudge on her cheek and dirt on the sleeve of her shirt, she looked like the lady of the manor. It was a heady feeling he could tell by the look on her face, and if this scenario played itself out, she'd never want to leave, however difficult the job of making the place livable. He had to put plan B into operation as soon as possible.

"I don't know wine the way you do, but I think it's aged well, don't you?" she asked him after they'd both tasted it.

"Not bad," he said and set his glass down on a ledge. "We won a bronze medal for this if I remember right."

"You must have won many medals."

"We have, but some contests are more important than others. The Gran Concorso Siciliano del Vini is coming up in a few weeks. We plan to take away a gold this year."

He didn't want to brag or look overconfident. But this was going to be their year. Winning the medal and getting the Azienda back. Two victories that would erase the losses of the past once and for all. He knew it. He felt it. If he kept a hawk eye on the land, the vines and the wine production, they'd end up with the prize and the best dessert wine Sicily could produce too.

He was proud of their wine, proud of the medals they'd

won. Nothing wrong with letting her know that. He turned to Isabel. "Now that you've seen the place, it's time to go."

"I haven't been upstairs yet."

What could he say? You won't like it? Knowing her, that would guarantee she'd insist she would like it. She didn't yet know about the bedroom off the kitchen where the servants once lived, and he sure wasn't going to tell her. Instead he led the way up the narrow staircase, Isabel following behind him. There it was, a small room with a narrow sagging mattress on a metal frame. And better yet, a huge gaping hole in the ceiling.

"It needs major roof repair," he said. As if she hadn't noticed. No one in their right mind could say anything positive about a hole in the roof. But she did.

"Why?" she said. "If it doesn't rain, it will be wonderful to look up at the stars at night."

He groaned silently. There was no point in telling her bats would fly into the room. She'd probably welcome them. He'd never met anyone like her. There wasn't a woman in Sicily who'd accept living under these conditions. What was it about this woman? Was she really capable or just stubborn and unrealistic?

"I know it needs work," she said, a trace of defiance in her voice. "I know there's no running water or electricity, but, as I said, I'm not afraid to pitch in and get things done. And I'd like to hire someone to help me."

"That won't be easy," Dario commented. It was true. All the able-bodied men were at work in the vineyards. "Most people are busy with the crush."

"Which reminds me, I want to see the vineyard."

"Of course." That, Dario thought, could help matters; she'd see how withered the vines were.

They went back downstairs and out into the hot sunshine

where they walked up and down the path between the old vines. Dario followed behind Isabel, noticing the way her hips swayed enticingly as she walked, how the perspiration dampened the back of her neck, admiring in spite of himself her red-gold hair, which she'd tied back, gleaming in the sunlight. But only as he would admire a painting by Titian, with cool detachment. His detachment was cool until his mind jumped to the thought of her as the half-clothed subject of a lush Titian painting.

A surprising jolt of desire hit him in his chest. He'd been immune to the allure of women since his affair with Magdalena had ended so disastrously. Could his libido be alive and well again? Maybe all it took was knowing he'd finally recovered and was back in charge of his life and his vineyards. And then a glimpse of a Titian-haired heiress didn't hurt as long as she didn't stay too long. All he asked was for life to return to the way it was—pre-drought, pre-fungus, pre-Magdalena. He was almost there. He felt a new surge of energy, a feeling of hope close at hand, as close as the vines on either side of the path.

Dario deliberately turned his attention to picking and tasting a grape here and there, much safer than watching the woman. Another surprise—the level of sugar in the neglected fruit. Soon they could be turned into the superb dessert wine they were famous for. If. If the woman would only be reasonable. They should win the gold this year for either a red or a white. They would be back on top, and the world would be theirs again.

Finding that Magdalena was deceiving him was one thing, but losing his head over her so that he'd been negligent in running the vineyards was ten times worse. He blamed himself for the whole mess. He'd learned a valuable lesson. No matter how tempting, he would never fall for any woman again. His family didn't believe that. They thought his turning into a loner this past year was only a phase. He didn't think so.

This year if all went well, they could be on top again with a win at the Concorso for their Ceravasuolo. Let his family call him obsessive. He didn't care. It was better than being careless. He buried himself in his work. It was his choice and his obligation. Someone had to worry about the wine and family's land holdings. His father was busy in Palermo, his grandfather was sick. So that person was him. Let his sisters suggest he get out and find a girlfriend. It wasn't going to happen. Not now. Not ever.

Isabel paused to pick some grapes and licked her lips. Even as a beginner unaccustomed to tasting wine grapes off the vine, she was struck by how sweet they were. She felt a quiver of excitement. These were special grapes. She'd read about super-sweet grapes, old grapes that had been neglected. Her grapes.

She turned to Dario, whose blue eyes were narrowed in the bright sun. "These are delicious," she said. "Are they the same grapes that produce the famous Amarado dessert wine?"

He hesitated. Didn't he know or didn't he want to tell her? Finally he nodded.

She realized he didn't want her to know. He wanted her to get discouraged and leave. Sell out to him. He was sorry she'd stumbled on her own high-quality grapes. She could tell by the way his mouth was set in a straight uncompromising line, and by the creases in his forehead that this was the last thing he wanted her to know.

"I've tasted that wine. It's delicious. After I did some research on the Azienda Spendora I went out and found a few bottles of old Amarado in an upscale beverage store. It's very expensive in the States, if you can even find it," she said thoughtfully. "A high-end wine. It could be a huge moneymaker."

"I wouldn't count on it."

She slanted a glance in his direction. He knew. He must know how valuable it was. "No wonder you want this vineyard so much. It's because of the Amarado. I can't believe it. These are all mine and I'll make this superb dessert wine. I *can* make a go of it. I know I can. I can make money. Live off the land and show the naysayers."

She paused, struck by the look on his face. What had she said to make him glare at her like that? A muscle in his temple twitched. Was she excessively bragging? Or was he just upset because they were hers and not his grapes? "You didn't tell me about these grapes."

"You didn't ask me," he said shortly. "Don't get too excited," he cautioned. "It takes more than just picking and fermenting the grapes to make a decent Amarado."

"You don't think I can do it. You don't think I have what it takes."

"Do you?"

Suddenly a shaft of uncertainty hit her. What made her think she could compete in a wine market where her competitors had been doing this for decades? Maybe she was dreaming. Maybe she was overconfident. He was right. It wasn't going to be easy.

"Yes. I'll make it work," she insisted. "Why shouldn't I?" She was proud of how certain she sounded when inside a small voice asked who she thought she was. How did she think she could compete as an outsider?

"Why? Because you can't possibly pick your own grapes," Dario said. "You have acres of vines. It's backbreaking work and you have to know what you're doing. You don't want to do work like that. That's not women's work."

Women's work? She frowned and bit back a retort, something like *Even in Sicily, haven't you heard of equal rights, equal pay and equal opportunities?*

It seemed as if he hadn't heard a word she'd said. Hadn't she made it clear she'd stick it out and produce the wine these grapes were famous for even if she had to pick the grapes herself?

"You can ruin the whole crop by doing it yourself or hiring unskilled laborers. What you should do is take a vacation then go back where you belong." He took her arm and half pulled her back to the driveway where his car was parked.

"I *am* where I belong," she said, stepping out of his grasp before she got into the car. Her face was hot. Perspiration dripped from her temples.

Once they were in the car, he drove so fast her hair was whipped around her face in the wind. "This is my land," she reminded him. "I don't care how hard it is, I'm going to get those grapes picked and make my own wine from them if I have to do it myself. Which I can't believe I will have to do. I don't know what kind of women you're used to dealing with or what work you expect them to do. I'm not a fragile flower who'll sit at home knitting, waiting for some man to come along and take care of me. And I'm not a tourist. I'm here to work and I'm here to stay."

"Fine," he said after taking a moment to digest this. "Stay. But stay somewhere else. I'm prepared to make you a generous offer. You can take the money and buy a house with a garden. Something you can manage on your own."

"I'm not interested in another house. I'm staying here on *my* land and in *my* house. My uncle wanted me to have it, not you. The Azienda Spendora is not for sale."

"You haven't heard our offer."

"I don't need to."

"Look," he said as he stopped the car and turned his head to turn his penetrating gaze on her. "I'll make a deal with you. Let me take you around the countryside to look at property for sale. If you don't see anything you like, anything that compares with the Azienda, then I'll give up. I'll stop bothering you. *Dio*, I'll even help you find the workers you need."

"And if I don't agree to this fruitless trip around the countryside? Because I can tell you right now…"

"If you don't agree, and you don't come with an open mind, then I promise things won't be easy for you. You have no idea how hard it is to find workers, and you won't find many friends either."

Her face paled. She tried to turn her glare at him but she couldn't keep her lower lip from trembling. Oh, she put on a game face, but he'd finally made a dent in her self-assurance. He'd threatened her. He must be desperate for the land. But not as desperate as she was to hang on to it.

"All right," she said. "I'll go with you, but I'm warning you…"

He almost looked amused. As if she had some nerve warning him when he'd just threatened her. He held up one hand, palm forward. "No warnings, no conditions. I'll pick you up at eight tomorrow morning."

"Wait," she said. "I never met any neighbors. You said…"

"Tomorrow is another day," he said. But he didn't apologize or make any promises. She had a feeling he never did. Then she saw she had a flat tire.

The next morning Isabel had half a mind to cancel. If she'd known Dario's phone number she might have. She dressed carefully in Capri pants and a tank top, then changed into a sundress, but after surveying her image in the full-length mirror in her hotel room, she changed into blue jeans and a T-shirt then back to the Capris.

As if it mattered. The man had barely glanced at her yesterday, and when he did look her way he didn't see a living breathing person who only wanted what she deserved, or even a pesky, tired, jetlagged tourist, he saw an obstacle standing in his way.

Take yesterday, when he'd fixed her flat tire for her. At first he'd looked at her as if she'd done it on purpose to annoy him. Without a word, he took his shirt off and opened the trunk of her car to remove the spare tire and a jack. She tried not to stare at his bare chest, since the sight of those well-toned muscles made her knees weak, but she couldn't help it. Since her auto club didn't have service in Italy, she had no choice but to watch him repair her tire. She hoped he didn't think she'd repay him for his work by selling him her vineyard.

She watched closely while he propped the jack into the fittings on the side of the car. Squatting next to the car, his broad shoulders were covered with a sheen of sweat as he started cranking the jack. He muttered something that she didn't understand. Probably something like "Damned helpless American women."

She kneeled down next to him, her skirt pulled to one side, her bare knees pressed against the hot pavement. All in the interest of learning how to change a tire by herself some day. Kneeling there, she was all too aware of the essence of earthy macho male emanating from his half-naked body. Just being that near him made her feel as if her insides were melting. Or was that just the temperature outside?

He handed her four small metal objects he'd taken off something, his rough palm brushing her fingers. He smelled like ripe grapes and the hot Italian sun. She felt faint. No wonder. It was way past lunch time and she hadn't had anything to eat for hours, just half a glass of wine. Maybe that's why she felt so lightheaded.

When he'd replaced the flat tire with the new one, she said *"Grazie,"* and gave him a grateful smile.

He didn't smile back. Didn't praise her attempt at speaking Italian. She didn't expect him to. He'd used up all the good will he had for her, if any. He hadn't introduced her to a single neighbor. Hadn't even introduced her to his brother. But, after him changing her tire, she could hardly complain. He might be the lord of the manor and the owner of all the land around here, but he wasn't too proud to do a menial job and she admired that about him. Another man might have called a garage and hired a mechanic. If only she'd told him then to forget about showing her other properties. It wouldn't do any good, but he'd made up his mind. Well, so had she.

CHAPTER THREE

AFTER a cup of delicious cappuccino and some hot rolls on the sun-dappled veranda of the lovely Hotel Cairoli the next morning, Isabel told herself to relax. Let him show her around the countryside. He'd soon realize he had no chance at all of her changing her mind. She'd simply treat it as an opportunity to see something of the area in the company of an attractive Italian man who knew his way around. And maybe finally meet some locals. Never mind the gorgeous Italian found nothing remotely attractive about her, especially her personality. That was his problem, not hers.

By the time he arrived, she'd almost convinced herself she could treat him like her driver and nothing more. But then she saw the heads turn when his impressive car pulled up and he got out wearing khaki cargo pants and an expensive polo shirt that matched his eyes and did nothing to conceal the taut muscles in his arms.

Before she could get up and go to meet him, he'd walked through the place like he owned it and taken a seat at her table. The waitress was scurrying to bring him a cup of coffee and a plate of fresh hot rolls. She was beaming at him as if he was her long-lost brother, and it seemed everyone in the place knew who he was and lost no time in either shaking his hand or putting their arms around him as if they hadn't seen him for years.

It was obvious he was not only part of a big family, he was part of a community as well. She felt a pang of envy. How long would it take for her to feel this way? She couldn't wait for twenty-six generations to pass by.

"Are you enjoying your stay?" he asked, his blue gaze zeroing in on Isabel as if she was the only one on the veranda. His attention was flattering. Or it would be if she didn't think he had an ulterior motive. He'd either decided to change his tactics, or he'd decided to enjoy the day and forget his only too apparent motive. Knowing him it must be the former.

"Very much. But I'm planning to move out either today or tomorrow."

"Why, what's wrong?" he asked with a quizzical lift of his eyebrows.

"Nothing, the people are nice and the beds are very comfortable. But I didn't come here to loll about in a luxury hotel when I have a perfectly good house of my own." She felt her cheeks redden. They both knew it wasn't "perfectly good." She braced herself for his retort.

"Ah," he said. But that was all. No mention of the lack of water, heat or electricity. Which only made her worry about these things more. It was much easier to be brave when she had to convince him at the same time. Without a rival to fight with, she felt strangely deflated.

"As you know, it's harvest time and I need to be picking grapes." She waited for his predictable comment about how hard the work was and how busy all the real workers were, but it didn't come.

Instead he drained his cup and said, "Ready?" then stood and pulled her chair out from the table. She had the feeling the whole hotel staff was standing there watching as if he were a movie star on location as she got into his car and pulled away. She had to admit he was better-looking than any movie star she'd ever seen.

Did his attention to her raise her status in the community she longed to be part of? Either the group on the terrace at the hotel were shaking their heads, thinking she was a fool for going off with the Sicilian playboy who might even be married or they were cheering her on, thinking she'd be a fool for not running off to spend a day with the sexiest man around these parts.

It didn't matter, this was not a date. He was not interested in her nor was she in him. He was showing her around only because he thought he'd achieve his own goal that way. She was spending the day with him for the same reason, to get what she wanted. But she couldn't help being curious about him and his family.

She leaned back against the soft leather upholstery and let the sun shine on her face. She felt no need to make conversation since he seemed to be lost in thought, maybe pretending she wasn't there. He'd insisted on showing her property, he hadn't said he'd enjoy it. His eyes were hidden behind his wraparound sunglasses, one suntanned arm braced on the open window. His mind was somewhere else, no doubt.

To distract herself from looking at Dario, thinking about him and admiring his hands on the wheel, his bronzed arms and his skillful driving, she tried to identify the different kinds of trees they passed—oak, elm, ash and maybe beech. There might even be cork and maple. In the hills above them, farm animals grazed. It was a peaceful and bucolic scene, one most tourists never saw. She told herself to sit back and enjoy it while she could. Tomorrow and the next day and every day after that she'd be at work in the vineyard.

Glancing at his profile out of the corner of her eye, she thought he was just as gorgeous from that viewpoint as he was full-on, with his broken nose, his solid jaw and high cheekbones. From a strictly impersonal viewpoint of course. If he wasn't married, she wondered why not. Was it his surly personality, or was that side of him reserved for her benefit?

He pointed to a village perched high on a hill. And finally he spoke. "Casale," he said, "one of the first towns taken by the Normans from the Arabs who took it from the Saracens who took it from the Byzantines."

"So I'm not the first foreigner to claim land here."

"Not at all. But you should know Sicilians are tough people. We may seem to give in at first, but we're just rolling with the punches. We may occasionally be defeated, but it's just temporary. We've been around for centuries through good times and bad. Everyone wants something we've got—our land, our crops and our climate. For six thousand years the Greeks, the Romans, the Arabs, the French and the Spanish, they've all come and seen and conquered. They've all left their marks. But eventually they moved on. And we stayed on. We're here for good."

Isabel took her time taking this all in. Not just the history lesson, but his taking the trouble to instruct her. "Of course you are," she said at last. "You're Italian and you belong here."

"I'm Sicilian," he said firmly. "The Italians are just the latest colonizers who've come to strip away our wealth." She knew what he thought. Whether Italian or American, she was in the same category as the other intruders. Was that the real reason he was taking her on this tour? To make her aware of her place in history? Where were the villas he wanted her to see? The land for sale?

"There's a rather nice Roman villa over there that was

buried in the mud for seven hundred years until it was discovered in 1950. You should see it."

"Why?" she said. "Is it for sale?"

One corner of his mouth twitched as if he might possibly smile. That would be a first. He shook his head. "Don't worry. I haven't forgotten why we're here. I'm glad you haven't either." He turned down a side road. The villa was open to tourists, but today there were only a few.

"Villas were more than simply vacation homes for the wealthy Romans," Dario explained, "there are outbuildings which could house more family and servants and workshops as well. The owner and his family lived in this section with fifteen rooms, an underground central heating system and mosaic flooring."

"Like your house?" she asked. How rich was he? How big was his house?

"Mine? I live by myself in the gatekeeper's cottage on the family property. It's pretty simple. No mosaics, no grand facade like you see here, where even the stables and servants' quarters are faced with some kind of beautiful stone frontage. The Romans wanted to make a statement, let the world know they were rich and powerful. Our family…" He paused as if he might be about to divulge a family secret. "Our family isn't like that."

Oh, no? she wanted to ask. Then why did they need her property? Why couldn't they be happy being the biggest landowners for miles around? Why did they have to have her tiny little vineyard?

Lived by himself, he said. She wanted to ask what he'd told his family about her. Maybe nothing. Why had his brother taken off yesterday before she could meet him? Was Dario protecting her or his brother? Maybe she was so insignificant she didn't even warrant an introduction. Just buy her off, she thought they'd say. We don't want to see her. Let us know when the sale is done and we can celebrate.

She paused to admire a well-preserved wall mosaic that pictured dolphins flanking a vase and a central rosette with a knot motif.

"Even the Romans loved dolphins," she murmured.

"Why not? They're intelligent, acrobatic, and they seem to like us humans. If you leave by ferry, you'll see them in the waters off Messina."

She stiffened. "Why do you assume I'm going to leave? I'm not. I'm staying." What did she have to do to prove to him how determined she was to stay? And why?

"Shall we go?" he asked without answering her question. Maybe he sensed her frustration. Maybe he even enjoyed pushing her, watching her respond, hoping she'd tire of fighting back. But she wouldn't. Her heart was hardened and her will power intact. She'd had years of practice.

She didn't even waver when he drove to the coast where white sandy beaches contrasted with the clear blue sea. There above the beach was a small cottage for sale with a balcony overlooking a garden. Standing on the stone terrace she caught her breath at the stunning beauty of the view.

The scent of lilies and wild herbs filled the air. The contrast to her own run-down house was striking and he knew it. This was the kind of place you could move into and never have to worry about a hole in the roof. She imagined a garden full of tiny tomatoes bursting with flavor, a kitchen with sauce simmering on the stove. For a moment she felt her heart longing to have all that and more.

Once she had wanted love too, but no longer. It was folly to think of having a family and sharing her life with them.

She'd tried that and it hadn't worked. In the past, every time she thought she'd found a family, they'd sent her on her way. When she grew up and finally fell in love, she'd thought her life had turned around. Her mistake. One she would never make again. She was on her own again and always would be. Now more than ever.

"The best part is that it's only a few kilometers from our largest archeological site. It was built by the Greeks and has the best example of Doric columns you'll see anywhere. If you're interested in that kind of thing."

What could she say? She didn't care about history? She was indifferent to archeology? On the contrary. She'd love to visit the site and study the relics of the past, but she had to make a living. No, it was better to say nothing negative, just tell him she'd think about it.

"How much is it?" she asked.

"Don't worry about that," he said. "Let's just say it would be an even trade."

"But how would I earn a living?"

He didn't have an answer for that. She knew what he was thinking, that she wasn't likely to make a living from her grapes either. But she'd show him. She'd make wine and she'd sell it if it was the last thing she did.

Instead he looked at his watch, which appeared to be a Swiss collector's timepiece with multiple dials and a view of the precision movements through the face. How like him to have a watch that matched his car—expensive, luxurious and well-appointed. He obviously had never known what it was like to need money the way she did. Except for that glitch when they had to sell her uncle their vineyard. She still didn't understand how that had come about. When she'd asked if it was a drought or fungus he'd said yes. But what had actually happened?

"Time for lunch," he said, expertly masking his disappointment, if he had any, to her reaction to the beach house. "You look hungry." If he thought an expensive restaurant lunch would soften her up to sell to him, he was wrong. That didn't mean she wasn't hungry and intrigued when he drove a half hour to the city of Pallena and parked just outside the old Roman walls.

She reminded herself this was his idea. But no matter how many historic sites they'd visit or how many fine lunches he'd treat her to, she couldn't be bought.

"This is a favorite restaurant of mine," he said, leading the way through an old arch and down a flight of steps to a narrow pathway that led to the walled city. "I hope you like it."

Like it? How could she not? There was an entrance to the place through a door in the medieval wall, where they passed through the lounge area to the large bustling restaurant upstairs.

"It was once a Gothic palace," he said, pointing to the high stone walls and graceful arches above them. As it was almost two o'clock the place was full of Sicilians who were talking, eating, drinking, and lingering over tiny glasses of Limoncello or small cups of strong coffee.

The smells of roasting meats and slow-cooked sauces filled the air. Isabel hadn't realized how hungry she was until she sat down across from Dario at a small table in the corner and looked at the menu.

She had no idea what to order. Were they supposed to have all five courses or just a salad or perhaps some pasta? She was relieved when he ordered lunch and wine for both of them.

Dario was curious to see what Isabel thought of the wine he'd ordered. It was his personal favorite. If he knew her, she'd have something to say, whether he agreed with it or not.

When it came to the table, he took a sip and nodded his approval. Isabel noticed the Montessori label.

"Your own wine," she noted. "Doesn't it bother you to have to pay for it?"

"Not at all. I'm glad to see they serve it here. It's a '97 Benolvio that my grandfather was especially proud of."

She sipped it slowly. But did she appreciate the subtle nuances in the taste? How could she? "Very nice," she said. "Did it ever win any prizes?"

"No, but it should have. We may make a wine aficionado out of you yet."

Surprised, she blurted, "Was that a compliment?"

He only shrugged. Maybe she'd learn to appreciate wine, maybe not. That wasn't his purpose in bringing her here. He didn't know exactly why he'd done that. Maybe because it was a place few tourists knew about. Or maybe because this was where he and Magdalena had often come and he wanted to exorcise the demons. To prove to himself he could enjoy the food and the atmosphere without thinking about her.

While Isabel was looking around the room, he glanced at her. She wasn't the beauty Magdalena was. But he wasn't the only man looking at her. Maybe it was because she was American, maybe it was her hair, a spot of riotous color in this dim restaurant. Other heads turned and other eyes watched her as she drank her wine along with drinking in the ambience.

If only he could get her to relax she might put aside her defenses and realize what everyone knew—the Azienda was not the place for her. He gave her credit for wanting it and wanting to make a go of it. Nothing wrong with a healthy dose of ambition. But she wouldn't last a week in that place. Maybe not even a day and a night. No matter how much gumption she had, she'd have to be rescued from the bats who flew into her bedroom and the boars that tore up the vines at night. Who else would do it but him?

Maybe it was the wine or the light from the sconces on the palace walls, but from across the table he thought she looked more at ease. Her shoulders were no longer stiff as if on military alert, her cheeks had a healthy flush and her warm gaze scanned the room. Maybe she just needed some time to get used to the idea of giving up the Azienda. He could only hope.

His gaze was fastened on her, studying her, trying to figure her out. He was glad he'd brought her here. She ought to see something of Sicily besides a worn-out vineyard. She should leave here with happy memories of the island and not feel she'd failed. He knew what that felt like and he wouldn't wish it on anyone. She'd go home with a pocketful of cash, enough to do whatever she wanted to do. Or even stay here, buy a cottage, one that needed no remodeling.

He was encouraged to see her let down her guard. And not just because it would make his job easier. She usually looked like she was braced for the worst. What had happened in her life to teach her to be on alert all the time?

"What did you do before you left California?" he asked. He'd planned to make polite conversation. But he found he was curious about her.

She set her glass down. "I was a graphic artist."

He glanced at her hand on the table, noticing her graceful tapered fingers. He could imagine her in front of an easel with a paintbrush in those delicate fingers. "You're an artist?"

"Of a sort. It's not like being a painter or a sculptor. I create images for the purpose of selling products for customers."

"Don't you ever want to paint or draw something for yourself?"

"I'm not good enough."

"Why don't you draw pictures of grapes instead of growing them? I guarantee it will be easier."

"I was thinking I could do both. I plan to design a wine label for myself and my wine." She picked up the bottle from the ice bucket on the table and studied it. "Look at this. The label doesn't say anything about your wine. And it's dated as well. You need something that tells the customer about your product. Something fresh and new. This is old."

"So is the wine," he said.

"It would make a big difference in customer perception. I could design something new for you if you like."

"Thanks, but no thanks. This is the Montessori label. It's what people know. What they're used to. And what they look for when they want a fine wine. May I remind you you know nothing about our wine or our tradition?"

"Maybe not, but I know something about labels and what sells." She leaned across the table, her eyes glowing, an intensity in her gaze he hadn't seen before. She was all earnest and eager to share her knowledge with him. She had confidence in herself, he gave her that.

"How are your sales?" she asked.

"Fine," he said brusquely. He would never admit to her they could be better. Why risk changing a label and bucking tradition on the slim hope sales might be improved? A gold medal would improve their sales. Nothing else.

"Then keep your labels," she said, "but when I bottle my wine…"

He felt as though a cold wind had blown across the table all the way from the Alps. She'd said *when* not *if*. She was a dreamer, and dreamers are not easily convinced to do the right thing. The practical thing. If he didn't find her a house to buy today, he'd promised to help her harvest her grapes. He'd better think of something irresistible to show her.

She was cut off in mid sentence when the waiter brought

the appetizer he'd ordered, a small plate of gnocchi in gor-
gonzola-and-pistachio sauce. Her eyes widened and she
inhaled the aroma of the rich sauce. She took a bite and
nodded slowly. At least she appreciated good food. Maybe
even good wine too, though he doubted it. How could she
when she hadn't been around it all her life?

After the waiter served them a salad of vine-ripened
tomatoes garnished with fruity olive oil and fresh basil,
Angelo, the owner came by to slap Dario on the back and tell
him it had been a long time, and he'd missed him. Fortunately
he didn't mention Magdalena. Even though he surely knew
what everyone knew—his fiancée had dumped him to marry
his cousin. The gossip and rumors were one reason he'd
avoided the restaurant and every other restaurant he used to
frequent. Maybe there was a new scandal to occupy
everyone's mind by now. If there was, Dario hadn't heard it.

He introduced the owner to Isabel. What else could he do?
By the way he looked at her, Angelo was clearly sizing her
up, comparing her to the beauty queen Dario used to bring to
the restaurant. The owner turned on the charm, asking Isabel
how she liked Sicily.

"It's beautiful. And I'm just learning some of the fascinating history," she said.

"Dario can teach you more than any guidebook," Angelo
said with an approving smile. "About everything. Wine and
food as well as history. Yes, you're in good hands."

Dario wanted to tell him she was not in his hands at all.
But all he could do was to sit there hoping the man would
quickly move on to greet other customers.

But Angelo was just getting warmed up. He told Dario he
should stop working so hard and come more often to the restaurant the way he used to, and bring the lovely American. He

suggested various dishes she should try and sights she should see in the neighborhood. A few minutes later he finally left them to their food.

"He's very friendly," Isabel noted. "Is he right about your working too hard?"

"In our business there's no such thing as working too hard. We suffered some losses during the drought and the fungus over a year ago, then grandfather got sick and frankly, I have no choice but to work hard. I'm in charge and it's the season of the crush. Everyone in the wine business is working hard." No one had as good a reason for hard work as Dario. No one needed to fill his days with backbreaking physical labor and his nights at his computer studying plans and projects and making spreadsheets. All that to try to make up for the past mistakes and to forget. Mostly to forget.

"I thought you said true Sicilians were easygoing."

"Most of the time, yes. Some of them all the time. I have an excuse for being different. Also it's my nature and the nature of owning a business. You'll see." If she was sensible and left and went home, she wouldn't have to face the hard work of owning a business.

He ate a tomato, then leaned back in his chair and studied her for a long moment. He'd talked quite enough about the Montessori fortunes or lack thereof. More than she needed to know.

Angelo must have noticed the contrast between his ex-fiancée, the stunning Magdalena, oozing self-confidence and bravado, and the plainly dressed American who sat across from him. Fortunately the name *Magdalena* was not mentioned. If he was lucky he'd get through the whole day without hearing it.

In a strange way it was a relief to be with someone who

hadn't lived here all her life, who didn't know everyone and their secrets from their past. It made him feel a sense of detachment, if only briefly, from his work and his family and the past and the pressures he put on himself.

This woman across the table from him with her red-gold hair and her casual American clothes was a stranger in a strange land. A blank tablet. She'd never seen the Roman ruins or eaten capellini Timballo or tasted Nero D'avola. He didn't want to like anything about her, but he couldn't help admiring her as she experienced these things for the first time. She had quite remarkable dark eyes that lit up at the sight of the old ruins or the taste of a superb wine. He liked it that she had no idea what really motivated him, what had really happened in the past, and if he had his way, she never would.

"You ask a lot of questions, but you keep quiet about yourself," he said.

"There's not much to say. As you know, I have no family except for my uncle, who's dead. I quit my job to come here. If everyone in the wine business is working hard now then I feel guilty taking you away from your grapes. You must have work to do. Perhaps we should leave."

He shook his head. "I work hard so the family can live, but even I don't live to work as you do in America."

"How do you know what we do in America?"

"I read. I've seen movies."

"Really? What have you seen?"

"We were talking about you. You left a job behind, anything else?"

"A rented apartment. Some friends."

"No boyfriend?" If she had one, there was a chance she'd go back to him.

"No boyfriend," she said brusquely. But a tell-tale flush

colored her cheeks. There was a story there she wasn't sharing. He knew something about that. As much as he respected her privacy, he couldn't help being curious.

"I'm surprised."

"That I'm independent?"

"That you're single at your age. What's wrong with American men?"

"Most of them are married," she explained. "Which is fine with me. Since I prefer being on my own." She looked down at the table, studying the silverware. Why did he have the feeling this was a painful subject despite her smooth explanation? Or it could be she found the flatware fascinating. Whatever it was, she recovered quickly and looked up, her face composed, her gaze steady. "I could ask you the same thing. If you're not married, why not? What's wrong with Italian women?"

He choked on a bitter laugh. "Ah, there's a subject. Italian women are loud and opinionated. Once you meet some of them you'll see." Fortunately she'd never met Magdalena, and she never would, because she'd moved to Milan. "They have power and they run the families. My mother can attest to that. She and my father are currently in Palermo to take care of some business. So my grandmother is running the house while Nonno recovers."

He stopped his speech about women when the waiter appeared to bring them a bubbling dish hot from the oven called Pasta Alla Norma, a combination of eggplant, tomatoes and ricotta cheese.

"Who was Norma?" she asked.

"The heroine of an opera by Bellini, Sicily's most famous son. Do you like opera?"

"I don't know, I've never seen one. What's it about?"

"Norma is in love with a man who's thrown her over for someone else. But she gets revenge. She ruins him and has him sentenced to death."

"Good for her."

"Except at the end, she jumps into the funeral pyre and dies with him."

"I prefer happy endings."

"So does everyone, but that's not life." If she didn't know that by now, she'd led a charmed life. "You'd like *The Marriage of Figaro* or *The Barber of Seville*. Or something by Puccini. Be sure to see an opera while you're here on vacation. Preferably a happy one."

"I don't think I'll have the time or the proper dress. And I'm *NOT* on vacation."

She was so predictable. All he had to do was refer to her temporary status or her departure and her cheeks turned pink and her eyes flashed as she glared angrily at him. He watched her high spirits and discomfort, knowing he'd caused it.

Taking his time he let his gaze wander from her face to her neck to her arms and breasts and tried to picture her in a formal evening gown at the opera. He was so engrossed he almost didn't notice the waiter who was offering an after-lunch drink from the bar. He shook his head and continued to muse about his companion. She just might enjoy a night at the opera. She certainly had the confidence to try new things. That much was clear. Under other circumstances, he might have offered to take such an attractive woman to the opera since there was absolutely no danger of his ever losing his head and heart to a woman again. He could see her dressed up and gauge her reaction. But she was right, she'd probably be too busy struggling to make a go of it to see an opera. How futile it was, how maddening that she wouldn't take his advice.

If her stay was as temporary as he hoped, she wouldn't be around for the opera season. The sooner she realized she should leave, the better. She'd never make it through a winter on that mountain. Never. As much as it was in his interest to send her packing, it was also the best thing for her as well.

Feeling more confident about the outcome, he signaled the waiter to order two cannolis and coffee. If she had any memories of Sicily when she returned to the States, he wanted them to be pleasant ones—of sightseeing and delicious food and wine. Not of cold nights and frost on the vines. It was the least he could do in exchange for his land.

"Are you sure we have time for this?" she asked.

"Of course. Everyone deserves a day off now and then. We're hard-working when we have to be, but in Italy everyone always has time to eat. And then we'll see some other properties I think you'll like."

She opened her mouth to protest, then closed it, realizing, he hoped, that there was no point in arguing. Maybe she was finally seeing the light. She didn't insist that she had no use for a new house with a solid roof and a clean kitchen. But he knew. He knew that she had a stubborn streak a mile wide. He knew she would initially refuse to consider any other property than the one she'd inherited. But he was just as stubborn.

In the meantime he watched her savor the creamy ricotta filling of the rich pastry. A tiny piece of crisp dough stuck to the corner of her mouth. It was all he could do to keep from reaching across the table to brush it away with his finger. Before he could make a move, she licked her lips and he felt his pulse accelerate wildly. What was wrong with him? Maybe his family was right when they said he'd been working too hard. He hadn't given a single woman a second look since

Magdalena had walked out on him over a year ago, let alone buy them lunch at his once-favorite restaurant. That was all that was wrong with him.

CHAPTER FOUR

ON THE WAY BACK to the town of Villarmosa, Dario showed Isabel several other villas, all attractive, all with intact roofs, some with gardens and others with patios. Isabel very politely but firmly told her guide she wasn't interested in any of them.

"Not interested?" he asked, sounding incredulous. She had the feeling he thought she was deliberately trying to thwart him, as if she was a bourgeois crass American who had no respect for fine living and no appreciation of his culture. He tilted his head to observe the frescoes on the ceiling of the next house he took her to. "The art work here alone is worth the price of the place."

She took a deep breath and tried once again to explain. "I'm sure it is. But it's not my art work. It didn't belong to my uncle. The house has no vines, no grapes, no challenging new career for me to undertake."

"But there is a pond and this one comes with swans instead of water snakes."

She sighed and glanced out the window. It was a lovely picturesque pond with graceful white-plumaged birds paddling by.

"Swans mate for life, you know," he said.

"Even in Italy?"

"Especially in Italy. Divorce is legal here, but not as common as other European countries. For one thing we marry late or not at all and most young people live close to their parents."

She nodded. How cozy it all sounded. How different from the families she'd lived with—single mothers, absentee dads and too many children on welfare. He was watching her to gauge her reaction to the house.

"This house just doesn't speak to me," she said at last. It was true. It was a nice house, the frescoes were beautiful, the swans a definite plus, but she couldn't see herself living there.

He might have rolled his eyes. Whatever he did, he effectively conveyed his dismay at her lack of good sense.

"What did you expect the house to say to you?" he asked, his voice tinged with sarcasm. "*Benvenuto?* Welcome? Make yourself at home? Glad you could make it?"

"I don't think you'll understand, but I need to feel something, a family connection, a feeling that I could live here, that I could belong here."

"Which is what you feel at the Azienda?" he asked. There was no mistaking the disbelief in his voice.

She nodded, but she knew that to him the Azienda was a terrible mess. It really didn't matter what he thought. She'd allowed him to show her around and now he had to do what he'd said he'd do for her.

To her great relief, after three more villas, each one desirable with assets like a deep well and a sturdy roof and even some furniture, he gave up when he saw her negative reaction. She kept her remarks to a minimum and her tone firm, and he finally drove her back to the hotel. She couldn't help feeling victorious. She'd successfully resisted his best efforts and now he owed her.

He walked her up to the door of the hotel and thanked her politely for accompanying him. He was probably furious with her for not caving in, if the frown lines between his eyebrows were any indication, but he said nothing.

Surely even he, incredibly rich, well-connected and sinfully handsome, didn't always get his way? She thanked him for lunch and the sightseeing, then she waited but he said nothing else. He just turned and headed for his car.

"I believe we had a deal," she said, raising her voice.

He looked back at her, seeming surprised. Could he really have forgotten? Not a shrewd businessman like him. He was hoping *she'd* forgotten.

"You said if I didn't see anything I liked, you'd help me find the workers I need."

"And I will. Of course. It may take a little time."

"I don't have time. My grapes are ripe. They need to be picked." She was only guessing. What did she know about grapes really? When he didn't contradict her, she had a feeling she was right. Those grapes were ready and so was she. She couldn't miss this harvest or she'd be behind a year in her quest for a new career.

"I'll see what I can do," he said. Then he got into his car and drove away without a backward glance. She stood there wondering if she'd ever see him again. He was disappointed that his plan hadn't worked. No, he was more than disappointed. He was angry. He couldn't believe she was still holding out on him. She wondered if he'd really keep his promise.

If he never came back, she'd have to scour the town, begging for workers in her broken Italian with the possibility she'd hired a crew of thieves and jailbirds. She needed his help. Badly.

She hated that feeling of being needy. Of depending on someone. It brought back the familiar empty feeling in the pit of her stomach she'd had when she moved from one house to another. From one family to another. No place to call home. No one to turn to. No one who cared about her.

She'd thought things would be different here. Her own house, her own business. She'd be in charge. No landlord, no boss. Instead, she was more vulnerable than she'd ever been.

She was too restless to hang around her hotel room studying her Italian audio tapes or reading how-to books about winemaking. All those chapters about yeast cells and tank-fermentation only made her feel more insecure and nervous about the future.

She took a shower to cool off, changed clothes and headed for the village to look around. For all she knew there might be a group of day laborers standing on the corner looking for work the way they did back in California. She put her Italian phrase book in her pocket, grabbed her camera case and walked the half mile to town down a road lined with lemon trees and almond groves. With the sun low in the sky, the air was deliciously cool.

Villarmosa wasn't a big town. Centered around the town square was everything one needed for the simple life. She took a few photos of the small, leafy park in the center of town and the cluster of old houses around it. Then she walked over to look at an ancient stone church, passed a post office, a garage and a handful of shops, one of which was a greengrocer's where the bins outside were filled with colorful cherries, ripe peaches and juicy melons.

The lawyer's office was located above a small café. She glanced up at the windows where she'd gotten the news about her inheritance, but the shades were drawn and it looked deserted. Maybe her uncle had been Signore Delfino's only client. She didn't see a single worker on any corner asking for jobs.

Her first stop was at a brightly lighted food shop with a

mouthwatering display in the window. Small jars of anchovies and sun-dried tomatoes were flanked by tall, hand-blown bell-shaped glass jars filled with colorful marinated vegetables. Figs, dried apricots and dates were strung like necklaces and hung from the ceiling. Isabel snapped some more pictures, then hung the camera around her neck.

There was no way she could walk by and not go in for a closer look and maybe even a small purchase. Even though she'd had a large and delicious lunch, her mouth was watering and she couldn't resist. Immediately behind the window was the counter where a portly man in a beard and a white apron was slicing prosciutto in paper-thin slices, carefully laying a piece of wax paper between each slice.

The air was redolent with the mingled scents—cured meats and flavorful cheeses. The whole place was like a shrine to the god Epicurus and she'd never seen anything like it. A bell rang when she opened the door and every customer turned to look at her, the new girl in town. Of course, her camera marked her as a tourist, but who was she going to fool anyway? She smiled tentatively.

While she waited in line she studied her phrase book to see how to ask for a small amount of what she wanted. When it was her turn she pointed to the prosciutto and the salami and two kinds of cheese as well as a carton of tiny black olives, and she even spoke a few well-chosen words of Italian.

Feeling proud and pleased with herself for her first foray into town, she followed one of the small old ladies dressed in black out to the street. The woman was bent over with a string bag in hand. Suddenly the bag broke and a half dozen peaches and a jar of honey went rolling down the brick sidewalk.

The woman let loose with a shriek, followed by *"L'oh il mio dio! Che cosa sono io che vado ora fare?"*

Isabel scooped up the slightly bruised peaches and the honey, which was still intact, from the smooth stone walkway, put them in her own camera bag and handed it to the woman, who beamed at her and said, *"Grazie così tanto. Siete molto gentili."*

"Prego," Isabel said.

Before Isabel could come up with another appropriate phrase in Italian, the woman waved frantically to someone in a large black car who pulled up and helped her into the back seat. Isabel stood watching as the car, the woman and her camera bag all drove away. Maybe she'd see her again some day or maybe not. Anyway, it was just a case she'd lost. Her camera was hanging around her neck.

Then she proceeded to the greengrocer where the woman must have bought her fruit. The produce was all beautifully arranged, piled high in a cornucopia of spiky artichokes and tomatoes, shiny purple eggplant and pencil-thin asparagus. She took more pictures.

She wanted to buy everything in the colorful display, but she had no way to carry anything else since the old lady had taken her bag. Never mind. She could always come back tomorrow and do some more shopping.

Back at the hotel she decided not to eat dinner in the dining room. Her room came with breakfast and dinner included so she looked at the menu and ordered that night's special dinner. She asked to have it sent up so she could eat in her room and not feel self-conscious about sitting alone while all around her were couples or families.

Just the idea of saying "Table for one" or "I'm alone," sent a lonely chill through her body. Why subject herself to pitying glances from other happy diners? She just couldn't face it, not after the day she'd had. Even though she'd had a good time seeing the sights and eating the food, she'd been afraid to let down her defenses for so much as a minute. She was afraid Dario would pounce on her and make her an offer she couldn't refuse.

Though everyone she'd met here had been nice—except for Dario Montessori and the lawyer—she didn't have the energy to sit down in a room full of strangers and try to make conversation in Italian with the friendly waiters. Here in her room she could relax and get back to studying viticulture and irregular Italian verbs.

First she had a long soak in the claw-foot tub, scrubbing with a sponge and some lemon-infused soap, letting the tension that came from verbal battles with her tour guide melt away. She took her *Guide to Sicily* with her into the tub and read a chapter about "Flora and Fauna." What she read there surprised and annoyed her so much she almost dropped her book in the hot water.

There was a knock on her door. Dinner already? She'd relaxed so much she'd lost track of time. She might have even dozed off, since she was still on California time and suffering from delayed jetlag. She slipped into the plush terry-cloth robe the hotel provided, wrapped a large towel around her wet hair and went to receive the tray from the maid.

Instead of the maid, it was Dario Montessori standing there, this time wearing a leather jacket, straight-leg denim jeans and brown leather loafers without socks. All of which she managed to take in despite the shock of seeing him there outside her door. It was easier and safer to focus on his expensive Italian clothes and shoes than on his craggy face half in shadow, half lit by the overhead fixture in the hall.

"What are you doing here?" she asked, tugging on the lapels of her robe. Why had she opened the door without asking who was there? She could only blame it on her sense of security here in this small hotel in this small town. Now that she realized it could have been a serial killer outside her door, she felt her face turn red with embarrassment. What must this man think of her? Not only did she appear to be a clueless heiress, but she was so naive and trusting she'd opened her hotel door without question to a stranger.

"I came to bring back your bag," he said while his gaze took in the wide-open lapels of her robe. "My grandmother told me how you saved her peaches and her honey. She said to thank you very much."

"Your grandmother? I had no idea. How did she know...?"

"That it was you? She didn't. But your name is inside the case."

"Oh," she said weakly trying to take it all in while she clutched at the front of her robe with one hand and tightened the towel around her head with the other. His grandmother was obviously the tiny little woman in the store.

She didn't invite him in, but Dario stepped inside the room anyway. "I have some news for you about your workers," he said, taking a small leather notebook from his jacket pocket. He must have noticed she wasn't dressed for company, but he didn't care. How typical of him to pursue his own ends and ignore whatever got in his way.

Purposefully he strode past the queen-size bed covered with a pale-green duvet and the antique writing desk, stopped at the round table at the window, took a seat and spread out some papers.

The only thing Isabel could do was sit down across from him as if they were having a business meeting, which they were, except she was hardly dressed or mentally prepared for one. If he'd planned to catch her unawares, and spring some new scheme on her, he'd picked the right time. Her brain was muddled and confused. But her resolve was as firm as ever.

She sat up ramrod-straight in the padded chair and tried to pay attention to what Dario said when all she could think about was how her skin tingled from the bath and how little distance was between the two of them. She felt trapped in the masculine aura that seemed to surround him. There was no way for her to escape or to try to change clothes without looking like a complete idiot. If it didn't bother him that she was wearing a robe and nothing else, why should it bother her? He surely wouldn't stay long.

"I found you a crew of workers." He pushed a list of names across the table in her direction.

"Good," she said. The names were a blur. "Who are they?"

"Old-timers. Men who know their way around the Azienda. They'll be up there tomorrow morning at eight."

"Fine." She breathed a sigh of relief. She might pull this off after all. "How much do they get paid?"

"That depends on their job. Some operate the crushing machine, some the fermenter. They're good men, but you have to be there to supervise them, otherwise they'll take advantage of you."

Isabel blinked rapidly. More men who wanted to take advantage of her? What had she gotten herself into? All she could see was fifty-dollar bottles of Amarado on the shelves without any clear idea of how they got there. She had to keep up a brave front.

"But where…how…?"

"The machinery is in the barn. As far as I know, it still works, but just barely."

"I didn't see any barn."

"You weren't looking. It's there behind the grove of trees behind the house."

"Oh, yes, of course," she said.

"The men expect to be paid in cash. I've written down the hourly rate for each man. Do you have a bank account?"

She shook her head. He must think she wasn't equipped to run a vineyard. Or to make wine. Or to change a tire. But she could learn. And she would.

"You'll want to open an account right away so you can write checks for your utilities. When you get them installed."

"Of course."

There was a soft knock on the door. Now what?

This time it was the maid with her dinner. She came in and set up the plates on the table. For some reason it appeared to be a dinner for two. Had the personnel seen Dario go up to her room and figured they would be expecting an intimate meal for two? Or had he told them he was staying for dinner? Dinner with the one woman he most wanted to get rid of? The woman he'd already had breakfast and lunch with? Hardly.

"Are you staying for dinner?" she asked.

"It looks that way," he said.

No "thank you." No polite refusal. Did he want to stay? Probably not. Then why do it? He must have his reasons. Did she want him to? Definitely not.

Whatever the reason, the maid seemed to know what she was doing, serving veal Madeira in a white-wine-and-mushroom sauce over creamy polenta from a silver chafing dish, along with sautéed fresh spinach. She poured two glasses from a bottle of Pinot Grigio and quietly left the room with a shy smile.

The whole scenario was surreal in the extreme. Was this really Isabel Morrison having dinner in nothing but a robe with the richest and best-looking man in all of Sicily? The same man she'd had lunch and breakfast with? If he shared her sense of the absurd, he didn't let it show. For all she knew, he dined with half-clad women in their hotel rooms every other night. The best she could do was to pretend to be at least that sophisticated herself.

She couldn't possibly change into her clothes at this point, but she did retreat to the bathroom to take the towel off her head, and run a comb through her tangled hair.

Dario looked up when she came back with her hair in a damp cloud of dark-red curls. He swirled some wine around in his glass to keep from staring at her bare legs and the way her robe gaped in front giving him a tantalizing glimpse of one pale breast.

Maybe he shouldn't have barged in this way and invited himself for dinner. It was only now he realized how bizarre the situation was. It had been a long time since he'd eaten dinner with a woman in her hotel room. The first time ever with a red-headed American woman in a robe in her hotel room. And he hadn't planned on her being a distraction, but she was.

The situation had its advantages over the expensive restaurants where he usually dined and where he might have taken her if he'd wanted to have dinner with her. No one but the night clerk knew he was here in her room. Also, he had to admit that any gown she might have worn for dinner would not be as sexy as this robe which covered most of her body, but left him free to imagine what was underneath it.

"I have to say they serve a decent wine," Dario said, tearing his gaze away from her for a moment. He really hadn't meant to stay for dinner. He'd only meant to hand over her camera case, thank her for helping his grandmother and tell her he'd hired some workers. But seeing her with the towel over her head looking like what he imagined a concubine in a harem would look like, had set his senses reeling.

Maybe it was the seductive smell of the soap that clung to her skin that had such a strange effect on him, or maybe he was losing his mind. He told himself to go, to get out of here before he did something stupid, but the voice in his head wasn't very loud or insistent. So then he told himself to shut up and relax.

No getting around it; Isabel looked very different from the enemy he knew she was. Instead she looked soft and warm and very feminine. The kind of woman you wanted to wrap your arms around and get into that queen-sized bed with. The kind of woman whose skin looked so soft and inviting you wanted to taste and touch it. If she wasn't who she was, and if he was someone else, he might be tempted. In fact, he *was* tempted.

How could this red-haired woman who knew nothing about winemaking, wearing only a bathrobe, be a threat to him or his family? She couldn't possibly be. She was as good as on her way home. He felt the guard he kept up around his heart and soul start slipping away. And why not? How threatening an adversary could she be? None at all.

So he stayed for dinner. And allowed himself to look at her between bites of the food, which looked delicious and probably was, but he didn't seem to be able to appreciate it the way he might have if she'd been a plain fifty-year-old spinster, which is what he'd hoped for when he'd heard about her inheritance.

It was late. He was hungry. The veal was tender and the sauce appeared to be exceptional. At the family home the talk would be all about the harvest which could be repetitive after a while. Truthfully, he hadn't seen much of his family in a long time. For one thing, his sisters always had some unmarried woman friend they wanted him to meet. He'd explained over and over why he wasn't interested, but they kept trying. Then he disagreed with them about the same issues, which they rehashed over and over. They just couldn't understand why his working so hard now was his way of making up for his past mistakes, so he gave up trying to explain and just tried to keep to himself. Having someone new in town, even someone he didn't want there but who needed his help, was like an unexpected shot in the arm.

Here was a woman who knew virtually nothing about wine, his family or their problems. He felt as though he'd been dropped down into a little part of America. He felt stimulated and refreshed and challenged for the first time in months. What had happened? Was it just her?

He saw no harm in having dinner with her. All he had to do was play along with her plans for a few days, a week or two at most. He'd even help her pick her grapes and make her wine. When she realized how hard it was and that it wasn't going to work, she wouldn't blame him, she couldn't. She'd just accept the fact she wasn't cut out to be a vintner, sell him the property and go home where she belonged. No hard feelings.

"I'm not sure how this happened," she said, indicating the food on the plates at the table.

"Did you order dinner in your room?"

"Yes, but just for me. I had no idea…"

He shrugged. "I stopped at the desk and asked for your room, maybe they thought…"

"I see," she said. But she looked confused. Maybe she thought he'd told them to make it dinner for two. If he'd known her skin was glowing, her toenails were painted pink and she was fresh from her bath and smelling like a fragrant essence of sweet-smelling herbs, he might have. What was the harm in dining with an attractive woman once in a while? No strings. No obligations. No anxious sisters asking him for a report: *Did he like Signorina X? Did he want to see her again? And if not, why not?* This was just dinner. A business dinner actually. It didn't happen that often. Not to him. Not anymore. Not since Magdalena.

"The food here is quite good," he said. As if that was a good enough excuse for him to stay. "Why would you want to move to the Azienda? No hot baths, no bathrobes. No sauces." He allowed himself still another frank yet leisurely look at the shapely body across the table from him.

"I told you—it's my home and I intend to live there. I didn't come here to stay in a hotel, however comfortable it is."

"Your home isn't quite set up for cooking either." That was the understatement of the year.

She looked around. "I'll miss the comforts here, but I don't need them. I want to live like the natives do. I believe there's a fire pit outside near my pond. I'll have picnics and cook over an open fire."

"Speaking of the natives, my grandmother is very grateful to you. She told me that you chased her peaches down the street for her. She didn't get a chance to thank you properly so she wants you to come to dinner at the house tomorrow night."

"Does she know who I am?"

"I told her." He paused. "You said you wanted to meet the neighbors. Here's your chance. Are you coming or not?"

"Well, I…yes, sure. Please thank her for me."

She poured more wine into her glass and then his. All of a sudden she'd become the hostess. Just as she had earlier today at the Azienda. He could have sworn a few minutes ago she'd wanted nothing more than to get rid of him. She probably still did, but now she was being polite.

"You said there was a long story behind your losing the Azienda," she asked. "What is it?"

CHAPTER FIVE

ISABEL knew he probably wouldn't answer her question no matter how many glasses of wine he drank. After a lifetime in Sicily he was probably able to drink wine all night and still keep a cool head. But she thought it was worth a try. Something must have happened. Something important enough that he didn't want to talk about it.

He probably thought it was none of her business. Maybe he was right. On the other hand, since she was going to live there on the property, with him as her neighbor, she wanted to know. He lifted his glass and considered the wine as a connoisseur would do. Or was he considering spilling the whole story? She held her breath. She waited. He still said nothing.

Finally he drained his glass and set it on the table. "It's not a very interesting story. But since you asked, here it is. Two years ago, I was engaged to a woman. It was, how do you say? A whirlwind time. We traveled from one end of the island to the other. Magdalena was Miss Sicily and she had appearances to make. Festivals to attend. We were wined and dined everywhere, Magdalena was treated like royalty, which she enjoyed and the truth of the matter is I forgot about work. Forgot about making wine. Forgot about checking the vines and following the weather forecast. Which meant I neglected the vineyards just when they needed my help most—during a drought and an infestation of fungus which attacked the plants."

He stopped suddenly. "I'm talking too much. Making excuses for myself. Trying to explain when there is no explanation and no excuse. The rest of the family were working round the clock trying to save the harvest, but I was gone enjoying myself. I let myself be distracted just when I shouldn't have. The result was a near disaster. A blight. The workers hadn't been paid. We had to raise money and quickly. We sold the Azienda to your uncle. All I can say is I regret the whole affair. I regret everything about it. And I assure you it won't happen again." He said the words with so much finality, she had no doubt he meant them.

He stood abruptly and looked down at her. "There you have it. I've talked too much and I hope I haven't bored you. Now I must go. It's late and you have a big day ahead of you."

"I'm looking forward to it," she said, while a million questions came to mind. What did he mean *it won't happen again?* Was he referring to the sale of the land or to getting engaged? What happened to the beauty queen Magdalena? Where was she now? Who broke it off and why?

She stifled the urge to ask these questions. He'd already said more than he'd intended. Instead she said, "It's the first day of my new life as a winemaker. And, by the way, if you ever want to swim in my pond, feel free. Because there are no water snakes in Sicily."

"Is that right?" he asked. A flash of something that might have been recognition of her knowledge of flora and fauna flickered in his eyes.

She stood and reached into the pocket of her robe for the book she'd been reading and opened it and read, "'Sicily's only poisonous snake, the viper, can be found in the forests and flatland in the south of the island.' As far as I know this is not the south of the island and the viper can't swim."

"I never said I was a herpetologist. I'm a vintner. I was trying to warn you about possible poisonous reptiles. For your own good," he said.

For her own good! She doubted that very much. She brushed past him and held the door open.

"Good luck," he said. Then he stood in the doorway, one arm braced against the door frame. He looked at her with a gleam in his eye as though he was about to say or do something, so she waited. And waited. The tension rose. Her cheeks were burning. The temperature in the room must have gone up ten degrees. His gaze held hers and she couldn't look away. All the breath had left her lungs. She couldn't stand there much longer. She had the strangest feeling he was going to do something rash like kiss her. But that was ridiculous. He didn't even like her. Finally after an eternity he seemed to switch gears, change his mind and the gleam in his eye disappeared.

"Thanks for dinner," he said briskly. Then he was gone.

Isabel closed the door and staggered backward. What was wrong with him? What was wrong with her, imagining him kissing her? Maybe it was a Sicilian custom, after dinner you kissed the hostess. Or at least thought about it. It would have meant nothing if he had kissed her. But he hadn't. She was not disappointed. She was relieved.

The next day she needed all the luck she could get and she didn't get much. First she went to the bank, but it wasn't open yet, so she proceeded straight to the Azienda. There, the foreman, whom Dario had assured her was the best in the business, was emerging from the wine cellar, and she suspected that he might have been sampling her vintage collection. At least he was cheerful which was more than she could say for the crew who all looked so glum she thought they must have just lost their best friend.

If only she could talk to them, but whenever she practiced her Italian on them, they just looked at her with a blank expression on their faces. Even without a common language she understood that the old trailer they found in the barn had a flat tire and without it they had no way of loading the grapes as they picked them.

The men handed her the tire and it was obvious they expected her to fix it. Or have it fixed. Fortunately she'd paid attention when Dario changed her tire, knowing he wouldn't always be around, and knowing she was too proud to impose on him again. She located an old spare tire in the barn then took the tools from the trunk of the car and after enlisting one of the workers to help her hold the tire in place, she actually replaced the old tire.

She might have imagined it, but she thought the workers looked impressed. It didn't matter. What mattered was that she'd done it herself. She needed supplies in town so she got in her car and headed down the hill, a feeling of pride swelling inside her.

But that feeling didn't last. One backward glance told her the men were glad for the lack of work. They were standing in her driveway, some leaning against trees, others lying on the ground as if they'd already had a hard day. They wouldn't mind if she never came back as long as they got paid at the end of the day, which would be difficult without a trip to the bank.

She remembered what Dario had said about keeping an eye on them or they'd take advantage of her, but what could she do? She was only one person, one person who had way too much to do and no real knowledge of how to do it.

In the small gas station she asked the owner for a tank of propane and a container of diesel oil. She was pacing up and down in front of the station as she waited when Dario drove by in his convertible. He pulled over and took off his sunglasses.

"Everything going well?" he asked. He must be working, but he looked as though for him it was just another day in paradise, and he didn't have a care in the world. Maybe some day she'd have the same calm, cool attitude, the same confidence, but right now she was frazzled, worried and nervous. And seeing him like this, all she could think about was his almost kissing her last night, even though he hadn't, and she knew it would have meant nothing if he had.

"Fine," she said briskly. Never show anxiety. Always project confidence. Never trust or rely on anyone but yourself. Lessons she'd learned early on. "Except for a few glitches."

"Glitches?"

"Problems." Sometimes she forgot he didn't know every American slang word. "Like the trailer had a flat tire."

"And…?"

"I found another and I changed it myself."

She bit back a little smile at the way his eyebrows shot up in surprise. He hadn't thought she could do it.

"I watched you, remember?" she reminded him.

"Good for you. You're a fast learner."

She blinked. Was that another compliment?

"The men all show up?" he asked.

"Yes, but they have nothing to do while I'm here doing errands."

"Nothing? What about picking the grapes and putting them into baskets?"

She gritted her teeth together. Why didn't she think of that? Because she didn't know there were baskets. She'd changed a tire, but there was more to be done. Much, much more.

"Yes, of course," she said. "That's what they're doing." She didn't think they were doing anything, but she didn't want to tell Dario that. Didn't want him to think she had a problem in the world that she couldn't solve. Didn't want him to think she couldn't manage her hired help by herself. Or at least command respect.

"I'll stop by and see what's happening," he said.

"You don't need to go up there. I have everything under control." She didn't want him acting as if he had the right to take over her job. It was her place and if she needed help, she'd rather get it from someone else. Someone neutral who didn't have something to gain when she failed.

"I'm going to the bank, then I'll head back up the mountain," she added.

"You haven't done that yet?"

What did he think she was, a robot?

"I did go, but they weren't open yet."

He shook his head as if he couldn't believe how stupid she was not to know the banking hours of a small-town bank in a strange country. She'd like to see him in America, challenged by the language, hiring a crew, moving into a house that needed repairs and starting a new business. That would be a very satisfying scenario—to watch him struggle with something…anything. Just a dent in his self-assurance—which bordered on arrogance—would improve her disposition. Just to know she wasn't the only one who made mistakes.

"While you're in town, you might want to negotiate with the company to turn the power back on, if you want electricity, that is. If you do, you'll need to run a wire from the nearest line. And pick up a tank of propane so you can use your stove."

"I'm just waiting for it now."

If he wanted to overwhelm and confuse her and make her

think she couldn't handle it, he was not going to succeed. Because she could and she would. The main thing was to let him know she was on top of everything.

"I don't need electricity just yet. I'll get some candles and I'm sure I'll be fine without lights for a while," she said loftily.

"And will you be fine without running water? You'll need diesel oil for the engine that pumps water to the tank from the well."

"Of course I know about diesel oil," she said, waving a hand at the pump. "I'm getting some here."

She had planned to skip the problem of running water because she'd buy a case of mineral water, but if he found out it would shout "spoiled American heiress" to him. She did want to live off the land if possible. "And I know I'll need electricity eventually."

"Only if you're really planning on living there."

"Oh, I am."

Some day she'd have everything under control just as he did. She'd have water and power and a roof without a hole in it. She'd be making prize-winning wine. She'd have friends and neighbors over to wonderful dinners cooked on her propane-fired stove. She'd invite local people who actually liked her and didn't resent her presence. And she'd smile at people instead of glaring at them, and she would refrain from telling them what to do. In other words she'd be the opposite of Dario Montessori.

He looked at her as if he knew what she was thinking, as if he knew she was dreaming a dream that would never come true. As if he knew she was going to fail and he'd be there to pick up the pieces. She tried to come up with a matching self-satisfied look, but she didn't have it in her. Not now.

The mechanic came out with her gasoline and propane and when she turned around Dario was gone. Then she headed to the bank. No problem there. They were open and glad to receive her money and open an account. It was a different story at the power company which was located above the bank in a small dusty office. There they didn't speak English and quoted what seemed an enormous amount of money. Maybe they didn't understand. All she wanted was a new connection or the old one repaired. They brought out several file folders with her uncle's name on them and had a long discussion in Italian.

Then they shook their heads. Maybe they'd come through. Or maybe she'd have to come back again. In the meantime she'd use bottled water and candles and propane. Her ancestors didn't have electricity and they survived. Of course, she wanted to do more than survive. She wanted to make a fine dessert wine and become part of this community. She wanted to be independent but not lonely. Would all these wishes come true? Or were they just impossible dreams?

When she got back to the Azienda, the workers were strolling leisurely up and down the rows of vines picking grapes and tossing them into baskets. That much they'd done on their own. But if they had to work this slowly it would take weeks to get her grapes picked. She consulted her dictionary and tried out a few commands, indicating that she needed them to work faster and harder.

When she lifted the heavy cylinder of propane out of the trunk of her car, suddenly one of the workmen appeared. They might not respect her, they might not understand her every word, but in Sicily chivalry was not dead yet. She pointed to the house, and he carried the tank to the kitchen where he left it next to the stove, which still tilted to one side. She motioned to the worker to lift up one corner of the cast-iron stove and she stuffed a piece of wood under the leg. It was now level and he left.

Now what? She studied a diagram on the side of the tank. Then she carefully attached the hose from the back of the stove to the cylinder. A picture of a valve with arrows showed her how to turn it on—and presto. She held the sparker to jets and they sent out blue flames. She jumped back from the stove, just in case.

It was magic. She had gas. She stood staring at the gas jets, smiling to herself as if she'd performed a miracle. She had. She could cook now. She could do anything.

She turned off the gas and went back outside, where she grabbed a basket and a knife and started picking along with the workers, hoping to set an example of speed. She set an example all right. She cut her finger and had to open one of her precious bottles of water to wash the cut. At noon the men all stopped working and pulled out huge hunks of bread, wedges of cheese, bottles of wine and slices of meat. They sat under a tall oak tree and spread out their food as if they were picnickers having a day in the country. Isabel hadn't thought to pack a lunch or buy any food. She had a working stove but no food to cook on it.

She was hot and tired and hungry. She longed to take a dip in her pond to cool off but she had no swimsuit and there were all these strangers there. When she saw Dario pull up in front of her house she sighed. She didn't want him telling her what to do and how to do it, so she kept picking and pretended she hadn't seen him.

"Hungry?" he asked when he met her head-on in the dusty row of vines.

She glanced up as coolly as possible. "Not really," she lied while her stomach protested. She'd never admit she couldn't manage her life without him, though she was dying to show off her newly working stove. "I have too much work to do to stop and eat." *And I have nothing to eat.*

"You need to drink something at least. And you need to pace yourself in this heat. You're not used to it. You look tired."

There's nothing like being told you look tired to make you *feel* tired, which is what happened—she was suddenly exhausted.

"I stopped at a farm stand and picked up some food. Stop and take a break." It was more an order than a suggestion and she didn't take orders well, she never had. If her back weren't aching and her forehead weren't pounding, she might have told him to take his food and leave her to pick grapes. But she didn't. Not with her stomach in knots and her throat parched. She wiped her hands on her pants and followed him to his car where he took a large box out of the front seat and walked with her around the back of the house to the overgrown patio with the ancient outdoor fire pit.

Setting the box on the weather-beaten picnic table in the shade of an old tree, he poured ice-cold sparkling water into real glasses. No paper cups for this Sicilian aristocrat.

Isabel sat down, took a long drink of water. "That's delicious," she murmured. Then she looked up at the spreading branches of the old tree for the first time. "Could that be a sycamore?"

"Here we call it a *platania* or plane tree. In the old days the bark and leaves were used for herbal medicine," he said as he uncorked a half bottle of chilled Montessori dry white wine. "Very useful. They even made fabric dye from the roots."

Isabel appreciated the information about the shady old tree, *her* shady old tree. It seemed Dario knew everything about everything. But it was the food that caught her attention. There was grilled lemon chicken fragrant with olive oil and rosemary and cubed provolone and marinated fresh mozzarella cheese. There were small tomatoes still warm from the vine. He set a small container of sweet roasted peppers and another of pesto sauce on the table. It seemed like an endless supply of gourmet items, each one better than the last. Finally there was a loaf of crusty ciabatta bread still warm from the oven.

"Where did you get all this?" she asked, tearing off a hunk of bread to eat with cheese.

"Here and there," he said with a casual wave of his hand. "Besides the farm stand, the bakery and the *deposito* in town. It was on my way."

"You shouldn't have," she said. "But I'm glad you did. I didn't realize how hungry I was. Thank you."

He sat across the narrow table from her with a look on his handsome face she couldn't decipher. It was partly curiosity, partly just landowner whose obligation was to feed the needy. Or maybe what he was doing was force-feeding the goose before it went to slaughter. After all, he surely hadn't changed his mind about wanting her gone.

"I owe you after you shared your dinner with me last night," he said.

"Oh, that," she said, as if she'd forgotten. There was no way she could have forgotten him after he'd left last night. She'd lain in bed picturing him standing there in the doorway, wondering what had gone through his mind. She knew what had gone through hers. She'd wanted him to kiss her. Just to find out what it was like to be kissed by a macho Sicilian. That's all. Today her mind was clear and she was glad he hadn't. She didn't need any more complications to this already awkward situation.

"Yes, that. Sorry I barged in on you."

She shrugged. What was she going to say? *I liked having someone to eat with, even if it was you. There's a side to you I didn't suspect—I'm surprised. That you fell so hard for a woman you neglected your duties. She must have been quite a woman. Why do I think of her in the past tense? For all I knew she's back in the gatehouse waiting for you with open arms.*

"Where do you usually have lunch?" she asked innocently, sipping the cold dry white wine he'd poured for her.

"Sometimes with the workers in the fields," he said. "Or I go home."

Aha, so she was there. "To eat with your family?" Isabel held her breath waiting for the answer.

"No."

That was it? Just no?

"They make a big deal of lunch. And dinner goes on for hours. No matter how busy they are. They want to talk. My sisters want to pry into my personal life. Make suggestions. In Sicily there is no concept of a personal space. I haven't got time for it."

Yet he had time to eat with her? The one person he'd like to see on the first plane out of here? Isabel dipped her bread in the fruity olive oil. Talking seemed to be a Sicilian pastime. And a nice one. Talking and eating fresh local food. She reminded herself not to pry any further into his personal life the way his family did, though of course that was exactly what she wanted to do.

"What's funny?" he asked with a frown on his face. It seemed she hadn't smothered her smile quite enough.

"Nothing. I'm very grateful you made time for me. I confess, I was hungry and envious of the workers with their lunches. I was feeling pretty sorry for myself when you showed up. Everything is wonderful. Delicious." She speared a chunk of ripe juicy melon with a fork he'd provided.

"What about tonight?" she asked. "Won't you have to spend time talking to your family at dinner?"

"My grandmother requested my presence tonight because of you, and no one says no to Nonna."

So he didn't want to be there. He was only going because he had to.

"Maybe I shouldn't have picked up the peaches and the honey for her if I've made things awkward for you."

"Dinner with my family will be a cultural event you should experience. I guarantee they'll be pleasant to you, more than I've been, in any case. And you'll see what Sicilian hospitality is like. Now I should be going. Grapes and more grapes. We only have a short time to get them off the vine."

Isabel got up, feeling guilty for sitting in the shade eating and talking and drinking wine and almost forgetting her problems—one of which was now standing across from her. Another was her house, literally falling down around her and then there were the vines and her workers.

She should never have spent all this time having lunch with Dario. He had work to do and so did she. But it felt so good to relax for a short time with the best-looking man in Sicily, maybe in all Italy and have him feed her with wonderful food and feed her mind with miscellaneous facts and opinions. A guidebook to Sicily can only teach a person so much. A Sicilian with impossibly blue flashing eyes, broad shoulders and a jaw of steel made every word he said about her adopted country seem fascinating and important.

He left the rest of the food, wine and water with her.

"Still no electricity?" he inquired.

"Not yet. I was concentrating on the propane and hooking up the stove."

"Who did that for you?"

"I did." A proud smile tugged at the corners of her mouth. She *was* proud of herself. "One of the workers carried the tank in for me, but I hooked it up. You're right, I do need electricity, but…I can only do so much in a day."

"You've done quite a lot," he said thoughtfully.

It was a good thing she was still sitting down because this too sounded suspiciously like yet another compliment and there were just so many a girl could take all at once.

"You still need to keep your food cold. I'll have some ice delivered," he said. "I'm sure the icebox hasn't been used in years, but it ought to keep things cool for a few days at least."

"Thank you," she said. Why was he being so nice? Must be the Sicilian hospitality kicking in whether he wanted it to or not. He couldn't help it. It was genetic.

Dario spoke to her workers picking grapes on his way to his car, asking them how the work was going. He wanted to be sure they were not taking advantage of Isabel just because she was a foreigner. Or because she didn't know what to expect from them. He was reassured when they indicated respect for her—her ability to try to communicate with them, and her willingness to work along with them.

He couldn't help being impressed too. No woman he knew would pick grapes herself, hook up the propane tank, change a tire or take on a dilapidated house. She'd managed to do it all so far. Maybe, just maybe she'd succeed here where her uncle had failed so badly. There was a look in her eyes that told him she wasn't an ordinary woman. Maybe the best thing for him to do now was to help her when he could with workers, ice, advice and food and back off about pressuring her to leave.

He had no idea what had made him talk about Magdalena last night when he hadn't so much as spoken her name in months. That was one reason he didn't join the family for dinners or just drop in at the house the way he used to. Somebody would always bring up his ex-fiancée. They wanted to know if he was over her. They knew what had happened. The whole town knew what she'd done. Of course he was over her. Did he really have to spell it out? Wasn't it obvious he'd moved on with his life?

The family tried to be tactful, but they wanted a sign that he was no longer carrying a torch for the beauty queen. A sign like taking up with a new woman. No question of that. Instead of stalling or changing the subject or out-and-out telling them it wasn't going to happen or it was none of their business, he chose to avoid the family and their questions. It was easier for him that way, easier to forget.

With Isabel there at dinner, they'd all be on their best behavior and the subject of Magdalena would not come up at all, God willing. Actually it would be good to see the family again. He'd missed his nieces and nephews. He'd always enjoyed their high spirits and their energy whether in a soccer game or a ride on the tractor at the vineyards. But work had been a good excuse for dropping out of sight as much as possible, even if the kids didn't completely understand it, the adults did, or should.

The family liked entertaining. They'd probably like meeting Isabel and would welcome her to the community. After all, they had no regrets about losing the Azienda, they all just accepted it as part of the ups and downs of the wine business. And they didn't understand why he felt so strongly about it. What was the use of trying to explain? So he didn't.

He wondered what would have happened if he hadn't brought the lunch today. Would Isabel have kept working until she collapsed?

If he knew her, that's exactly what might have happened. She was that determined to prove she could do it on her own.

He couldn't just stand by and watch her faint from hunger or get dehydrated. He drove slowly back to his crushing station, thinking about her while he passed acres of ripe grapes, golden wheat waving under a hot cloudless sky and gnarled olive trees. It was possible that she actually deserved this property after all. That was a revolutionary thought, but one he couldn't shake off.

By the end of the day, despite the break she'd taken for lunch, Isabel's back was stiff, her fingers were numb, her neck and arms were sunburned and she'd barely filled one basket. When the men looked into her basket they shook their heads. Of course she couldn't compete with them. But she had to try. She had to show them she wasn't a spoiled American heiress. They quit promptly at five o'clock and asked for their money. As soon as she'd paid them they piled into the back of a truck and they were off to spend their earnings. She envied them.

She realized just how much she was looking forward to a long soak in a bathtub and a change of clothes. And how when she moved up here she'd be roughing it. No hot baths, no clean clothes. She'd give herself one more day. She'd wallow in luxury a little longer, then she'd move up here. She could do it. She could make her little house comfortable. As soon as the grapes were picked and crushed, she'd get busy on the house. She'd make it look like home. Put it back in shape—the shape it must have been in long ago. She could picture it being a blend of old-fashioned charm and modern improvements.

When the ice was delivered all the way to her ancient icebox, she felt a wave of gratitude toward Dario. He didn't have to do that for her. Now she was that much closer to moving in. She opened another bottle of sparkling water, then she went back to the hotel.

She had no idea when and where she was expected for dinner at his family's home or who would be there besides Dario and his grandmother. She hoped it would be a big group, because with a large family his presence would be diluted. Sitting across the table from him, eating bread and cheese and drinking wine at lunch while bumping knees from time to time was enough for one day. He made her uneasy. She wasn't sure why he was being so helpful when it went directly against what he wanted.

He was too big, too strong, too Sicilian, too confident, too sure of himself and of course too good-looking. How could any woman resist him? He and Miss Sicily must have made a striking couple. She'd been part of a couple once, but no one had said they were striking. But that was because no one knew they were together.

Isabel wanted to make a good impression tonight. Not just because these were Dario's relatives, but because they were big landowners, they'd been here for generations and they were her neighbors. She pulled out of her suitcase the one and only dress she'd brought with her, a blue-green cotton sundress with tiny straps and a slim skirt. Was it appropriate? Her nerves were getting to her. Her imagination was running wild tonight. It was fatigue, it was worry and it was him. She was seeing entirely too much of someone she wanted to avoid and who wanted to avoid her. She could only hope his family would show her the famed Sicilian hospitality he'd promised.

Dario went to the hotel at seven to pick up Isabel. The sun was low in the sky and the air had cooled a little. He paused at the front desk and asked if the *signorina* was in. She was. Now that the dinner was looming, he almost wished she'd turned down the invitation for some reason, then he could avoid the scene completely.

He'd made his position clear to his family. As far as he was concerned, there was only one way to make up for losing the land and that was to get it back. But he hadn't considered that Isabel could possibly deserve the land as much as he did. Now, after seeing her toiling away as he'd never seen anyone work, he wondered. Maybe she did.

He had the clerk call up to Isabel Morrison's room and say he would be in the bar waiting for her. He couldn't risk another face-to-face encounter with her in her robe. He'd sworn off women, all women, after Magdalena had walked out on him, but he wasn't made of stone. That much was clear. Then what had possessed him to bring her lunch today? Simply repaying her for the dinner last night. After all, Sicilians had never let their enemies starve, whether they were Phoenicians, Normans, Vandals or American heiresses.

At that moment he looked up when Isobel entered the bar. She looked stunning. The total opposite from the last time he'd seen her only hours ago at lunch, her face sunburned, her hair damp, her face dripping perspiration. Tonight she looked as though she'd stepped right out of an American movie in a turquoise-colored dress that set off her fiery red hair. A more amazing transformation from disheveled and frustrated vineyard worker to glamorous woman he'd never seen. His gaze met hers and held for a long moment while he just stood and stared. The voices in the bar faded.

He'd planned to maintain whatever distance was necessary, however much he admired her determination, that's all he wanted to admire, but at that moment all his plans were forgotten as he appreciated her for what she was, a stunning apparition who stood out even in a crowd of attractive Italian women at the bar. It was her copper-colored hair, and it was her body wrapped in a blue-green dress that showed her curves to everyone in the bar. They turned to gawk at the newcomer. They'd have to be blind not to notice her.

He noticed too. In fact it was impossible for him to look away. In her face he saw hesitation, a hint of unease. After all, she was the stranger here. He had to force himself to stay where he was instead of rushing over to her and claiming her as his guest, or whatever she was. Certainly she wasn't his date, since he didn't date and didn't intend to.

"Ready to go?" he said, and set his empty glass on the bar before leading her outside to his car.

"The hotel owner is very nice," Isabel said as Dario opened the car door for her. "He was telling me about the big wine competition coming up. Sounds exciting and quite important."

"That's right." She wouldn't have any wine to enter this year. She'd be a spectator. She'd see Montessori recapture the gold this year, if the judges knew what they were doing. And next year? Would she be his competitor then?

"I suppose you'll enter."

"Of course. It's important to take away a medal, the gold if possible."

"I'd like to enter. Maybe next year…" She looked away with a dreamy look in her eyes. "Oh, and he told me I need to have a Blessing of the Grapes ceremony."

"That's true." Once her grapes were blessed there was no turning back. She'd be hooked, she'd have respect, a place in the community and she'd never leave no matter what happened. Maybe it was time to recognize the facts and get on the train before it left the station without him.

As he drove he was struck by the sweet smell of jasmine. Just when it was best to keep his distance from her, he wanted to get closer. He wanted to inhale her skin and find out where the scent came from. Was it her bare shoulders? Her neck, her throat? Or was it the flame-colored hair that brushed against her shoulders? He shouldn't have had that drink in the bar. He needed his brain and all his senses on the alert for this evening with his family.

For so long he hadn't looked at another woman. He had a permanent pain in his chest where his heart was and he had vowed never to be taken in again, a vow that was easy to keep. He hadn't been tempted. Not once.

He told himself there was no chance it could happen again. Magdalena had aimed a spear right through his heart. Every time he took a deep breath, every time he woke up in the night thinking of his colossal mistake, he felt the pain in his chest, and he didn't expect it ever to go away. Why should it? He deserved it. It was a constant reminder of how naive he'd been to fall for someone like her.

The American woman was a slight diversion, which he needed. Nothing major. There was no harm in admiring her for what she was or in helping her out when she needed it. His family was right. He'd been working too hard. He needed a break from time to time. Whether sparring with her or feeding her or admiring her determination, he found Isabel a change from his all-work-and-no-play lifestyle. That was all it was. No need to worry. He told himself to give it a rest.

"I'm glad you enjoyed speaking to the hotel owner. The hotel bar is a gathering spot for the neighborhood, which is another reason I strongly recommend you stay there." Why should she deprive herself of the comfort of the hotel and brave the rigors of living at the Azienda?

"You have a point," she said. "I've heard a lot of neighborhood news there."

He wondered exactly what she'd heard. Gossip traveled fast in a small town. He was glad he'd already told her his story, and she'd heard it from him. He normally hated talking about his past mistakes. But last night was different. Maybe it was the wine talking, maybe some long-repressed desire to get his story out from where it festered inside, and lay it on the table. It was a chapter in his life he wanted everyone to forget. Especially himself. But so far it stuck like a bone in his throat.

Isabel shifted in her seat and her skirt pulled to one side giving him an extra-good look at her beautiful long legs. He dragged his gaze away. Wasn't there temptation enough without her legs on display?

"I have nothing against the hotel," she said. "But as you know I'm in the middle of an important process and I should be up at my vineyard 24/7," she said. "By the way, I'm very grateful to you for the lunch and the ice."

"Lunch there is fine, but I wouldn't stay overnight if I were you," he said. "Apart from the lack of running water and electricity, there is always the threat of wild boars."

Her eyes widened. Then she turned to give him a skeptical look. "Are they worse than the poisonous vipers in the pond?" she asked pointedly.

"Much worse," he said without apologizing for his white lie about the snakes. "They come at night in packs and uproot your vines."

"Then I'll just have to move up there so I can scare them off," she said.

"Good idea," he said. Obviously she didn't believe him after the snake story. He believed she should be warned, if she was planning to stay up there after dark. Then he shot a skeptical look at her. "How exactly were you going to do that?"

"How do you do it?"

"I use a shotgun."

Isabel pressed her lips together to keep from telling him he'd lost his credibility with her after the snake story. She refused to let him scare her, though the thought of a bunch of wild boars rooting through her vineyard caused goosebumps to pop out on her arms. That and the thought of using a gun. She knew she could never shoot an animal, even if it was destroying her crops. She felt a shiver of fear go up her spine. Just how big were these boars? When should she expect them? How *would* she scare them away?

"It seems," she said as he pulled away from the hotel, "that considering the threat from these wild beasts to my vines, I should definitely be on the site, I mean to move there permanently as soon as possible. What if they come rooting while I'm not there?"

"Hire a night watchman?" he suggested.

"I'm not going to spend money hiring someone to do something I can do myself," she said. "I can tell you are not used to seeing women change tires or hook up their propane stoves. Or scare wild boar either."

"I'm not. I admit it. I look forward to you facing off the wild boars. I have no doubt you'll send them running for their lives."

"I appreciate your confidence in me," she said with a matching touch of sarcasm. He didn't think she could face a wild boar without flinching, and truthfully she didn't either. But she'd never admit it to him.

First she'd give it a try. After all, she'd spent a lifetime standing on her own two feet and learning not to depend on anyone. She didn't want him to think she needed him to help her. He'd already done enough what with the lunch he'd provided, and the ice and the workers he'd sent up.

Thanks to him, so far she'd met some friendly people and

enjoyed talking to them. There would surely be other friendly people as soon as she had some leisure time to circulate and socialize. She felt encouraged for the first time in days.

"Are all your friends in the wine business too?" she asked.

"More or less," he said. "Are all *your* friends in the design business?" he asked.

"No, not at all. And I'm not in the design business anymore. I'm in the wine business."

"I thought you were going to design a wine label for yourself?"

"I am. And I'll design a new one for you too, if you change your mind."

"Go ahead," he said.

"Really? You'd give me a chance? I don't know if you'll like what I come up with, but since you've been so helpful to me, showing me around the countryside and everything and bringing me a picnic lunch, I owe it to you."

She didn't know why he'd changed his mind, but she was glad he had. Her mind was spinning with ideas for a new, enticing label for him. Her fingers itched for a paper and pencil to get started.

After a long drive toward the outskirts of town, she said, "I've been thinking about moving to the Azienda right away. You're not just trying to scare me away with the story about the boars are you? Are they really a threat?"

"They really are. Not every night. Not every season. But it's only fair to warn you. They're fairly large with no enemies. They'll eat everything in sight, especially the roots of your vines."

"What about people?"

"They love people, especially fresh, newly arrived Americans."

She gasped and he gave her a rueful half smile. He was teasing her! That was a good sign. And totally unexpected.

"Which is why if the boars come and rip you to shreds while you're out defending your vines," he continued, "no one will know. The workers will find nobody there in the morning. Then the whole community will blame me for not telling you about them. It's not just the boars. There's that hole in your roof. What if the rain fell through the hole in the roof, you contracted pneumonia and had to be airlifted out to a medical facility? How would I feel then? I'd be responsible for not warning you."

"Thank you. I stand warned on both counts," she said. She hoped he wasn't back to being serious. She shot a glance in his direction but his expression gave nothing away.

"Why do I have the feeling that the minute I was airlifted out of here, you'd be there on the tarmac waving to me with the deed to the property for me to sign over to you?"

He smiled again. Twice in one night. Maybe he was human after all. Tonight when he'd met her in the bar, the smoldering look he'd given her had made her feel hot on the outside and shivery inside. She wasn't sure how to interpret it.

"You may not believe this," he said, "but I'm beginning to think you have what it takes to make it there after all, despite the boars, bats and the hole in the roof."

"Really?" Her eyes widened. A warm feeling suffused her bare shoulders and crept up her neck to her face.

"Don't get me wrong. I'd still like to see the land back in our family, but I'm willing to help you fight off the pests because maintaining the vines is important to me. I can see you appreciate the place almost as much as I do. But you have to get a telephone so you can call me if anything goes wrong."

"That's very generous," she said. "But I couldn't impose. You've already done enough for me."

"I just want you to know I've been honest about everything I've told you. I don't know everything. I *thought* there were poisonous snakes in the pond. I was wrong. It's not the first time. Go ahead and swim there."

"I will," she assured him. "Just as soon as I buy a swimsuit." It was a good feeling knowing she'd won his respect.

"What about you?" he asked. "Haven't you ever been wrong about anything?"

"Wrong? Oh, yes. I've been very very wrong. And I've made my share of mistakes." She pressed her lips together. She'd come all this way to get away from the past, why go into it now? But instead of keeping it to herself, she found she couldn't stop talking now that she'd started. "I trusted someone I shouldn't have. After all the things that happened to me in my childhood, all the disappointments, all the moving from family to family, despite all the dashed hopes that I'd find a home and a family, I still let myself believe someone loved me…." Her voice trembled and she stopped and took a deep breath wishing she hadn't blurted out the part about love.

"Nothing. It doesn't matter now." That was a lie. It still mattered. It shouldn't but it did. It mattered terribly. She'd fallen in love, given her heart away when she knew better. It was the last straw. "It taught me a lesson. More than one. I won't make the same mistake again. But it led to my coming here and starting a new life. The inheritance from my uncle came just when I needed it the most. It was a godsend. Do you believe in miracles?"

"No," he said shortly.

"I don't either, but why, just when things looked the bleakest, did my uncle leave me the vineyard? Doesn't that sound like a miracle? If it isn't, I don't know what else to call it."

He didn't say anything, and she wondered if she'd talked

too much about miracles and getting the Azienda. Of course he didn't believe she'd received it in the form of a miracle. He believed she'd received it because her uncle was a failure as a vintner. She just wanted him to know how much her inheritance and coming to Sicily meant to her.

He turned off the main road and onto a long lane lined with cypress trees and ending at a magnificent white stucco house. It was like a travel poster with Come to Sicily written on it and it took her breath away. She'd never seen anything so beautiful and so inviting. The fragrance of heavy-laden orange and lemon trees filled the air. Late-afternoon shadows fell across the lane.

"Your house?" Why did she even ask? Of course it was.

"My family's house. Very old and lived-in."

"So they don't know who I am?"

"I told my grandmother. She knows."

CHAPTER SIX

IT WAS more than a house. It was an estate with gardens, patios, outbuildings, cottages and one beautiful main house. Isabel had known it would be nice. She hadn't known it would be a dream house straight out of *Italian House Beautiful* magazine. It was surrounded by citrus trees and twisted ancient olive groves. It had everything an Italian villa should have, including the children who came running from all directions, playing with their large shaggy dog and shrieking as if they hadn't seen their uncle Dario for years.

They threw themselves at him, and he hoisted one little boy onto his shoulders. Two others grabbed his legs and tried to hang on. Isabel stared at the sight of the man she would have voted "most likely to avoid children and animals."

She couldn't be more surprised to find that he was so popular with this group. And he apparently liked them as much as they liked him. So he wasn't always all about business. He'd said he didn't live to work. Maybe it was true.

If anyone had asked her, she would have sworn he was a loner, in fact hadn't he as much as told her so? She assumed that because he kept to himself and avoided his family, he wouldn't want to play or laugh with anyone, including kids or dogs. How wrong she was. His deep laughter echoed in the summer air. It was a rich, warm sound that left her dazed, standing there alone with her mouth open. Dario, children and pets. She couldn't have been more surprised to see them all together, getting along famously.

A short pretty woman in a simple but well-made blue cotton dress and leather thonged sandals intercepted Dario and the children.

"Dario," she said, hugging her brother. "You came."

"Of course I came," he said. "Nonna's orders." He turned and waved to Isabel. "Isabel Morrison, this is my sister Lucia."

"Welcome to El Encanto," Lucia said.

By then the children's entreaties were getting louder. Dario excused himself and he and the kids walked across the lawn.

Lucia watched her brother go. "I'm so glad you could come to dinner. I can't believe Dario came too." She was still staring off in the distance as if she was afraid he was an apparition, and if she took her eyes away, he'd disappear.

"But I thought…"

"You thought we all ate together every night like a big happy Italian family? Some of us do, but Dario has been absent from family gatherings ever since…for a long time. We have you to thank for bringing him here tonight."

She sounded truly grateful, as if Isabel was responsible for Dario's presence when it had been his grandmother's orders that brought him.

"Thank you for inviting me. Your house is lovely."

"It's old and been in the family for generations. Come and have a tour. You'll have to excuse Dario for taking off, my children are so excited he's here. They haven't seen much of him lately. As I said, his visits are rather rare."

"I understand the crush is keeping everyone busy," Isabel said.

"We're all busy," his sister said, a frown creasing her brow. "But we still make time for family. At least the rest of us do."

Isabel didn't know what to say. Fortunately, Lucia filled in. "It's the children who miss him the most. He's always been their favorite uncle and they don't understand where he's been and why he doesn't come around to see them. Do you have children?" she asked.

"Uh, no. I'm not married." Why did Italians think every woman her age should be married?

"I see. Well, they've dragged my brother off to have a look at the new tennis court and they'll try to persuade him to play a game or two with them. When it comes to the children, he's their hero and there's no one else they'd rather see. He's *Babbo Natale,* our Father Christmas and Paolo Maldini, our most famous soccer player, rolled into one. Though I warned them he is busy and might need to leave early tonight they just don't understand. They only remember when he'd come by just to see them. He hasn't been the same…for quite a while."

Isabel was certainly getting a new perspective on Lucia's brother. He didn't seem like the type of man children would adore or drag off to play tennis with. And yet, according to his sister, who ought to know, he was. He'd told Isabel his family was too intrusive and demanding. Maybe it was more than that. Or less. Maybe it had more to do with his former fiancée.

Lucia led Isabel through the heavy oak front door into the house with its brightly tiled floors, comfortable couches and antique pieces and into the kitchen. There, standing on a stool so she could reach the stove, and stirring a pot of sauce was the old woman she'd met at the market. She looked up and smiled broadly.

"Ciao. Benvenuto alla nostra casa."

"Grazie per ivitarlo," Isabel said.

The grandmother let out a torrent of Italian words directed to her daughter while Isabel stood and admired the kitchen with its rough red-tiled floor and the brass pots and pans hanging from the ceiling.

"She says she hopes you like Sicilian food."

"I'm sure I will. Does she do all the cooking here?"

"Oh, no. We have a cook who's been with the family for years. But she oversees it all, the sausage stuffing, the rolling out of the pasta, making the cheese that comes from the goats my grandfather raises. And when we have a special guest like you, she has to be right here in the kitchen to make sure everything turns out right. Actually my family and I live nearby but we love coming for dinner at least once a week. So did Dario once. Before he became a workaholic."

"What a nice custom," Isabel murmured, ignoring the part about Dario and his work habits. She knew if she had a grandmother and a big family she would be here once a week at least. But then she hadn't been through a drought and a fungus attack and the sale of her land as well as a personal problem like a broken engagement. Maybe he just needed time out from his family. Since she had no family, it wasn't easy to imagine. It certainly sounded like he'd been avoiding them for some time.

One day she would have a tradition like this. She wouldn't have grandchildren, but she could have friends. She could have a garden, maybe even a goat or two. She already had a pond and a vineyard. She had more than most people she knew.

"Come and see the garden. Nonna is very proud of her Romano beans, eggplants, figs, zucchini and Italian chiles. But the roses are all Nonno's. Before he had his stroke he poured all his energy into them. I'm sorry you won't meet him tonight. He's having dinner in his room. He overdid it today, and he needs rest."

Stepping outside through a lovely shaded patio with hanging pots of bright geraniums, Lucia took Isabel to the garden and pointed out the different types of roses her grandfather had planted. "These are Balkan double yellow, over there pink Queen Isabella. Your namesake," she said with a smile. "They almost take the place of grapes in his life, but not quite."

"He must have plenty of grapes as well. Your Montessori Cabernet and Merlot wines are famous. Dario told me he is especially proud of—what was it? A Benolvio we had at a restaurant."

Lucia gave her a surprised look. "Where was that?"

"I don't know the name of it, it was an old palace at one time, I believe."

Lucia nodded. "The Palazzo, yes it's a wonderful restaurant, a special place, I'm glad he took you there. And surprised. He always tells us he has no time to spare."

"This was actually more of a business lunch," Isabel said, hoping she hadn't spoken out of line. "I have a lot to learn from him about growing grapes and making wine." She was sure it was a business lunch as far as Dario was concerned. He'd never have taken her to lunch if he hadn't been trying to get her to buy another property instead of the Azienda.

Lucia paused and gave Isabel a curious glance, then she picked some lovely pink Queen Isabella blooms. She tore off some faded petals as the heady fragrance filled the air. It was time for Isabel to level with his sister.

"You see, I'm in the wine business too. I inherited the Azienda Spendora from my uncle."

"Oh," Lucia said. "So you're the one."

"Yes, I'm the one." What had she heard about her? That she was unreasonable? That she didn't deserve the property?

Lucia gave Isabel a long look, then she smiled and said, *"Benvenuto in Sicilia."*

"Grazie," Isabel said, relieved at her reaction, so different from her brother's the day she'd arrived. She seemed as friendly as she'd be to any newcomer to the area.

"How did you meet Dario?" Lucia asked

"Not only did he give me directions on my first day," Isabel said, "but he was kind enough to take me to the property himself." At the time the word *kind* hadn't crossed her mind.

"I see," Lucia said thoughtfully. "How nice."

Just then a woman wearing an apron came out and rang a little bell. She spoke a few words to Lucia and Lucia said, "It's time for dinner."

The bell seemed to work well. Children came running from every direction along with several adults, including Dario, who had joined his grandmother and was deep in a serious conversation with her. They made quite a striking pair, the small, black-clothed old woman and her handsome strapping grandson. From the way she was talking to him, it seemed more of a lecture on her part than a conversation. Isabel would have given much to be able to understand it. Anyone who could lecture Dario must be a figure to be reckoned with.

Before he took a seat, Dario greeted his brothers and sisters, their husbands and wives, who all seemed delighted and surprised to see him. They hugged him, kissed him on both cheeks and were peppering him with questions which he interrupted to introduce them to Isabel as the new owner of the Azienda, in case someone hadn't gotten the word. Then he took a seat at the outdoor table under the arbor across from her.

There was no mistaking the looks she got. They'd heard about her and now they wanted to see for themselves. There were somewhere between fifteen and twenty at the table and she had a hard time remembering who was Maria, who was Paolo, which girl was Francesca and which was Angela.

They all talked at once in rapid Italian while the maid served bowls of a light creamy soup. Just one taste and Isabel was convinced she was in heaven.

"Do you like it?" Dario asked from across the table.

"It's wonderful. What is it?"

"*Maccu*, a Sicilian specialty. Made from our own home-grown beans. Grandmother wanted to make a special dinner for you. She's convinced no restaurant or hotel can come up with the true Sicilian cuisine."

"Tell her thank you. I'm very grateful to be included at your family dinner. It's not the same as eating at the hotel."

"Although the food at the Cairoli isn't bad," Dario said with a pointed glance at Isabel. "They make a very decent veal Madeira. They even have room service."

The knowing look he gave her told her he hadn't forgotten the intimate dinner they'd shared. Or not kissing her. She hoped his family didn't think she'd invited him to that intimate dinner, when his arrival had been a complete surprise to her. In fact, he had a disconcerting way of seeming to see right through her clothes, as he did right now, when his intense gaze seemed to strip away her sundress.

She shivered in the warm air and concentrated on the soup in front of her. Did anyone notice this casual flirtation on his part? Or was she mistaken? That was not flirting, Sicilian-style, it was just…something else. Or was it what they expected from him? More likely they had once been used to him bringing women to dinner for the family to meet and scrutinize, at least in the days before his engagement. What did they think of his ex-fiancée?

"Nonna told us how you helped her last evening at the market. I'm afraid shopping is rather limited around here," Angela said.

"Not at all. I bought some wonderful meat and cheese. And the fruits and vegetables we had for lunch today were beautiful," she said to Dario.

His sisters exchanged looks. Maybe she shouldn't have said anything about their lunch. Maybe they'd get the wrong idea, think that she and their brother were spending quite a lot of time together. *It's just business*, she wanted to say. But was it?

"I mean, I'm not yet set up for housekeeping, so Dario brought me some food, or I don't think I could have made it through the day," she said, feeling her cheeks grow hot as she struggled to make less of the lunch than it was.

"How do you like the Azienda?" his sister Caterina asked politely.

"Very much. It needs work, but it has lots of potential."

Again, looks were exchanged around the table. What did they expect? That she was a spoiled heiress who was so discouraged she might turn around and go back to America? Maybe that's what Dario had told them.

Dario said nothing. He couldn't be surprised since he'd heard her say the same thing before. Instead he took a large helping of the caponata, a classic mixture of eggplant, capers and olives.

His grandmother looked around the table at her family who were unusually quiet. *"Que es male? No le gradite?"* she asked.

"It's delicious, Nonna," Dario assured her. He got up and poured red wine from a carafe for everyone. "Isabel is interested in history. Of course Sicily is the ideal place to study the past since we've been colonized for six thousand years by everyone who came sailing in the Mediterranean. I showed her the ruins at Casale since they're close by."

"I thought you were too busy for sightseeing," his brother Cosmo said from the end of the table. "Now we see the reason you suddenly find a time in your schedule for someone, but not your beloved family." He shot an admiring glance in Isabel's direction.

Dario, back in his seat, poured some fruity olive oil into a small dish. "Never too busy to give a newcomer a tour of the countryside," he said.

"And how do you like our wine?" his brother Cosmo asked. "Or should I say *your* wine?"

She reminded herself this was the brother who'd been at the Azienda the other day.

"It's held up well," she said. "I'm no wine expert. But I know what I like. Your family's wines are superb. You must be very proud of them."

When she looked up Dario was looking at her. His blue eyes were deep and unfathomable like the Mediterranean. If he was trying to send her a message, she had no idea what it might be. Maybe it was that she'd said the right thing or maybe the wrong thing. She only knew that his intense gaze sent a tingling up and down her arms and a strange feeling in her head as if her brain was on vacation. She wasn't thinking clearly. It was hard to concentrate. She was glad the adults all spoke English, because it was all she could do to concentrate on saying the right thing in her own language.

His sister Lucia who was at the end of the table with her two children, said, "We've been doing this so long, sometimes we take our wine for granted. That's why the *concorso* is so important."

"The competition. I've heard about it. You're sure to win."

Dario changed the subject. "Isabel is an artist," he said. "And she's volunteered to design a new label for Montessori wines."

"An artist?" Lucia said. "Then she's come to the right place. There are some beautiful scenes to paint here. You must show her Nonno's paintings. The ones you hung on your wall. She'll appreciate them."

"I'd love to see them." Isabel looked around the table at the smiling faces. She'd never felt so welcome before. As a child she'd been used to being shunned by the other kids in her foster families, who were afraid she would siphon off scarce supplies of food and affection. What a contrast to the warm-hearted Sicilians. This new experience made her feel warm all over.

The next course was a crisp grilled snapper served with small new potatoes and fresh-picked asparagus garnished with toasted prosciutto. The children got restless as the meal stretched on and dusk fell over the patio and the gardens. The crush was on, this was a critical time in the vineyards, but this wine family was sitting around enjoying dinner as if they didn't have a care in the world, just as Dario had said they would. But he didn't look as if he was wasting time and wanted to leave. Maybe tonight he'd let himself slip back into the Sicilian way—work hard but enjoy life too. And if by some chance you're not enjoying life, act as though you are.

Maybe some day she'd be able to adopt this lifestyle and have a leisurely dinner every night with friends. Now that she had a functioning stove and ice in the icebox, she was getting closer. If only she didn't have to worry about making wine and making a living. Not to mention the Blessing of the Grapes ceremony she was supposed to host.

When the children got up and pulled Dario up from his seat, he said, "The kids want to play tennis on the new court to try out the night lights." He turned to Isabel. "Do you play?"

"Not very well," she said.

"Then we'll give you a lesson," he said. "Come with us."

Leaving the rest of the family behind, they trooped down a limestone path through the garden, past a grove of olive trees, past a turquoise swimming pool with underground lights, to the illuminated tennis court. It was a beautiful location, surrounded by towering cypress trees and paved with red clay.

One of the nephews handed Isabel a racket and told her to take off her shoes.

"He wants to be your partner," Dario explained. "They all do."

"You'd better tell them I'm not very good."

Dario sent the kids to practice volleying back and forth across the net. "They don't care. My nephew thinks you're pretty. I'm sure you've heard that before."

She hoped he couldn't see her blush in the gathering darkness. "More often I'm told I'm stubborn."

"That doesn't surprise me. Is that why you've never married?"

"No," she said, bouncing the ball against the clay surface. "I believe we've already had this discussion. Maybe I prefer to be single, just like you. For your information, I was engaged once, but it fell through. Why are you so interested in my personal life?"

"Most Sicilian women your age are married. That's all I'm saying."

"In America women marry late and sometimes not at all. Women can be whatever they want. They can live alone or with a partner. Marriage isn't essential for happiness." *If I really believe that, then why did I make such a terrible mistake by rushing into an engagement?* "Maybe you have a more traditional idea of marriage and family."

"Not me. I know things don't always work out. As you see, my sisters are all happily married with children, and no doubt my brother Cosmo will also settle down one day. That leaves me."

"You mean you've given up on marriage?" she asked.

"Marriage is not in the cards for me. Tonight you saw family life at its best. No arguments, no disputes. Everyone was relaxed and having a good time. We're good hosts and you're a good guest. We tried to show how wonderful family life in Sicily can be. And it can. Make no mistake about that.

"Now they're sitting around the table talking about the crush, the fermentation, the bottling and the advertising campaign. There's rehashing of past harvests, going back one hundred years or more. It can get very tedious. It's worse when the conversation turns personal. 'Don't give up, Dario,' they'll say. 'There's the Benvolio girl who's looking for a husband. What about Maria Del Popolo? Or Angelina Spano or...' All I mean is we live in a small world here where everyone's involved in everyone else's life whether they want them to be or not."

"As someone who has no family, it doesn't sound so bad," she said. In fact, she'd be willing to accept a little interference in her personal life in exchange for a group of relatives and a small world.

She was relieved when they stopped talking about marriage and family and started a game of tennis. But first there was a dispute about who was playing on whose side, and Dario repeated that all the kids wanted to play with her.

"I thought you were their favorite uncle."

"I am, but you're the new girl in town. How can I compete with that?" he asked, a half smile on his face.

She didn't know what to say to that. Just the hint of his smile had her feeling as though she'd just had the rug pulled out from under her, if they had rugs on tennis courts. It was so unexpected. Is that what the kids did to him? Made him relax and feel young again, even though he said he didn't want to spend time with his family?

Though she hadn't played for a long time, she managed to get in a few good shots that went past Dario. The children clapped and he looked mildly surprised each time she did it, but the next time he hit back with such force she didn't have a chance to return it. If she'd doubted his competitive nature before tonight, she had no more doubts. Perhaps he had the same impression of her. She didn't like to lose, on the court or in the vineyard.

When they pronounced the game a draw, Isabel and Dario walked back to the house behind the children who ran on ahead. "You're not bad. Where did you learn to play?" he asked.

"In high school. I took a tennis class. First time I'd ever been on a court. It was fun. It came sort of naturally. The teacher loaned me a racket and taught me a lot. She said I had a good stroke."

"I'll second that."

"She encouraged me to try out for the school team, but then I had to move. My new school didn't have a tennis team. And I didn't have any equipment."

"Did you move often?"

"All the time. I had to go wherever a family was available to take me in."

"That must have been difficult."

"Not really," she said. "It was interesting meeting the different families, attending different schools, making new friends." That last part was a lie. It was so difficult making new friends every school year, she had finally stopped trying and spent her free time studying and her lunch hours in the library because she knew she'd have to win a scholarship if she wanted to go to college. "I suppose you've lived here all your life."

"I spent some summers away playing sports, even a summer at tennis camp, though you wouldn't know it from my game tonight. Then I went to university in Milan and studied finance. But I knew I could never live there. This is my home."

"Your sister said they haven't seen much of you lately."

"I've been busy," he said shortly. "It doesn't mean I don't care about them. I thought they understood that."

"Family ties are important in America too, it's just that I didn't have any. Which makes it easier for me to move across the ocean and make my home here." It didn't mean she wasn't envious of him. Who wouldn't be? Still, she owned a house and a vineyard, and he wouldn't hear her complain.

When they returned to the house, lights were glowing from every room. Framed in the windows were various family members. Isabel felt a wave of homesickness wash over her as if she had a home to be homesick for.

She missed being a part of a home and a family, no matter how happy she was to have a house at last. She blinked back a sudden tear, grateful for the darkness falling. She couldn't let Dario see even a hint of sadness or envy. She'd been called a crybaby too many times until she learned to control her emotions. No matter how bad the insults or the abuse she'd suffered, she'd learned never to give anyone the satisfaction of seeing her cry.

"I promised to say goodnight to the kids," he said. "Then I must leave. Come with me if you like."

She couldn't help being touched at this gesture to include her. She was also touched and surprised by his relationship with his nieces and nephews. They obviously liked him tremendously, and he seemed to have fun with them. It was a whole different side to him, one that caught her off guard. Maybe she'd judged him too hastily.

At first she'd thought he was a hard-hearted, greedy land-owner who'd do anything to get rid of her and get his hands on her property, but then he'd stayed for dinner in her room, confided in her and brought her lunch when he didn't need to. He'd ordered ice for her instead of letting her food spoil. And now here he was playing with dogs and kids. What next?

The children were gathered in the large bedroom on the second floor for a sleep-over, cousins and brothers and sisters, some perched on their beds, others on a thick carpet on the floor where they'd made room for Dario to sit. The scene was straight out of one of Isabel's fantasies. She wondered if they knew how lucky they were to be a part of this family. Probably not. Most children took for granted being loved and well cared for. She hadn't.

They cheered loudly when Dario came in. He grinned at them. She couldn't believe this was the same man who had glared at her only a short time ago. He took his place while she sat on the edge of a bed as he told them their favorite story which he translated into English for her as he went along.

"The history of our island goes back to thirteen thousand BC," he said. "That's when this land was inhabited by a group of powerful giants who were descended from the god Zeus.

"The giants thought they were smarter and more powerful than the gods. The gods were so angry they banished the giants and sent them to the underworld below the volcanoes to make weapons for them, like thunderbolts. Are the giants still there?" he asked.

"Yes," the children chorused.

"How do you know?" Dario asked.

"We hear them when the volcanoes erupt."

"They're struggling, trying to get back to earth, but the mountains are too heavy."

Just then Caterina came to the door and told the children it was bedtime.

"But he didn't tell the part about how Sicily got its name," her son protested.

"Or how it got to be the bread basket of Europe."

"Another time," Dario said. Maybe he'd finally had enough family time.

The kids moaned and groaned, but before they turned out the lights, one of the children, a little girl named Ana-Maria kissed Isabel good-night. One hundred painful memories knifed through her, of missed hugs and kisses, of bedtimes without anyone to say goodnight to her.

Isabel stood at the door for one last look inside the bedroom. She'd never seen such an idyllic scene. Lamps turned low, children sleepy-eyed and tired from a summer day of play in the sun. She caught her breath and longed for her camera or her sketchpad. Maybe she didn't need it. It was a scene she wouldn't soon forget.

She wondered if Dario ever longed for kids of his own. She'd given up on that dream. It sounded as though he had too.

She went to find his grandmother to say good-bye and thank her. She was in the kitchen sitting in a rocking chair and talking with a woman who must be the cook. Isabel told her in her best halting Italian how delicious the dinner was and how beautiful her house was and how she admired her gardens. The old lady hugged Isabel and said something that might have been "Come again," or "I hope my grandson treated you well," or something entirely different. But the smile on her small round face was unmistakably warm and friendly.

Isabel looked around at the huge restaurant-size oven, the open shelves stacked with old plates and the well-worn chopping block in the middle of the room and she longed for a kitchen exactly like that, laden with memories, handed down from generation to generation.

She wanted to have bread rising on the stone counter, and smell the yeasty fragrance. She would do it. She would make the kitchen at the Azienda such a place. Smaller of course, and without any family mementos, but it would be all hers.

When his sisters came into the kitchen carrying coffee cups, she thanked them for their hospitality. Impressed by their friendliness, Isabel took a seat on a stool at the counter.

"I've had a wonderful time tonight," she said. "I hope next time I can invite you to the Azienda."

"You mean you're going to stay there?"

"Yes, of course."

"Alone?"

Isabel nodded. She hoped she wouldn't get another lecture on the dangers of wild animals. "I've been alone since I was eighteen. So it's nothing new. Except that now I have a house of my own. I know it's in bad shape, but I plan to fix it up. I have a lot of work to do," she said. "First comes the harvest of course."

"Welcome to the winegrowers of Sicily," they chorused, lifting their glasses in a spontaneous toast.

Isabel felt a rush of gratitude. They barely knew her and yet they'd welcomed her with so much warmth she swallowed over a lump in her throat.

"I didn't know how you'd feel about my inheriting the land that used to be yours. I didn't know what to expect. I'm an outsider. My uncle didn't do much for the place. You have every reason to resent my barging in like this…"

"Is that what Dario told you?" Lucia said, her hands on her hips, a frown on her face.

"Well…"

"We sold the land to your uncle, and it's yours now," Francesca said. "You have every right to it. Dario may have a different opinion…"

"Because of what happened," Maria said. "He lost his heart to that…horrible woman…! Then she…"

"Don't even speak of her," Francesca interrupted, her mouth curved down in disgust. "She is dead to us. Dario lost his heart yes, and the land as well. What of it? It's over. No one blames him. He's Sicilian, after all. We are emotional people. We fall in love and give our all and if we make a mistake, so be it! He'll get over it. Maybe not today or tomorrow, but some day."

Lucia turned to her sisters and announced, "Dario took Isabel to the Palazzo for lunch. It's where he used to take Magdalena, remember? That's a good sign he may be getting over her. I thought he'd never go there again. And he brought you here tonight." She looked around the room at her sisters and sisters-in-law. They nodded vigorously.

"I think that was your grandmother's idea," Isabel said.

"No matter. I believe you must be good for him," Lucia said with a smile. "He needed a distraction. What about you? You're not engaged to someone back in America, are you?"

Isabel was a little startled at their personal question. But flattered too, that they felt they could ask her.

"I was once, but…it didn't work out." It never works out when the person you're engaged to is already married. "Just when I was at a low point and needed a change in my life, I got the letter from the lawyer about my inheritance."

Lucia clapped her hands. "A miracle," she exclaimed.

Isabel beamed. "Exactly."

"Dario can help you with everything," Francesca said. "He knows about making the Amarado wine."

"He can give you Italian lessons," Lucia added.

"He's already helped me more than I expected," she said. "Considering how he feels about the Azienda."

"It's not only losing the Azienda he suffers from," Maria said. "It's what Magdalena did to him."

"He is the oldest son and he feels guilty for what happened," Lucia added. "Too much. He's supposed to look out for us all. But he takes his responsibility too seriously. Ever since, he hasn't been himself. We've moved on. He hasn't. Maybe you can help him forget…" She looked at Isabel with a hopeful smile.

Isabel didn't have the heart to tell her *Maybe nothing*. She was in no position to help Dario forget anything. She was a foreigner alone in the world, still suffering from the fresh wounds of betrayal herself. She was the last person to help someone else recover.

She was going to say goodnight and thank them for a memorable evening when they mentioned the Blessing of the Grapes.

"Your first harvest at the Azienda. You must have one."

"We'll talk to Father Guiseppi. He'll sprinkle the holy water over the grapes."

"The holy water?" Isabel had thought maybe it was just a party, but it sounded like a serious religious ceremony.

"You should choose a date. And it must be soon so the blessing can take effect, and you'll have a good harvest."

Out on the terrace, Dario was talking to his brothers and brothers-in-law. They all stopped talking when she appeared and stood to either shake her hand or kiss her on the cheek and wish her well.

"Don't forget to show Isabel Nonno's paintings. They're very realistic," his sister said. "Even if she's never seen the volcano, she'll recognize it right away."

Dario nodded, but Isabel didn't want to presume on his improved attitude toward her any more. He'd already spent quite a lot of time with her today. He'd come here tonight as a favor to his grandmother and had seemed to have a good time with his family, but maybe he was just putting up a good act to make the evening a pleasant one for everyone, which he had, at least for her. Just seeing Dario in this setting made her evening one she wouldn't forget. He was standing at the door, staring up at the starry sky as if he'd never seen it before.

"What did you think of them?" Dario asked when she got into the car. "They can be overwhelming."

"They were nice. Very nice indeed. I didn't know what to expect, but they're wonderful. They couldn't be more warm and friendly."

"They liked you too," Dario said. "They're impressed with how you try to speak Italian, how friendly you are and of course they like the color of your hair. 'Like the sunset,' they say."

She felt a flush color her cheeks. "That's nice to hear." She took a deep breath. She knew she shouldn't spoil the mood, but she had to know. "I wonder if they like me so much because I'm not Magdalena."

Dario pulled up in front of his house. The car jerked to a stop and he turned to look at her. She met his gaze reluctantly, sorry she'd said anything.

"It's true they didn't like her," he said brusquely.

"They believe she hurt you." Nervous, she turned and stared straight ahead.

"That's not true," he said after a long silence. "I was disappointed, not hurt. No one can hurt you unless you let them. Unless you let down your guard. In my case it was my fault, not hers. I was wrong. I should have known Magdalena wasn't right for me. Everyone else knew. Not me, I was blind. I didn't want an ordinary girl. And she was far from ordinary." There was irony in his tone. Isabel could only guess at what he meant, knowing that she was a beauty queen and was treated like royalty. "I was greedy. Ordinary women weren't good enough for me. I wanted someone different. I wanted her but she wanted more than I could give her. I don't expect you to understand," Dario said. "You're from a different world."

"But I do understand. I was even stupider than you. I fell in love with my boss. He was married with no intention of getting a divorce. I wasn't the first woman he'd romanced while still married. Everyone else knew all about him, but not me."

"Why didn't they tell you?" Dario demanded.

"No one knew we were seeing each other. They had a rule at the company—no inter-office dating. So we had to sneak around, never going out in public, always meeting on the sly. It was exciting at first and I was flattered by his attention. I was a nobody, just one of many, a graphic artist in a big company. He was a big shot, in charge of the whole opera-tion, rich and powerful. I thought...I don't know what I thought," she said, stumbling over her words.

"You thought he loved you," Dario said. This was some-thing he understood. "Didn't you?"

She nodded. "That's what he said. And I believed him. Stupid, stupid me. What was wrong with me?"

"Nothing. Nothing's wrong with you." He reached for her hand and held it between his own. Her fingers were cold and stiff. He would like to meet this rich powerful guy who'd lied to her. He'd like to knock him across the field and show him he couldn't treat people that way, no matter who he was. "You were too trusting, that's all," he assured her. "Sometimes it takes a shock to make a change in your life. You learn to deal with disappointment by moving on. You gain something knowing it can never happen again. You won't ever let down your defenses again."

"You're right. I won't," she said. "Have you really recovered?"

"I'm fine," he said flatly. He didn't want her to think he was still suffering. Or that he'd ever suffered at all. He hoped his sisters hadn't said anything like that. "I know one thing. I will never fall in love again. Not after what I've been through."

She withdrew her hand. He got out of the car, came around and opened the door for her. When she got out he slammed the car door shut.

"Enough of the past," he said as if he was slamming the door on it too. "It's over. Come in. I want you to see the paintings." Dario wanted to change the scene, change the subject and forget the past for a while. Both hers and his. He hadn't meant to talk about Magdalena and he knew it was hard for her to talk about her boss. He could tell by the way her voice shook and how cold her fingers felt.

He seized on the opportunity to show her Nonno's paintings to have something else to talk about. She'd made an effort to get along with his family and he appreciated that. Magdalena had sneered at his family for being bourgeois country people.

He wanted to see Isabel in a different atmosphere, in his house with no family around. No woman had been there since Magdalena, who'd thought it was "rustic," and totally unlivable. If ever there was a woman who was the exact opposite of the pampered city girl he'd been engaged to, it was the down-to-earth American.

His family liked Isabel, but was it true they liked her because they'd like anyone who wasn't Magdalena? They'd been polite and impressed by Magdalena's title of Miss Sicily, but that was all. They thought she was cold and self-centered and definitely not good enough for him. Funny, because Magdalena thought she was too good for him.

Tonight he wanted to see what Isabel thought of his house. She had the most expressive face he'd ever seen. If she thought it was rustic he'd know. Right now she was taking it all in from the desk piled high with bills and paperwork to the over-stuffed chairs and the sturdy coffee table with industry magazines stacked there.

Isabel stood on the hand-woven carpet with the geometric design and looked around. The room was spacious and snug at the same time, with the scent of leather and wood in the air.

Dario switched on the lights and opened the windows. A cool evening breeze wafted into the room. Isabel drew in a quick breath. There was music playing from somewhere. A woman was singing a plaintive song. Even though she couldn't understand the words, she understood the feeling, so familiar, so touching.

"Opera?" she asked.

"Puccini. Do you like it?"

"It's beautiful. But it sounds sad."

"It is sad. Her lover has left her."

No wonder Isabel could identify with the song. "I'm beginning to see it's true that Italians are very emotional people," she said.

"We're also proud and loud and impulsive and passionate." He had an intense look in his eyes that told her he was all of those things, perhaps the reason he'd fallen so hard for Miss Sicily. She, on the other hand, was trying to be sensible. Passion and runaway emotions were what had got her in trouble. She too had learned a hard lesson.

She bit her lower lip and looked away. Too many impressions were all crowding in on her. There was way too much to take in—the kids and Dario, Dario and his family, Dario and his past. She'd seen a different side of him tonight, a softer, caring side he hid from the world. He'd finally opened up about his affair. Just enough for her to guess he'd been hurt, no matter how much he denied it.

A rush of mixed emotions left her feeling shaky and confused. Who was he? What did he want besides making wine, winning wine contests and moving ahead with his life? He'd been a different person tonight. He hadn't mentioned wine or her land at all. Maybe she was different too.

"What a wonderful house you have," she said, tearing her gaze away from him to look up at the rough-hewn timbers on the ceiling and the wide-planked wood floors.

"It's better in daylight when you can see the fields and the hills from the front windows."

"It's nice at night too," she said, admiring the huge picture window and the stone fireplace, picturing a fire blazing there in the winter. Did he and Magdalena spend any time here or were they always on the go?

"I haven't done much to it since I moved in two years ago. Just moved a few walls to make it seem bigger."

The room, with the colorful rugs on the floor and leather ottomans, reflected his personality and his country. She'd never seen him relax, but she could imagine him reclining in one of those big chairs gazing at the view or at a fire on the hearth.

She was uneasy being so close to him, his masculine aura so much a part of him he was oblivious to it, but she wasn't. She was only too aware of the way he towered over her five-foot-ten-inch height, the strength of his grip on her arm, the warmth of his hand when he held hers, his strong features and his equally strong will. She walked across the room to look at some photographs in frames on a high table. They were pictures of a vineyard and people all holding wineglasses with a priest in the center wearing his clerical robe.

"Could that be a Blessing of the Grapes?" she asked.

"From a few years ago, yes."

"I suppose I'll go ahead and have one at the Azienda. I want to do what's expected."

"What's expected is a party for everyone in the village. The priest blesses the grapes, everyone sits down to a large feast and they toast you and the harvest."

She sighed. "It sounds overwhelming. Along with picking grapes and remodeling the house, I'm not sure I could manage a party."

"If you don't, you risk a bad harvest," he said. "It's not that complicated. I'll help you set it up."

"You'd do that for me?" She stared at him for a long moment then turned to look at the paintings. After all, it *was* the paintings she'd come to see. Instead she was getting a different look at a side of Dario that she'd never seen before, and she wasn't sure she wanted to. It was an eye-opening experience to see where he lived and find out so much more about him. What she learned made him more intriguing than ever. It would be better for her equilibrium if it made him look less attractive, less interesting. But it was just her luck he was probably the most attractive and unavailable man in Sicily.

"Your grandfather's very good," she said, walking up for a closer look at the towering volcano and its purple shadow in the picture. "Does he still paint?"

"No. It's too bad. Maybe he'll get back to it when he recovers. He hasn't been the same since he had a stroke."

"He must be an amazing man, making wine, growing roses and painting pictures. I hope I'll get a chance to meet him."

"He'd like to meet you, I'm sure. But I warn you, he doesn't mince words. He speaks his mind. He can be charming when he wants to be. He's always had a weakness for pretty women. It runs in the family." He paused. "Not the charm but the weakness."

Her cheeks burned. Not just at the unexpected compliment, but at the significance of the remark.

He stepped forward, a look in his eyes that made her knees weak. It was the same look she'd seen last night when she'd thought he was going to kiss her.

"I don't know about the weakness," she murmured, "but I'd say you've inherited your share of the charm." Would she have said that yesterday, before he brought her lunch, before she met his family, before she heard what he had to say about his ex-fiancée?

He smiled. A slow smile that spread to his intense blue eyes. Her heart thudded. If he touched her her skin would sizzle. That's how hot she was.

The sound of the Puccini aria rose and filled the air. She didn't know what the words meant, but she understood pure passion when she heard it and when she felt it. Isabel's heart raced. The longing in the song matched the longing in her heart. A longing to hold and be held. To kiss and be kissed. That's all.

He was going to kiss her this time. She knew it.

CHAPTER SEVEN

WHEN HIS LIPS came down to claim hers she was ready. If truth be told, she'd been wanting him to kiss her since the first time she'd seen him when she'd thought he was a humble field worker. His kiss was so hot she thought she might burn up. She felt his arms tighten around her. His strong, muscled thighs pressed against her. She moaned softly, wanting more. Her heart banged in her chest and she kissed him back.

He groaned deep in his throat and pressed her back a few steps to the wall where she could lean against the smooth stones, all without breaking the kiss, even intensifying it. Then the rhythm changed just as the music did. He invaded her mouth with his tongue, taking and giving her so much pleasure she wanted to sink to the floor and take him with her.

He splayed his hands on her bare shoulders. Then he pulled away and looked at her as if he was seeing her for the first time. The cool skeptical look he once wore was gone. Instead there was white-hot desire, burning with a blue flame. He didn't say a word, but the questions in his eyes were clear. Do you want this as much as I do?

She wanted it as much as he did. Needed it. Needed to feel whole again, desirable again, if only for the moment. If only for tonight. She didn't hesitate. She put her arms around his neck and kissed him again. The answer to his unspoken question was hot feverish kisses she couldn't stop. He reached for the strap on her dress and teased it off her shoulder. She gasped and realized he could peel the straps off along with her dress and make love to her tonight on the floor or in his bedroom and no one would find it strange. In fact, maybe the whole family assumed that's what they were doing. They might think it would be good for him. Good for her.

Yes, she thought. Yes. She was alive in every pore of her body. More than that, she felt warm and feminine and desirable for the first time in a long time. It was a heady and delirious feeling. It shocked her, but at the same time she never wanted it to stop.

Dario was like no other man she'd ever known. He was Sicilian. He was passionate and proud and impulsive. He tasted like wine and smelled earthy and masculine and he felt hard and solid. He felt like the kind of man you could lean on. If she were someone else. Or if he were someone else. But he wasn't, and neither was she. She wouldn't and she shouldn't lean on anyone—not on him, of all people. He wasn't in the market for a relationship and neither was she. Just a flirtation. There was nothing wrong with that, was there?

Her breath was coming in short bursts. Her face was flaming. With one finger he stroked the rounded curve of her breast through the cotton fabric of her dress. She could only imagine how it would feel if she could shed the dress and let it fall to the floor at her feet. His hands would caress her heated skin, teasing…soothing, exciting. She didn't want him to stop. She wanted this feeling to go on forever. She wanted to stay there in his arms, to take the next step wherever it led.

Her whole body throbbed with anticipation. But somewhere in the back of her mind she knew she had to stop. With shaking fingers she adjusted her strap, then put her hands on his shoulders and held him at arm's length. She was gasping for breath, trying to fill her lungs with air. Trying to regain her self-consciousness.

"I…I think I'd better go home," she said, only half aware she didn't really have a home to go to. Not yet. "I'm afraid I lost my head for a moment." If only she had a better excuse.

"Nothing wrong with that," he said. "I thought it was about time for this to happen." His voice was so deep and low she had to strain to catch the words. "You're a very attractive woman and I've resisted up until now, but it hasn't been easy. Blame it on the night, the wine or the dress you're wearing. Or blame it on me."

She shook her head. "It was my fault. I know better. Or I should know better. Now I should go."

"Sit down for a minute," he said.

Obediently she sank into one of the leather chairs at the fireplace. Every muscle ached and her skin was covered with goosebumps. He stood with an elbow against the stone mantel, looking down at her. She had no idea what was on his mind. Her brain was racing, trying to anticipate. She was trying not to show how much his kisses affected her. They made her melt inside. They made her wonder if they meant anything to him. She knotted her fingers together and waited. There was a long silence before he finally spoke.

"I have to apologize," he said at last.

"Please don't. I wanted you to kiss me."

A hint of a smile tugged at one corner of his mouth making him look more gorgeous than ever. He leaned forward and focused his intense blue gaze on her. "Not for that. For trying to pressure you to sell the land when it was obvious you have more of a right to it than I do. The important thing is that you want the best for it. I do too. You'll pick grapes and you'll make prize-winning wine. And if you need help, you can call on me. When I saw you on the road for the first time and I realized who you were, I confess I wanted nothing more than for you to leave. I'd been through a bad time since Magdalena left. I'd been betrayed and, what was worse, the whole world knew it. I was angry, not just with Magdalena, but with everyone in the world. With friends who told me it wouldn't last, with my family who warned me she was wrong for me. And most of all with myself for being blind." He shook his head as if he couldn't believe what had happened.

Isabel wanted to get up and throw her arms around him and tell him he wasn't blind, he was just human. He was Sicilian, proud, passionate and emotional.

"For a long time I hid out from my friends and family," he said. "I didn't want to see anyone. I didn't want to be the object of their pity or their scorn. You came along. You knew nothing about what happened. You forced me to take action. At first I did everything to discourage you. I thought you were another opportunist, a gold digger, out to take advantage of our family."

"So you told me there were snakes."

"Snakes, mice, bats, boar…whatever it took. They weren't all lies. But I underestimated you." He gave her a wry smile.

She nodded. "It happens to me a lot. I'm used to it. No one thought I'd amount to anything being tossed about as a child, no parents, no money, nothing. But I got an education, a job and now a vineyard. And I made it on my own. With the help of my uncle of course." Maybe it sounded like bragging; she hoped he'd accept it for what it was—the truth.

He went to the sideboard, opened a bottle of an amber liquid and poured two fingers worth into two glasses. He handed her one and touched his glass to hers.

"To your uncle," he said, "for leaving the grapes to you."

"To you," she said. "For the food, the ice and the workers." *And the kisses. Oh, those earth-shaking kisses.* "What would I have done without you?"

She sipped the rich warm flavor of aged Scotch and felt it burn a trail right through her body.

"You'd be fine. You don't need me. You have what it takes to make things work. You've got more determination than anyone I know."

His words warmed her heart along with the Scotch. But she did need him. Badly. "I have a feeling I'll need all the determination I can get. So far I haven't spent a night at the Azienda or fought off the wild boar—which I'm sure are real. So maybe you should save your praise until I do."

He shrugged. "All right."

She forced herself to stand and look at the door. She had to leave even though she wanted to stay. It was wrong even to consider staying and she knew it. She'd been badly burned and she knew enough to stay away from the fire. Falling for Dario would be the worst thing she could do. Just a taste of having someone to kiss, someone to talk to, someone to share her thoughts with, someone to lean on when things went wrong and someone to share the work with made her want more.

She who prided herself on her confidence, her ability to stand on her own, was feeling vulnerable tonight. Tomorrow she'd be back to her self-reliant personality. She had to be.

The breeze from the open window had cooled her overheated face, the music had died down and she had to leave. He didn't try to stop her. He picked up his car keys and they left the house. She turned to look back, wondering if she'd come back to his house. Wondering if he'd ever share it with anyone. Wondering what this evening meant to him. Maybe it was just a transition from Magdalena to the world of available women again. Maybe she was just the first on his road to recovery. Maybe she was just a bridge, nothing more, nothing less.

For her it was just a few kisses, and some exchanged confidences, that's all it could possibly be. She might be tempted, but she'd never trust, never love and never let her guard down again. Not for anyone. Especially not for a passionate Sicilian who was out of her reach. He'd made it clear he felt the same.

In his car on the way to the hotel, with the scent of roses in the air, she decided to set matters straight now that she was in command of her brain again.

"I have to tell you, after what I've been through, I don't indulge in casual flirtations," she said.

"I never thought you did," he said soberly. "My kissing you was spontaneous and rash. I told you it's a Sicilian fault. It had something to do with the way you look tonight. And the way you play tennis. The way you watch me repair a flat tire. The way you eat melon and drink white wine. All those things made me want to kiss you. And the way your chin sticks up in the air when you're angry. It was an impulse, that's all. At least on my part. I can't answer for you." He slanted a look at her that said he was aware that the kisses they'd shared were not one-sided. "I haven't any other excuses. It won't happen again unless you want it to."

What could she say to that that wouldn't sound desperate? Of course she wanted it to. Of course she'd deny it. She was shaky and tense and on the edge of her seat all the way home in his car. She hadn't meant to get carried away, but what did he expect? He was the sexiest man she'd ever known. He radiated heat and masculine strength in ways she'd never experienced. She'd have to be made of stone not to respond.

What a day it had been. Filled with unexpected discoveries and obstacles, a dinner with sparkling conversation, followed by mutual baring of the souls and emotional upheaval, physical and emotional intimacy and now this. Her mind was spinning and she longed for a hot bath and a soft bed. How would she cope with a hard bed and no hot water? How would she cope with wild boar and an overwhelming attraction to the one man she should avoid getting involved with?

CHAPTER EIGHT

DARIO DROVE as fast as he could on the winding road back to the Montessori estate. He tried to put Isabel Morrison out of his mind, but he couldn't erase the taste of her lips on his, the feeling of her body pressed against his and the touch of her skin, as smooth as silk.

Even though he'd told her and himself it wouldn't happen again, even though he knew it shouldn't, he wanted it to. He wanted to see her eyes full of desire, feel her body tremble in his arms, inhale the scent of her hair, and hear her sigh deep in her throat. Just a taste of her only made him want more. She excited him, challenged him and tantalized him. She made him feel alive again for the first time in a year. Maybe she didn't want a casual flirtation, but he was starting to think that was exactly what he wanted.

She was probably going to stay; he'd come to terms with that fact. The two of them were both young and unattached. They were in the same business. He'd offered to help her. There was no way they could avoid each other even if they wanted to, which he didn't. As long as she didn't expect anything from him except support in the vineyards. That he could give. Anything else—promises or commitments—was out of the question. He'd learned his lesson, as he'd told

Isabel, and learned it the hard way. But an affair didn't have to mean forever. It could mean for now. It could be good for both of them. She needed to forget about the guy who'd treated her badly just as much as he needed to forget about his past, move on.

He dropped back in at the family house before going home. Just to see what they had to say about Isabel. As if he didn't know. He'd seen the approving smiles on their faces before he left tonight. The family had a tendency to jump to conclusions and have him married off before he knew it. Before things got out of hand, it was time he made it clear to them that while Isabel was attractive and admirable, there was no room in his life for a permanent woman, not now, not ever. As for a girlfriend... As for an affair... He was beginning to think that was a different matter.

The family was in the living room, everyone but his nonna, who'd gone to bed. As soon as he walked in the door, just as he anticipated, they started.

"This Isabel is a beautiful woman, Dario. She likes you. Why I don't know," his brother teased. "So what are you waiting for?"

"We liked her. The kids liked her too," Lucia added pointedly.

He knew what she was referring to. The kids hadn't liked Magdalena. And she hadn't liked them. *They're so loud. Always in the way*, she'd said. *Let's not go to the house. It's all about them. So many of them. All the time.... We can never be alone.*

"As far as we're concerned, Dario, Magdalena is gone and forgotten," Maria burst in. "No one blames you for what happened. Let's forget the past and welcome Isabel by helping her with the Blessing. I'll talk to Father about it and we'll all be there to celebrate. It's the least we can do for a newcomer."

"I'm sure she'll be grateful for your help," he said. The

Blessing was fine, as long as they didn't think Isabel was another potential fiancée. There would never be another one of those in his life and he was glad of it. But Isabel was good for him. He'd readily admit that. She'd made him feel as if he'd had a jolt of electric power shot into him. The kisses they'd exchanged had left an imprint on his mouth and his mind. She was obviously what he needed, even though he hadn't known it. An affair, a romance. He had to persuade Isabel that they could have one, and he had to make it clear to his family that that was all it could ever be. Not tonight though. He didn't want to start a discussion about his future, so he said good-night and left before they could continue to sing Isabel's praises.

Back at his house, the living room seemed large and empty. He looked around, picturing Isabel in front of the mantel, seeing her face when she heard the music and imagining her standing there, her dress on the floor, in nothing but briefs and a bra and then...

He was trying to see the place through her eyes wondering how it looked to her. Too severe, too masculine, too subdued?

He saw her as she was, standing breathless, her eyes half-closed, one strap off her shoulder, looking so soft, so desirable... He didn't know what would have happened if she hadn't stopped him. Would she still be here?

Dario fell into a dreamless sleep for the first time in months. He was no longer haunted by disturbing negative memories of Magdalena, instead there were visions of Isabel passing through his subconscious, walking through the vineyards, her hips swaying, her glorious hair shining like copper in the sunlight.

Isabel didn't see Dario or any member of his family the next day. She didn't expect to, but she wondered, would he act as if nothing had happened? Would she? What did the evening mean? Was it the beginning of an affair or the end of their dispute? Or was it both?

The question kept her awake half the night. That and the memory of how his kisses felt on her lips and in her mind. She replayed his words over and over—*an impulse...spontaneous and rash...* Which would mean that it probably wouldn't happen again. The idea left her feeling low. She knew it was wrong, but she wanted more. How much more, she didn't know. How would she handle another relationship? This time she would not get her heart broken. She was too smart. She'd been through too much.

It was good to have a day without seeing him. Even if it seemed like a day without sunshine. But she didn't want to rely on him and she certainly didn't want to think about him all the time. He was an attractive man and a different man from the one she'd met the first day. He'd changed his mind about her and about the Azienda. She'd changed her mind about him.

She hadn't come to Sicily to have an affair with anyone, least of all the richest and sexiest but most unavailable man in the area. He'd already been burned by a beauty queen. He should be off limits. Until last night she'd thought he was. She'd told him that she didn't indulge in casual flirtations. Now she couldn't help but wonder if the attraction between them could lead anywhere, whether a casual flirtation could be better for her than a serious relationship...

She spent the day at the vineyard supervising and picking grapes with the workers, but she kept listening for his car, watching the driveway and trying not to feel let down when he didn't come by with food, drinks and advice. And hot, sizzling kisses that rivaled the sky-high Sicilian summer temperatures.

In the evening she was restless. She decided she couldn't stay at the hotel anymore no matter how much she wanted a hot bath and a soft bed. So she had an early dinner of spicy pasta arrabiata and a crisp salad by herself in the hotel dining room. She was the only customer since most Italians didn't eat dinner until ten o'clock.

She kept her eye on the door but no one else came to eat at that early hour. No tall, handsome Sicilian came looking for her, to join her and share food with her. She ate alone, determined to enjoy it. But what a contrast with her meals with Dario. The hotel dinner at the small table where their knees bumped and she tried to act normally while dressed in a robe, the family dinner where he sat across from her looking like an Italian movie star while she sipped Sicilian soup.

Then she checked out of the hotel before it got dark and she lost her nerve. Without a backward look at the charming Hotel Cairoli she drove resolutely back to the Azienda. It was dusk and the sun turned the fields on both sides of the road to gold.

Tonight the Montessori family would again be gathered around a big table laughing and talking and sharing their experiences with each other. Would Dario be there too? Had he changed his solitary ways and rejoined his family? Or was he eating alone as she had?

Was it a foolish dream to think she'd ever be at home here the way his family was? Maybe after about one hundred years. Should she consider selling the place to his family? Never. In fact, not one of them had even mentioned the possibility. As night fell she couldn't see the broken tiles on the roof or the hole above the bedroom. This was her home, flaws and all.

After scrubbing her kitchen with some of her precious bottled water by the light of a gas lantern one of the workers had brought her, she climbed the stairs to her bedroom, tired, sore and just a little lonely. She, who'd spent her whole life alone, was feeling lonelier than ever.

She lay in the narrow bed that she'd covered with layers of foam and blankets, then the new sheets and more blankets that she'd bought at the dry goods store in town. Too tired and too full of anxious thoughts to sleep, she stared up at the stars through the hole in the roof. It wasn't quite as romantic as she'd hoped it would be. In fact, it was a little scary being alone in the dark, hearing strange rustling sounds from somewhere outside, though nothing, not even wild boars, would let her admit her fears to anyone, especially Dario. Where was he tonight? Probably not at his grandmother's house. Out with friends at the hotel bar? Or back at his house tackling the mountain of paperwork she'd seen on his desk and listening to opera? She tried to forget the sound of the music, the touch of his hands on her shoulders, and the warmth of his lips on hers. Did he know she'd checked out and was staying here at last? Was he thinking of her?

She could blame her lack of sleepiness on the bed or the strange house, but it was more likely she just couldn't turn off her brain.

As for her feelings… They were what was keeping her awake tonight. His kisses had awakened something deep inside her that she had thought was long buried. She knew better than to get carried away by another attractive man, but she wasn't made of granite. She couldn't turn off her attraction for him so easily. He was Sicilian, she was in Sicily and she loved the land, the climate, the food and the people. It would be so easy to fall hard for a Sicilian and jump into an affair for the full Sicilian experience. If she was a fool that is. She finally fell asleep while thoughts of boars invaded her dreams.

Isabel told herself every day that her job and her life would get easier. She told herself not to expect Dario to keep turning up when she needed him. But after a few days passed without him dropping by or running into her in town she began to wonder when she'd see him again—especially at night when she lay in her lumpy bed thinking of what a huge project she was facing, harvesting grapes and making wine by herself.

Her thoughts bouncing around in her brain kept her sleepless night after night. But one night it was more than her thoughts that had her wide awake. There were noises outside, getting louder, a strange cacophony of low growling and grunting. Finally she couldn't pretend it was just the wind in the trees any longer. She jumped out of her narrow bed and went to the window that overlooked the vineyard.

She shone her powerful flashlight onto the field below, and there they were! She jerked up and bumped her head on the window frame at the sight of the big brown animals with short legs and large heads running pell-mell through the vines. She pulled back from the window and rubbed her head.

Every instinct told her to close the window, go back to bed and let them destroy her vines. How could she alone defend her grapes from the wild marauders? And there went her future wine sales just like that. But she had no gun, no crew, no way to scare them off. She could go down there and yell at them, but what if they turned on her with their tusks and speared her leaving her alone and bleeding in the dirt?

She'd sounded brave when discussing the boars with Dario, but that was all talk to impress him. She wasn't brave at all now with the actual animals in sight. The beasts with their dark fur and huge snouts were after the roots on her vines and would destroy her whole crop unless she did something about it.

"Go," she shouted at them. "Get out. Get lost. Those are my grapes." Her voice shook. Her cries were swallowed up in the night air.

Above the noise of the boars, she heard a car. A few minutes later she was blinded by a flashlight shining up at her from beneath her window. She shaded her eyes and saw Dario looking up at her. He had a shotgun over his shoulder. She felt a surge of the same relief a settler in the old West would have felt at the arrival of the cavalry. She braced herself against the window frame.

"What are you doing here?" she asked, as if she didn't know.

"I heard the boars were around tonight. I thought I'd better come by and scare them off," he said.

"I'll be right down."

Barefoot, she hurried down the narrow staircase to meet him at the edge of the vineyard.

"Did you know I was here?"

"I knew you weren't at the hotel. They told me you'd checked out a few days ago. Why didn't you tell me?"

"I…uh…I was busy." That was better than telling him how desperately glad she was to see him. Why hadn't he come looking for her? Because *he* was busy. And she'd had no right to expect him.

She was so glad to see him she had to fight off the urge to throw her arms around him and let him hold her and tell her everything was going to be okay. He was so big, so solid and so confident. He looked as though he could handle any emergency.

"Let's go," he said and led the way to the vineyard. It was like a safari, walking single file behind him, stalking the wild boar while he shot pellets at them. Her heart pounded. Her bare feet hit the dirt that sifted between her toes. Her mouth was dry. It was scary and exciting. Dario would let loose a rain of pellets, the boar would scatter, run and then more would take their place.

Dario explained that though the pellets bounced off their

fur, they stung and the more they shot the faster the boar would run out of the vineyard. After a long hour, the beasts had finally run off and the vineyard was eerily quiet again. It was over. Isabel's knees wobbled and her hands shook even though she'd done nothing but watch and stalk.

"I hope this doesn't happen every night," she said weakly. "Thank you. You saved me. Maybe they haven't done too much damage." It was too dark to see how many vines had been uprooted.

"I think we caught them in time."

He said *we* but she hadn't done anything but yell at them ineffectually from her window.

She glanced at him. Now that her eyes were used to the dark, she could see his dark hair, a flash of white teeth, his wide mouth and his crooked nose clearly.

"I'll have to get a gun like yours," she said. "And learn to shoot it."

"Another day," he said with a glance at her nightgown. She'd almost forgotten she was wearing a long, sheer cotton gown. His eyes seemed to smolder as he surveyed her body. She could feel the heat right through the cloth and she was afraid she might catch on fire from the sparks between them.

The smell of crushed ripe grapes filled the air and a soft breeze caressed her overheated body. She ached to feel his arms around her. She wanted to share the triumph of defeating the wild animals even though he'd done all the work. She had no idea how long they'd been out there. The first rays of sun were creeping over the hills.

Impulsively she reached for his arms and pulled him towards her and kissed him. Kisses tinged with relief and gratitude and something else she didn't want to name.

His arms tightened around her and her body was pressed

against his. She told herself to pull away though it felt so good to feel his heart beat in time with hers. She told herself to let him go. Thanks were enough. Falling for Dario was the stupidest thing she could do. He could never return her love even if she offered it to him. He'd made that very clear.

But the voice of reason was drowned out by the pounding in her head. There was even a buzzing in her ears. She reminded herself she wasn't falling in love. This was not love. It was lust. It was longing. Anything but love. She would never love again. She knew the painful consequences. She knew how humiliating it was to fall for someone who wasn't available. What was happening now was that she was just having fun for the first time in a year. She didn't want a serious relationship any more than he did. An affair. An affair to remember when winter came and there were no more grapes to pick and no more excuse to see Dario. That's all this attraction could become.

His kisses and the look in his eyes made her feel like the bravest and the most beautiful woman in the world. Made her want to rip off her nightgown and run through the vines and jump into the pond with him. Feel the cool water around their bodies.

Finally it was he who broke the kiss and held her at arm's length. He was breathing hard and there was a shuttered look in his eyes she couldn't decipher. "I'd better let you get some sleep."

"Sleep?" She looked around. Sleep was the last thing she wanted. She was full of energy. "It's morning. Would you like some coffee?"

She noted his look of surprise and said, "Follow me."

The air was still cool and a fine mist hovered over the vines as they walked to the house, straight through to the kitchen where she lit the stove with the sparker. He took in the new propane cylinder, then picked up and inspected an ancient but well-scrubbed saucepan on the stove.

"You've been busy," he said. There was admiration in his voice and she treasured it. She opened the small packets of coffee she'd taken from her hotel room into the two tin cups she'd found in the pantry. When the water boiled she put both cups on a tray and carried them out to the picnic table prouder than if she'd been serving tea in china cups at the Palace Hotel in San Francisco. The smell of the coffee mingled with the smell of the dew on the overgrown grass poking up around ancient stepping stones. Dario was watching her so intently she almost dropped the tray.

"It's just coffee," she said modestly. "Next time I'll make bread. Now that I have a working oven."

He sipped his coffee. "Not bad," he said with a smile that melted her heart. She smiled in return, proud of herself for achieving a way to heat water. The coffee was hot and strong and on top of the adrenaline pumping through her veins, she was ready for a full day's work.

Then there was his smile. Another stimulant. With just his smile she needed no coffee. Not to mention his company. He kept her entertained with stories of how he learnt to make wine and the times he had had to chase off the wild boars. But when he finally left she sat on an old wooden chair on the patio, suddenly as limp as a rag doll, exhausted and light-headed and more confused than ever. They kissed each other again— beautiful kisses that made her feel amazing—but what did it mean? Had they begun a relationship, an affair? She didn't ask when she'd see him again and he didn't say. She wished she didn't care so much.

Dario drove slowly down the road toward town. He'd done what he had to do, what anyone would do for a neighbor, he'd chased off the boars. But Isabel wasn't just any neighbor; she was like a magnet and it was hard to resist a magnetic force. He'd resisted for a few days, but he still hadn't been able to push her out of his mind. He'd finally given in and come here and now he knew he couldn't stay away.

It wasn't just the way she looked in a turquoise dress or in a nightgown or the fact that she changed a tire by herself. It wasn't just the way she followed him through the vines as he shot pellets at the boars instead of watching from the window like any other woman would do. It wasn't only her pride in making coffee in an old kitchen with nothing but a few packets. It was her determination in the face of obstacles and the fact that he could not let her face these obstacles alone. It was all of these things put together. And something more. Something he refused to analyze.

That night he was back at the Azienda, telling himself and her that the boars were likely to come again. It was true, they were determined and hungry beasts. He wasn't the only one who thought so, all the growers were on alert. It was only prudent to be prepared. This time he was so prepared that he brought steaks, potatoes and a bottle of Chianti.

"I owe you a dinner since you shared yours with me at the hotel," he explained. The smile she gave him made him regret the nights he'd stayed away. He could have been here with her, feeling the warm radiance of that smile.

They cooked outside at the fire pit. There was plenty of old firewood stacked in the barn. He was being a good neighbor. It was a tradition. In Sicily you don't let your neighbor go hungry.

They ate on the weathered oak picnic table behind the house. In the middle of the table was a pitcher with the pink fragrant Queen Isabella roses his sister had given her. How aptly named, he thought. Isabel was like a rose, so pink and lovely he wanted to inhale her fragrance.

They talked about the harvest and the grapes, then he asked about life in California. She told him San Francisco was full of fit, bright young people who enjoyed the outdoors, ate salads and fresh Dungeness crab out of the ocean.

"California sounds like paradise," he said. "What made you leave? I know, a miracle happened and you inherited a vineyard. But what really made you leave? Was it because of your boss? The one who lied to you?"

Isabel turned her wineglass around in her hand before she spoke.

"That's right. I was ready for a big change after I got fired for breaking the company rule, no inter-office dating."

"You were fired? I thought no one knew."

"I thought so, too."

"What happened to him?"

"Nothing at all. He's still there."

"But he broke the rule, too."

"I know what you're thinking. It's not fair. But if I have learned anything it is that life is not fair. Was it fair my parents died? Was it fair the foster families didn't want me? But my luck changed when my uncle left me this place. Was it fair he left it to me and didn't sell it to you? I don't know, but I'm not going to complain, not about anything." She folded her arms across her waist as if she was still protecting herself from any more hurt.

He leaned across the table to brush a tendril of red-gold hair from her cheek.

"I have no excuse for what happened between me and him. After years of telling myself not to believe, not to trust anyone but myself, I knew I was on my own and always would be. Then I forgot it all and made a huge mistake. I thought I'd never get over it."

"But you did," he insisted. "You're back on your feet. You've got gumption and drive and you're the hardest worker I've ever seen." *And you're beautiful, bright and courageous.*

She blushed at the compliment, her cheeks turning pink. She was the most amazing combination of modesty and confidence. The thought of anyone hurting her filled him with rage.

"Thanks to my uncle and this vineyard, which gave me something to do. A reason to try. A new place, a new job. Everything I needed but didn't know it. That's the miracle I was telling you about. When I got the letter from the lawyer I thought it was a message from heaven. It was my ticket to a new life, a life I could live without help from anyone." She stopped and looked at him. "Except you. I don't know what I would do without you to help me."

He wanted to take her in his arms and tell her he'd always help her, that she'd never be alone again. But he couldn't say that. He couldn't make any such promises, not to her, not to anyone.

"Anyone would have done it. I just happened to be around." As if he would be there with dinner if it had been someone else. She'd broken through his reserve the way no one else could have. "Next thing, you should learn Italian," he said.

"I know. Every day I realize how difficult life is when you don't speak the language. I can't even read the newspaper."

In a moment she was back with the local newspaper. He opened it up and together they translated an article. He couldn't help laughing at her pronunciation of certain words in Italian. He was afraid he'd hurt her feelings, but she laughed with him. What a woman. What a remarkable woman. She seemed to be without an ego. Yes, he knew she was wounded and vulnerable, but tonight she seemed happy and relaxed and so sexy with her tousled hair and her sunburned face. Keep it neighborly, he told himself. Unless you can be sure she's ready for more.

"I think you're ready for advanced Italian tomorrow," he said.

"I need advanced Italian, but first I need running water. I got motor oil and gasoline and diesel for the pump, but…" She trailed off.

"Let's have a look at it." He got up and stretched. It was a good excuse to stop staring at Isabel, watching her lips as she pronounced the words in Italian, knowing how her mouth felt pressed against his, knowing how she felt in his arms and how she smelled like wildflowers. Much safer for his state of mind to face off against an ancient pump and try to make it work than to imagine holding her in his arms all night.

Isabel went to get the motor oil she'd bought and her flashlight and met him at the old pumphouse behind the wine cellar. She felt guilty prevailing on him to help her after he'd brought the dinner. But sitting across the table from him, sharing food, could become a habit she shouldn't get used to. Hadn't she confessed how stupid she'd been to fall for the wrong man?

Dario kneeled next to the antique cast-iron engine. "I'm not sure this old relic will run again. Shine the light down here. Now we need the wrenches. They should be in the toolbox in the wine cellar."

When she returned with the toolbox he struggled with the rusty drain plug, but it appeared to be frozen from years of disuse. She sighed with despair. She had the oil, the wrench and the expert and still no luck.

"This could be trouble. If we can't change the oil, we can't run the pump."

"Never mind, I'll bathe in mineral water after all."

He looked up and grinned at her. A real grin. Instead of criticizing her for being extravagant he just smiled. Her heart drummed against her ribs. She'd rather have him smile like that than have all the running water in the world.

"Just joking," she said. "What can I do to help?"

"Sit down." He motioned for her to take a position on the dirt floor opposite him. "I'll push on the wrench from this side, you pull from the other. Okay, pull!"

Together Isabel pulled and Dario pushed, their hands squeezed together on the wrench. Dario's straining calf pressed against her thigh. But the plug didn't budge. They rested. They tried again. Isabel's hair was hanging in damp tendrils; her face was dripping with sweat. She had to do her part. They had to make it work. She had to have running water if she was going to live here.

This time she put all her energy into it, pulling as hard as she could. Suddenly the plug broke free. Dario's straining body lunged forward and he fell against Isabel, who was now spreadeagled on her back. His chest pressed against hers, his legs on top of hers. For a long moment he didn't move and she didn't speak. She couldn't catch her breath and she didn't know what she would say if she could.

"Are you hurt?" he asked, his voice low and as intimate as his position on top of her.

"No."

Instead of taking advantage of the situation, the way she wished he would, he got up, then extended his hand to help her up. "Very good job, *signorina*," he said, "you'd make an excellent plumber."

She nodded, too tired to speak. And just a little disappointed he hadn't kissed her again. But it wasn't over yet. Next they drained the old oil into an olive-oil can and put the fresh fuel Isabel had bought into the engine's tank.

"Now comes the moment of truth, when we find out if we can wake up this creature from its sleep." He wound the starter cord around the pulley. If Dario couldn't make it work, no one could. But after several more tries, Dario was panting and nothing was happening.

"Can I try?" she asked anxiously.

He wrapped the cord around the pulley and handed her the wooden handle on the end. Then he stood behind her and wrapped his warm hand around hers. "Pull gently but firmly. Like this." She sighed. Life didn't get much better than that. Working together, learning together, making something happen.

His hand tightened on hers and they pulled together. The flywheel slowly turned as the cord unwound. The engine gave a little cough.

"Did you hear that?" she asked, her heart pounding.

"I think she's got some life in her yet," he said and poured some gasoline into the carburetor. "Stand back," he ordered. Then with one powerful pull on the cord the engine roared to life. He gave Isabel a thumbs-up and she'd never been so proud of herself in her life.

They primed the pump and she could hear the beautiful sound of water gurgling in the pipes. On the roof, which they reached by a long wooden ladder, she could see the water was now filling the tank.

"I think you may be able to have a shower tonight," he said.

She definitely needed a shower after being caked with dirt and sweat. Just as soon as he left. But he didn't leave. He said he was afraid the boars would be back.

"It's the season, you know. You can't take a chance on losing your vines."

Before she could protest that there was nowhere for him to sleep, he said there was a room for the servants behind a door in the kitchen she'd never opened. Inside was a bed and Dario said he'd be fine staying there.

By that time Isabel didn't have the energy to argue, and

why should she tell the man who had provided her with food and water to leave when she didn't want him to? Fortunately she'd bought extra sheets, a pillow and blankets, almost as if she knew something like this would happen. And she did feel safer having him there. Not only safer but happier.

He promised to hook up a tankless flash hot water for her the next day, but she thought a cold shower would feel wonderful. And it did. From the top of the stairs, she called to him.

"It's your turn," she said, wrapped in a towel.

He stood at the foot of the stairs and looked up at her. His face, only half-lit by the gas lantern, was all sharp lines and deep hollows. She sucked in a deep breath. There was a long silence. Their eyes locked and held. She told herself to move, to go to her room, but her feet wouldn't obey. Her skin tingled from the cold shower but his smoldering gaze made her feel as if she was burning up.

Was he thinking about how few steps stood between the two of them? Was he thinking of how few seconds it would take for her to walk down and throw herself into his arms? Or for him to climb up the steps and wrap his arms around her? She knew what it would feel like. Like heaven. But heaven was not what was in store for her. She knew it. She'd tried to find it before but it was always outside her grasp.

She had a house and a new life—more than she'd expected. She wouldn't wish for more. Her job was to stand on her own two feet. Nothing wrong with accepting help, but never should she count on it. Nothing wrong with a few kisses. As long as that's all it was. She was proud of her self-control.

Finally she relaxed her shoulders, then she sighed and turned and went to her bedroom with the hole in the roof and stared at the stars while he showered. She tried to think about the Milky Way and the constellations, but instead she thought about how he must look with the water coursing over his body, the drops catching in the hair on his chest. No wonder she couldn't sleep.

Later, Dario lay in the bed in the old servants' quarters on top of a blanket he kept in his car. The window was wide open and he didn't need any cover. He wanted to feel the breeze on his bare body and think about Isabel upstairs. Was she having as much trouble sleeping as he was? Was she thinking what he was thinking? Why hold back when they were attracted to each other? Why stop when they were in the prime of life with normal passions kept buried too long?

They were both mature adults with realistic expectations, that is to say, none at all. They were sleeping under the same roof, working toward the same goal—producing fine wine— his family liked her and she continued to amaze and surprise him. After she'd been betrayed by the married man, she'd suffered, but then she'd rebounded remarkably. It was good to know she wasn't interested in a long-term relationship any more than he was.

Too restless to stay in bed, he pulled on his jeans and went to the kitchen where he found a bottle of cold sparkling water. When he heard footsteps on the stairs he set the bottle down and leaned back against the counter. Had she heard him come into the kitchen?

It was the second time he'd seen Isabel in her sheer night-gown, so transparent he could see her breasts, her stomach, and her long legs in the bright moonlight that shone through the window. He grabbed the back of a chair to keep his balance. How was a man supposed to resist this kind of temptation? She stood in the doorway blinking in surprise. Every fiber of his being called out to her, but his voice was silent— until he finally said, "You can't sleep either?"

"Just thirsty," she said in a half whisper, half sigh.

He held out his bottle. She took it.

"What about you? That bed must be hard as cement."

"It's not the bed. It's you. I was thinking about you." He paused. "You're good for me. You've made me break out of the shell I was in."

"What did Magdalena do to you?" she asked softly.

He sucked in a deep breath. She'd told him about her ex, and he'd already told her about Magdalena, but it was time he came completely clean about what had happened. He pulled out a chair and straddled it. She sat across the table from him, her chin propped in her hand. Her hair was in a tangle around her face. She smelled like fine-milled soap and she looked as though she'd just stepped out of his dream.

"I told you she and I went off together when she was crowned Miss Sicily and I neglected the vineyards. That was bad enough. I justified it by thinking we would eventually get married and settle down here at Encanto on the family estate. Then I'd have no more distractions. Magdalena's reign as Miss Sicily would be over and she'd be as happy as I was to stay home.

"But that was not the future Magdalena wanted. To her, Sicily was the last outpost of civilization. She wanted out of the island altogether, but she didn't tell me or anyone that or she'd lose her title. So she finished out the year and then ran off with my cousin Georgio from Milan. He's a very well-to-do businessman who came to our engagement party and made a pass at her without my knowing. She saw he was her ticket out of here and she took it. I was blindsided. Completely fooled. I had no idea." He buried his head in his hands. "Sometimes it still feels like it happened yesterday," he said.

"I'm sorry," she said. "I think I know how you must have felt."

He raised his head. He stared off into space. "Like the

volcano had erupted and buried me in hot ashes. Like all the color had been drained from the world. Everything was in black and white. Mostly black. Some gray. I walked around, I went to work in the fields, I managed the harvest, but at the end of each day I had no idea how I'd gotten through it. My mind was blank. It was the only way I knew to survive. I felt nothing, not the heat or the cold or the rain. I was numb. You could have done open-heart surgery on me without an anesthetic." He gave a hollow laugh. "Maybe that's what happened. They opened me up, looked at my heart and saw it was broken, cracked in half. They shook their heads and said, 'No chance of repair.'"

"Oh, Dario," she said, reaching for his hand. There was sympathy and understanding in her eyes, but no pity. If anyone understood it would be Isabel and he was grateful.

He stared off into space. "I never told anyone what I was going through, but the family guessed, which is why they hold such a grudge against Magdalena." He rubbed his chin. "I did survive, as you see. Color came back to the fields and the vines. The sky was blue again. The sun rose and set a few hundred times and I was an older, wiser man, I hope. So don't feel sorry for me."

She shook her head.

They sat there for a few minutes, then she touched his cheek, as soft as a feather, and she stood and reached for his hand. He didn't have to ask what it meant. The answer was in her face, in the way she clasped his hand. She wanted him as much as he wanted her. They both knew what would happen next as they walked up the narrow stairway to the bedroom and the narrow bed meant for one. Meant for one, but just right for two people who'd been waiting for this moment since the first time they'd met on that dusty road.

As the stars faded and the sky grew light, they lay together, wedged at the hip, legs entwined, arms flung around each other. Lying there, happier than she ever remembered, with Dario's face half buried in the pillow, Isabel relived the night spent making glorious, passionate love with Dario under the stars, the most amazing night she'd ever had. She said a prayer to the heavens and whatever gods were listening—*Please, please don't let me fall in love with him.*

But it was too late.

CHAPTER NINE

THE NEXT DAY was Saturday. Isabel didn't expect her workers but she heard a truck in her driveway in the morning. She looked at Dario, sleepy-eyed, his hair falling across his forehead. He raised his head, propped himself on his elbow and kissed her. If she'd thought last night was a dream, she knew now it was real. He was real and she was ecstatic. But a little worried too. What did it mean? What happened next?

"The bed's a little small," she said.

He grinned at her and her heart beat to a crazy rhythm. "Seemed just right to me," he said. "Although you're welcome to try mine the next time."

So there would be a next time. She returned his smile, then she remembered.

"Someone's here," she whispered as if afraid someone would hear and someone would know. A hangover from the old days, she knew, when an affair must be kept secret from the world. Some day she'd get over it, but not now. Not yet.

She jumped out of bed, surprised she'd slept at all, let alone so late. She felt his eyes on her as she stood naked in the small room and her sensitive skin burned. She dressed quickly in a pair of shorts and an old T-shirt.

"I'll go see who it is."

When she went to the front door she saw his sister Lucia standing on the steps with a basket in her hands. "I heard you'd checked out of the hotel and I was afraid you didn't have any food."

Isabel felt a moment of panic. Would she find out her brother was here? What would she think? More importantly what would *he* think if the word spread he was spending the night? "How nice. Thank you." She should invite her in, but if she ran into Dario, it could cause problems.

Lucia turned to look down the driveway. "That looks like Dario's car down there."

"Uh, yes, you see, he was afraid there'd be boars in the vineyards so he came by…" Her mind was racing so fast trying to come up with a plausible explanation, that she stumbled and her mind went blank.

"You don't have to explain to me," Lucia said with a small knowing smile on her lips. "I'll be off now, but I wanted to say I've spoken to the priest and he's free on a Saturday to do the Blessing if that's okay with you. He's also available for other ceremonies…like a wedding," she added with a gleam in her eye.

Isabel hoped Dario didn't hear her say that. Surely Lucia knew he'd never commit to another relationship. Neither would Isabel. And yet, despite the brick wall she'd so carefully built around her heart, she had a sudden vision of herself walking through the vineyard in a long white dress. She closed her eyes and forced herself to be strong. No wedding dreams, no letting her imagination run away with her. That was a sure way of getting caught in a melt-down she'd never recover from.

"Thank you. That should be fine," she told Lucia. "The Blessing I mean," she added hastily.

Lucia's gaze drifted to somewhere over Isabel's shoulder.

"Lucia, what are you doing here?" Dario asked. Isabel whirled around. Just as Lucia was about to leave, he had to appear. But he didn't sound angry at being caught in a compromising position, just surprised. Just one glance at his bare chest, his low-slung jeans and his hair standing on end made Isabel's heart leap and told her as well as his sister that he'd just gotten up and that he'd definitely, without question, spent the night with her. He didn't seem to care what anyone thought. What a change from her last affair, where the anxiety of being caught had left Isabel with a nagging pain in her chest.

"Lucia's brought us some food," Isabel said brightly. All she could think was that he looked so sexy with his eyes still filled with sleep that her pulse was racing. She had an urge to run her hand around the outline of his rough jaw. She wanted to press her cheek against his bronzed chest and listen to his heart to see if it was beating as fast as hers. Instead she clenched her hands into fists and told herself to be strong.

"Thanks," Dario said casually to his sister.

Feeling as relaxed as he seemed to be, Isabel said to Lucia, "Won't you come in for some coffee?"

Lucia said she had to go home, then she headed back down the driveway. Before she got into her car, she turned to look at them for a long moment. Isabel waved.

"I don't know what she must think," she said to Dario, still slightly anxious.

"She thinks we're having an affair."

"Are we?" Waiting for his answer, her heart hammered so loudly she was afraid Lucia could hear it from where she stood.

"Aren't we?" he answered with a devastating smile that warmed her heart and curled her bare toes.

Isabel breathed a sigh of relief. The contrast between him and Neil, her one-time fiancé, was startling in every way. Her ex-boss had worried constantly about being found out. When they had been found out, it was she who'd suffered, not him.

He pulled her tightly against him and kissed her throat, her chin, her eyelids and finally her mouth.

"Why not have an affair?" he asked when he let her go at last. "We get along well, if last night was any indication."

She blushed. Yes they got along extremely well.

"We're both free of obligations," he continued.

"As long as we both know we can come and go at will. That is, no strings," she said firmly. "No promises. No commitment." She said these things for herself to hear as well as for him. The rules had to be agreed on, whether she liked them or not.

He nodded solemnly, put his arm around her and they went inside.

She asked herself how could anything that felt this good be bad? As long as no one got hurt, and Isabel knew better than to let herself get hurt. She needed his help on the vineyard. He wanted to help her. Instead of fighting for the property, they were both working toward one goal—to turn the grapes into fine wine. It was as simple as that.

After eating a half dozen delicious *cornetti*, the crescent-shaped local pastries Lucia had brought, and drinking more coffee, Dario walked out to the vineyard. The sun was shining on a run-down house and rows of neglected vines, and the world had never looked so good to him. Isabel was beautiful, wonderful, kind and generous, and for now she was all his. Before he let himself wallow in contentment, he saw with alarm that there was water gushing up from the ancient water pipe buried under the ground. Just when he'd repaired the pump, gotten water into the house and filled the tank on top of the roof, now this. He turned off the water at the pumphouse, got a shovel from the shed and dug down to expose a length of pipe. But he couldn't tell where the break was.

"The water pipe's broken," he called to Isabel. She came running from the house. "I need you."

"What happened?" she asked breathlessly.

"The pipe's old, it sprang a leak so the water's not getting to the vines. We'll have to replace it." Even in the heat of the battle with the leaky pipe, he realized he'd said *we* when he meant *you*. After all, it was her pipe.

"You stay here. I'll turn the water back on and you tell me where it's coming from."

She nodded. A few minutes later he heard her shriek. He ran back and found her drenched in water from the spray.

"Good, you found it," he said, his gaze riveted to her shirt plastered to her breasts and her shorts clinging to her hips.

She looked so surprised with her hair dripping down her face and her shirt and shorts soaked to her body, he burst out laughing despite the situation.

She laughed too and they stood looking at each other, water gushing from the pipe, until the laughter died and she was in his arms again, where she belonged, her breasts pressed against his chest, his shirt wet. He knew right away he was ready to go back up to the bedroom and continue where they'd left off. In fact, they might still be there if his sister hadn't appeared.

It was a good thing they had an agreement. Nothing serious. He'd been hurt, so had she. This affair of theirs was part of the healing process, and he'd never felt so happy as when he had Isabel in his arms. Still, there was good reason not to lose their heads. He'd never take a chance on love again and she wouldn't either. He'd learned the hard way. Besides, there was work to be done here. "I'd better get this thing repaired," he said abruptly.

"Need my help?" she asked, stepping backwards.

He shook his head. "You go change." Because if she didn't change into dry clothes, and he couldn't stop holding her and planning about how he'd like to take her clothes off and make love all afternoon, then he'd better get out of here. And that was something he didn't want to do.

After the pipe repair, Dario went up to the roof to get his mind back to work, while Isabel whitewashed the cellar. When she started painting the front of the house, he held the ladder for her.

"You're brave," he noted. "The ladder hasn't been used for years."

"I'm only brave when there are no boars around," she said from her perch under the shingles of the roof.

That night they searched the basket Lucia brought and found homemade pasta, pesto sauce, fresh tomatoes, Parmesan cheese and sausage his grandfather had made. But first they each had a refreshing shower, now available with either hot or cold running water. He thought it best to wait outside the house until she had finished showering. Then he changed his mind. The sound of running water and the picture of her standing naked under the shower had a profound effect on him. Why wait for her to finish her shower when it would save water if they showered together? As he bounded up the stairs, he wondered where Dario the workaholic had gone? He'd changed since she arrived. That much he knew.

It bothered him to remember that the last time he'd changed was when he'd followed Magdalena from one end of the island to the other allowing his vineyards to go to ruins. But this was different. He wasn't neglecting anything. As long as he was in control of the situation, no worry. He knocked on the bathroom door, tossed his clothes on the floor and joined her in the shower.

"It's more than I expected," she said when they came down-stairs after the shower. Dario's hair was still wet, his body still responding to hers in the most primitive way. She sat outside while she dried her hair in the late-afternoon sun. "Cold water would have made me happy, but make that hot water and you add it up to pure bliss."

Bliss is what she radiated. Bliss is what he felt too. Dario couldn't take his eyes from her face and the sight of her copper-colored hair gleaming in the sun. He hadn't smiled much for at least a year. But now, every day and every hour, something Isabel said or did made his mouth curve upward.

She was so warm, so generous, that he felt like a new person in a new world, a world he was getting used to. He already knew she was gutsy, dedicated, and determined to get the house in order as well as supervise the harvest. She was also so much fun to be with he sometimes stopped working just to watch her standing on the top of the ladder, a smudge of paint on her nose, and he'd catch himself staring at her won-dering how long this could last.

Days went by. Long sunny days followed by balmy starlit nights together in her narrow bed. She painted the kitchen and made curtains for the bedroom. He worked on his own harvest in the morning, but joined her every day for a long lunch. "It's a Sicilian tradition," he explained. It was also a Sicilian tra-dition to make love in the afternoon on long summer days. Then back to work.

In the evening he'd return for dinner laden with supplies and they cooked together, ate together, talked together, laughed and kissed and fell into bed at night, tired, but never too tired to take their relationship to a new level of intimacy. As long as they both knew the rules.

Sometimes, even when Dario wasn't helping her out at the

Azienda, he felt as if he was standing on the top of a ladder. Not only on top of the ladder, but on top of the world. He had no idea how long his mood would last. One week passed, then two weeks and he was still on top of the world. But the last time he'd been this close to a woman their happy affair had come crashing down around him. The warning voice inside his head got more muted each day. He knew it wouldn't happen again because he would never let himself go the way he had. He was holding back, keeping his heart and soul locked away.

Of course, Isabel was a different kind of woman than Magdalena and he was a different man than he was then. He was a man with defenses firmly in place around his heart. If he still had a heart, which he sometimes doubted, it had hardened into Sicilian granite. Which wasn't a bad thing under the circumstances.

But waking up each morning in bed with Isabel was something else. He liked seeing her every morning, her glorious red hair tousled, her eyes sleepy. He liked seeing her every night, her hair damp from the shower, and just before she fell asleep she murmured *buona notte* to him. It seemed natural. It seemed right.

The approval of his family when they learned he was spending even more time at the Azienda with Isabel was a nice change from their worried frowns and negative remarks during the Magdalena era.

But still, he knew this affair wouldn't last. They had a goal—to prepare the place for the Blessing of the Grapes. After that something would change. Either he'd go back to his house full time or… By then she'd have power and water and a telephone and she wouldn't need him to stay there anymore. She wouldn't need him at all. That was a good thing. At least he'd thought so until today, over two weeks since the first night he'd spent there. Now he wondered how much he would miss not being needed, miss being a part of her daily life.

Sitting at the picnic table after dinner when the air was cool, drinking wine and talking or just sitting there as night fell and the breeze came up made him feel that life couldn't get much better than this. Isabel had cooked the whole dinner after a hard day of work grouting the bathroom floor because he was late.

"Tomorrow night I'm taking you to the hotel for dinner," he said. "For a change. You've been working so hard here, you need a break."

She looked up, her eyes wide, her cheeks flushed in the light from the gas lantern hanging from a branch of the sycamore tree.

"You don't have to do that," she said.

"But I want to show you off. You'll wear your blue dress and I'll even wear a clean shirt. I want everyone to see me having dinner with the beautiful American winemaker."

CHAPTER TEN

THE NEXT NIGHT Isabel showered and scrubbed the paint off her fingers before putting on her one and only dress. She loved cooking with Dario and for Dario in her own rustic kitchen every night, but when he'd invited her to dinner at the hotel, she'd had to stop abruptly and think. This was a date. They were having an affair, but this was their first date. She hadn't had a real date for years. Certainly not with Neil.

Her mind was still reeling. He wanted to show her off. He wanted people to see them together. It was all so new, so amazingly different from her last affair. It made her feel wanted and desired…but not loved. If he loved her she'd know it. But he didn't. His words echoed in her brain—*it won't happen again*. She understood that. He'd loved Magdalena, but he'd never love again. She felt the same. It didn't matter. Love was greatly oversold.

When she came downstairs he turned to look at her. His mouth fell open. He looked as stunned as if he'd never seen her before, when he'd seen her every day of the past fourteen.

"What's wrong?" she asked, nervously adjusting the spaghetti strap of her dress. She hadn't worn it since that night at his house. She hadn't been back there since.

"You look beautiful," he said soberly.

Then it was her turn to stare. He was so gorgeous in a white shirt that contrasted with his dark hair and showed off his tan that she felt as though she'd never seen him before.

The wind whipped her hair against her cheek as they drove down the hill to the hotel. He took his eyes off the road from time to time to look at her and she felt the heat from his gaze.

They had drinks in the bar. Dario ordered Bellinis for them, ripe white peaches mixed with champagne, and he introduced her to several of his friends. They made small talk about wine and grapes until they went into the dining room.

"So much has happened since I left this hotel," she said looking around at the familiar white tablecloths and the flowers on every table. "I hardly feel like the same person who bumbled her way to the Azienda. I have you to thank for taking me there and making me feel at home."

He shook his head. "You did it on your own. You wouldn't let anyone or anything stand in your way. Anyone else would have turned around and gone home after one look at the Azienda. Not you." He sent her a dazzling smile with no hint of regret in it, at least that's what she wanted to think.

Before they ordered, a bottle of dry sparkling white wine was brought to the table and a waiter in a black vest poured two glasses.

"To the future," Dario said, tapping his glass against hers. "But first we have to bury the past. I've told you more than you want to know about my past and Magdalena, but you haven't told me how you got fired."

She took a sip of wine then set her glass down. "I'd rather not talk about it. I'd rather forget it."

"You can't forget something until it's gone, dead and buried and out of sight." He paused. "Believe me, I know. Some other time then," he said with a shrug.

She knew it was time to come clean with the whole story, no matter how painful. It was only fair. He'd told her about Magdalena and now it was her turn. But when the *calamare fritti* came with a delicious spicy sauce she didn't want to spoil the mood or the dinner so she changed the subject. The salad was her favorite, made of spinach with ribbons of *pancetta* and sprinkled with chunks of creamy gorgonzola cheese. It was so delicious and he was being so entertaining and making her smile with stories of his childhood, she couldn't change the subject and start talking about her disastrous affair. Especially when the main course arrived— pasta with smoked salmon in a brandy cream sauce. She sighed with contentment as she spooned the last drop of sauce from her plate.

"The last time I ate dinner here was the night I moved to the Azienda," she said. "It was early and I was the only one in the dining room." What a difference. Tonight she was eating with the best-looking, most desirable man in Sicily. Tonight the place was full of couples and families, happily talking, drinking and eating. Not a single person was alone. It was almost a crime in Sicily to eat alone. Food was for sharing. Life was for sharing. How far she'd come in just a few weeks. How much farther would she go?

After coffee they strolled out to his car. She still hadn't answered his questions. She didn't know how to start. So she waited until they got back to the Azienda and were sitting on the newly painted front veranda, on a large swing he'd brought her as a housewarming present.

They sat in companionable silence for a long time swinging back and forth while the stars glittered in the sky above them. *Tell him, tell him,* said the voice inside her head. *It's not going to get any easier.*

"All right," she said at last, unable to prolong the silence any more. "You asked me how I got fired. His wife found out. I don't know how. But one day she burst into his office while I was there. We weren't doing anything, just talking. But she was furious. She screamed at me, called me names. I tried to tell her I was as shocked as she was, I'd had no idea that Neil was married. The next day I had fifteen minutes to clear my desk and leave the building. I was humiliated, and I was angry. *Why me,* I thought. Especially when I learned he hadn't been fired, he hadn't even been punished. In fact, he got promoted."

The memory of the shame and humiliation caused all the air in her lungs to leave. She took a deep breath. "The next week I dressed in a suit and went to see him to get a recommendation I knew I'd need if I ever applied for a job again. I thought it was the least he could do."

She hated talking about it. And yet, Dario was right. It was time to bury the past. If she couldn't tell Dario, then she couldn't tell anyone.

"He said he couldn't do it. He treated me as if *I'd* seduced *him.* As if it was all my fault. He said I deserved to be fired. I felt so sick I rushed out to the street. I started to believe he was right, that somehow I deserved what had happened to me. That was still my mood when I got the letter from the lawyer. After job-hunting for months, avoiding friends and sinking deeper and deeper into depression, I got the letter. I was an heiress. I had someplace to go and something to do. I studied Italian, I read up on winemaking. I had a goal, a purpose to my life."

He put his arm around her shoulders and held her tightly against him, her head on his shoulder. She could have stayed there forever.

"You wonder how I could ever have loved somebody like that," she said. "You have to realize that he not only told me I was a brilliant designer, he said I was beautiful and he loved me."

She leaned back, still feeling the support of Dario's arm around her. "No one had ever treated me that way before. No one had loved me before. One thing I'd learned long ago and that was not to cry. When it all fell apart, the day his wife found out and confronted us, I didn't cry. Because, if you cry, people will mock you or feel sorry for you. I'm not sure what is worst."

"So you came to Sicily."

"Thanks to my uncle."

"But it still hurts." It wasn't a question. It was as if he knew.

She turned her head to look up at him. His eyes were deep pools of understanding. "Yes. No. Not as much." *Not since you came into my life.* "I have other things to think about now. The grapes, the harvest, the Blessing, the house." *And you.*

And then she broke the one rule she'd always lived by. She started to cry. After all these years and all the rejections, all the hurt feelings, all the insults and all the sleepless nights she'd kept the tears from flowing. Maybe it was the night or Dario or the memories she'd uncovered. Whatever it was, once she started she couldn't stop. A lifetime of tears poured from her eyes onto his shoulder, onto his chest, dampening his beautiful clean white shirt.

"Tesoro don' grido di t…" he said. She didn't understand the words, but they made her feel better anyway. After an eternity, when she was finally cried out, she lay exhausted with her head in his lap looking up at the stars. And saying to herself the same prayer she said every night. *Please God, don't let me fall in love again.*

The Saturday of the Blessing was a brilliant, hot sunny day, like all the others. The early-morning mist that hung over the vines had disappeared by eight in the morning when the workers arrived with huge steel drums to fill with charcoal and cook the meat over a makeshift grill. Isabel stood at the edge of the vineyard, looking out at the fields below, her heart pounding with anticipation when Dario came up behind her and put his arms around her.

"Excited?" he said.

"And a little worried. What if the priest forgets to come? What if the wine from the cellar isn't good enough? What if I didn't order enough food." *What if I've fallen in love with you and you don't love me back?* It was her worst fear and her current nightmare. After two glorious weeks together— working together, eating together and sleeping together and getting things ready for the Blessing—today was the pinnacle. It would be a turning point. They'd either go forward or backward. She studied Dario's face for a clue to how he felt. At the end of the day, would he take his clothes and his tools and go home? Or would he tell her the words she wanted to hear. *I love you Isabel. I want to spend my life with you. Not just two weeks, but forever.*

He turned her around in his arms and pressed his finger against her lips.

"It's going to be a perfect day," he said. "You'll see. It's not the end, it's just the beginning."

She nodded. If only he meant that the way she wanted him to mean it. She had high hopes for the day, a beautiful ceremony, delicious food and wonderful new friends to share it with. It should be enough, but she wanted more. She wanted Dario.

What was wrong with her? Why couldn't she be happy with what she had? A house and a working vineyard. She didn't want to admit it, but she knew she'd made a terrible mistake. She'd fallen in love with Dario. When did it happen?

The night he came to shoot the boars? The night he took her to his house and kissed her? Or was it that first day when she saw him standing by the side of the road?

Whenever it was, she'd have to get over it. Unless he felt the same. Today she'd tell him how she felt. How else would she know if he loved her too? If he didn't, why had he moved into her house, why had he fed her, helped her, fixed her roof, repaired her water heater? Held her, kissed her, made love to her and let the world see they were a couple?

If he didn't love her, would she continue her life without him? She couldn't go on seeing him day and night like this if there was no future for them. If he didn't love her now he never would. It was time to find out the truth before it was too late for her to recuperate.

People started arriving mid morning, wearing their Sunday best, all Dario's relatives, including his grandfather in a wheelchair. They assembled in the meadow. The priest was there in his flowing robe. Dario was wearing a suit and Isabel almost fainted when she saw how gorgeous he looked in the white shirt and contrasting dark jacket and tie. His face was sun-browned and his eyes bluer than ever.

"You look beautiful," he said to her, his gaze lingering on the bodice of her turquoise dress, the same dress she'd worn at his house, the same dress she'd worn the night she'd finally let down her defenses and told him what had happened to her. She managed a little smile, too nervous and excited to compliment him in return. Or to tell him she loved him. Or ask if he loved her.

The tantalizing smell of pork roasting on a spit blended with the warm grass, the sweet smell of crushed grapes and the summer sunshine. The priest took his place at the edge of the clearing facing the crowd.

"God watereth the hills from above: the earth is filled with the fruit of thy works. He bringeth forth grass for the cattle, and green herb for the service of man: that he may bring food out of the earth; and wine that maketh glad the heart of man. Psalms 104: 13-14." When he blessed a basket of Amarado grapes Isabel felt a rush of emotion so strong she almost fainted. It was all so beautiful. So bittersweet. The beginning of her life as a winemaker on her own and the end of being Dario's protégée, always able to count on him being around. Unless…unless…

After the short service, Isabel saw Dario deep in conversation with his brother, Cosmo, and two sisters. He was frowning. His sister had her hand on his shoulder. She felt a slight shiver of fear go up her spine. Something had happened. Something was wrong.

She kissed the guests on both cheeks, she thanked them all for coming, she served the food and all the while she kept Dario and his family in view, wondering and worrying.

Finally he broke away from his relatives and joined her at the edge of the clearing.

"I have to leave," he said. "There's a problem. The dock workers in Palermo are on strike and our wine has been sitting on the dock for two weeks. It's my fault. I've been out of touch. The family didn't want to bother me while I was with you, they thought they could handle it." He paused. "They can't."

Isabel felt cold all over despite the heat from the noonday sun. She had a terrible feeling that history was repeating itself. Once again Dario had been distracted from his work by a woman. Her. And he felt guilty, maybe he even resented her for keeping him here helping her when he should have been paying attention to Montessori wine instead of her.

"I'm heading for Palermo now, today." He glanced around

at the party in full swing, the friends and neighbors eating and drinking together, but she wondered if he even noticed them with his mind on his problem.

"Dario, I'll miss you," she said softly. Now was not the time to tell him she loved him. Maybe after he got back.

"I'll be back in a week or two if all goes well. But you'll be fine without me," he said. "You're on your way. The house is livable and the grapes are ripe. You'll have a great harvest. You're strong. You're capable."

I may be capable, but I need you every day in every way, she thought, her heart pounding. What he was really saying was good-bye. Things would never be the same. He left without kissing her good-bye. His mind was hundreds of miles away. While she had been falling in love he had been just helping a neighbor. The truth hit her like a barrel of aged wine. Once again she'd fooled herself into thinking the man she loved loved her in return.

When everyone left, and the sun was setting over the hills in the distance, silence descended on the Azienda. Isabel looked around from the house to the vines. She sat down on a wooden chair at the edge of the vineyard, suddenly so tired and weak she felt as if she'd just run a marathon instead of hosting a party.

For the first time in two weeks, she was alone. She'd been spoiled. She'd let herself get used to having Dario there every night and every morning. Worst of all, she'd let herself fall in love with him. Finally she stood and went into her house, her cold, empty, lonely house.

During the next week Isabel took her grapes to be crushed. She continued to paint and plaster. She managed to buy food for herself, but she didn't feel like eating it. She went to bed every night and lay tossing and turning and thinking about how stupid she'd been until it got light. Life on the Azienda was no longer beautiful. It was flat and uninteresting without Dario. She gave herself stern warnings about standing strong, but she buried her head in her pillow and tuned them out.

Another week went by during which she talked to no one but her workers, and their conversation was limited by her lack of Italian. She was anxious to know how Dario was doing in Palermo, but she had no way to find out except by calling him on his cell phone, and she couldn't do that. She had her pride, after all.

If he wanted to get in touch with her, he knew where to find her. One day she ran into Lucia at the town square. Dario's sister greeted her warmly.

"How's Dario doing?" Isabel asked, swallowing what little pride she had left.

"Still in Palermo. The problems are more serious than we thought. He's working night and day to negotiate a new contract with the workers' union. Who knows how long it will take? In the meantime Cosmo is taking over some of his work here. It's good for him. Dario was always the big brother. Always in charge. Cosmo never had a chance to show what he can do. Now's his chance."

Isabel felt sick. He'd updated his family, but hadn't called her.

"Are you all right?" Lucia asked. "You look a little pale."

Isabel managed a smile. "I'm fine."

Lucia looked at her and Isabel was afraid she could guess that she'd been suffering. "You know I was hoping you and Dario…"

"We were just friends, that's all," Isabel assured her.

"It's too bad," Lucia said softly. "You were good for him. I don't understand what happened."

Isabel understood perfectly. He'd made the same mistake

with her that he had with Magdalena except that he'd been in love with Magdalena. He was once again making up for his lack of attention to work by burying himself in it. This time for good. No one can recover from two mistakes in a row. Not Dario and not her either. It was time to do something different. She couldn't continue to live and work where Dario's face and his voice and his hands infused in every square inch of the house and land. Everywhere she looked she saw his smile, heard his voice and listened for his car. Every surface she touched, she felt him. It was an illusion. He wasn't there and he would never be there again, not the way she wanted him to be. She had to pull herself together and stop thinking about him night and day. She had to make decisions based on what was best for her and her state of mind. Hard decisions.

Dario was exhausted. He'd been working nonstop since he got to Palermo. He'd been up for the last twenty-four hours haggling over details with the union organizers. The days had all blended together since he'd left home. Home. Where was home? When he thought about it, the Azienda came into his mind. The Azienda and Isabel.

He tried not to think about her, but the sound of her voice, the look on her face before she woke up in the morning, the smell of fresh paint on her house, the taste of the coffee she made for him in the morning haunted him day and night. He couldn't shake the image of how she had looked when he'd said he was leaving. She'd tried to smile, but her lips had trembled. He'd thought he had no choice but to go. His mind was already there, settling the dispute. Fixing the problem by himself the way he always did.

He'd thought no one could handle the situation but him, but

his brother-in-law had arrived the night before with new energy and fresh ideas, so maybe he was wrong. He'd thought no one could manage the harvest without him, but Cosmo seemed to be doing fine. Maybe his family was right. He was a control freak who couldn't let go. But he couldn't do everything by himself. It was time to go home. He knew where home was. It was the Azienda. It was wherever Isabel was. He needed her. Without her he could never be whole. Never be happy.

Finally the answer came to Isabel. She had to leave. But how could she when she loved the Azienda, every crack in the foundation, every spiderweb, every dripping faucet. With all its flaws, it was the only home she'd ever had. Still, the pain was unbearable. The loneliness worse than ever. She'd been alone before, but that was before she met Dario. That was before she'd shared this house and her bed and her life with him. She could be alone again, but not here. He'd made it impossible for her to stay.

She went to Dario's house and looked in the window. She saw the stone fireplace and the matching leather chairs and the pile of papers untouched on his desk. She remembered how she'd felt the night he'd brought her here to see his grand-father's paintings and had kissed her for the first time.

There was no music playing today. The windows were closed. She slid the note she'd written under his front door. When he walked in it would be the first thing he'd see. She was glad he wasn't there. If he were, he'd try to convince her to stay. He'd give her all the reasons why she should stay, except for the one she wanted to hear. She leaned against his front door, her head pressed against the hard wood panel. *What am I doing?* She asked herself. *I can't leave.* She had to retrieve the note. But she couldn't reach it. She'd write another one, she'd say—*Disregard the previous note. I'm not leaving after all. It's nothing personal. Nothing to do with you. I just can't leave a house I've spent so much time and energy on.*

Then she reminded herself he hadn't called her since he'd left. He didn't miss her. He didn't love her. It was obvious. The brusque way he'd left her the day of the Blessing was like a fresh wound in her heart. He didn't seem at all sorry he had to go. He appeared almost eager for a new challenge. Why had she not realized what it meant? Once again she'd fallen in love by herself. It was time to go or to consign herself to suffering even more than she was now. Or should she wait and tell him in person? She went to her car and sat there for an hour, torn between going and staying.

Dario returned from Palermo that night. He had to see Isabel. He had to see her right now. He'd thought he didn't need her. He'd thought he'd lost his head again, along with his work ethic. Instead he'd found what was important. More important than the land or the harvest or anything. It was her. He went straight to the Azienda, but she wasn't there. The door was unlocked but the house was empty. Puzzled and confused, with a sense of dread gnawing at his gut, he went to his house.

When he saw her note lying on his floor he dumped his valise on the ground and sat down at his desk, his heart pounding, his vision blurred as he read her words.

"...can't stay here any longer...too difficult...I understand...Azienda all yours..." He crumpled the note in his hand and threw it across the room. What was wrong with her? Why did she leave? Was it because he'd gone to Palermo and she needed him? Why didn't she get in touch with him then? She'd never called him once while he was gone. The note was full of explanations, but none of them made any sense.

He was in a state of shock. He'd been working too hard, not eating enough, not sleeping enough, then driving here too fast, thinking about her too much.

He stared at the empty fireplace filled with cold ashes. He retrieved the note and smoothed the wrinkles in it with his palm. He walked outside and looked at the sky. The sun was still shining even though Isabel wasn't here. She'd gone back to California. But when and how?

He was filled with anger. Anger at her for leaving without telling him. Anger at himself because of all the things he'd never done. Never taken her to see the volcano. Never taken her to see the *cathedrale* at Monreale or to the opera to hear Puccini.

He stood for a long moment trying to get it through his head that she was gone. She wouldn't be there to share dinner cooked over an outdoor fire pit with him. She wouldn't be there to take a shower with him or put her arms around him to keep from rolling out of the narrow bed they'd shared.

He thought of the Azienda. Her touch and her smell were everywhere as if she'd just stepped out for a moment. Maybe she had. Maybe she'd just left. Maybe she wouldn't be able to get a ticket home. He could only hope. Missing her caused a dull ache in his heart, the heart he'd thought was encased in stone. So he ran back to his car and drove as fast as he could to the airport. He, the ultimate loner, the guy who lived alone was racing down the highway to try to persuade a woman to share her life with him. Forever.

Isabel was at the ticket counter where she'd been waiting for hours while the agent checked the flights to the U.S. again and again. Nothing. There was nothing today. Maybe *domani*… tomorrow?

She couldn't wait until tomorrow. She'd lose her nerve. She was already having second and third thoughts. If she didn't get on a plane now what would she do? Return to the Azienda? Go to a hotel? Buy a ticket to someplace else? No, no no. She paced the floor, bought a magazine and went to the airport *caffee* and ordered a cappuccino. If Dario were here he'd insist she get a gelato too. He wanted her to taste and experience everything Sicilian.

But he wasn't here. He was in Palermo working. That's where he wanted to be. The time he'd spent with her at the Azienda was just a blip on the screen of his life, only a short sequence that had been fun but that couldn't last. If it weren't for the family business emergency, it would have been something else. Yes, it was best she leave. If not today then tomorrow. And if not tomorrow…

"*Ciao, signorina,*" he said, in a voice she recognized with a jolt.

She swiveled around on her chair and stared. There he was easing into a chair across the table as if this had all been planned. She gripped the spoon in her hand so tightly her knuckles turned white. She opened her mouth but no sound came out. He very casually ordered a coffee, so casually that she was convinced he'd seen her note and he had just come to say good-bye.

She braced herself against the back of the chair while her heart pounded and the whole room spun around. "What are you doing here?" she asked, her voice so strained she sounded like a rusty gate. It must be a dream. Dario at the airport.

He rested his elbows on the table and leaned toward her. He was so close she saw the fine lines at the corners of his eyes and the shadow of a beard that lined his jaw. He looked as if he hadn't slept for days. But he still looked amazing in his Italian jeans and his blue shirt. He was so close she felt her bones melt.

"I might ask you the same thing," he said. "What are you doing here?"

"I'm thinking of returning to California. But all the flights are full."

"Why?" he said, his blue eyes glittering like the sea on a stormy day.

"Why are they full?" she asked with a frown. "Maybe because it's Friday."

"Why are you leaving?" he asked, with an obvious effort to be patient with her.

"I wrote you a note," she explained

"I got your note. But I want to hear it from you. Straight from your mouth. I thought you liked it here."

"I did. I do. But I can't stay." She pressed her lips together and willed herself not to cry. She must stay calm and explain why she was leaving. If only she could make it clear in her own head. "I thought I could manage the Azienda by myself, but when you left I realized I couldn't."

"It's not like you to quit something you cared about so much."

"It wasn't an easy decision." That was the truth. In fact, she was still wavering.

"At least you could have waited until I got back to tell me in person. I thought I meant more to you than that." His mouth twisted into a frown. "You could have called me. I never heard from you."

"You didn't call *me*. If I hadn't run into your sister I wouldn't have known you were still alive."

"I'm sorry. I should have kept in touch. The work was

overwhelming, but that's no excuse. I thought about you. And I missed you." He looked deep into her eyes, so deeply she was afraid he could see the real reason she was leaving.

Isabel blinked back a tear. These were the words she longed to hear.

"I missed you too," she said softly.

"I shouldn't have gone. I should have sent someone else," he said, shaking his head. "I thought I was indispensable, the only one capable of doing the job, but when Guillermo came to relieve me I realized he was even better qualified than I was. He had the energy I had run out of. And Cosmo has taken over back here and done a great job. So maybe it was good I left as far as he was concerned. It's been a humbling experience to find I'm not as important as I thought. Except for one thing. You too decided you didn't need me."

"That's not true," she blurted. "The reason I'm leaving is that I need you too much." Now was the time to tell him how she felt. Then she could leave knowing she'd done her best and been honest with him. She'd have no regrets. She took a deep breath. " I...I...know we thought we were just having a good time, a summer fling, no strings, but somehow, even though I knew the rules, I couldn't help myself. I fell in love with you, Dario. Please don't say anything. I don't expect you to love me. I know how you feel. I know how much you've been hurt."

He reached across the table and took her hands in his. "I thought I'd never love again, you're right. I'd made such a colossal mistake, I lost all confidence in my judgment. I had myself convinced it was my destiny to be a loner, the black sheep in the family, the favorite uncle with no kids of his own. Then you came along and you changed my mind and you changed my life.

"I'll never forget that first day when you were determined to get to the Azienda in your ridiculous sandals and catch a ride back to town on a road that no one used. You just had to fix your own tires and grow your own grapes. I kept waiting for you to fail. But you always bounced back. I'd never met anyone like you. I didn't believe you could make it on your own."

"I can't," she said soberly.

"Yes, you can," he said and squeezed her hand. "But you don't have to. I want to be there for you whatever you want to do. I want to run the Azienda with you. I love you, Isabel. I want to marry you. I want to watch our children grow up together at the Azienda."

Isabel tilted her head to one side as if to see better, because her hearing must be affected. She thought she'd just heard Dario say he loved her.

After a long silence he spoke again. "Of course, if you don't feel the same…if you really want to get on that plane…" He stared at her as if willing her to tell him what he wanted to hear.

"No. No. I want to stay here with you. I came here to claim my inheritance and to find myself. A girl who'd never had a family or a home of her own. I wasn't sure I could manage by myself. Then you came along. You showed me how to scare off the wild boar, how to know when the grapes are ripe, how to change a tire and how to love again. You gave me the courage to do things I never thought I could. You introduced me to your family who I love as if they were my own. You challenged me and I hope you always will. I love you Dario. I loved you from the first moment I saw you picking grapes. I loved you even when you tried to talk me into buying another house. You wanted me to have an easier time."

"I confess, I wanted the Azienda. But I have something better. I have you. I should have known you'd choose the hard way. My stubborn Isabel. My darling Isabel." He brought her hands to his lips and kissed her fingers. "Don't cry," he said, with alarm as the tears gathered in her eyes. She'd tried so hard to be brave. She knew the penalty for crying. She'd learned early and learned well. But now the dam had burst she couldn't stop. She sobbed so loudly that other passengers turned and looked at her with sympathy.

Dario handed her his handkerchief. "Don't cry, Isabel. I love you. I can't promise you an easy life, but I can promise you a life that will never be boring." He stood and helped her out of her seat.

"Let's go home," he said, drawing her to him. "There are grapes to be picked, bells to ring and a wedding to plan." She threw her arms around him and kissed him as a flight to America was being announced on the loud speaker. It was a flight she would not be taking. Not today. Not without Dario.

EPILOGUE

ON A SUNNY October day, the small stone church on the Villarmosa town square was full of friends and relatives for the wedding of Dario Montessori and his American bride, Isabel Morrison. No one who had ever seen them together in the weeks before their wedding could doubt they were meant for each other. They radiated happiness wherever they went, from the Azienda to his family home to the town of Agrigento where he bought her wedding ring and where they attended a performance of *The Marriage of Figaro*. The music made Isabel feel as romantic as any Sicilian in the audience. Everyone remarked that they made a perfect couple. Everyone seemed to have known they were meant for each other before the couple knew—especially the Montessori family.

He was rich, strong, tall and dazzlingly handsome in his black tuxedo and white shirt. She was beautiful, rich in spirit, and wore an ivory satin dress that set off her fiery auburn hair, the color of a Sicilian sunset.

They said their vows in English and Italian, then kissed while all the women watching dabbed the tears from their eyes and all the men smiled broadly. Dario Montessori had finally met his match. After the ceremony the bride showed off the results of her Italian lessons by engaging Dario's grandfather in conversation.

"*Sono cosi felice di fare parte della vostra famiglia,*" she said.

The old man beamed at her from his wheelchair.

Then it was off to the reception at the Azienda, now in the middle of reconstruction. Soon there would be a huge addition to the old house as well as a tasting room for visitors. Tables covered with white cloths and flowers were set up outside in the vineyard. A string quartet played Italian love songs. There were toasts in two languages. A temporary dance floor had been constructed with a view of the surrounding countryside.

After Dario toasted his bride, he took her aside and said, "Signora Montessori, I haven't given you your wedding present yet." He reached into his pocket and handed her a small black velvet box.

Inside was a small picture frame with a photo of a man with red hair. "Your uncle," he said. "I found the photo in the newspaper office. I'm sure if he knew what you've done to his vineyard, he would be proud of you. No one could deserve it more. No one could have done more for it than you. And there's no one I owe more to for bringing you to me."

"Thank you," she said, with a smile. "Now I know what he looked like. My only relative. I too thank him for bringing me here to Sicily and the Azienda."

He lifted his champagne glass. "To Uncle Antonio."

She tapped her glass against his.

"Your only relative until now. As of today you now have dozens." He gave a wide gesture toward the family members, all part of the wedding party from the flower girls and the ring bearers to the bridesmaids and groomsmen.

"I found an account of how he arrived a few years ago from America to make his way to Sicily," Dario said. He studied the tendrils of red-gold hair that framed her face. "I think I see a family resemblance."

"You mean the hair. I hope you're prepared for red-haired children."

"The more the better," he said, holding her so close she felt his heart beating in time with hers. "This will be a wonderful place for them to grow up. By the way, isn't it time to leave for our honeymoon?"

She looked around at the rows of vines, at the house with the new roof and the scaffolding and the framework for the addition. Her home. *Their* home. A wonderful place to live. A wonderful place for their children to grow up. A dream come true. When they returned from their honeymoon in Florence they'd move into his cottage until the remodeling was finished.

"I have a present for you too." She reached into the embroidered lace bodice of her gown and handed him a small gold key. "The key to my heart," she said.

He pressed the key to his lips, put it in his pocket and thanked whatever fates had sent him Isabel—his life and his love.

HIRED:
THE ITALIAN'S BRIDE
Donna Alward

Dear Reader,

For nearly twelve years I lived in Alberta, Canada, with my husband and children. My mum would come to visit us annually and her visit always included a trip to the Rocky Mountains and, more often than not, lunch at the fabulously decadent Banff Springs Hotel. I always thought there was something magical about it. It's perched at the pinnacle of town, a great stone castle looking up at Cascade Mountain and down the Bow River Valley. At Christmas there's a replica of it made of gingerbread on display inside. The food is excellent, the atmosphere even better. When I thought of putting a heroine somewhere to reclaim her life, the town of Banff simply fitted the bill.

Of course I needed a hotel and a to-die-for handsome hero. I found him in Italian Luca Fiori. Luca is heir to the Fiori hotel empire and is sent to Banff to oversee the newest company acquisition, the Fiori Cascade. The Cascade is a place for relaxation and rejuvenation, for a bit of decadence and specialness. Luca says it is to 'remember the romance'.

As I write this letter, I've just returned home from a wedding…my mum's wedding, after many years on her own. I couldn't be happier that she has 'remembered the romance', and that she and her new husband 'found' each other. It just goes to show that there is always, *always*, room for love.

I'd love to hear from you… You can e-mail me at donna@donnaalward.com or care of my publisher.

With my very best wishes,

Donna

A busy wife and mother of three (two daughters and the family dog), **Donna Alward** believes hers is the best job in the world: a combination of stay-at-home mum and romance novelist. An avid reader since childhood, Donna always made up her own stories. She completed her Arts Degree in English Literature in 1994, but it wasn't until 2001 that she penned her first full-length novel and found herself hooked on writing romance. In 2006 she sold her first manuscript and now writes warm, emotional stories for Mills & Boon®'s Romance line.

In her new home office in Nova Scotia, Donna loves being back on the east coast of Canada after nearly twelve years in Alberta, where her career began, writing about cowboys and the west. Donna's debut Romance, *Hired by The Cowboy*, was awarded the Booksellers Best Award in 2008 for Best Traditional Romance.

With the Atlantic Ocean only minutes from her doorstep, Donna has found a fresh take on life and promises even more great romances in the near future!

Donna loves to hear from readers. You can contact her through her website at www.donnaalward.com, visit her myspace page at www.myspace.com/dalward or through her publisher.

For Mum and Harold

CHAPTER ONE

"Ms. Ross? Mr. Fiori has arrived."

He was here.

"Thank you, Becky. Show him in."

Mari ran a hand over her already smooth hair, trying hard not to resent a man she'd never met. Luca Fiori, golden son of the Fiori Resort empire. Rich, powerful, and according to her online research, a bit of a playboy.

Just what she—and the hotel—needed. Not.

She could just make out the sound of his voice, smooth and warm, coming from the reception area. The sound sent a flutter through her tummy. Becky would be bringing him back any moment. Perhaps she should go out to meet him. Yes, that would probably be the genial, professional thing to do. But her feet wouldn't move. Instead she turned her head to both sides, assessing the office as if through a stranger's eyes. Her new office, though she couldn't help feeling a bit of an interloper. What Fiori needed to see was a woman confident in her new position. Even if she wasn't, she had to give that appearance. She made sure everything was in its place. Not a speck of dust or scrap of paper. Everything had to be perfect. The only thing that revealed she'd even been there that morning was her mug, half-full of cold tea, a faint half-moon of lipstick marring the cream-colored ceramic.

Mari inhaled, then let it out slowly, trying to relax her shoulders. She carried all her tension there and right now they were sitting close to her ears, she was so nervous. She pushed them down and attempted a smile. She had to show him she was up to the job…the job she'd had for exactly two weeks and three days.

Seconds later Becky returned, extending a hand and showing Luca into the office.

All Mari's practiced greetings flew out of her head.

"Mr. Fiori."

The pictures didn't do him justice, she realized, as her heart gave a definitive *thud*. He was taller than he seemed from the online pictures. He was wearing a suit, but with such a casual flair she wasn't sure it actually could be called a suit at all. Black trousers and shoes and a white shirt, open at the collar, with a black jacket worn carelessly over top. The unbuttoned collar revealed a slice of tanned skin and she saw his hand tuck into his trouser pocket just before she lifted her eyes to his face.

She'd been caught assessing. His twinkling eyes told her so and the crooked, cocky smile confirmed it. Her cheeks flushed as her gaze skittered away.

"Ms. Ross, the acting manager, I presume?"

She wet her lips and pasted on a smile, trying hard to ignore the heat that blossomed anew in her face at the sound of his smooth, rich voice. She extended her hand. "Yes. Welcome to the Bow Valley Inn."

"You mean the Fiori Cascade."

Mari went cold. Of course. She'd received the memo about the name change and had simply forgotten it in her nervousness. She looked up at Luca's mouth. He was smiling, at least, not angry with her for the slip.

She pulled her hand out of his, attempting to keep the polite turn of her lips in place. "Yes, of course. Old habits."

She gestured to a small seating area. "Come in and sit down. I'll ask Becky for some refreshment."

"Why don't we go to the lounge, instead?" He raised one eyebrow at her. "I passed one as I came through the lobby. It'll help give me a feel of the place. And the lounge will be much more intimate, don't you think?"

Mari's hand froze on the handset of the phone. This wasn't what she'd planned. Her pulse drummed at the word "intimate." She'd wanted coffee and the chef's signature scones, followed by a brief presentation of what she considered the Inn's finest points and some basic proposals for changes and upgrades. She'd spent hours getting it the way she wanted—flawless. And with an appropriate amount of distance between them.

"Is something wrong, Ms. Ross?"

She rubbed her lips together. "No, not at all." Her voice came out thin and reedy and she cleared her throat, stretching her lips in a smile again. "Coffee in the Athabasca Room would be fine." She'd simply have to remember what she'd put in her report and make her points as they went along.

"I look forward to hearing your ideas. Perhaps you'd take me on a tour later?" He stepped aside, letting her exit first. His voice was smooth, his smile charming. Mari exhaled again, trying to keep her shoulders down. She could do this. She wasn't used to thinking on her feet, but she could do it. She'd just ignore what she knew about his reputation. Or the fact that he fairly exuded charm without even trying.

The lounge was nearly empty at ten in the morning. Two other couples sat at tables, sipping from large mugs and chatting quietly. Mari led him past the main bar to a smaller corner one, perching on one of the backed stools, making sure there were several inches between them. Luca took the seat next to her and the scent of his expensive cologne reached her nose. There was no mistaking the confident ease with which he carried himself. This was a man completely out of her league. Not that she was looking. She wasn't even close to looking, not when the very thought of any physical contact with a man sent chills down her spine.

"This might be my favorite view in the whole hotel," she began, focusing on her job, determined he see the Inn…the Cascade…at its best. The way she was turned, she could look out over the hotel front grounds and down over the valley, the turquoise-blue of the Bow River a shining snake through the gold and green hues of autumn. "And our coffee is superior. We import it from—"

"The scenery *is* spectacular." He interrupted her and she realized that he wasn't looking at the view at all, but at her. Nerves tumbled in her stomach and her voice trailed off, unsure of how to continue. He must think her provincial, not the standard of management *Fiori* employed. Certainly not up to bantering, like he seemed to expect.

Mari turned back to the bar and put her hand on the coffeepot that was set out. It didn't matter. This was her job and she wanted to keep it. Wanted it more than anything else in the world.

"Coffee, Mr. Fiori?"

She looked up when he remained silent and their eyes met.

Her hand shook on the handle of the pot. He was watching her steadily, so unwavering that tightness cinched her chest. She willed it away, telling herself it was his power as her boss that had her so unsettled. It wasn't his fault that he was so handsome. Wasn't his fault that his eyes were the color of melted molasses toffee, only a slightly deeper shade than his hair. He wasn't responsible for the perfectly shaped lips, either, or the way he spoke, with flawless inflection and just a hint of Italian accent. He was possibly more magnetic than he was in the pictures on the computer or in the industry magazines she kept filed on her bookshelf. She would imagine he got his way often simply from his looks and charm. But not here, not with her. There were important things at stake.

"Call me Luca, please," he answered finally.

She forced herself to pour the coffee as the waitress returned with a basket of warm scones. "Luca, then."

"You're not going to tell me your first name."

She raised an eyebrow, cautiously determined not to let him ride roughshod over her. "You own this hotel. Don't you know it already?"

He laughed, the sound devoid of any pretence. A genuine laugh that nearly warmed her from the inside out. "Remind me, then."

A smile crept up her lips; she couldn't help it. She'd expected him to be practiced, but the truth was everything about him was natural. From the way he wore his clothes to his manners to his easy chuckle. There was nothing fake about Luca Fiori. His charm was innate and genuine.

And therein lay the danger, she realized. In her books, charm equaled trouble. She didn't need trouble. In any form.

"Mari. My first name is Mari."

"Oh, Mari, I believe you've short-changed me."

She picked up a spoon and stirred sugar—a heaping teaspoon of it—into her coffee. "Short-changed you? How?"

"Because I know your name is really Mariella."

Her fingers gripped the spoon. She much preferred Mari now. She'd been Mari ever since moving to Banff three years ago. No more Mariella. Mariella had been scared and obedient and faceless. She hadn't been a person at all.

"I go by Mari. Or you may continue calling me Ms. Ross." She didn't even attempt to keep the cool out of her voice.

Luca split a scone and buttered it. "Mariella is a lovely Italian name. It means *beloved*."

"I know what it means."

Undaunted, he continued. "It was also my grandmother's name."

Mari swallowed a mouthful of coffee too fast and it burned all the way down her throat. His grandmother's name wasn't what was important right now; it didn't even register on her radar. She was Mari, manager of a four-star resort and she'd had to leave a lot of pain behind to get here. *Mariella* reminded her of things she kept trying to forget. How many times had her mother told her about her father's so-called family? The family she'd never known?

A family she never would know. Not now. It was just one of the missing gaps in her childhood.

"Mr. Fiori…" At his raised eyebrow she reluctantly amended, "Luca, I don't mean to sound impolite, but you are here as a representative of Fiori Resorts, here to evaluate your latest acquisition. My first name should be of little importance. Perhaps we should begin the tour now."

Luca took another bite of scone and considered how to answer. The general manager was a prickly sort, but pretty. And he did enjoy a challenge. "And miss out on this superior blend? I think not. We'll get to the rest. In time."

He sipped his coffee thoughtfully, letting his eyes roam over her. Her dark hair was pulled back into a simple, elegant twist, not a hair out of place. She had great legs, but she hid them beneath a conservative navy skirt and completed the look with an equally plain jacket. She gave new meaning to the words "power suit." Even her shoes…*dio mio*. His sister would have had a fit at the sight. Her shoes were plain, unadorned navy pumps. Hardly inspired. All in all she was a package that screamed "stay away."

Until she finally looked into his eyes, and then he knew.

Hers were stunning, nothing at all like the cold, efficient package she presented. They were gray-blue and smoky, soft and sexy, holding a lifetime of secrets.

"Mariella…" He let his voice soften and was gratified to see her turn those eyes on him again. This was more than a challenge. This was unvarnished curiosity, something unusual for him. He was generally happy to skim the surface. On his arm was just about close enough for any woman to get. But there was something in Mari's eyes that drew him in. A mystery begging to be solved.

"Mari," she corrected coolly.

He frowned. Usually that soft tone worked on women. There was more to her than frosty order and sensible shoes, he could sense it. But as her eyes blazed at him, refusing to let him use her full name, he knew that this was one time his charm was going to fail him. With it came the unholy urge to laugh, along with grudging respect.

Who would have thought a trip to Canada would turn out to be so intriguing?

He had the most incredible desire to reach out and rest his fingers on her belligerent cheek. Even sitting on the stool, she was several inches below his face. So petite and feminine, even when she was standing her ground. What would she do if he tried such a thing? Blush? He didn't think so. Some of the women he knew would slap his face in a bout of indignant passion, but he didn't think Mari was the type for that, either.

No, an icy diatribe was more her style and he almost did it just to see what would happen. To see the sparks ignite, and flare.

Something held him back.

That wasn't why he was here. He was away from Italy, away from the constant demands and in a place where he alone could call the shots. He'd let himself be distracted before and it hadn't been pretty. It had cost him. Not quite so much as it had cost his father when his mother had walked out on them, but it had been adequately messy. He'd let Ellie make a fool of him. He'd risked his heart and had lost. No, his initial instinct was right. He would enjoy himself, but not take it any further than that.

He was here to make the Bow Valley Inn into the Fiori Cascade and in order to do that he had to *work* with Mariella Ross.

He stepped back. "Show me the rest, Mariella. And we'll see about taking the Fiori Cascade to a whole new level of opulence."

Luca stared at the papers once more, leaning back against the plush sofa and crossing his ankles on the coffee table. There was nothing really *wrong* with the hotel, not really. It was a nice establishment, comfortable, good service.

But *good* wasn't *Fiori*. His father had taught him that.

The new manager was something else, too. Mariella. Right now it appeared the only thing she shared with his grandmother was her name. She'd let down her guard for a few moments, but she was a woman bound up in rules and boundaries, that much was crystal clear. All through the tour she'd mentioned how profitable or efficient their amenities were. Which was all well and good—he wanted to make a profit. But it wasn't the be all and end all. There was more to the Fiori brand than a balance sheet. It was what set Fiori apart from the rest.

He put the papers down and wandered over to his balcony. He slid open the door, crossing his arms against the chill of mountain fall air. Listening, he caught the whispered rustle of the wind through the gold-coin leaves of the trees below. He hadn't missed the way she kept putting distance between them, either. After that preliminary handshake, it had been like there was an invisible shield around her. The woman was a big contradiction. A sexy woman wrapped up in bubble-wrap. He wondered why.

And he really had to stop thinking about her.

He leaned against the railing, looking out over the white-capped range before him. He liked the gray stone exterior of the hotel, the way it mimicked the slate color of the peaks surrounding them. It reminded him of a small castle, a retreat tucked into the side of a mountain. A fortress.

A knock at the door shook him from his musings and he went back inside to answer it.

Mari had to struggle to keep her mouth from falling open when he opened the door. She completely forgot about the file in her hand or her reason for going to the suite as soon as she saw him. Gone was the suit of earlier. Instead he wore jeans, old ones. The hem was slightly frayed, the thighs faded. And he'd changed into a sweater, a ribbed tan pullover that accentuated his lean build and complemented his dark coloring. He looked completely approachable. Delicious.

This was ridiculous. She was staring at a virtual stranger like he was a piece of the chef's *sachertorte.* Good looks were just that. Good looks. They said nothing about the man, nothing at all. A man could hide behind his good looks. An all too familiar ache spread through her chest.

"Mari. Come in."

He'd acquiesced and used the shortened version of her name. She should have been grateful, but the way he said it, the way the simple syllables rolled off his tongue, sent flutters over her skin.

He reached out and took her hand and the skitters fled, replaced by an automatic reaction. She pulled her hand back, couching it along her side, and took a step away from him.

His brows furrowed in the middle. Of course he wouldn't understand.

Handshakes were a matter of business etiquette and she tolerated it, but that was the extent of the personal contact she could tolerate. Taking her hand probably meant nothing to him. But to her it meant taking a huge personal liberty. She couldn't help her reaction any more than she could change the past. She couldn't stop the fear, even when it was irrational as it was now. It didn't matter how much time went by, it was impossible to stop the instinctive reactions. He'd done nothing to make her believe he'd hurt her, but it didn't matter. The trigger was the same.

"I brought you the financial statements." She covered the uncomfortable moment by holding out the manila folder.

"You're serious?"

It was her turn to be confused, and she gratefully switched her focus to business. "Of course I am. I thought you'd need them."

"Are we in the black?"

"Of course we are!" When he didn't take the file, she lowered her arm again, hiding behind it.

"Then that's all I need to know."

"It is?"

"Please, sit down. Would you like a drink?"

"No, thank you."

She perched on the edge of an armchair like a bird waiting to take flight, while he walked over to the small bar. She noticed he was in his bare feet and for a moment her gaze was drawn to the frayed hem of his jeans, the way it rested against the skin of his heel.

She couldn't let his good looks distract her. She'd bet anything he was aware of his appearance and used it to his advantage all the time. But it wouldn't work with her. She wasn't so naive as that.

He wasn't interested in the numbers? Worry plunged through her stomach. What was he going to do to the hotel? Run it into the ground? Every decision she'd made in the last two and a half years had been carefully thought out, balanced against the pros and cons. What to do, where to live, what to wear and say... And he was treating this whole thing like it was no big deal. More and more he was bearing out her initial judgment. That for him this whole thing was a rich boy's game. But it was her livelihood. It was all she had. She'd built it from nothing. And he'd been given everything—life on a silver platter.

"What are your plans for the Cascade?" She spoke to his back as he poured a glass of red wine, filling a second glass despite her decline.

He returned and handed her the glass, then perched on the arm of the sofa. "I have many plans. I think revamping the hotel is going to be fun."

Fun? Her heart sank further. Great. He was charming, handsome. There was no denying it. In fact he was the first man she'd responded to physically ever since leaving Toronto. Her eyes narrowed. Acknowledging his good looks meant nothing except that she still had eyes to see with. Taking her livelihood in his hands for *fun* didn't sit well.

"Don't you think those sorts of decisions should be examined, weighed?"

"What's the fun in that?" His lips tipped up as he sipped his wine. "Aren't you going to have any? I brought it with me. It's Nico—the vineyards of my best friend, Dante Nicoletti. You'll like it—it's a fine Montepulciano. And it's a staple on all Fiori lists."

She dutifully sipped and looked down as the rich flavor surrounded her tongue. Oh, it was nice. Very nice. But that was hardly the point.

"I take my job seriously, Mr. Fiori. Not something to enjoy on a whim."

"Sometimes whims are the very best things." He smiled disarmingly and she found she actually had to work at not being charmed. Damn him!

She sipped again, sliding further back in the chair and crossing her legs. "I like what I do." Would she have called it fun? Probably not. But it gave her a sense of accomplishment. Working in a hotel in the majesty of the Rockies suited her wallflower qualities to a tee. She could glimpse the fairy tale while still being able to watch from the sidelines. She felt protected, and yet had room to breathe. But fun?

She wasn't sure she knew what fun was.

"But that's not the same thing. Tell me, Mari, what drives you? What makes you get up in the morning?"

The fact that I can.

She pushed the automatic answer away. She didn't have to justify her choices to him. He didn't need to know how she'd had a narrow escape, how it could have turned out so very differently years earlier.

"This isn't about me, it's about what's going to happen to this hotel. Paul Verbeek resigned when you bought the hotel. How much more is going to change? Staff is already upset at the possibility of change and insecurity. If I start handing out pink slips, morale's going to take a serious dip."

"That's the first thing you've said that I agree with."

She bristled. He waltzed in here and after what, four hours? decided she was wrong about just about everything. She knew how to do her job and she did it well, despite being new at it. This was going to be another case of owners sending in an emissary, turning everything upside down, then leaving the mess for local management to clean up. She sighed. Everything had been going fine. Why did this have to happen now?

"I don't know what to say. We obviously have differing opinions yet I have no wish to cause any discord. You're the boss." She folded her hands. One of them had to keep a logical head.

"Describe the Cascade in three words."

She squeezed her left fingers in her right hand. "Are you serious?"

"Perfectly. What are the first three words you think of when you think of this hotel?"

"Efficient. Class. Profitable." She shot the words out confidently. She prided herself—and the hotel—on them. It was the image she tried to portray every day.

He stopped pacing and sighed. "I was afraid of that."

"What's wrong with that? We have an efficient staff, an elegant establishment and we make a profit. You should be happy with all those things."

"Come here." He went to the balcony door again and slid it open. She followed, bringing the wine with her and cradling her glass in her hands. What on earth was he doing now?

"Look out over there."

The afternoon was waning and the sun's rays filtered through trees and shadows. Goose bumps rose on her skin at the chill in the air and she shivered.

"Just a minute," he murmured, disappearing back inside.

When he returned he draped a soft blanket over her shoulders and took the glass out of her hands. She tensed at his casual touch.

"Now look. And tell me, what do you see?"

"The valley, poplar trees, the river."

"No, Mari."

His body was close, too close and she fought against the panic rising instinctively in her chest. *Please don't touch me,* she prayed, torn between fear and an unfamiliar longing that he'd disobey her silent wishes. What would it feel like to have him cradle her body between his arms? Torture, or heaven? The way her heart was pounding, she recognized the sensation for what it was—fear.

As if he sensed her tension, he stepped to the side and gripped the iron railing. He breathed deeply, closed his eyes. When he opened them again he gazed over the vista before them.

"Freedom. Right now, what I'm feeling is freedom." His smile was wide and relaxed. "Look at this place. Look at where we are. There's no place in the world like *this* place. The Cascade can be a jewel in a beautiful kingdom. Wild and free on the outside. And inside…a place to rest, rejuvenate, to fall in love. Can't you feel it seducing you, Mari?"

Tears pricked her eyes but she blinked them away, gripping the edges of the blanket closely around her in a protective embrace.

Freedom. Rest. Rejuvenation. All the things she had spent years searching for, and exactly how she felt about her new life in this tiny resort town.

And with his good intentions, Luca Fiori was about to ruin it all.

CHAPTER TWO

"I DON'T understand."

Mari stepped back from the railing, away from the whispering trees and Luca's warm voice. He was talking castles and falling in love? She'd stopped believing in fairy tales a long time ago. "How exactly do you intend on accomplishing this?"

Before he could answer she scuttled back inside, removed the blanket from her shoulders and kept her hands busy by folding it. Having it around her shoulders had felt too much like an embrace and that didn't sit well. It was becoming increasingly clear that she and Luca were two very different people. She was firmly grounded in reality. Full stop.

He followed her, watching her from the glass door until she put the blanket down and then he stepped forward, giving her back the wine.

"I'm just working on impressions, for now."

"I prefer to work with facts, and so far all I've heard from you are nebulous statements of…of grandeur," she finished, faltering a little. Her heart pounded in her ears as she fought back the feeling that she was crossing an invisible line.

It was beginning to feel like an argument and she forced herself to relax, taking slow breaths and picturing the stress leaving through the soles of her feet. She hated conflict. With a passion. She'd learned to stick up for herself over the last few years but it didn't mean it came easily to her. If it weren't for the rest of the employees looking to her for leadership, she'd be tempted to back away and let him have a go at it rather than argue.

But she was the manager and if she wanted to keep that job, she needed to fight the battles that needed to be fought. People were depending on her. People who had been there for her since she'd made this her home, whether they knew it or not. She steeled her spine and made herself look up again.

"That's the problem with the Cascade," Luca explained. He poured a little more wine in his glass, took a sip and smiled a little. "Everything's been compartmentalized. One room says cool elegance and another is modern and another is rustic comfort…all admirable designs and styles, but without unity."

Unity?

His hand spread wide. "We need to decide what the Cascade is. What it means…what we want to achieve…and then work around that. If we work on one area at a time, it means less disturbance to everyone. The goal is to make everything exemplify Fiori Cascade."

Mari's eyes widened. "That will cost a fortune."

"Fiori has deep pockets."

"Of course…I'm just…weighing the cost versus the benefit. The Bow Val…I mean the Cascade is already doing well. Look at the numbers—we have excellent capacity even for this time of year."

"That's not remotely the point."

And there was where they differed. She realized that they did not see *anything* the same way. Maybe it was having money and security that made the difference. Luca didn't have to worry where his next meal was coming from, or where he'd sleep, or what the future held because his was there waiting for him. It always had been. But her life wasn't that way. It was planning and dollars and cents and making the most out of less, rocking the boat as little as possible. It was staying in the background, out of notice, causing little trouble. And there was nothing wrong with that. It had gotten her where she was. She worked quietly but effectively and she'd been rewarded for it through steady promotion.

"If you implement all these great ideas, when can we expect the memo from head office telling us to downsize our staff?"

"That won't happen."

"Will you guarantee that in writing? Because I've seen it happen, the expenditures are too great to sustain staffing and layoffs occur. Are you planning on closing us down during renovations? What are these people to do then? They count on their pay to put food on the table. Have you considered that?"

A smile flickered on Luca's face and Mari steeled herself against the onslaught of charm she knew was coming. This was important. As much as she wanted to back away and say, "Yes sir, whatever you want sir," she wouldn't.

"Of course I'm not shutting the hotel down, don't be ridiculous. And if any employees aren't required during refurbishing, they'll get paid vacation. Will that suit you?"

"I want it in writing," Mari reiterated, and put down her wineglass. He was the boss, and she was treading perilously close to insubordination. She thought back to the timid girl who had started working here only a few years ago. It was the people in this very hotel that had helped her. She wouldn't let them down now.

"You are a sharp one." His voice held a touch of irritation and she felt the warm thread of slight victory infuse her. She'd gotten to him, then. His implacable charm was faltering and it emboldened her.

"I'm no one's yes-man."

"I'm beginning to see that." His gaze appraised her and she felt a flush climb her cheeks. It felt as though the air in her chest expanded. No, no, no. She had to keep focused on work!

"Perhaps tomorrow we might schedule a meeting to go over the preliminary details."

"I have a better idea."

Mari met his eyes yet again, and for a moment the air seemed to hum between them. The annoyance of moments ago was dispelled as he slid one hand into his jeans pocket. His eyes were warm, crinkled at the corners as he smiled at her.

"Have dinner with me tonight."

She took two steps back as sure footing flew out the window. Alarm bells started ringing in her head. "Absolutely not."

"Here, in the hotel. It'll be a business supper. What is it you say…scout's honor? Strictly work." He lifted a finger to his forehead.

"It's two fingers, and dinner is hardly a business meeting."

Luca stepped forward, putting his glass down on a side table with a small click that echoed in the silence.

He was too close again. Part of her held the thread of panic and the other part was drawn to him, plain and simple, which meant that nothing was simple at *all*. It was much easier when they were disagreeing. Easier to keep him at a distance. She wasn't equipped to deal with his charm. He didn't even seem to know he possessed it.

"Bring your day planner if that makes you happy." Happy? Huh. He was flirting, and she didn't flirt. Ever!

"I think my office tomorrow would be much better."

"Yes, but you see I need to get a complete picture, and that includes the quality of the dining experience. And eating alone does not constitute a fine dining experience, in my opinion."

Oh, he was good. Smooth and persuasive and actually logical! She couldn't find a good argument. How could she tell him why she didn't go out to dinner with anyone? How she went home each night and made a meal for one and ate it with Tommy, her dog? Flimsy at best. And the real reason was none of his business. Not his, not anyone's. No one here knew how she'd run away. How she still looked over her shoulder.

"A working dinner."

"Of course."

There was no polite way out of it. He was here, all the way from Italy, he was her boss and he was calling the shots. Like it or not. She'd pushed him as far as she'd dared just now and her victory was thin. If they were to work together for the next several weeks, months even…her heart quivered at the thought… then somehow they needed to reach an amicable status quo. She swallowed. He had to know she was not afraid. He had to know she put the hotel and its employees first.

"One dinner, that's all. And we discuss work."

"Naturally."

Mari took a few sidesteps, thankful the door was within reach. "I'll meet you in the Panorama Room at six."

"Perfect."

When he walked toward her she pulled open the door, a little too quickly to be poised. His hand gripped the door frame above her shoulder and she felt the heat from his body. Too close. She wasn't sure if the tripping of her pulse was fear or exhilaration. She slid out the opening as fast as she possibly could, clinging to whatever grace she could muster.

"I'll see you then," Luca said softly.

She fled for the elevator without looking back.

It was 5:57 when Mari stopped before the entrance of the dining room and smoothed her dress.

She paused in the door, scanning the room, but he wasn't there. Relief warred with annoyance. She didn't have to worry about making an entrance this way, but at least he could be on time. She wanted to get this over with. It was irritating to have her initial impressions of him confirmed so accurately. Luca was unfocused, cavalier about the whole thing. He was every bit the playboy she'd read about. Sexy and smooth. Working together was going to drive her crazy.

She was shown to the best table in the room. She took her seat with surprise, looked outside at the mountains and trees being thrown into shadow by twilight. She hadn't asked for this particular table; it was one usually reserved for guests requesting something "special." It would be very wrong of them to monopolize the table when there was likely a paying guest waiting for it.

She sipped her drink and waited. By ten past six her toes had joined her nails, tapping with impatience. Only to stop abruptly when he stepped in the room.

God, he was beautiful. She could admit it when he was a room away from her and they weren't embroiled in business. He was safe there. Safe and devastatingly sexy in black trousers and a white shirt. She shook her head, sighing. It was one of those tailored shirts that was meant to be untucked, emphasizing his narrow waist and moving up to broad shoulders. One hand slid casually into his pocket in a gesture she somehow already knew intimately. He said something to the hostess at the front, and the two of them laughed.

Luca Fiori was every woman's dream. Everyone's but hers. Dreams like that simply didn't last. But it didn't mean she couldn't appreciate the package. It *was* a lovely package. And for a very quick moment, she wished. Wishing wasn't a luxury she afforded herself. But looking at Luca, with his bronzed skin and easy smile, she wished she knew how to be that free. To be able to accept, and to give.

He approached the table with an easy stride. "I'm sorry I'm late. I got caught up in e-mails my father sent and lost track of time."

She pursed her lips, determined not to let him off easily, but he leaned over and pressed an informal kiss of greeting to her cheek.

She froze.

Seemingly unaware of her reaction, Luca took the chair across from her. "You look beautiful. Have you ordered?"

Beautiful? Her? She'd gone home to change and feed Tommy and then he'd drooled over the front of her outfit, causing a wardrobe change. Gone was the tailored charcoal trouser suit she'd picked and in its place was her generic little black dress—simply cut, black velvet with long fitted sleeves and with a hem ending just above the knee.

It wasn't as businesslike as she'd have preferred, but it worked and while classy there wasn't much sexy about it. It seemed compliments rolled off his tongue as easily as assurances.

"Thank you, and no, I was enjoying a drink and the music." Mari struggled to make her voice sound less strangled than she felt.

A recent jazz CD played over the speakers. She hadn't paid it a whit of attention but needed to cover. It was becoming clear that Luca was a toucher. He was comfortable with easy, physical gestures like polite kisses and hand clasps. It should help, knowing they were impersonal, but Mari knew she could never be that tactile with people. It was simply too difficult. Yet to explain was unthinkable. She'd just have to muddle through.

"I ordered us some wine on the way in. I'm looking forward to tasting something more local."

Brenda came back with a bottle and moved to uncork it, but Luca took it from her hands. "Thank you, Brenda, but I can do this."

Mari looked at him, tilting her head as he applied the corkscrew to the bottle. He was new, and likely jet-lagged, but he'd remembered Brenda's name. She couldn't help but be impressed. It showed an attention to detail that surprised her, and people didn't often surprise her.

He pulled out the cork with a minimum of fuss and put the bottle down briefly. "You haven't said anything."

"I'm waiting to get to the business portion of the meal."

She set her lips and looked him dead in the eye. A deal was a deal. As long as he kept it about the Cascade they'd have no problems.

He chuckled as he poured wine into two glasses. "Single-minded. I like that. It means you're focused, driven."

"A compliment."

"Perhaps. I'm reserving judgment. Waiting to see if you're also rigid, stubborn and always need to be right."

Mari grabbed her tonic water as her face flamed. Of all the nerve!

"I don't apologize for being organized or efficient."

"Nor should you. They're admirable qualities."

Mari looked out the window and away from him. She'd never met a man like him. She couldn't quite pin him down and that threw her off balance. Normally she could typecast a person within moments of meeting. She put them in a file in her mind and dealt with them accordingly.

But not Luca. There was something different about him that she couldn't put her finger on. He was very urban with his carefully messed hair, the way he left his collar open so that Mari was treated to a tempting glimpse of the tanned hollow of his throat. As he lifted his glass she spied a ring on his right hand...plain, not ostentatious at all. It almost looked antique. In the centre of the flat gold oval was the imprint of a lily. The same imprint that she recognized from the company logo. It was the only jewelry he wore. His entire demeanor suggested playboy, but there was something more.

"Let's order," he suggested, his voice drawing her eyes away from the ring. "We'll talk about the food and brainstorm about what the Cascade will become."

He flipped open his menu, skimmed it and shut it again.

"Just like that?"

"Absolutely."

Mari looked down at her own menu, though she could recite it without seeing the words. Everything about him threw her off her stride. Just when she credited him with not making decisions, he surprised her by being annoyingly definitive.

"We should switch tables. There's usually a wait for this one and our guests do come first."

Luca regarded her over his glass. "No need. I took care of it."

"And how, may I ask, did you do that?"

His smile was disarming. She noticed again the sensual curve of his lips and wondered what cruel joke the universe was playing, sending such a man for her to deal with. She was completely out of her depth and drowning fast.

"I called the room, spoke to a lovely gentleman who is here celebrating his twentieth anniversary with his wife. I explained who I was and said that the hotel would be happy to treat him—and his wife—to a five-course meal in their room, along with a bottle of champagne."

Mari's lips dropped open before she could help it. Mentally she added up the cost of such a thing. It was selfish. Indulgent. All so he could have the best table.

"It would have been easier, and cheaper, for us to simply eat at a different table."

Luca ran a finger down the leather spine of the menu, a smile playing on his lips. "Perhaps. But they get an anniversary to remember and I get to enjoy the sight of you at the best table in the house. It is…how do you put it? A no-brainer."

She ignored the compliment. "It's self-indulgent."

"Of course. Shouldn't the Cascade be about indulgence?"

She lowered her voice to a whisper that hissed across the table. "You're going to indulge us right out of business!"

A waiter came to take their order. Without missing a beat, Luca ordered the Harvest Squash Soup and Pancetta Salmon, while she scanned the menu once more. In the heat of the discussion, she'd forgotten what she wanted, and the gap of silence was awkward.

"The pasta, Ms. Ross?" the waiter suggested. She closed the leather cover and nodded. When the menus were taken away, Luca leaned forward, close enough she could smell the light, masculine scent of his cologne. Exclusive, expensive and somehow perfectly Luca. Her pupils widened as he took the finger that had caressed the menu and ran it lightly over her wrist. The action surprised her so much she couldn't even think to pull away.

"Mr. and Mrs. Townsend will have an incomparable anniversary night. Mr. Townsend is a prominent attorney, did you know that? His wife is involved in several charities. What do you think they'll say to their friends when they return home? That the room was lovely? That the mountains were splendid? That could be said of nearly every hotel in this area." He withdrew his finger from the delicate skin of her wrist and looked in her eyes. "They will remark at how special they felt. The delightful meal served in their room by attentive staff. The complimentary champagne and the single red rose presented to Mrs. Townsend."

He sat back, satisfied. "Don't underestimate the power of

a happy customer, Mari. We'll more than earn back what dinner cost. The Townsends will come back. And they'll likely bring a trail of friends and associates with them. They'll remember the romance."

His eyebrows lifted as it dawned. "That's it. That's what the Cascade needs to become. Get out your day planner, Mari."

He changed tack so often she was having difficulty following. "What on earth are you talking about?"

"The Fiori Cascade. Remember the Romance." He clapped his hands together then reached for his wine. "This room—the Panorama. It's romantic, don't you think?" He didn't wait for her answer. "Look at the color, the furnishings. Timeless, nostalgic, reminiscent of a golden age. Gleaming wood, rich scarlet and gold. A place where women feel beautiful and wooed. A place to slow down, be indulged, pampered. Chandeliers and fine wine and…"

He paused.

"You're not saying anything."

"I can't get a word in edgewise." Mari left her planner right where it was. By tomorrow his ideas could have changed a half dozen times, for all she knew.

"You don't like it? You don't agree?"

"I think you're getting carried away with an idea."

"Oh, but, Mari ideas are the best part." He reached out and clasped her hand. "There is nothing more exciting than looking and seeing all the possibilities."

She pulled her hand away, cradling it in her lap. Luca carried on as if he hadn't noticed her abrupt withdrawal. "Taking a vision and making it reality is the best part of my job."

Their first course was served. Mari watched as Luca tried the soup, closed his eyes and murmured, "Mmm."

She stared at the full curve of his lips, shocked to feel the stirrings of attraction in the midst of such animosity. Instantly those stirrings were followed by numbing fear. It wouldn't matter. She wasn't capable of relationships. She was done with trusting and taking risks. That she'd suddenly gone from physical appreciation to attraction startled her sufficiently to keep her on task. She stabbed at her greens like she was wielding a pitchfork.

He looked around and Mari tried to see what he was seeing. People enjoying fine food in an elegant setting. It's what they paid for, what they expected. How would the rest of the hotel look, if it followed in the tradition of this room?

"What are you thinking?" He put down his spoon and she felt his eyes on her.

"Just wondering." The trouble was, she *could* see it. Could see how stunning, marvelous it would be. Like stepping back in time.

"Trust me, Mari."

She dropped her eyes and focused on spearing a large chunk of walnut from her salad. "I can't."

"Don't you feel the beauty here? This room...this is what the Cascade should embody. It's warm, it's cozy, yet it's rich and opulent at the same time. From the outside it's a castle. On the inside...it needs to be an embrace. When guests are here they need to be soaked in beauty."

"Please." That one word was ripe with disdain. She could not be wooed by pretty words, and he'd been doling out more than his share. Pretty words did not keep a four-star hotel profitable. Pretty words did not...would not keep her in line.

"You're worried about the money. And details."

"Bingo."

Luca picked up his spoon again, ate some soup. "I'll tell you what, Mari. I'll start making some notes. I'll even put some preliminary figures together...just for you."

"You're too kind." She didn't attempt to disguise the sarcasm. It was becoming increasingly clear that Luca was full of grand schemes and she was going to have her hands full keeping him out of the clouds and on the ground.

"Mari?"

She raised her eyebrows.

"Why are you so determined to dislike me?"

She looked away from the steady gaze. There was nothing condemning in it, just a curiosity that burned through her.

It wasn't that she didn't want to like him or dislike him. It was more a matter of self-preservation. She didn't like change, didn't work well with change. And it was everything Luca represented. She'd worked so hard to get where she was, to feel comfortable and established and…safe. And he waltzed in, in his expensive clothes and sexy smile and wanted to change everything. And with a method that made no sense to her. All of a sudden *safe* wasn't a sure thing.

"It's not about liking or disliking, Luca. It's about the changes. You're changing more than the name. You're changing things that some of us have worked very hard to maintain. I've put a lot of time and energy into this hotel and perhaps I feel like that's being swept away without a moment's consideration. Meanwhile all of us here will remain long after you're gone. When you're done, you can wash your hands of it. We're left to deal with what comes after." He'd blow through like a whirlwind, and what destruction would be left in his wake?

Luca leaned forward, linking his hands on the white cloth on the table. "I understand that, really I do. But this is where you have to trust me. This is what I do, Mari. This is what my family has done for decades. I know my job and I'm good at it. If I weren't, Fiori wouldn't be nearly as successful as it is.

I'm not going to throw you…or the staff…out along with the old carpet. I promise."

And oh, she wanted to believe him. Desperately. But trust was a very rare commodity.

"You also need to consider how this will affect us financially. The reality of it. It cannot be ignored." *I can't be ignored,* she thought, but swallowed it away. This wasn't about her, not really.

"Reality is overrated. What we're selling is an experience, an escape, a fantasy."

He leaned over so that the enticing scent of his cologne tickled her nose once more. His toffee-eyes captured hers. "When was the last time you indulged in a fantasy, Mari?"

CHAPTER THREE

MARI stopped, smoothed her skirt first and then her hair, before knocking on the door that used to be to her office before she became general manager.

"Come in."

It was odd, finding her new boss sitting in her old chair, but she pushed the feeling aside. He needed a working area and she was now in the general manager's office. It didn't make sense to feel he was taking over her space. She was the one with the big office now.

She'd had to push a lot of feelings aside this morning, like the lingering fear that flickered in her belly when she remembered her dream of last night. There was no sense worrying about the fact that the dream was back. She would just chalk it up to the chocolate she'd indulged in last night at dessert. That, paired to the chaos that was rapidly becoming her life, explained it away. Even if she couldn't quite shake the darkness of it from her system. Considering the letter she'd received two days ago, it wasn't surprising. She hated the thought of Robert being up for parole. Hated the way the mere mention of his name paralyzed her. Focusing on work was the only thing keeping her sane. And Luca wasn't making it any easier. He'd featured in her dream as well. But she had to shake it and be objective.

This was about today, about figuring out what it was Luca planned to do and exerting some of her own caution over the procedure. He would do whatever he wanted. She'd realized that after their dinner last night. But she was no pushover. Not anymore. She would keep things logical, reasonable. Within boundaries. In *all* ways.

"Mari! Good morning." He gave a click of the mouse before pushing back his chair. "I was just sending an e-mail to my sister in Florence. Sharing my ideas and getting her input. She's got a fantastic eye."

"Then why didn't *she* come?" The question was out before Mari could think and her cheeks bloomed at her rudeness.

"Because she has a three-year-old and a baby to look after. I'm hoping she'll make it out next summer, when the refurbishing is complete and the landscaping done. As it is, she's nagging me to be back home for Christmas."

"You think we'll be done that soon?"

"Shoulder season is the best time to renovate. I can always come back after the holiday and finish things off."

Mari stood awkwardly in the doorway, unsure of how to proceed. Her blazer pocket contained half a dozen messages she should answer and she knew there were matters that needed her attention on her desk. So why didn't she get to it?

"Did you need something in particular?" Luca posed the question, raising his eyebrows and Mari felt even more awkward.

"No, not really. I'll just, um, go to my office, and if you need me for anything you can find me there."

"I'm waiting for a call from a designer. He did some work for us when we bought the Colorado Springs property and with the similarity in settings, I thought bringing him up here would be a good idea. I know what I want, but I'm at a loss when it comes to deciding fabrics and tapestries and…well, it's Dean's job to take my vision and put it all together."

Her mouth went dry. Nine o'clock in the morning and he was already moving forward without even discussing things with her. Was this all going to happen without her, then? "And what's my job in all this?"

For a moment she was afraid he was going to get up and her fingers felt for the handle of the door. Briefly she remembered the touch of his finger on her wrist last night. But he merely crossed an ankle over his knee and smiled up at her. "Your job is to keep the hotel running as seamlessly as possible for our guests and staff. I can already see you're good at it. And your job is also to help me. I do want your input, Mari."

When the phone on his desk rang, his attention slid away from her completely, and she felt like a child dismissed from the principal's office. Damn, she'd come in here hoping to get some insight into his plans, figure out a way to retain at least some control over the whole business. And she was leaving with nothing.

Mari made her way to the manager's office in a daze. It was clear she wasn't needed when it came to whatever changes were impending. As far as Luca was concerned, she was there to keep people happy.

She shut her office door firmly and threw her purse on her chair. She hadn't worked this hard to build up her life to have someone dismiss it like it didn't matter. Her years of being a doormat were over. She thought of the court proceedings happening this very moment and lifted her chin. She smoothed her hands over her cheeks, trying to soothe away the nagging feeling of inadequacy. She wouldn't let him do this to her. This was *her* life now, and she would hold on to it with both hands.

He was bringing in a designer, of course he was. That was logical. But it was all happening so quickly. She wanted everything back the way it was.

Luca would consult with this designer and she'd be out of the decision-making process. She couldn't let that happen. If she did he'd start making unilateral decisions that affected everyone. He'd have all the control and the thought terrified her.

But how could she hold her ground, when the very thought of asserting herself into the situation made her stomach tremble and her knees watery?

She had to come up with something that showed her value. When the idea hit she was shocked she hadn't thought of it before. The hotel had an attic. And with every renovation, she knew certain things had been placed there for storage. She was sure there was a trove of antiques from the original design up there. She remembered what he'd said last night about returning to a "golden age." Rich fabrics and natural wood. If she remembered correctly, there was an old chandelier, and who knew what other treasures she'd find?

She jumped up from her chair, ignoring the open file on her desk and grabbing instead a ring of keys from the back of her desk drawer. She was just turning into the hall when she ran smack-dab into the solid wall of his chest.

"*Allentare!*" He gripped her arms to steady her and she stiffened beneath his fingers. "Mari, slow down! Are you all right?"

"Let me go. I'm fine." She shook off his hands and straightened her shoulders.

The woman was as prickly as a cactus. Luca stood back, nonplussed. She'd nearly knocked him over and now stood glaring at him like it was his fault that she'd come storming out of her office, not looking where she was going.

"I am glad to hear it."

Her face softened just a bit. "I beg your pardon, it was my fault."

"It doesn't matter. I was just coming to see you."

He watched as she slowly relaxed. First a deep breath, then her shoulders lowered and the taut lines of her face disappeared. She was wound as tight as a top. She had been last night, too. Her cheek had been cold when he'd kissed it in greeting and the tiny touch on her wrist seemed to turn her to stone. The woman needed to deflate before she imploded.

She placed a polite smile on her lips, one he knew was put there for show and not genuine. It was a cover. But what was she covering? He'd never met a woman so uptight and rigid. He had a feeling if he said black, she'd say white just to be contrary. In that way, he thought ruefully, she wasn't that different from his father. He held back the sigh gathering in his lungs. The Cascade was his baby. He'd demanded full authority over everything. And when it was over he'd be able to take the credit and finally step out within the company in his own right. He loved his father, he did. It didn't mean he wanted to work under his thumb for the rest of his life. It was the one thing that kept things tense between them.

"Did you need something?"

At the sound of her voice he dragged his gaze from her lips. "Need? I heard back from the designer, Dean Shiffling." He couldn't keep the annoyance out of his voice. "He can't make it until day after tomorrow. I told him we'd send a car to meet him at the airport."

They'd taken half a dozen steps down the hall but she halted abruptly. "Luca, we don't have a car. We have a shuttle van."

"Fiori does not herd guests into a, what did you call it? A shuttle van." He muttered something under his breath. There was much to be said for the old Inn, but things needed to change to bring it up to Fiori standards. "I shall look after getting us proper transportation."

He started walking again, knowing she'd have no choice but to follow after him. Already he could see the adding machine whirring in her head, working sums. A smile played with the corners of his lips. Perhaps it was wrong, but he had to admit he enjoyed putting her off balance. It had been too long since he'd had a worthy opponent to butt heads with and he got the feeling that Mari would be up to the challenge. It was worth it to see that firelight in her gray-blue eyes and her color rise. So much better than her icy withdrawal.

They stepped into the lobby area. "What did you want to see me about?" he asked, surveying the lobby. He looked at the floor. They'd get rid of some of those fussy carpets, polish the stone beneath. And the lighting was wrong. This lobby was comfortable but cluttered. It needed space, and light amongst the richness. Let them play off each other.

"I didn't. You ran into me, remember?"

"Ah, yes. A happy accident indeed." He let his eyes twinkle at her. "And you were in a spectacular rush."

"I thought of something this morning that may come in handy during your redecorating."

"Yes?" She had his attention.

"And you're noticeably agitated that your designer isn't at your beck and call within the hour."

His eyebrow raised at that. She was going to keep him on his toes. She was correct. He'd wanted to get started right away and he was being forced to wait.

"Perhaps."

"And people always do what you tell them."

"Usually, yes. With a notable exception." He aimed a pointed glare at her.

She held up a key.

She was playing with him now and it amused him as much as annoyed him. She'd never once in their meetings shown a fun side. "I'm assuming that is to a door. A door you're going to tell me about."

The faintest of smiles cracked her face. She looked very different when she put away that cold façade. Her eyes lightened and she seemed almost like a precocious child. Like there was more to her than fusty suits that covered as much skin as possible and prim hairstyles. He stared at the utilitarian twist and wondered what it would look like if she let it down. If it would be soft and pliant. Like her skin. He remembered the feel of the nearly translucent skin just beneath her palm. Would the rest of her be as fragile and soft?

Now that wouldn't be wise at all. Even if a man couldn't help but wonder.

"I was going to check it out first, but I suppose you want to come along. It's to the attic."

"You've an attic?"

Her smile grew as she nodded. "We do. And if we find what I think is there, you're going to be happy I thought of it. Then you can stop obsessing about getting your designer in and focus on something else."

He ignored the barb, too excited by the idea of a treasure hunt. "Then lead on, by all means."

They took the service elevator to the top floor. Stepping out into a windowless corridor, Mari stepped to the right toward a large double door. "This is our storage area. I remembered it this morning. Something you said last night twigged with me, about a golden age." She turned the key in the lock and pushed the door open.

Inside was like finding buried treasure. A film of dust covered everything: chairs, tables, desks, divans, even paintings and sculptures. A room full of potential, waiting to be rediscovered. The hotel must have been a glory in its early days, Luca thought, before someone came along and decided to change it. His eyes lit on a particularly fine tallboy. Whoever had relegated it to the attic should have been whipped. It was too fine, too valuable, to be hidden away in an airless, forgotten room.

"Dear God." Luca stepped inside. There was little order to it, but he knew already she'd uncovered a gold mine. Excitement drummed in his veins. He wasn't changing the hotel at all. He was restoring it. The idea thrilled him. He enjoyed the creating part of his job so much more than the management. It was a large reason why he wanted to step out of his father's shadow. "Why are these things not displayed?"

"I can only assume that renovations over the years have relegated them to the bench."

"The bench?"

"You know, when sports players aren't on the field. They're benched."

"Right." He stepped around an old rolltop desk, a layer of dust hiding what he knew would be a gleaming walnut finish. "Feel it, Mari. There's history in this room. So much history." If only Dean could be here sooner. They'd take an inventory and choose which pieces would be used in the decoration. Luca wanted to start right now.

But perhaps now was the time to explore.

He looked over at Mari. Prickly as thorns, but he could tell she was enjoying this. It was in the way her eyes lit up, or her fingers daintily touched the back of a tufted chair. She was picking her way to the far right, stepping gingerly and careful not to disturb the dust. She was a careful one, he was coming to understand. Always a deliberate move. Always a purpose. He wondered why. What had made her so cautious, when it was clear that inside she had vision fighting to get out?

"Here it is."

He gave a plush wine velvet divan a longing look as he passed by, making his way to her. Only to find her standing beside a huge gilt and crystal chandelier that had been hidden by two armoires.

"It's seen better days. But I thought I remembered it here."

Luca reached out and touched a large teardrop shaped crystal, sending it tinkling against identical drops. "It's stunning. It's perfect."

"It *is* lovely."

Luca looked up at her. Ah, so the chandelier's magic wasn't all lost on her. The wistful turn of her lips told him so. A tendril of hair had come loose from her ever-present bun and kissed her cheek. She looked up at him and their eyes met, held. He could already picture the chandelier gracing the ballroom, the shots of light glancing off the crystals on to the gleaming floor and polished wood. Could picture Mari in the middle of it, slim and elegant in a golden evening dress, smiling at him. She was, he realized, cool class and grace. Timeless. His ingénue.

"You love it, too. I can see it on your face."

Something changed at his words, breaking the spell. Her eyes cooled and she straightened her shoulders, looking away. "It makes perfect sense to use these things if they fit in with your renovations. Much cheaper than purchasing new."

"Oh, it's not about the money, don't pretend otherwise. Look at this place." He turned, laughing to himself to shake away the intensity he'd felt in the moment. At least she was consistent, protesting about the bottom line. But he'd seen the look of longing in her eyes and he'd wanted her to look at him that way. Every moment she intrigued him more, but he was also increasingly aware that she wasn't the kind of woman a man trifled with. He forced himself back to the task. "Each of these pieces has a story, can't you feel it?"

He took a few steps and stopped in front of a gilded mirror. He swiped a hand over the glass, clearing a stripe of dust away. "Oh, Mari, such beautiful pieces. Neglected for so long, forgotten. Just waiting for someone to discover them and make them new again. To make them shine."

When she said nothing, he looked back. She was trapped with the armoires on one side, the chandelier on the other and he was blocking her path back to the door. She was standing so very still, as if he'd struck her, and he didn't know why. He got the sense that she was crying, but that was ridiculous because her eyes were bone-dry in her pale face. For some odd reason he wanted to erase the distance between them and take her in his arms. As soon as he thought it, he mentally stepped backward.

Enjoying playing cat and mouse was one thing. Having fanciful thoughts was well and good. Acting on it was another. And this situation was already complicated enough without him adding to it by getting involved with the hotel manager. It wouldn't be suitable. It would be messy. And he didn't do messy relationships. He didn't do *any* relationships at all, beyond the no-strings-attached ones. He'd determined long ago not to let his heart get involved with a woman. He never wanted to give a woman the power to destroy him the way his mother had his father. The way Ellie had nearly destroyed him.

"Please excuse me, I need to get back. If you'll lock the door when you leave…"

She took halting steps toward him, cueing him to move out of the way. But he couldn't, not hearing that cold, dry tone in her voice. He didn't know what he'd said to cause such a re-action but he knew for certain that she was not all right and that superceded his own concerns.

She stopped a few feet from him. "Please, excuse me," she repeated, her eyes gray against her washed-out pallor.

He started to step aside so she could pass, but at the last moment he couldn't let her go without checking she was okay. He moved forward, reached out, clasped her elbow.

"Get your hands off me."

She said it quietly, calmly, but the underlying venom in it shocked him so much that he stepped back, immediately releasing her elbow. He hadn't thought it possible but she paled even further.

"Don't ever touch me again," she said stridently, as she quickly picked a path around the scattered forgotten furniture. She scrambled out the door, leaving it open. Seconds later he heard the elevator pause, open and close again.

He sat down on the nearest chair, releasing a puff of dust. He'd only been trying to be a gentleman when she was clearly in distress. It was obvious that whatever attraction he'd felt earlier was not reciprocated. She was cold, irritating, dictatorial. Nothing but a complication. He should fire her and get on with turning the Fiori Cascade into the hotel it was meant to be.

But he couldn't do that. She was good at what she did, he could tell. He'd promised her no one would lose their jobs. That had included her.

And Luca Fiori was a man of his word.

When he went back to the administration offices, her door was closed. He knocked, then opened it.

It was like the scene upstairs had never happened. Her suit was straight, brushed of any dust. Her color was back, enhanced by fresh lipstick and her hair was tidied, even more severely pinned in place, if that were possible.

The sting of the insult had worn away and he'd been left with the very empty knowledge that for some unknown reason, Mari was afraid of him.

"I wanted to make sure you were all right."

She looked up from what she was writing and pasted on what he was rapidly coming to understand was her face-the-public smile. "I'm fine, thank you. A little behind after our tour, though." She looked back down at her paper and began writing again.

He wrinkled his brow. The woman before him was cool,

assured, in control. A direct contrast to the woman who'd nearly come unglued the moment he'd put a hand on her elbow. A woman practiced at hiding her feelings, who happened to have slipped and let him witness a weak moment.

He should nod and walk away. It was none of his business. But then he remembered the stark look of nakedness he'd seen on her face when he'd spoken of the antiques. She'd looked like a woman who'd been stripped bare. He couldn't ignore that, even if he wanted to. If he let this go now, it would stand between them the entire time they worked together. It would be far better to get it out in the open. Move on.

"Do you want to talk about it, Mari?"

With a sigh she put down the pen, placed her hands flat on her desk and crossed her legs. "Talk about what, Luca?"

"About what happened in the attic."

She looked away. "No, I don't."

"You were frightened. I want to know why."

"I was not frightened. I happen to be…claustrophobic."

It was paltry and he saw through it. But he could not make her talk and he hardly knew her well enough to pry. Still…

"I did not realize that when I reached for your arm."

Her hands remained flat on the blotter and she met his eyes coolly. "Luca, I am a person who does not like her personal space invaded. I'm not a touchy person. That's all. I'm sorry if that is blunt, or rude."

"It is honest, and I appreciate it. So it is not just me you don't want to touch you, it is everyone."

Her cheeks flamed. "That's correct."

"It's nothing personal."

She swallowed, and his gaze was drawn to the curve of her throat. Damn, it sure felt personal right now.

"Nothing personal," she echoed weakly.

"I'm glad, because we will be working together closely and it will be difficult if there is animosity between us."

Animosity?

Mari swallowed and forced the cool, neutral expression to remain on her face. He had no idea about what had happened in the attic. How his words touched her, mirrored so many of her own emotions. How she'd suddenly felt strangled and had to get out.

He'd touched her.

She hated being touched. And when he'd gripped her elbow, something had shot through her that terrified her.

But it wasn't memory. It was longing. Something she hadn't felt for so long the very presence of it undid her. She *liked* the feel of his hand on her elbow, connecting them. Liked it so much she'd wanted to slide forward into his arms and let them surround her. Protect her.

She'd vowed no man would touch her ever again, and until now she'd never wanted one to. Oh, nothing made sense! She'd had to escape, pull herself together.

She risked a look up. He was watching her steadily and she knew there was something *very* personal between them, like it or not. Something she refused to acknowledge further than she already had. She wasn't equipped for more than accepting there was a small level of attraction. Anything more would be pointless.

"I assure you, it has nothing to do with you." And the bottom line was, it didn't. It had to do with her and with Robert and that was all.

"Then I won't take it personally. I merely wanted to be sure you were all right."

"I am, and thank you for asking."

When she smiled this time it was without the frosty veneer.

He had accepted what she'd said with politeness and grace. She was touched that someone cared enough to be concerned about her. No one worried about her, because she'd reinvented her life that way. But without even knowing her, Luca seemed to care. It was unexpected, and though she suspected he'd hate the thought, it was sweet.

He stepped forward and laid the key on her desk. "I thought you might want this back."

She left it where he'd placed it and he stepped away.

He was nearly to the door when he turned back. "Oh, and Mari, I'd like for you to sit in on the meeting with Dean once I've given him the tour and my initial ideas. We'll work up a preliminary budget and tentative schedule, get the ball rolling so to speak, and that's your forte. I also would like us to send out a joint memo before then to all the staff. Something to say that over the next months there will be changes and adjustments, but that no one will lose their position. That every effort will be made to make this as seamless as possible for both staff and guests. I keep my promises, Mari. I hope you remember that."

He was keeping his word. It pleased her that he remembered. When she least expected it, he showed consideration to those around him. Perhaps he was more than she'd initially suspected. Perhaps the playboy from the glossy magazines had a little more substance than she'd given him credit for.

"I'll draft one up today and e-mail it to you."

"Thank you, Mari."

She got up from her desk finally, knowing that she owed him something, even if she didn't know what. She picked up the key and held it out. When he reached with his hand, she pressed the key into his palm.

"Keep it. I have another somewhere."

His fingers closed over hers slightly as he cupped the key

in his hand. She tried very hard to ignore the tingles shivering up her arm at the warmth of his fingers.

"You're sure?"

Mari remembered his face as he'd walked into the attic. She'd put up walls because she'd resented the easy joy he'd had, seeing the dusty antiques. She didn't let herself feel things like that anymore. It would be petty to deprive him of it. It was his hotel, and he was keeping his end of the bargain.

"I'm sure, Luca. And when Mr. Shiffling arrives, we'll meet and discuss how best to approach the changes to come."

"Then I'll hear from you later today."

He pulled his hand from hers and pocketed the key. He walked back to his office, and moments later she heard the door click. But she stood in the middle of her own, wondering how on earth she was going to handle the roller coaster that was rapidly becoming her life.

Luca Fiori got to her. In every way.

CHAPTER FOUR

"I THOUGHT we were storing the furniture in the Green Conference room, and the rest in the storage area off the south corridor."

Mari looked up, knowing she looked harried because she was. Yesterday she'd received another letter. She'd hardly slept last night thinking about what it said. Hating how the past still had this hold over her.

Now, this was the second time Luca had interfered with clearing out the lounge. He stood beside her, not a bead of sweat or hair out of place or a wrinkle in his trousers or his chocolate-brown shirt, calmly issuing edicts.

"You said the *other* conference room. The Mount Baker." She knew it was hard for Luca to remember, but all the rooms were named after peaks in the Rockies and she was determined to use the proper names, not identify them by color.

"The Mount Baker is being used for meetings."

"When did that happen?"

"When I scheduled them."

She took deep breaths to hold on to her temper. Everything was in flux and it was starting to get to her. Now he was changing his mind and she was just supposed to go with it.

"You scheduled them? Why not use another room?"

"Because the company I hired to renovate our spa wanted a room where they could use a projector."

Her head spun. A spa? They'd have to discuss that one, but not now. Now she had a dozen employees moving furniture and putting it in the wrong place.

"Luca, do you think you could get out of my hair long enough to let me do my job?"

"Certainly. I have calls to make."

Cool as a cucumber. Mari scowled after him. Luca was infuriating. Nothing seemed to faze him, and she could hardly keep her balance.

She put her hands on her hips and took a moment to redirect the staff—again—that was emptying the Athabasca Lounge of furniture. Once they were back on track, she sighed and pushed her hair out of her face. Her twist had long since been in tatters and she'd resorted to anchoring it with an elastic, except pieces kept escaping and getting in her way.

The more she knew of Luca, the more she didn't quite know what to make of him. Her playboy image of him had been reshaped and a new version in its place. Oh, the charm was still very present, hard as she tried to ignore it. But she was coming to discover that he was used to getting his own way. Only a week after his arrival and already things were changing, shifting, strange workmen appeared from out of nowhere, and she was signing for deliveries. He'd definitely taken charge. She certainly couldn't say he was lackadaisical about the job. He seemed completely committed to the Cascade.

And he'd definitely taken to ordering *her* around. This morning was just another in a long line of commands he'd issued. She caught sight of him now, talking to a man in dark green trousers and a lighter green shirt. A laborer of some sort by his uniform. Luca's arms spread wide and his eyes danced as he spoke to the man.

She had to admit things were never dull anymore. Every day there was a new discovery to be made. Adjustments to be made. The lack of routine threw her off her stride. And when he went at something, he did it all the way. That included making her chafe at the bit at being ordered around when she was, in fact, the manager of the hotel.

Yet all it had taken was one bit of information to make her feel like a complete fraud. To make her return to being the scared little girl she'd been for so long.

A crash echoed through the room and she jumped, pressing a hand to her heart. Her head jerked toward the sound as a flash of a memory raced before her eyes. Glass after glass, shattered against the kitchen wall as she cowered in the corner. Her heart pounded against her ribs and she struggled to keep her composure. This was not *then,* and no one had thrown anything at her. A table holding glassware had been bumped, sending vases and pitchers teetering over the edge. That was all.

With a sigh, she grabbed a spare box and started picking up pieces. But when an employee passed by and said, "Sorry, Ms. Ross," she lost her grip on the thin edge of her control.

"Sorry? Why can't you watch where you're going?" She huffed out a disgusted sigh. "Look at this mess!" Her eyes stung suddenly, mortified. How often had those words rung in *her* ears? Her regret was instant.

The girl faltered, her lips twisting. "I'll help you clean it up."

"Is something wrong?"

Mari looked up from her crouched position. Luca stood over her, his usually smiling lips flat with disapproval.

"Besides careless employees breaking hundreds of dollars of crystal? Not at all."

The girl's eyes filled with tears at the dressing down and Luca's gaze fell on Mari, steady and disapproving. Guilt slipped through her; she knew she'd been out of line with her tone. She was manager of the Cascade. The staff had to know she was still in charge. But that didn't mean she had to be a bully. Her, of all people! Shame reddened her cheeks.

"Lisa, I'm so sorry." She looked up at the young woman, mollified and contrite. "I know it was an accident. Please... my tone with you was inexcusable."

"I *am* sorry, Miss Ross! Please let me do that. It was my fault."

"Go back to work, Lisa, and don't worry, we'll get this straightened out." Luca's voice was calmly reasonable, completely unemotional and she hated him for it. She tried to ignore his body just behind her and focused on putting broken pieces of glass in the box. And all the while a voice in the back of her head was chanting, *he's out, he's out, he's out.*

"Yelling at the staff isn't the way to get them to work better."

Oh, as if she didn't already know that. Apparently he didn't understand that the constant changes and adjustments needed meant that she was juggling twice her normal workload. He had no idea of the other stresses she was under, that kept her awake into the dark hours of the night. "I don't need *you* to tell *me* how to do *my* job."

"Leave the glass and come with me."

"God Luca, stop ordering me around!" She looked up again and let her eyes flash at him. Frustration bubbled up and out. "I'm tired of it. You've bossed me around all week."

His eyes darkened and she knew she'd pushed the anger button. Crossed the insubordinate line. Dread curled in her stomach. How many times had she let this happen? How many times had she let her temper get the better of her and then have to pay the price for it? All the lessons she'd learned flew out of her head when he glared at her.

"In my office, if you please." The words were gritted out.

"No." She nearly choked on the word, and backed up a few steps. But the thought of following him into his office to be called to the carpet for her actions was more than she could bear. She would cry. She would beg, like she had so many times before. And then she'd hate him for it.

"Ms. Ross, unless you want this to happen in front of your staff, you'll come with me now." His voice was dangerously low and smooth. Sweat pooled at the base of her spine as she rose and brushed her hands down her trousers.

She could handle this. She could. Luca was not Robert. He couldn't be Robert.

She followed him into his office and while he sat in one of the chairs, she stood by the door. A means of escape if she needed it. Logically she knew this was just an argument. It didn't mean…but it didn't stop the physical reaction. That fight-or-flight response. And she knew her choice was always flight.

"Mari, *what* is going on with you?"

"I don't know what you mean." She worked hard at not fidgeting with her hands.

"You've been out of sorts all week. Tense, irritated. Short with the staff. What happened today was an accident, and you blew it out of proportion. The same as you did when Christopher put the Maxwells in the wrong room. It was easily fixed."

"What happened today was staff being careless. And I know I snapped at her, and I apologized."

"And the Mari I met a week ago, the one so concerned for her people, wouldn't have handled it by shouting at them."

She looked away. He was right. She was so tired of him being right. But telling him the truth—that the man who had terrorized her was out on parole—that just wasn't an option.

"We need to be able to work together, Mari. We need to be on the same page."

She took a breath and exhaled, glad of the diversion from the real problem. "Maybe that's it, Luca. I don't feel that we're working together. You're giving orders and expecting them to be carried out. I haven't had one single input into what's happening here other than writing the memo to staff."

"You've been at every meeting Dean and I have held."

"Yes, but why bother? I never get to say anything or weigh in on discussions. The two of you go on your merry way and leave me out of it. All you do is issue orders about what you want done and when. Never mind increased workload or trying to make adjustments. What's it like, Luca, being at the top? You don't have to try to finesse the little changes to keep things running as smoothly as possible."

"I beg your pardon." His voice was stiff and formal. "I believe you said that was your job."

Oh, the man made her blood boil. Using that against her. "It is. But I'm still only one person and the volume of work has increased significantly. And you also said you wanted my input."

"Is there anything we've done you don't agree with?"

She paused. The truth was she *did* like all the ideas and changes so far.

"That's hardly the point. You've set me up as your traffic cop, directing people here and there. Seven impossible things to be done before breakfast is even served."

"If you can't handle the job…"

Panic threaded through her. This was what she hadn't wanted to happen and she'd been working day and night so it wouldn't. She needed this job. She wanted this job and the life she'd built back. She'd thought that she would simply have to work extra hard for this short period of time and all would be well. And it had only been a week and they were at each other's throats.

"I can handle the job. *My* job. But I'm only one person, Luca."

"So you're angry at me, and not with Lisa. You're not the only one putting in long hours, Mari. I don't ask anything of my staff that I don't ask of myself."

"Then perhaps you expect too much."

"Yet here we are. And I'm not the one throwing a tantrum."

She let out a sound of frustration. "You are infuriating!"

A slow smile curled up his cheek. "So I've been told."

The cajoling did nothing to lighten her mood, only darkened it. Her tone was biting. "Probably by your legions of swooning women."

"Legions?" He smiled at that, too.

"Would you stop smiling? I read the magazines."

He laughed then, a rich lazy chuckle that did things to her insides. She immediately hated him for it. She was trying to stay angry! It was easier than actually *liking* him. Watching him work the past week, she'd come dangerously close to admiring his enthusiasm and dedication.

"Oh, Mari, are you jealous?"

"Hardly." She said with so much contempt she thought he must believe her. Her? Jealous of his women? Why on earth would she be? His eyes sparkled at her and she ground her teeth. It wasn't fair that his shirt today matched the exact rich brown of his eyes. *So what,* she thought. He had nice eyes, he was sex-on-a-stick gorgeous. But he drove her crazy. She wasn't in the market for a man, and even if she were, it wouldn't be a dictatorial womanizer like Luca. She curled her lip. "Trust me, Luca. I have no desire to be a notch on your bedpost."

Her heart trembled as the words echoed through the office. What did she think she was doing, challenging him!

His smile faded. "That's clear enough. And let me be clear, Mari. If you have an idea, a problem with anything happening here, you need to speak up. My education did not include mind reading."

But she wasn't used to speaking up. She was used to order and routine. She'd gotten where she was by being good at her job, not by running over the top of people to get there. She knew what happened when you rocked the boat.

Slowly, in the silence, she felt her anger dissipate. "I don't like arguing."

"I love it." He smiled suddenly, the corners of his eyes crinkling. She stared at him. He loved it? Her stomach tied in knots at the very thought of confrontation and she was completely stressed now that she seemed to be dealing with it nearly every day. And he claimed to enjoy it?

"How can you say that?"

"Don't you feel better?"

"I don't follow."

He stood up, but leaned back against his desk, stretching out his long legs and crossing them at the ankle as he braced his hands on the edge of the wood. "Having an honest, open argument is much better than holding frustrations and resentments inside. Clears the air. It doesn't fester. It's healthy."

"I'm sorry if I don't quite get the concept of healthy confrontation. To me there's nothing healthy about shouting at each other, hurling insults. In the end someone always ends up getting hurt because one person doesn't know when to stop." She said it all in one breath, but couldn't look at him while she did it. And she steeled herself, willing away the shaking that happened every time she thought about Robert. Knowing he was out there somewhere, and free.

Something clicked in Luca's head. A seed of an idea that was suddenly so clear he didn't know why he hadn't put two and two together before. Maybe because he'd been so focused on his job that he hadn't given it priority.

Mari had been hurt. Someone had hurt her and now she was afraid.

It made sense. He'd missed the signs but he could see them now. Her aversion to touching, to arguing. The way she'd looked at him in the attic, the way she stood now, by the door, like she was ready to flee. The way her eyes wouldn't meet his, keeping her distance. In his family, arguing was something done often and passionately, the same as loving. One didn't negate the other. He couldn't live life with his sister and father and not argue, it was part of who they were. But he'd been right about the loving, too. As much as he chafed at his father's control of Fiori, it didn't stop the love between them. It was the love that had made them safe. But he could see now that somehow, with Mari, someone had taught her differently. Someone had taught her that love hurt.

But he couldn't broach the topic. They hardly knew each other. He was her boss, and it would be crossing a personal line. But he couldn't help but wonder what—or who—had made her so afraid. The last thing he wanted was for her to be afraid of him. He was no threat.

"Mari, I'm sorry. I certainly didn't mean to upset you. We've both been under some stress." He decided a little insight into himself wouldn't hurt, to put her at ease. He smiled at her. "I'm Italian. In my family we argue as passionately as we love each other. We know that we'll be there for each other, no matter how much we disagree. I didn't think that perhaps not everyone is the same way."

She turned her eyes on him and he was caught for a brief moment. The same as that day in the attic, her eyes shone like gray dawn at him and he saw there was much more to Mari than he'd imagined. He could see the pain. The pain she thought she kept hidden inside behind the wall she'd built around herself. He'd seen that kind of ache before. In his father's eyes, and in his sister Gina's. It was, he realized, the look of the death of hope. As hard as he'd tried over the years, he'd never been able to make that look go away for them completely. "I'm sorry," he repeated.

Her voice was soft. "And I lost my temper before and owe you an apology."

"Accepted."

They couldn't go on being at each other's throats all the time. It wouldn't be good for the hotel, or the staff, or for either of them. And the first step was for him to offer her an olive branch. "It's a beautiful day outside and from what I hear, one of the last. Let me treat you to lunch. Now that we've cleared the air."

"I don't think that's a good idea."

He began to hold out his hand, but pulled it back. He normally would have taken her fingers in his, but he remembered her aversion to touching.

"I'm offering a truce, Mari. I would like us to be friends. I'd like for you to be comfortable enough with me that you can feel free to offer an opinion. You know this area. You know the staff far better than I. You are a great asset to the Cascade, Mari, and it won't be good for either of us if we cannot find a way to work together. We can't have more arguments like we did today. It's counterproductive."

"Luca, I appreciate the gesture, but I have a list of phone calls to make, not to mention the actual running of the hotel. We're shuffling so many things around I'm having to adjust everywhere…"

"You need to take a break and come back refreshed. A little relaxation now means higher productivity later. Besides, I'm hungry. You have to eat. I insist."

For someone who didn't like orders, she seemed to understand them well enough. He saw her capitulate as her shoulders slumped slightly.

"Oh, all right."

He smiled, his mind already working. She was still uptight—they both were. This wasn't finished. The best plan was to get away from the hotel altogether, somewhere they could meet on middle ground. He wanted her to look at him without the guard she put up all the time.

He wanted her to trust him.

"Meet me in the courtyard. And bring a sweater."

"The courtyard?"

He went to her, reaching around and opening the door. "Fifteen minutes, *si?*"

She stepped outside into the courtyard, her boots making dull sounds on the cobbled walk. He was standing by a bench to the right, by the remains of the rose garden. Now that most of her anger had dissipated, she felt that unfamiliar crawl again. No matter how hard she tried, he pushed her buttons. Either one extreme or the other. And she didn't know which was more difficult—fighting with him or fighting the attraction that seemed to be budding. He'd been completely right this morning, and then had offered an apology. To her recollection, no man had ever apologized to her before. Damn it, she was starting to *like* him.

He was talking to another couple—Mari recognized them as the Townsends, the anniversary couple—and it took a lot of effort not to turn around and go back inside. The morning, combined with their argument and then apology had left her exhausted and off balance. She wasn't sure what to say.

He'd apologized for arguing with her. He wanted to establish a better working relationship. And she knew by Christmas he'd be gone back to Italy and everything would go back to normal. It was only for the short-term. It all should have made her feel much better. But it didn't.

She approached with a smile. "Good afternoon."

"Ah, Ms. Ross. You've met Mr. and Mrs. Townsend?"

She appreciated Luca using her surname. She held out her hand. "It's nice to see you again. Are you enjoying your stay with us?"

Mrs. Townsend beamed. "We are. It's just beautiful here. And that dinner the other night…what a lovely way to celebrate our anniversary. Thank you so much."

Mari smiled. "You are very welcome. Such a milestone deserves special treatment."

"Indeed it does," Luca remarked.

Mr. Townsend noticed the picnic basket. "We're keeping you."

Luca smiled back. "Not at all. We're just testing out a new program we may implement, and the day was too beautiful to waste."

Mr. Townsend lifted a hand in farewell. "Enjoy then. And thank you for a memorable week."

"Congratulations," Luca and Mari said together, then looked at each other and smiled. As the Townsends walked off, Mari lowered her gaze as she felt her cheeks bloom.

"Thank you for coming."

"When the boss gives an order…" She chanced a look up. Their brief encounter with the Townsends only served to remind her of how personable he was. He remembered details, and knew how to put people at ease. She admired that; it was a quality she'd never mastered. She tried hard to ignore the older couple's smiles as they'd seen Luca holding the picnic basket. A warmth spread through her at the thought of them paired together.

He laughed shortly. "I thought you said I wasn't to give orders anymore."

"I don't think you can help it…it's in your nature. Where are we going? I'm hungry." She wasn't, really, but knew her body needed nourishment. More than a muffin and several cups of coffee, which was all she'd eaten so far today. The sooner she got this over with, the sooner she could get back.

He stood to the side, revealing a wicker picnic basket. "I had the kitchens put together a meal for us. And if you'll follow me, I have the car waiting to take us to our destination."

"A picnic." Mari wasn't sure if she should be happy or aghast. What would the staff say if they went gallivanting away on a picnic for two?

"Colleagues and friends enjoying a late fall day. Nothing shocking about that."

"Can't we eat here?" She looked around. The gardens were filled with benches and grassy expanses. It would certainly be more seemly. She was still trying to grasp the fact that he'd referred to them as *friends*.

"Mari, we're changing more than cosmetics here. Remember what I said to you that night at dinner?" He turned slightly, lifting his arm to encompass the gardens. "Remember the Romance. Restoring the Cascade is more than furniture and fabrics. It's also services, special touches. Imagine being here in this town, with the man you love. Venturing out on a sunny day to a mountain meadow where you share lunch, a bottle of wine."

With the man you love. She *couldn't* actually imagine it. She couldn't imagine letting herself be in love, giving someone that much power. This…this magnetism to Luca was just that. Magnetism. She stared at his chest, which was a mistake as she couldn't help wondering what was beneath the sweater he'd put on against the brisk autumn chill. She had to deflect the intimate mood somehow.

"As long as you don't share lunch with the bears. Or elk. They can be mean this time of year, you know. The elk."

Luca's jaw tightened; he wasn't amused. "Fine, Mari. Don't go if you've not a mind to."

He picked up the basket.

She closed her eyes, frustrated. "Luca, wait. I'm sorry. I just find this…awkward. I'm not used to catered picnics with my boss." That wasn't all. The very idea of being alone, secluded…it made her feel closed in, defenseless.

"I thought we could both use an hour away from the hotel. A chance to see something else. I've hardly seen any of the townsite yet. I thought you would be a good tour guide."

Mari's level of discomfort grew. Here at the hotel they were surrounded by staff. It was her turf, as well as his. But this picnic, it was completely organized by him and she had no idea where they were going. She wasn't great at following someone else's plans.

"Maybe I could pick the place, then," she blurted out. At least then she would feel more comfortable. "As you said, I do know the area."

He carried the basket and she led the way out to the new luxury car he'd purchased for the hotel. The most senior of their shuttle bus drivers had taken over chauffeur duties and he opened her door with a smile, "Ms. Ross."

"Thank you, Charlie," she murmured, sliding in, sinking into the soft leather seats.

Luca slid in beside her after placing the basket in the trunk. "Where to?"

"To my place, if you could." Mari leaned forward. "You remember the way?"

"Sure do, Ms. Ross."

"Your place?"

She felt Luca's eyes on her and she nodded without looking at him. Her place, her turf. A tiny element of protection. "Yes. I'd like to change into jeans and a sweater. And introduce you to someone."

CHAPTER FIVE

IT WAS only a matter of a few minutes until the car pulled up outside a stone cottage, perched on the side of a hill dotted with spruce trees and shrubs. Charlie opened her door and she got out. "Would it be too much to ask you to wait for us, Charlie?"

"You're the boss, Miss Ross."

She smiled at him then. She was glad Luca had chosen him as their driver. He'd been driving shuttle bus for several years, and she'd always enjoyed his anecdotes about his grandchildren. Charlie was one of the few men she felt very comfortable around.

"You may as well come down, too, Luca. We'll walk to the spot from here."

She walked down the stone path to her door while Luca retrieved the basket from the car. As soon as her feet hit the veranda the barking started and she smiled. As she opened the door, she called out, "It's just me!" and was greeted by happy licks and tail wags.

Tommy. Her companion, her protection, her one bright spot of unconditional love.

"You wanna go for a walk, boy?"

More butt wiggling as his tail beat a furious pace. Then he spied Luca at the top of the path and leaped out the door.

"Tommy!"

For once he ignored her command, reached the top of the path and with a loud bark, jumped up on Luca, planting firm paws on Luca's chest.

What next?

Luca rubbed Tommy's blond ears. "Aren't you handsome." He called down to Mari. "I didn't know you had a dog!"

At least he wasn't angry. Even if she was mortified that her dog had met him with more exuberance than he should have.

"Tommy. Come."

At her sharp command, the Labrador slunk back down the stone steps to where she stood on the veranda. "Lie down."

He dropped by her feet.

"If he's that well trained, I can only assume you whispered something in his ear as he went out the door." Luca's teasing voice came closer as he descended to the cottage.

"I'm sorry about your sweater."

"It's not even dirty. Besides, that's what laundry service is for."

"Tommy, stay." She left the dog on the porch floor and opened the screen door. "I'll just be a moment."

"So this is who you wanted me to meet?"

She paused. "Yeah. I figured if we're going to be lunching outside, it would be a good chance to let him out for a run. He's such a good boy, staying in all day and waiting for me." She knelt down and rubbed the top of his head. "It would be a big treat for him to get out in the middle of the day for a romp."

"You don't leave him out in your garden?"

Mari ceased patting and looked up. "I know it sounds cruel, leaving him shut up all day. And I probably could leave him out, but I don't trust the bears." She leaned her forehead against Tommy's warm neck. "I don't know what I'd do if anything happened to him."

He was also a level of protection for her. Nothing would

hurt her while Tommy was close by. He wasn't vicious by any stretch, but he was big and he was loyal.

"We'll wait for you, then. Enjoy the outside and get acquainted." Luca put the basket down and sat on a deck chair, rubbing Tommy's silky ears in his fingers.

Mari went into the bedroom and pulled jeans and a soft sweater out of her closet. It felt strangely intimate, undressing and knowing Luca was only a few steps away. She slid the jeans over her panties, pulled the sweater over her head and re-did her ponytail.

All the while aware that he was out on her porch, with her dog and a picnic.

This could technically be classified as a date.

She sat heavily on the bed. No, it was a working lunch, that was all. A break from the craziness that had become the Cascade and testing out guest services. They could eat and still classify it as work. They could forge a truce of sorts. That was what Luca had said, right? That he wanted to be friends. She was torn. She wanted friends, she did. And yet the idea of getting close to people frightened her. She wished she were different. That she could leave the past where it belonged, behind her. That she could shed all the hurt and fear and live a normal life. Instead she tied herself into knots over the mere thought of being alone with her boss for a simple lunch.

Mari wasn't prepared for the tumbling feeling in her belly when he came into a room. She'd spent so long on her own, focused on getting her life together that it was a new and unsettling experience. Bringing him here today wasn't an accident. Knowing Tommy was with them—between them—would help. He was her reinforcement. Charlie would be waiting here, with the car. She would not be alone. And perhaps with this one lunch Mari and Luca could finally set a consistent tone. Perhaps they could come to some agreement on how to deal with each other during the coming weeks. He was right about that. They had to find a way to work together.

"Mari? Are you all right?"

She startled at the sound of his voice. She'd been day-dreaming for several minutes, leaving him to his own devices on her veranda.

"Coming," she called out, standing and smoothing her clothing. He hadn't made this into anything other than lunch. It was Mari who was off balance. She either sniped at him or stared at him stupidly. It was her imagination running wild because he caused her temperature to rise a little bit each time he was around.

And because she hadn't felt like this in such a long time the novelty was jarring.

She met them back on the porch. "Let's go. Tommy, come."

The dog fell in step at her heels, while Luca carried the basket, and the black Cadillac rested down the hill from them.

She led him across the lane and up a small, single track path. Little traffic ventured along here, but she could always see her little cottage just below. The grass was drying, golden in the noontime light. When she reached the crest of the hill, she stopped, picked up a stick and threw it a short distance for Tommy, who bounded off and then brought it back, tail wagging.

From the crest of the hill they could see down the valley. Her cottage and their car lay below them; the hollow was cra-dled by spruces and pines and the ever-present poplars and birches that were rapidly losing their plumage. The nearly round leaves scattered everywhere, forming a golden carpet, while the air held the sharp tang of evergreen. "Is this okay?"

Luca put down the basket and reached inside for a blanket. "It's perfect."

She sat down on the blanket, throwing the stick for the dog again. "We won't have many more days like this," she murmured, feeling the sun warm her face. "I'm surprised it's held on this long."

"Then we must make the most of it." He began unpacking the basket. "Tomato bocconcini and peppers, marinated lamb and minted potato salad, and I'm not telling you what's for dessert because good girls eat their vegetables first." He laid out real china and silverware along with their parcels and said, "If you'll serve, Mari, I'll pour the wine."

For a few minutes they busied themselves with laying out the picnic. Mari sat with her legs crossed, arranging the meal on the plates. Already she could feel the stress of work ebbing away and filled with a newer, sweeter problem—the fact that she was, indeed, enjoying his company. She tilted her chin up to the sun, letting its warmth absorb into her sweater. She was glad to be here with him, sharing something as simple as a picnic on a fall day. But that was as far as it could go. She had to remember why she had come. To establish some sort of truce. Some sort of equilibrium between them. She wasn't capable of anything more.

"Fresh air and good food does wonders for stress." Luca's voice came from beside her and she turned to look at him, squinting against the sun.

"This is one of those times I'm going to have to admit you're right again." She handed him his plate, smiling. "I didn't realize how tense I was. I've been so focused on trying to get everything accomplished with the same number of hours in the day."

Tommy had played himself out bounding through the grass, and collapsed in a contented heap a few feet away. "I haven't been doing this with him enough lately. I need to or he's going to get fat and lazy."

"Everyone needs downtime like this. Outside, peace and quiet, something simple and restorative. It's what I hope people find at the Cascade. A break from the…what's the term… the rat race. Time to smell the roses. For some, this is a way of life."

"For someone like you, you mean?"

He smiled and took a bite of bocconcini. "Someone like me?"

She gave him a significant look and he grinned. "Oh, you mean the idle rich."

She took a drink of the mellow chardonnay, enjoying the light teasing between them. "I will concede that you are definitely not idle. You've proved that this last week."

"You thought I was?"

She looked down over the valley. "Oh come on, the golden son of Fiori Resorts? I've read the magazines, you know. Life handed to you on a silver platter? Fancy cars and fast women… or is that fast cars and fancy women?" She couldn't stop the teasing quiver of her mouth.

"Either way," he admitted dryly.

"You're incorrigible," she giggled, leaning a little sideways and jostling his shoulder.

And sighed into her wine.

"Have I been pushing too hard, then?"

She eyed him carefully. Had he? He never looked tense or flustered or tired, but she knew for a fact that he was up and working by the time she arrived in the morning, and just last night when she had gone home late, he was still on his computer in his office.

"I don't think you've been pushing anyone harder than yourself. But maybe the Cascade staff isn't used to that pace."

"Staff like you?"

She put off answering by nibbling on her potato salad. But his gaze remained on her face and she swallowed.

"I didn't get where I am without putting in the hours," she replied. She was tired. It was no secret. But part of the fatigue was due to the fact that things were changing and she was unsettled. She was under stresses he knew nothing about, nor would he. She was waking more in the night than she usually did. The nightmares had returned. She was looking over her shoulder. It meant she started most days already at an energy deficit.

"I wouldn't have asked so much of you if I weren't sure you could handle it, Mari."

And she couldn't help the warmth that spread through her at his words of confidence.

"And I thank you for that. As well as thanking you for realizing I needed a breather."

When Mari pushed away her plate, Luca reached into the basket one more time.

"I know I probably shouldn't have, but I got them to sneak in dessert." He removed a ceramic pot and a spoon, held them up.

"You thought of everything."

"Not everything. They only sent one spoon."

She stared at the single utensil. What sort of game was he playing? She thought he'd simply hand her the dish and that would be it. But instead he dipped the spoon in and out, a smile playing on his lips.

"I told you that there was simple beauty to be found. That the Cascade meant an *experience,* more than providing a service. What if we weren't running the hotel? What if we were guests? We wouldn't be thinking of whether or not this was profitable, we'd be thinking of how wonderful the afternoon has been. We'd be opening our senses, our minds. We'd be thinking of ourselves and enjoyment and not worrying about a thing."

Her heart tripped over itself as he held up the spoon, rounded with crème brûlée.

"Close your eyes, Mari."

Oh God. This wasn't putting up boundaries at all, or establishing a status quo. It was blowing it all to smithereens and she wasn't sure she could do it.

He held the spoon, waiting. She was caught by his warm gaze, as lazy and seductive as the creamy concoction on the spoon.

And she closed her eyes.

The cold spoon touched her lips and she instinctively opened them. Felt the cool richness of the dessert enfold her tongue. Smooth, soft, sweet.

As the spoon left her lips, she opened her eyes.

Luca dipped the spoon again, but this time tasted it himself, his gaze never leaving hers.

"It's good," he murmured, presenting her with the spoon once more.

The spoon that had just been in his mouth. It was silly that the thought would have such an effect on her, but it felt like seduction. She opened her mouth and let him feed her, feeling more and more like she was completely out of her mind and her element. She didn't know what to do with romance. And this was clearly romance.

"It really is exquisite." Not only the dessert, but being here with him, and she had to find a way to divert the mood. It was sheer craziness that she'd let herself fall under his spell, but she knew what came next. Before she knew it they'd be kissing. The very idea made her tremble, from want and fear. She was not equipped for an affair, and she was smart enough to know an affair was all there would be with Luca. He was a limited time fantasy, and she couldn't afford to buy into it.

She had to bring it back to the business of the hotel somehow. Mari started fussing with plates and silverware to avoid being fed any more of the decadent dessert. "I think we could develop a selection of picnic items."

Luca helped himself to one more spoonful and Mari forced herself to look away from how his lips encircled the spoon.

He put the dish down and picked up his wine. "Interesting idea. Maybe offer a selection to choose from. Don't want the bocconcini? Have a shrimp and rice salad, perhaps. Herbed chicken instead of lamb. Gunther's chocolate terrine instead of crème brûlée. What do you think?"

What Mari thought was that test driving a sports car wasn't the same as owning one, and doing a dry run for a romantic picnic wasn't like being on one. But...the potential was still there and she could use her imagination. Especially after the last few moments.

If she were in love with Luca, and he with her, and they were in this setting, eating decadently, growing lazy on fine wine...

A couple in love would be romanced. And they'd end the afternoon in a very different way than she would with Luca. And that would be part of the Cascade experience.

And how would such a couple end the day? Mari's hand paused over the dishes. Perhaps they'd return to the hotel and order in room service. Or they'd dress in fine clothing and have dinner at the best tables, dancing on the gleaming parquet floor with the scent of fresh flowers falling around them. He'd smile and hold out his hand, his brown eyes shining down at her because she was so lovely...

"Mari?"

"I think that sounds wonderful," she answered, fussing with the blanket beside her feet, knowing that such a scenario was not possible, even as longing suffused her. A chill blew in with the breeze and she shivered. She had to stop thinking of him this way. Everything would go sideways and there'd be no graceful way out. If she couldn't even stand his hand on her arm, how could she possibly relax enough for there to be more? She was simply tired and her defenses were down. She was muddled from the wine. It had to be about the Cascade, not about them.

But she'd have to go back to the hotel with Luca and the thought of walking back through the lobby with him and a picnic basket sent quivers through her stomach. They didn't need rumors circulating amongst the staff. Even over something as innocent as a picnic. She desperately needed to put the tone back to business.

"We could do a variation on a winter picnic. Soup in a thermal container, bread and cheese, hot cocoa and a dessert."

Luca grabbed the basket and began repacking the dishes she'd gathered into the basket. "That's brilliant. We can adjust it and make it seasonal. The Rocky Mountains in winter. See, I knew you'd catch on."

Maybe to the concept, but definitely not the execution. Falling in love and being romanced was fine for some people, but not for her. Not anymore. She looked over at Luca's profile as he wrapped the now-empty wineglasses in linens to keep them safe. Never would she let someone take over her life so much that it wasn't hers anymore. She wouldn't give anyone that much control ever again.

It was just as well Luca was only here for a few weeks, certainly he'd be gone by the new year. In a way that made him safe, too. Any attraction she felt wouldn't matter. She wouldn't have to worry about feelings deepening and things being awkward. She just had to hold out until he was gone and she could get the life she'd built back. Her safe life. A life where no one had the power to hurt her again.

"Why don't you take the rest of the afternoon off?"

Luca stood, holding the basket. Mari hopped up, grabbing the blanket and folding it into an imprecise square. It was tempting. But her car was still at the hotel and she'd dallied enough today. There was still work to be done and she didn't want to take advantage. It was important for her to end the day with their work relationship at the fore, not the lazy intimacy of the picnic.

"Thanks for the offer, but my car's still there anyway."

They walked back down the hill, Tommy trotting happily ahead. The stress headache that had been lurking behind her eyes was completely gone. Perhaps Luca was right. She did need to relax more. She certainly had relaxed with him. Perhaps too much.

"I'll be back in a few moments," she murmured as they reached the cottage. She put Tommy in the house and checked his water bowl before locking the door and leaving again.

Charlie drove up and opened the door for her. Luca got in again, and her eyes were drawn to how the fabric of his trousers hugged his thigh. As the car pulled away and back down the mountain, she leaned back and studied him without being obvious. He wore his clothes like he belonged in them. He was at ease, comfortable with himself, and it came across as confidence. She blinked slowly, wishing she had that sort of self-assurance. She agonized over every piece of her wardrobe, yet he seemed so at home in whatever he wore, whether it was jeans and a T-shirt, or dress trousers with his trendy shirts. She imagined he'd be equally handsome in evening wear. Looking like she'd imagined earlier. A picnic like today, then an elegant dinner, only it wasn't guests she envisioned but the two of them. Stepping out on their dance floor, with her on his arm...

"We're here."

Mari heard the words but the fabric against her cheek was soft and warm. She snuggled into it further.

"Mari, I hate to wake you but we can't sit in the car forever."

The voice intruded again and she realized it was Luca. Then she realized she was leaned against the breadth of his arm. It was wider and stronger than she'd anticipated. And his scent came through with each slow breath.

She sat up abruptly, putting distance between them. Her last thought had been of him dressed in a tuxedo. Now she was intimately couched in the back seat of a luxury car with him. She edged over further. "I fell asleep."

His smile was lazy, indulgent. "You did. Almost as soon as the car began to move."

"I'm so sorry."

"Don't be. It's perfectly all right."

Embarrassment flamed in her face. "But it's an eight-minute drive from my place."

"Obviously you were tired. And relaxed. Shall we?"

Charlie had opened the door with a bland look on his face.

She got out into the refreshing mountain air, its bite going a long way to clearing her head. Luca said something to Charlie and then he touched her elbow and they walked toward the lobby doors together. Just before they reached the entrance, Luca quipped, "Don't let it get around that my company put you to sleep. I have a reputation to uphold."

As she let out an unexpected splutter of laughter, he opened the door and held it as she passed through. He followed her in, both of them chuckling.

"Luca."

Both their steps halted as they turned together toward the voice. Mari stared at the most beautiful woman she'd ever seen. She was the picture of class, elegance, style. She was dressed in a trouser suit of dove-gray silk with matching heels, her nearly black hair flawlessly styled around a heart-shaped face, dominated by brown eyes and the thickest set of natural lashes Mari had ever seen.

"Gina."

Mari could only gape as Luca dropped the picnic basket and crossed the floor with long strides, gathered the woman up in his arms, and swung her around.

When he put her down, she laughed out loud. "I missed you." She cupped his face and kissed one side, then the other.

"And I you. What are you doing here?"

"I came to see you. Aren't I allowed?" The smile on her face was filled with teasing.

The Italian accent was clear. Mari didn't understand the spurt of jealousy she felt nor did she like standing in the middle of the lobby looking daft. She bent to pick up the abandoned basket. The picnic had been two co-workers, not lovers, so there was no reason for her to be jealous now. She had work to do. She'd return this to the kitchen and go back to her office.

As she bent down, the woman spied her. "Luca, introduce me to your friend."

Mari straightened slowly.

"Of course." Tugging the woman's hand, he led her to where Mari was standing. She felt more stupid by the second, embarrassed. Here she was, the manager of the hotel, in jeans, a sweater, with her hair in a windblown tangle, talking to a woman who looked as though she wouldn't be caught dead in such a state. Not only that, but the scenario was so predictable it even made *her* wince. Of course Luca would have a girlfriend. She should have foreseen. Instead she was caught looking provincial and awkward. A caricature.

"Gina, this is Mariella Ross, the manager of the hotel."

Gina held out a hand. Mari shook it and then looked down. She'd expected soft, perfectly manicured hands with sculpted talons for nails. Instead the hands were gentle but plain, with neatly trimmed nails painted only with clear polish.

"Mari, this is my sister, Gina."

Mari's flush deepened. Oh, would she ever stop feeling stupid?

Gina's light laugh echoed. "Luca, I'm offended. You didn't tell her you had a sister?

Mari looked up but to her relief Gina's eyes held nothing but humor. She should have seen the resemblance straight off. The same color eyes, the same shaped lips. "He hasn't said a word about his family."

Gina swatted Luca's arm with her matching clutch purse. "Of course he didn't. Men. All about work."

"What are you doing here, Gina?"

Luca stood by Mari as he asked the question again. This time Mari noticed the brunette's eyes dim as she said something in rapid-fire Italian and Luca answered back, his cheeks suddenly drawn. Mari wrinkled her nose. Happy, carefree Luca? He looked positively thunderous.

"Is something wrong?"

Luca spared her a glance. "A family issue."

"I'm sorry. I'll leave you two alone." Mari picked up the basket again, prepared to leave.

"Mariella?"

Mari didn't have the heart to correct Gina. It didn't matter right now. There was clearly something going on between Luca and Gina that any explanations of her name could wait.

When she paused, Gina continued. "I do hope you'll join Luca and me for dinner tonight. I'd love to hear about your plans for the hotel. Luca thinks he has the only eye for decoration, but he underestimates his sister."

"Perhaps you need time to catch up. You needn't feel obligated."

"It's no obligation at all. Tell her, Luca." Gina smiled up at her brother, who was scowling back at her.

Luca turned his head and stared down into her eyes, his expression softening. Despite her fears and misgivings, she wanted to hear him say the words. It made no sense. What they'd shared, first in the attic, and now on the picnic, scared her. She would be foolish to want more. She should refuse and go the other way. Instead she wanted him to ask her. Wanted to hear him say he wanted to spend time with her. How on earth had this happened?

"We would both like it," he said, and her gaze dropped to his lips for a brief second. "I would like it. Please, come."

"I will."

"Wonderful." Gina smiled. "It will give me a chance to wear the new dress I bought in Milan."

Mari felt her insides blanch. She couldn't go like this. This wasn't her business supper of a week ago where a skirt and blazer were the order of the day. There was suddenly a standard to uphold and she wasn't sure she was up to it.

"If I'm joining you, then I must excuse myself. I have so much to do…if you'll excuse me."

She didn't dare look up into Luca's face. If she did she'd be caught. Instead she hurried away, mentally assessing her wardrobe and wondering what on earth would be suitable.

Luca watched her go. She hadn't said as much, but from her blush she'd thought Gina was his lover. A wrinkle formed between his brows. Interesting. Perhaps Mari wasn't as immune as she pretended to be.

"She's lovely, Luca. I can't imagine why you haven't mentioned her."

Gina's voice diverted him and he spun back around. "There's nothing to mention. Unlike yourself. Let's go to my suite so you can tell me why you're here, Gina."

Once in the rooms, Luca went to a cabinet and opened the door. "Wine or brandy?"

Gina smiled. "Neither. Oh, it's good to see you. You travel too much and I never see you anymore."

He led her to the sofa, then sat on the arm of a nearby chair. "Father sent you?"

"Father sent the sculpture you asked for. I chaperoned it."

Luca held his annoyance. He hadn't seen Gina in weeks and he didn't want to argue.

"And you, I suppose, had to get your finger in the pot."

She grinned cheekily. "Darling, it's what I do best. I'd be a horrible sister if I didn't help at least a little with our newest acquisition."

"I thought you were busy with *your* newest acquisition." He slid off the arm and down into the cushions, crossing his ankle over his knee. "How is my new niece?"

"Growing. And her brother is turning my hair gray."

"Good. You deserve it."

She snorted out a laugh. "I have missed you, Luca."

"And I you. But you have Angelo and the children now. You didn't need to come."

"I still have an interest in Fiori, Luca. Father sent me with the sculpture and to see if you needed a fresh set of eyes. And resources."

"You need to be with your family."

"I left the children with Carmela, the nanny, at Father's. Traveling with two small children…" Gina shook her head. "It will be a grand holiday for them, with Carmela to keep them in line and Papa to spoil them. It makes me feel needed. Something of my own."

"And where is Angelo?"

"He is in Zurich, seeing to a new project. He will be back in a few days, and then Carmela and the children will go back to our villa. You worry too much, Luca."

Luca smiled, though his heart wasn't in it. Gina tried hard to be the exception. She insisted she and Angelo had found each other and now they had two beautiful children. Yet he'd always had the feeling that Angelo wasn't good enough for her. He had a difficult time believing it was enough to last.

He couldn't help but wonder if down the road his sister was in for heartbreak. The same way their father had been.

Perhaps he was just being overprotective. He always had been where Gina was concerned.

Gina yawned, covering her mouth with a hand. "I'm sorry. It was a long flight."

"You are exhausted, Gina. Why don't you nap now." He stood and urged her down onto the plush cushions. "You don't want circles beneath your eyes tonight, or to be yawning through dinner. You can rest here, since I have work to finish downstairs. When I get back, I'll wake you and we can get ready, hmm?"

"And discuss the Cascade, don't forget." She winked at him. "*Grazie,* Luca."

"*Prego.* Rest now." He took the blanket—the same one he'd wrapped over Mari's arms—and laid it gently over her as her lids drooped.

His fingers grazed the soft blanket and he remembered Mari's eyes, closed, as he'd fed her crème brûlée. Remembered the feel of her, warm and soft against him in the limo today as she'd slept. He'd wanted to slide his arm around her and pull her on to his lap, feel her curled around him.

She had no idea what drove him. No idea why he worked so hard to prove himself. But Gina's comment about wanting something of her own made sense to him. He wanted to prove himself, to step forward and take a larger role at Fiori. His father had shouldered all the burden of the company, and family, as he and Gina had grown up. Luca had worked hard to take some of that burden, and now he just wanted what was his due.

In the beginning he'd thought it would be fun to make Mari see life was more than a balance sheet. It had seemed like a game. And admittedly he was good at games. But it had backfired. He hadn't counted on feeling attracted to her himself.

CHAPTER SIX

WHEN she walked into the room it was like someone punched him in the solar plexus, strangling all the air from his lungs.

Mari wasn't Mari tonight. She deserved the fullness of her name. She was Mariella. Every inch of her, from her hair to her toes, was elegance and shy sexuality. He hadn't known she could look like that. He had imagined what would happen if she let her hair down and left her tidy suits in her closet. But even that image had fallen woefully short.

"She is beautiful, Luca. An ingénue."

Gina's voice interrupted beside him as they watched Mari speak a moment to the hostess, a smile lighting her face.

"She keeps me on my toes."

"There *is* something between you then." She put her hand on his arm.

He shook his head. "No, Gina. She's the manager here and she's good at what she does. We work together. That's it."

Mari turned from the hostess and made her way to them. Luca tried to ignore the thrumming of his pulse at the gentle sway of her hips. Mari had legs. Yards of them, it seemed. Navy silk draped and clung in all the right places in the wrap-style dress, revealing shapely calves that curved elegantly into matching strappy heels. The neckline rose up from a V to cover her shoulders with barely an inch of strap.

"I see how you look at her, Luca. Trust me, you'll be happy that I'm here to free up some of your time."

Luca tore his eyes from Mari's image and glared at Gina. "If you think you're going to hang around here and be a thorn in my side…"

Gina smiled sweetly. "Dear brother, I consider it a family duty. She looks at you the same way."

Mari stopped in front of them and smiled, and for a moment his heart stopped.

"I hope I haven't kept you waiting."

It was Gina who replied when Luca remained silent. "Not at all. We just arrived ourselves. I had a refreshing nap and now I'm ready to sample your chef's delights."

Luca moved to pull out Mari's chair first.

"Thank you," she murmured, and he caught the first scent of her perfume.

"That dress is stunning. You have fabulous taste, Mari." Gina smiled disarmingly. "I hope Luca's not bullying you into making all *his* changes."

Mari smiled. "Thank you. And he tries, believe me."

Luca sat down. "I'm very fortunate to be sitting with the two most beautiful ladies in the room."

Gina laughed lightly. "Only the room? Mariella, I think we should be insulted."

But Luca's eyes had locked with Mari's. She'd left her hair down and his fingers itched to touch it, to be buried in the mahogany richness of it. It curved around her face and shoulders, and as she brushed a little of it back, he caught sight of her necklace, a silly little creation of silver and sapphire leaves.

He wanted to lift her tiny hand and press a kiss to it, but

he knew she'd frown on it. "I can see I won't stand a chance with the two of you."

Mari smiled and her eyes twinkled at him. "Somehow I think you can hold your own."

Luca ordered champagne and sat back, listening to Mari and Gina speak as if they'd known each other forever. But Gina had always had that way about her. Open and interesting. She had the grace and ease about her that brought Mari out of her shell like he hadn't been able to. And seeing Mari relaxed made her shine. She was open in a way she'd never been with him.

They were partway through the second course when one of the waitstaff approached Mari with a problem.

"I'll get it, you enjoy yourself," Luca said, beginning to push back his chair.

"No, I will." She smiled easily. "It is my job, after all. I won't be a minute."

He stood while she rose from her chair and sat again, watching her as she followed the staff member toward the kitchen.

He looked over at his sister, who kept insisting she was happy in her marriage. Was Luca the only one who could see what she was doing? She kept saying Angelo was her happy ending and he wouldn't be the one to shatter the illusion. He wanted it for her, after all they'd been through as children when their mother had abandoned them. He remembered holding her when she was little, when she cried for their mother in the night and didn't want Papa to hear. Remembered the summer he'd suspected there was something between her and Dante. But then Dante had gone to Paris with him and when they'd returned, she'd been engaged to Angelo. And he'd known she was trying to make up for the life they hadn't had and he'd been powerless to stop it.

He'd been by her side during the darkest time in her life. He'd been the older one. He'd understood more. He sincerely hoped Gina wasn't in for the same heartbreak again. *He* certainly wasn't in the market for a fairy tale happy ending. Neither were the women he usually dated, and that suited him just fine.

When Mari returned, he let his gaze fall on her as she and Gina spoke of the internal workings of the hotel business.

Mari was different. He couldn't explain it, but somehow all the jaded thoughts from the past faded away when she was near. There could never be anything permanent between them, but the brittle sense of skepticism he usually carried dissolved when she was around. He'd seen her eyes light up as she spoke to Gina, laughing easily in a way he hadn't seen before.

It was mesmerizing. This was Mari, unguarded. He'd wondered if she could ever be this way. Now he wondered if she could ever be this way *with him*.

"Luca, you must dance with me."

Gina issued the command and Luca sighed. "Gina."

"You know you want to. Besides, who else am I going to dance with? I don't see you for months on end. And this really is a quick trip."

Mari looked at Luca and a reluctant smile crawled up her cheek at his mulish expression.

She'd smiled more today than she could recall smiling in a long time. Seeing Luca being bossed around by his little sister was enjoyable. She'd gotten so used to him giving orders that she was delighted he knew how to indulge his sister.

"Ah, the family guilt," Mari teased him. "The same no matter what nationality you are."

"Oh, we Italians are particularly well-versed in it," Gina replied jauntily. "Let's go, Luca."

Mari watched, wishing she had the natural ease and grace that the Fioris seemed to possess. She'd insisted that Luca dance with Gina, and it was fun watching them. He took a wide step and spun his sister around, and the sound of her tinkling laughter reached Mari's ears. This was a man she could warm to. Like she had during their picnic, dinner with Gina seemed to have released the tension he'd been holding in. It made him even more attractive. She wet her lips. Not in a million years, would she have expected to be feeling a physical attraction to a man. Especially not now, when she knew Robert was out there, and free.

She knew her mother must know that he was out on parole, and for the first time, she wondered what Anne was doing, where she was. After the trial Mariella had walked away, not looking back. She couldn't. But through the years and silence between them, there was no denying that her mum had had to deal with the same thing. Perhaps even more than Mariella, she must be feeling like it wasn't ever truly over. For the first time in a long time, she felt sorry for her mother.

Breathless, Gina and Luca returned to the table. Gina sat but Luca looked down at Mari. She forced a smile, but she knew it was too late. He'd seen her melancholy. His eyes softened with concern and he held out his hand. "Mari? Dance?"

Mari stared at his extended palm. Could she? The scene was eerily close to her musings just before she'd dozed off in the limo. But now, faced with the reality, her stomach twisted in knots at the thought of being held so closely in his arms. She wanted to dance, she discovered. But she didn't trust herself to handle it. Not when the mere thought of Robert caused the trembling to start. The last thing she wanted to do was have the proximity of his body trigger her panic. For once, she was unsure of her own reaction and she hesitated.

"Go on, Mari, dance. Luca's actually a very good dancer." Gina narrowed her eyes at her brother. "But if you repeat that, I'll deny it."

Mari let out a breath and carefully put her hand in Luca's as she rose from her chair. Immediately she felt the warmth of his hand radiate up her arm. "I suppose I could dance, once."

He led her to the dim floor. Her heels echoed on the parquet and he turned, pulling her gently into his arms. She felt like she was in a dream. Gone was the Luca of before, the man of casual flair, of style and flirtation. In his place was a gentleman. He seemed to know how she felt about touching and kept a polite distance between them. Knowing he did it out of respect for her drew her to him in ways that his innate charm never could. Even so, one hand was warm at her waist, and he cupped her right hand within his, a perfect fit.

He was dashing tonight, dressed in a dark suit, his tie precisely knotted, his hair slicked back, reminiscent of the golden age days he so wanted the hotel to represent. The song was slow and jazzy, the singer's voice smooth and rich like melted caramel. Luca's arm cradled her waist as he lifted their joined hands close to his shoulder. "Relax," he whispered, and their feet started to move to the music.

Unlike when he danced with Gina, now Luca didn't say a word. Mari swallowed, closing her eyes and letting the music in, guiding her feet around the intimate floor. Their steps grew lazy and Mari drew his scent in, that expensive, man-scent that she knew she'd always recognize as his. Their bodies were closer now than before, and the trembling in her body wasn't fear. Perhaps it was, she thought, but not fear of her safety.

Fear of Luca and the way he made her feel. Because he was making her feel things she'd never wanted to feel at all.

Vulnerable. Wanting, dear lord. Wanting to give a part of herself to him, rather than closet it away.

His hips swayed against hers and she longed to rest her cheek against the fabric of his dinner jacket. His hand slid up her back, leaving a warm trail in its wake. This then, was what it felt like to feel cherished.

Breath caught in her throat. She'd felt safe once before only to have it go very wrong. As much as her heart told her she was safe with Luca, she couldn't be sure. Couldn't take that risk. She couldn't survive it again.

It was very good he was a short-term complication.

The music ended and Luca pulled away. "Let's walk."

"But Gina…"

"Gina has gone to bed."

His voice was warm in her ear and goose bumps erupted on her skin. She jerked her head to look back at their table, but he was right. It was empty, save for the remnants of their dessert.

He took her hand and led her to the balcony doors. As they stepped outside, the cool autumn air assaulted them and Mari welcomed it. It would clear her head. This was crazy.

The music was muted as Luca shut the doors behind them. Mari walked to the railing, resting against the sandstone and looking down over the valley. The moonshine glittered over the winding river.

"Why did Gina leave? I thought she was enjoying herself."

Luca's voice came, deep and smooth, from behind her. "I believe she thought we could use some time alone."

Everything in her dropped to her feet.

"Luca, I don't think this is a good idea." The words came out strangled, shaky.

"I know it's not."

She turned her head at his response. Having him admit it was wrong somehow made it all the more tempting. He was standing a few feet behind her, so tall and strong with the façade of the hotel behind him.

"Then what are we doing?"

"I brought you out here because…" He paused.

"Because…" Her voice was a whisper.

He turned away, abruptly. "I'm sorry, Mari. It was a mistake."

Disappointment cooled her warm skin, and she wrapped her arms around herself. Evenings on the terrace were very romantic, except for when it was only a few degrees Celsius above freezing and one was wearing a sleeveless dress. And when the man in question turned away. It amazed her to realize she didn't want him to.

She shivered and he looked back at her. "You're cold." Without hesitation, Luca removed his jacket and came forward, draping it around her shoulders. For a moment she wondered if he'd pull her into his arms as his hands gripped the lapels. But he released them and stood back.

His shirt stood out, crisp and white in the moonlight and Mari thought again how perfect he looked. And how looks could be deceiving.

"I thought you said Gina had children and couldn't come."

"She does. They are at our father's, with their nanny."

"I see."

"Do you?"

She tilted her head to look up at him. "Not really." She smiled. "What is clear is that you love her. And she loves you. I—" She broke off, wondering how much was safe to tell him. "I envy you. I never had a brother or sister, or much of a family at all."

"Where's your family now? What about your mother and father?"

He came to stand beside her at the balustrade and they looked out over the hulking shadows of the mountains together.

"I never knew my father, and I haven't spoken to my mother in several years."

"Does it have something to do with why you're so afraid of me?"

She bit on her lip. She couldn't look at him, not now. He wouldn't understand about Robert, and her mother, and it would only make things awkward between them. Her feelings might be changing, but Luca definitely wouldn't be interested in someone with so much baggage. He had a father and sister, and his whole business was based on family. They were from two very different worlds.

"It doesn't matter, Luca."

He linked his fingers with hers, and her heart soared. In ten minutes he'd treated her to more tender, caring touches than she remembered getting in her lifetime.

It would be too easy to fall for him.

"What about you? You must have a girlfriend…or girl-friends…lurking about somewhere."

She thought he'd take his hand away from hers, but he didn't. "Not really."

"Oh, that's right. You like playing the singles game. Do you really think you can do that forever?"

He did pull away then, and his jaw tightened. She wanted him close to her so badly she knew she had to push him away. "I don't particularly believe in love, Mari."

She smiled, but it was barely a curving of her lips. "That makes two of us."

His eyes, deep and dark, rested on her. The scent of his cologne wafted from his jacket so that she felt like he was touching her even when his hands were in his pockets. "What did it for you?"

He would walk away, but perhaps that was best anyway. He didn't need to know the story; he wouldn't be here long enough for it to matter. "When the one person who should love you doesn't, it tends to shape you whether you want it to or not. So I came here, and built my own life. It's all I have, Luca."

He nodded slowly. "And you think I will take it away from you."

She confirmed it by simply remaining where she was, her gaze steady on his.

"I won't."

"I won't let you."

That tripped a ghost of a smile.

"What about you, Luca? Why don't you believe in love?"

"My mother abandoned us…all of us…when we were children. I heard Gina crying herself to sleep every night. I saw my father's anguish…and yet he still loved her. She divorced him and he gave her a settlement, but not once in all these years has she come to see Gina, or me. Or father. She walked off to a whole other life."

"You haven't seen her since?"

"Not once. Not even when Gina was married, or when her children were born."

"I'm sorry, Luca." Mari's heart ached for him. She knew what it was to feel insignificant in the eyes of a parent. "But your father…"

"He did a wonderful job raising us, and running Fiori. But in the absence of her, Fiori became his bride. He's fierce about keeping it under his control."

Mari reached out and touched his sleeve. "He doesn't trust you."

"He thinks he does."

Luca wanted more. He wanted something for himself. Perhaps they had more in common than she originally thought.

"So you came here to prove something."

He nodded, again slowly. She was mesmerized by the

motion. The whole evening felt somehow like she was waking from a nightmare, complete with a sense of the surreal. He had touched her, and she hadn't flinched or been afraid. He was only here for a short time, and somehow being with him helped. She'd be a fool to question that, wouldn't she?

"I never, never want to be in the position that father was. I don't need any great psychoanalysis. I don't trust love, not the long-lasting kind."

"So you satisfy yourself with temporary flings."

"I tried something more once. It only ended up hurting both of us. It's better this way."

"What happened?"

Luca hesitated and she sensed his hurt. Perhaps she shouldn't pry. But an *open* Luca...it wasn't likely to happen again. She wanted to know. It was so unlike her, but she wanted to know about him, the little details that had shaped him into the man he was. Here in the starlight it was like she couldn't get enough.

Luca met her eyes. "I had an affair with a woman I worked with. It didn't end well."

"Who did the ending?"

His lips tipped up slightly, but there was little warmth in the pseudosmile. "She did. Unofficially, and for someone else."

The quirk of his eyebrow told her as much as any words could. Her lips dropped open. "You mean you caught her with another man?"

"Indeed."

"I see."

"It is just better for everyone to keep things up-front and honest. No unrealistic expectations. Don't you agree?"

At least they were on the same page. It should have been a comforting thought, but it wasn't. Not in the least. Her brows puckered. She didn't want a relationship, nor a fling.

And yet there was something within her that wanted to explore this thing that was growing between them.

"What are you thinking, Mariella Ross, standing there in the moonlight?"

She swallowed. Held his gaze not because she wanted to but because she could not look away. "What are *you* thinking?"

His voice was rich silk. "I think I'm about to make a big mistake." He took a step closer.

Mari saw immediately where this was heading and alarm bells started pealing madly. "Luca, I don't think…"

"Relax, Mari. I'm not interested in falling in love. Love only results in people being hurt."

She should be feeling relief. Those were her thoughts exactly. She didn't understand why she was slightly deflated at his statement. "We can agree on that, then."

She backed up against the stone railing, closing her eyes. "Mari."

When she opened her eyes he was directly in front of her, his warm gaze steady on hers.

"I know you've been hurt badly." Her eyes widened but he continued in that same, soft, hypnotic tone. "I can see it in you. I realized it after that day in the attic. I won't hurt you, Mari. We'll keep our eyes open. I promise."

He lifted his hand and his fingers disappeared beneath her hair. Her breath caught as she fought against the urge to lean into the pressure of his hand. Luca kept his promises. Eyes open.

"Beautiful Mari. I cannot deny there is something between us. I feel it. You feel it, too. We both felt it today, in the meadow. I could see it in your eyes. But the difference is we set the limits. We set the boundaries."

"I can't sleep with you, Luca." It came out on a rush of breath.

A smile teased his mouth. "Perhaps a kiss."

He was close enough now that she had to tip her chin up to meet his eyes. It was a struggle to keep them open as his fingertips moved through her hair. "Kiss."

"Surely you've kissed before?"

Mari's insides trembled. She had, but not for a very long time. Not without utter fear.

"A time or two."

His face was so close his breath warmed her cheeks. Her fingers tightened around the edges of his jacket. Surely, if she could make it through a first kiss, it would all be fine. "Kiss me, Mariella."

Their gazes held for a second. He was waiting for her, she realized. He understood she'd been hurt and he was letting her make the first move. It was unexpected. She was used to him bossing her around. Now he was giving her the power and it made him even more difficult to resist.

She leaned into his hand, tilted her face up, and with her heart in her throat, touched her lips to his.

For a split second she let them rest there, testing. Their eyes were open, and the connection between them was so strong it rocked her core. His lips were warm, soft, waiting. She let go of the jacket and rested a hand against his heart and she felt the thunder beneath her palm.

The simple movement changed everything. Her breath came out in a rush as Luca's hand commanded her head, tilting it gently to the side and he opened his lips. Her lashes fluttered shut. The kiss was deliberate but soft, easing into the passion slowly, building the fire with teasing nips.

For the first time since leaving her old life behind, she threw caution to the wind, wrapping her arms around his torso and pulling him closer.

The moment she did it, everything changed. His hand swept from beneath her hair and dragged her close. His tongue swept into her mouth and she wilted against him. The jacket fell from her shoulders to the floor of the terrace and his hands warmed her skin as they roamed over the bare flesh of her arms.

Glory.

He broke off the kiss, resting his forehead against hers.

Mariella pulled out of his arms, immediately feeling the cool air and the bite of cold reality. "Thank you."

His eyes glittered at her knowingly. "Thank you?"

She had to take a step backward. She'd been swept away in the magic of the moment and had forgotten. She was supposed to be afraid. She was supposed to keep personal distance. She was not supposed to let herself be vulnerable. She could not… a sob built in her chest. She could not allow herself to *feel*.

She wanted to deny it, but he'd know she was running away from it, and him. And to acknowledge it had affected her deeply was to take things where she didn't want them to go.

"As you said, there's a certain amount of chemistry." She lifted her chin, daring him to contradict her.

Instead he laughed, reaching out and grazing her cheek with a knuckle.

"You are a strong woman, Mari. You do my grandmother's name justice. She was a strong woman, too."

Mari swallowed. Coming on the heels of the kiss, she was seeing a whole new side to Luca. Whether he recognized it or not, he carried around his own scars, ones indelibly scraped on his heart.

She turned away, leaving him staring at her back as she rested her elbows on the balustrade.

"You remind me of her." He paused for a moment. "Why did you not correct Gina when she called you by your full name?"

Mari shrugged. "It would have been rude of me. We'd just met."

"But you didn't mind being rude to me."

She heard the dull sound of his shoes on the stone floor as he came closer. "You can take it."

"I appreciate you being kind to my sister. Annoyance that she is."

Mari held her breath as his hands appeared on either side of her and he leaned closer, not quite an embrace, but with his chest leaning warm and secure against her back.

"Mariella."

Mari's eyelids drifted shut. The soft way he said it was sweet seduction. But it was no better as his image appeared behind her eyes. The way he looked tonight, the way the expensive cut of his suit emphasized his physique, making him look like a movie star from bygone days. Too much like the man from her dreams. She had to resist him. Had to. This was madness. She was supposed to be afraid. Repulsed. She wasn't supposed to be feeling like this.

His lips touched the back of her neck and she quivered. Tilted her head without thinking, allowing him access to the gentle curve.

His arms tightened around her and his wide hands rested just below her waist, their warmth seeping through to her skin.

"You didn't correct me just now."

"No, I didn't." The words came out on a breathy whisper. How could she possibly explain that the way he said it sounded different? How could she do that without making this more than either of them wanted?

"You would honor me if you let me use your given name,

Mariella. It was the name of a woman I loved very much and I've missed the sound of it on my lips."

Her lips parted but no sound came out. How could she refuse him now? They'd moved this far out of the realm of strictly business and she wasn't at all sure how it had happened. She only knew they had a connection. Knew that somehow tonight they had shared more than simple family history. Somehow, in between the main course and this moment, she'd started to trust Luca. She'd let him in, whether he realized it or not.

She swallowed, opened her eyes and turned so that she was still in his arms, but facing him.

"You really mean that. That's not a line, is it."

He shook his head. "My *nonna* was very special to me. And she would have liked you, Mariella. She'd have liked you very much."

Mari would have answered, but Luca bent his head and kissed her again, sending all her words scattering into the starlight.

CHAPTER SEVEN

"You wanted to see me, Mari?"

Mari looked up as Luca stopped at the door to her office. The smooth sound of his voice sent flutters over her skin and she shook them away. The intimate whispers of last night weren't real. Today was what was real. She had to set the tone.

Last night had been a fantasy, dressed up in finery, gazing at stars from balconies. But today they had to get back to business. Gone was the dashing movie-star gorgeous hero, and in his place was the real Luca. The one in regular trousers and trendy shirts that showed off the lean physique of his upper body. She couldn't stop the visceral reaction to his appearance any more than she could stop the instant knowledge that kissing him had been a terrible mistake.

No matter how wonderful.

"Luca, come in."

He ambled into the office. She'd been here early, had made sure of it. Yesterday had been a one-off. Gallivanting on picnics and romantic dinners. Being held in his arms and kissing beneath the stars. That wasn't reality. Reality was the Cascade and the job at hand. How easily she'd forgotten. How completely he'd managed to distract her.

He took a seat across from her desk, crossing an ankle over

his knee. "I'm sorry I wasn't here earlier. I had breakfast with Gina. And she doesn't rise early. If I had known you wanted to see me…"

"You'd have what?" She folded her hands on top of the papers neatly arranged in front of her.

"I'd have made myself available."

The dizzying thought of Luca making himself *available* to her spun through her veins, the anticipation of possibility seducing her away from her goal. No one had ever made her a priority. No one had put something off for her before. But for all she knew that could just be pretty words.

"You're here now. And since we were out yesterday afternoon, there's a lot to catch up on."

She began explaining about contractors and unions while he was looking at her. She stuttered over a word, realizing he was gazing at her face, her neck, the buttons on her jacket. He wasn't paying attention. Scratch that. He was paying too much attention!

"Luca, are you listening?"

He straightened his shoulders and leaned forward a little. "Intently."

Oh, indeed he was. She blinked, forced herself to keep to the topic at hand. "I needed to see you about these invoices." She held out a sheaf of papers. "Luca, those numbers can't possibly be correct." He'd mentioned upgrading the spa facilities, but the numbers coming in didn't make any sense to her.

He glanced down at the sheets. "Yes, that's right." He tossed off the matter. "What's on your schedule for this afternoon?"

Her face blanched as she ignored his last question and focused on the fact that he'd said the invoices were accurate. "Look again. That decimal point can't be right."

He handed them back to her. "It's all in order, Mari."

She tapped her pen against the blotter, unsure of how to

proceed. Surely he could see the folly in laying out so much money in addition to all the other things he was adding. She had seen the bill for the new draperies for the Athabasca Room and had nearly fainted. It had gone way beyond what they'd agreed when they'd laid out the budget. Now this…

"This is not what we budgeted. And you went over our budget for the drapes by nearly thirty percent!"

"It was a great price for a much higher quality fabric. Gina found it and…"

"Gina?" Mari stopped fidgeting and put down her pen. Fighting Luca was difficult enough. But now she had two Fioris to keep up with. Gina had delivered a sculpture, but she also did much of the interior design detail for Fiori Resorts. Trying to keep Gina from spending them into the ground was yet another tick on her to-do list. She couldn't take them both on. She took a deep breath.

"I told you she was persistent."

Then she caught a hint of a smile at the corners of his mouth.

And she remembered that mouth on hers.

And his hands on her skin.

And how everything else had vacated her mind during those moments.

He tried to charm her and then ignored the plans they'd already set out for the Cascade. He'd done it more than once already. This was one time when his charm wasn't going to work.

They had set out a plan. A plan to enhance the hotel while looking after her staff. It was up to her to keep it, especially if he kept looking at her in *that* way.

She ran a hand over her hair, though not a strand had dared to escape her precisely arranged knot. "Luca, we can't possibly afford the draperies, let alone the spa. The plans already mean incorporating other space into this expanded spa vision.

Need I remind you how expensive that restructure is going to be? But this…this is beyond exorbitant. It's *criminal*."

"I assure you it's not." He continued on, unfazed. As cool as could be. "This isn't a third-class hotel, Mariella. It's a *world-class* hotel. That means going with the best." He lowered his chin and pinned her with his gaze. "Fiori always chooses the best."

She heaved a sigh, ignoring what she knew he intended to be a disarming compliment. "There must be a way to trim these costs. You promised no shutdowns or layoffs. With something of this magnitude…you won't be able to avoid it. The money has to come from somewhere."

"I won't?" He grinned suddenly. "Oh, Mari, that sounds like a challenge. And I do like a challenge."

Her heart slammed against her ribs, but she narrowed her eyes. He hadn't had to say the words to know that he considered *her* a challenge. And she didn't like that, not one bit. She'd been a challenge to Robert, she understood that now. She'd been independent and free and she knew the challenge had been for her stepfather to break her. And he'd done a fabulous job of that, for a long time.

But last night she'd proved that his power over her wasn't absolute. She'd enjoyed Luca's touch. She'd come alive beneath his hands and had welcomed his kiss. And somehow that made her feel just a little bit powerful. She wouldn't be under anyone's thumb ever again. But she refused to be a challenge for Luca.

The trouble was, she *wanted* to trust him. So far he'd kept to his word about the changes to the hotel, despite his exorbitant taste. And the staff was, for the most part, happy. Luca had a way about him. Even when he'd explained to some staff that in order to stay, they'd have to do different tasks than was the norm, they'd greeted the news enthusiastically. No one had been dismissed or made redundant. In fact, the whole place was running remarkably smoothly, considering.

And the fact that his sudden smile had her entire body warming didn't help, either. It drew her eyes to his mouth again. And that made her remember last night and how magical his mouth had felt on hers.

For once, in those moments in Luca's arms, she'd forgotten Robert Langston even existed. And he'd been a constant for the last twenty years, present or not. For once she'd felt sheltered and protected and not defined by what had happened to her before. The world had opened up for her in the moment she'd twined her arms around Luca's ribs. And it had been exhilarating and terrifying.

Now in the cool light of day, it seemed impossible. For nothing had really changed. Robert was still out there, and nothing could change the things he'd done to her, or her mother. Luca would still be leaving in a matter of weeks and her goal had to be the big picture. Wasn't that what Luca had said? And the big picture was holding on to this job that she'd worked so hard for.

"It's not a challenge, it's fact." She bolstered her argument with numbers. If they could just keep this about the hotel, and not about them, then she might stand a hope of keeping things clear and professional. "This invoice alone is for over a hundred thousand dollars."

"And every guest who comes out of our spa will feel like a million."

"I doubt it."

Mari watched as Luca ran a finger beneath his bottom lip and she remembered how their bodies had been close. How she'd shamelessly wrapped her arms around his ribs and pulled him in so that the warmth of his body pulsed through her. That couldn't happen again. A relationship was out of the question. Boundaries. He'd said they could set the boundaries. She wished he'd let her.

"Have you ever had a spa day, Mariella?"

"I've had facials and pedicures, sure." Once, when she'd first moved here and had treated herself. When she'd been re-inventing herself.

"No, not that kind. The kind where you spend a whole day. You are massaged and buffed and polished from head to toe, so that when you're done you feel like you own an entirely new body."

She shook her head.

"You must. I'll talk to Gina."

Gina again.

She was losing ground quickly. Somehow this conversation had gotten away from the topic of expenditures and she had to bring it back.

"I do not have time for a spa day, Gina or not."

His smile was crafty. "But if you're with Gina, she's out of my hair."

"And conveniently, so am I." She raised her brows so he knew she was on to him. "You made these changes without even consulting me."

"I *am* the owner."

Mari unclenched her fingers, relieved they were back to the safe topic of talking about the hotel again. "As I'm well aware." She smiled coolly. "I have to run these figures again, if they are, as you say, correct. Find a way to trim costs some-where else." She didn't add that she blamed him for the extra work; there was no need. He never seemed to listen to her cautions about money. He simply forged ahead with whatever scheme he had in mind. And he was a great one for schemes.

"Mariella, you are going to worry yourself into the ground. Take the day. Enjoy it." He reached over and put his hand over hers. "You're no good to me or the employees here if you're out on stress leave because you've pushed yourself too hard."

Words seemed to strangle when she tried to talk and she paused. He wasn't goading her or criticizing. His eyes were sincere. He actually sounded like he cared.

He was so hard to resist when he was this way. It had been easier for her to deal with the work this morning than think about the what-if's with Luca. But he was here now and work didn't solve a thing. If anything it only served to increase her awareness of him. To highlight how often during the day they were together. To remind her of how much she'd lost herself in his arms last night. To remind her of how much she longed to trust someone, to have them fill that empty space she'd become so adept at ignoring.

Luca saw her face change, saw that little hint of vulnerability she tried to keep hidden. He recognized that look. Gina had had it, less now that she had her own family, but he'd seen it enough growing up. In his days here, he hadn't seen Mariella with any friends. She never talked about her family. She was, to his recollection, the most *alone* person he'd ever met. And something told him she had it that way on purpose.

It would be good for her to have a day with Gina. Moreover, it would get them both out of his hair for a blessed few hours so he could work in peace.

"I want to do this for you, Mariella. I want you to take the rest of the morning and treat yourself to a massage or a wrap or whatever you like." And he lifted her hand and kissed the back.

It was a mistake. The scent of her skin as he touched it with his lips made him remember the feel of her last night, soft and pliant in his arms. It had affected him more than he'd expected, but he'd been unable to resist going to her on the balcony. There was nothing brash about her, she had no agenda, and that set her apart from most of the women he escorted to various functions. But that wasn't all.

It would be very easy to care for Mari, to care too much. She seemed to need it, but he wasn't the one to give it. He would be leaving. She was different. He knew she wasn't the kind of woman to string along. And he didn't have it in him to give her anything more.

He dropped her hand and sauntered to the door. As he reached the threshold, he turned his head back. "Oh, if you could, be back at two-thirty. I've made us an appointment to see some artwork at a local gallery."

He shut the door behind him. Mari could never know that the attraction was becoming very real for him. It would complicate everything, and right now he needed to keep things simple.

At two-thirty Mari met Luca in the lobby.

"What, no Gina?" She'd left Luca's sister after their hot stone massages, refusing an invitation to lunch and instead working in her office, desperate to keep up with the workload.

"Gina sends her apologies, but Charlie has taken her back to Calgary to catch a flight home."

She caught the small furrow between his eyebrows. "Has something happened? Is it your father?"

"Why would you ask about my father?" The wrinkle deepened.

She looked up at him and put her hand on his arm. "You said her children were staying with him."

He sighed, and put his hand over hers. "No, it's not Papa. I rather think it's Gina and Angelo, but she wouldn't tell me."

"I'm sorry."

He put on a smile, though she saw through it to the worry. How long had he been shouldering the weight of his family? The thought came to her and she realized it fit. Luca felt responsible. He hid it behind a playboy-type façade, but after the way he'd spoken about his father and now his sister, she was sure of it.

"Let's not worry about that now. You look lovely. The spa clearly agreed with you."

Mari began to lift her hand to smooth her hair again but stopped. It had been wonderful, being fussed over and pampered. The stress had melted away with the heat of the rocks. She straightened her shoulders. "Thank you."

Yet she knew days at the spa and art shopping trips were things she couldn't get used to. She was Mari Ross of small town Ontario. Luca was Fiori of Fiori Resorts, used to glamour and a lifestyle very different from hers. It was understandable why she'd find that seductive. But it was also a reminder of why it was temporary.

Things like this simply didn't last.

When they reached the car, he leaned over and kissed her temple before she got in. "You look radiant," he murmured in her ear.

The spot on her scalp where he'd pressed his lips burned. He was acting as though they did this every day, for Pete's sake! All the feelings from last night's fairy tale came rushing back, and she tried to push them away. "It's the facial," she replied curtly, sliding over and buckling her seat belt.

They started with a small gallery tucked in behind Banff Avenue. Mari examined piece by piece, from soapstone sculptures to paintings to spectacular photographic work. As the visit continued, Mari felt like she was swept along with a whirlwind…only everywhere she turned, there was Luca, a few steps behind her. Always aware of him, the sound of his voice as he spoke to the proprietor. And using softer, more intimate tones for her.

It was hard to ignore him. Even if she really wanted to.

The saleslady was off to wrap a few of their smaller purchases to take with them, when Luca's hands draped over her shoulders, his fingers gripping the ends of her scarf. She jumped at the contact.

"Nervous?"

If only he knew. She wasn't sure she'd ever get used to sudden moves like that, even if it were Luca doing it. She breathed away the adrenaline rush. "I didn't see you behind me."

"This is lovely. The shade brings out the gray in your eyes."

"My eyes are ordinary blue."

She turned around to face him, expecting to see him smiling at her. Instead he was gazing at her, a serious expression clouding his eyes.

"Your eyes, Mariella, are anything but ordinary," he murmured, and before she could catch her breath, he dipped his head and touched her lips with his.

Her fingers gripped his arm as the gentle contact seared through her. His lips were soft as they explored her mouth, undemanding yet beguiling. He pulled away slightly, their breath mingling, waiting. Mari dimly remembered they were standing in the middle of a shop, but the noise faded away to a distant hum as she leaned in the inch and a half to kiss him again. Her eyelids drifted closed and Luca's free hand cupped her cheek.

The tenderness of it made her want to weep.

She hadn't realized, hadn't thought that the absence of affection had left such a huge hole. She hadn't wanted contact, or tenderness, or even kindness. Hadn't wanted to make herself vulnerable. She still didn't. But when Luca touched her this way, kissed her this way, like she was precious, she craved more of it. Like gentle, steady rain after a long drought.

He broke the kiss when a car horn honked outside on the street.

"Luca," she whispered. She'd come here to keep an eye on

his purchases. To make sure he didn't outspend them again. To make sure she still had a say in the decisions being made.

Only it had backfired. She'd allowed him in and...dear God. She had *feelings* for him. Alarm thudded through her. She didn't do feelings! She had to keep things level. Luca wasn't really interested in *her,* she wasn't his type of woman. She knew that. Thank goodness one of them was thinking rationally.

Yet the thought that Luca wasn't interested in her at all left her crushed with disappointment. How could that be, when it was what she wanted? She didn't want to be closer to him, did she?

She lifted her confused eyes to his.

And was shocked to see her feelings mirrored back at her. He didn't say anything. But she knew. She knew she hadn't been alone in being affected by the kiss.

"There you go." The saleslady held out two bags, smiling like finding them in an embrace was a sweet secret. "The rest of your purchases will be shipped to the hotel."

Mari felt Luca's body behind her as she turned, the solid wall of him against her back as he put his arm around her, cradling her against him as he rested his chin atop her head. Mari wanted to beg him, *please don't be so kind.* And somehow she heard his unspoken answer: *Let me in.*

They left the shop and ventured on foot to the next, cradled between two restaurants on the busy main street. As he held the door for her, he murmured, "That's probably not a good idea, letting that happen again."

She stepped inside the door, the scent of vanilla and lavender teasing her nose. "No?"

"You're the manager, and I'm the owner. It wouldn't be good for appearances."

Mari nearly laughed. Luca, concerned about appearances? He was the one who wandered through the hotel in jeans instead of business suits. He was the one who asked for picnics and dinners and shunned anything traditional. He was the one who had his picture in magazines with a new woman on his arm every month, it seemed. "If I remember correctly, *you* kissed *me*."

"I believe you kissed me back."

Something in the last few days had caused something to break free in Mari. Instead of backing off she lifted her chin. "That's hardly the point now, is it."

"Fiori does have an image to uphold, Mariella."

Mari goggled.

"Who are you and what have you done with Luca?"

He only offered a tight smile in response. Mari stepped inside the gallery, immediately surrounded by pieces by local artists. She was secretly pleased he wanted to showcase local art. It was part of what the Cascade should be about. She was beginning to see that. This place was like no other place on earth. It deserved to be showcased as such.

She found some particularly interesting carvings and when she looked up, Luca had moved on. She spied him in a side room, his hands in his pockets as he looked at paintings. She sighed. He was so…something. He was just so Luca. He made no apologies for it. The self-assurance was sexy, she realized. He'd been molded and shaped long ago, when his mother had left all of them. Now he knew who he was. She envied that.

When she reached him, he didn't look at her but simply said, "There are some wonderful pieces here."

For a moment she wondered about the cost of adding original art to the hotel. But put it aside for once. How could she worry about dollars and cents for her livelihood, when she'd splurged for perfectly selfish reasons today?

"I haven't been in here before."

"Don't you like art?"

He stopped his perusal and turned his head. The kiss they'd shared was suddenly in the front of her mind.

"I haven't given it much thought."

He turned back to the painting before him.

She found a bench and put down her bags. It was true. She hadn't had time for things like art appreciation. In the last store she'd merely followed his lead. She'd had more immediate needs, more pressing concerns. Like getting her life back. Taking charge. Moving forward instead of being paralyzed by fear.

And she'd done quite well, until that phone call. The one telling her Robert had served his time. Had fulfilled his debt to society. It was no solace at all—what about his debt to her? To her mother? Where was he now? She could swear up and down she'd rebuilt her life, but all she'd done was run. Run and pretend. Now she didn't even know where her mother was. If she'd run, as well. If she was even okay. She'd gone years telling herself it didn't matter, but now with Robert out of prison, her thoughts kept turning back to the one parent she had.

Luca didn't get any of that. Nor would he. She couldn't bring herself to explain it to him. Despite their newfound closeness, she certainly didn't know him, or trust him enough to fill him in on the sordid details.

"Are you feeling well?"

"Excuse me?"

Luca was close to her shoulder. "Mariella, you are pale as a ghost. Are you all right?"

"I'm fine. Show me the paintings you like." She had to stop giving her stepfather any power. She'd left that life behind.

He took her hand and showed her his favorites. She dutifully nodded and commented. She ignored the way he looked at her with his brows meeting in the middle.

She bluffed her way through it, going through the motions as best she could. The paintings he liked were lovely, she could see that. They were mostly landscapes, and with the Rocky Mountains being their backyard, sweeping mountain scenes were prevalent. He favored those over the wildlifes or stills, she noticed numbly.

"Whichever ones you want will be fine."

He stopped in his tracks. "You have no opinion? You're not going to pull out your calculator and quote budgets to me?"

Mari swallowed. "You're going to do what you wish anyway, Luca. Why argue?"

"Because it's what we do best," he replied.

"I don't want to argue. The paintings are fine with me. They are very nice."

He stepped closer, his face puzzled. "But how do they make you feel, Mari?"

Feel? "Luca, it's paint on canvas." She didn't want to talk about how she felt. Today she'd felt like she was the girl she'd always wanted to be but hadn't been allowed. She could do what she wanted, buy what she wanted, feel what she wanted, and no one would punish her for it. She could take a morning off and no one would berate her. She could splurge on vanity and it was fine. The self-indulgence had been heady. Then reality had crashed in and she felt alone again, too weary to fight. Luca could make her forget, and it was wonderful while it lasted. But coming back to earth was a big thud and it hurt a little more each time.

"Yes, and the Cascade is a hunk of rock on a hillside. Even you know better than that."

"I'm afraid I'm not an art aficionado."

"You don't have to be to have feelings, Mari."

"Of course I have feelings!" she snapped.

She turned away, ashamed. Even-tempered, reliable Mari

was suddenly all over the place. One moment she was sighing into his eyes and the next she was so overwhelmed she was biting his head off. She didn't know who she was anymore. He kept pushing at her, demanding things of her and her well-ordered life wasn't so black and white. She certainly didn't feel up to dealing with everything she was feeling.

He led her around a corner. "Look at these. Tell me what you feel. Let them speak to you. You'll know it when you see it."

She sighed, put upon. When he got like this, there was no deterring him. She had learned that already. She may as well humor him.

These were no landscapes. The paintings here were different, angled shapes and colors and impressions. Mari walked past, feeling no connections. Longing simply to return to the hotel. She was tired. She was drained. The whole day had been something special, but she doubted he'd understand how much it had meant to her. She'd felt a part of something.

Something based on a lie.

And then she turned a corner and saw it. Sweeps of blue with a brilliant core of red, exploding out from the middle in splashes.

It made no sense. But something about it spoke to her and she stepped ahead, lifting her fingers, coming close but not actually touching the canvas.

"Mari?"

Mari ignored his voice, but knew he'd been right all along. As hard as she'd fought, he'd been sure of himself. There was something inside her that Luca had set free, and it was right here in oil and canvas, looking back at her. She couldn't explain why, but she knew she had to have it.

CHAPTER EIGHT

"You like it."

She nodded, her eyes roving over the blend of paint and canvas. "I don't know why…it isn't even of anything at all."

"But…" he prompted.

She looked over her shoulder. "But it speaks to me somehow. I can't tell you what this is a painting of. I can only tell you that I feel connected to it somehow."

She turned back to the painting, her eyes drawn to the scarlet centre.

"So my Mari feels first and thinks later. I'm surprised." His words, his breath caressed the skin behind her ear, sending a delicious shiver down her spine. A warmth flooded her at being called *his*. It made her feel protected, like she belonged somewhere. And that with belonging, a sort of freedom she hadn't expected. She remembered how he'd described the view from his suite that very first day. Freedom. Little had she imagined then. Had she ever felt this way before, in her entire life? Like around every corner was an open door?

Had Luca changed her *that* much? How had he snuck past all her defenses so easily?

She half turned. "Surprised? Didn't you think I had feelings, Luca?" She did have feelings, so many of them that she refused to show the world. Letting people see inside her gave them *power.* It was much better to think, and wait. She'd been thinking a lot about Luca lately, and letting him in bit by bit, despite reservations. She couldn't seem to help herself, and couldn't pinpoint it any more than she could say exactly what it was about the painting that was so striking.

"Of course I did." He tucked an errant hair behind her ear. "I merely wondered what would finally make them break free."

She paused slightly, but she was growing bolder; dealing with him on a daily basis and having to stick up for herself had achieved that. She'd learned to trust him a little, and trust was uncharacteristic of her. And yes, he drove her crazy when he bossed her around. But he also touched her heart when he was gentle with her, as if he already knew her secrets.

After years of planning every moment, every aspect of her life, the ability to break out of the box was exciting. She wished he'd kiss her again, like he had on the balcony after dinner the other night. Like he had just minutes ago. She looked up and met his eyes boldly. "What if I told you it was you?"

His golden eyes met hers. Clung. Without anything happening between them she felt the power of their earlier kiss. Swayed closer to him.

"Tell me why this painting." He broke the connection and faced the work of art.

She looked back at it, her heart thudding. The opportunity was gone but she hadn't imagined the link between them.

She wasn't sure why this particular painting spoke so strongly to her. It wasn't a painting of anything concrete at all, just a swirl of color. It wasn't of people that reminded her of someone, or mountains or lakes or places. It was a vertical rectangle with the color of twilight forming the background, the tones and shades swirling together in an ocean of blues. And bisecting it, a splash of deep, throbbing red.

"It's peace," she murmured, taking a step closer to it. Without thinking she reached down and took his hand in hers. "It's tranquillity and contentment and a thudding heart." When she looked at it, it made her ache. Made her hope, and that was something she'd given up on long ago. Hope was about the future, and she lived day to day. Luca would think that silly, she was sure, so she kept the last to herself.

Luca smiled, though he was unusually unsettled. He'd called her "his" Mari without thinking, and it shocked him to realize he thought of her that way. He'd meant to share the art with her, but it had become more very quickly and he felt the need to back away. The way she'd looked up at him, the way she'd credited him with her response, sent warning bells crashing through him.

It was all his fault. He'd ignored the signs and had told himself that he wasn't getting in too deep. Because he'd sworn not to.

He was about casual liaisons, but nothing about his feelings for Mari were simple or casual. It was a miscalculation he hadn't counted on. He'd be a liar if he didn't admit he had looked for an excuse to see her today. The kiss last night had affected him more than he'd expected. And he'd enjoyed knowing it had affected her, too, seeing her back in form when he'd arrived this morning. He'd taken pleasure knowing he'd gotten to her, seeing her trussed up in her suit and with her hair pulled back. Wearing her battle armor. Keeping him at arm's length. She had been right about one thing. He did enjoy a challenge.

But something had changed. It was more than enjoying her company, of matching wits. There was a connection with Mari that he hadn't anticipated. He felt it when she'd reacted to the painting. And when their eyes had met moments ago. And when he'd kissed her earlier this afternoon.

He took a step back, his brows pulling together as he stared at her back. "That's the meaning of art, Mari. It doesn't have to make sense. It just needs to mean something."

She stepped up to the canvas and looked at the price. "That's insane."

He looked at the number. It wasn't exorbitant, but he remembered again that he was used to Fiori money and that such a sum was nothing to him. For someone in Mari's situation, he imagined it was quite different.

"Think of how it elicited such a reaction from you, and then try to quantify it. Can you put a price on that?"

"I can and have." She smiled, even as she gazed wistfully at the canvas.

He laughed, he couldn't help it. Mari was so charmingly practical. It reminded him how far apart they were and he took a little comfort in it. She was not for him. He was not for her. She was the kind of woman who looked for long-term stability, and he traveled around the world with his job, settling nowhere. This was just a blip on the radar.

"I could afford it, if I didn't eat for the next year. This is why art is in museums rather than living rooms."

She started to walk away. "I don't know why I was so struck by it anyway."

"You don't need to know why. Sometimes understanding takes all the magic away."

Once he'd said the words he considered them. Mari moved down the wall, looking at the next pieces and he watched her. Maybe he was making this too complicated. An attraction did not a fairy tale make. And he was the last person on earth to believe in fairy tales. Gina believed enough for the two of them and he was happy for her. But it wasn't something he was willing to risk himself.

Gina had been young and full of her own grief at their

mother's abandonment. Luca had been a little older. He had seen the toll it had taken on his father. He'd realized his father had truly loved his mother. Time and again he'd seen his father try to win her love only to fail, and in the end losing her had broken Papa's heart. Luca had never wanted to put himself through that anguish.

Maybe it was doing this job for too long that had him dissatisfied. Tired of the endless travel and rootlessness, of living out of a suitcase and only going home for holidays. Maybe that was what intrigued him about Mari. She knew her place and was happy in it.

He was smart enough to know it wasn't him she was enamored with. She was taken with the changes; with experiencing new things and it was breathtaking to watch her blossom. But he wasn't fool enough to believe it was him, as she said.

He wouldn't take it further than it had already gone, and in the end they'd part as friends. He'd return to Italy.

The idea didn't seem as charming as it had a few weeks ago. What was waiting for him at home seemed flat and lackluster now. More than ever he longed to break free and take his own place within the company. To step out of the shadows. To be Luca, not just the son and brother.

Mari returned to his side. "Have you finished?" She placed her hand on his sleeve. "I thought I'd do a little shopping of my own before the stores close. But if you're not…I can stay."

He wanted her to stay with him, he realized. And he didn't like knowing it. Didn't like knowing he'd somehow lost control of the situation he himself had orchestrated. He had to keep it to their original agreement. So that no one got hurt in the end. Maybe he wasn't looking for love, but he sure wasn't looking to hurt anyone, either.

"No, you go. I'll see you tomorrow."

"You're sure?"

He leaned over and on impulse dropped a light kiss on Mari's lips, wondering why in the world they tasted like strawberries. "I'm positive." He aimed a winning smile at her.

"All right then. Don't forget, we have a meeting in the morning with the landscape designer for our spring plans."

"I'll be there."

She squeezed his hand and grabbed her shopping bags. He turned around and looked at the painting again, but for the life of him he didn't see a beating heart.

Mari took a moment to roll her shoulders back and forth, easing out the tension. There had been too many long days in a row, she realized. There had been no more kisses, and she had told herself that was for the best even as she felt the dull ache of disappointment. Reminded herself of it even as she caught herself staring at his perfect lips in meetings or when they met in his office or hers about the renovations.

Once she walked in while he had Gina on speakerphone. She'd paused, unsure of what to do, but Luca had waved her in. His hair stood up in rows where his fingers had run through it and the scowl line was back between his brows. They were speaking in Italian, but at the end, his voice softened. "I love you, Gigi. *Ciao*."

The line was disconnected.

"You're worried about her. Is everything okay?"

His smile was thin. "It will be. She says hello, by the way."

Their obvious closeness made her wish once more for the family she'd never had. Seeing Luca with his sister, teasing, arguing, and like today—always supportive—made her long for it.

For the first time, she felt free to be herself. Luca had no expectations of her and that was liberating. The way he smiled seemed as if it were just for her. The way he'd held her hand felt like it had always been that way. And his kisses had taken her breath away. Even knowing it was imprudent, she couldn't help but wish he'd do it again.

The clincher had been when the delivery man had arrived on Saturday morning.

She'd carefully unwrapped the package, staring down at the painting she'd admired during their trip to the gallery. The fact that he had spent so much money to buy it and give it to her said it all. It didn't require a note, but there was a brief one anyway, scrawled on a plain white card...

When it speaks to your heart, you know it's the right one.

No one had ever given her such a gift. And it wasn't the money. She knew now that the price tag meant nothing to Luca. And it hadn't been for appearances; if he'd wanted to impress he would have given her jewelry. This was more personal. It was perfect.

She had yet to thank him, though. Saturday had rolled into Sunday and she'd spent the day cleaning and picking up groceries...she hadn't noticed the fridge, but she had noticed Tommy's empty food bowl. Now it was Monday and the opportunity hadn't arisen.

She wasn't sure what she'd say. She'd glimpsed him this morning, walking through the lobby and her heart had given a little leap just at the sight of him. She was falling for him. She hadn't wanted a relationship and even now it wasn't a real one, but she couldn't help her feelings. She saw so many things in Luca to love. She knew now she'd seen them in the beginning, but hadn't recognized them as they'd been blanketed in her own fears and insecurities. The truth was, he was a conscientious, caring boss who worked hard and was extremely capable. Luca wasn't the irresponsible playboy she'd expected. He was nothing like.

If she thanked him for the painting now, she'd probably make a complete fool of herself and say something sentimental.

She had to keep her head. Soon Luca would be gone. She'd get over her feelings. She'd be fine. She'd look back on it all as a beautiful time.

Mari stepped into the lobby, her eyes taking in the changes that were ongoing. The lobby was, for all intents and purposes, operating in half its usual square footage while the other half underwent its transformation. Even though they'd cordoned off the area being worked on, there was still mess and disorder, and she wondered if it would have been better to close the hotel for a few months. On the other hand...she looked at the staff. They were doing a fantastic job of adjusting. More than one had mentioned to her how excited they were to be able to take part in it all. And while she'd felt duty-bound to try to keep a check on the plans, she could admit to herself that Luca had been right. He *was* good at his job. The hotel was going to be stunning when it was completed.

But as she turned, she caught sight of a man at the make-shift reception desk. Something about him unnerved Mari. She couldn't pinpoint it, but a cold feeling of uneasiness swept through her. Colleen, the employee behind the desk, had a smile pasted on her face but Mari could tell it was forced. The man gestured with his hands and Mari heard his raised voice carry across the lobby, over the construction noise.

But it was her job to deal with this sort of thing, no matter how distasteful. She gave her shoulders one last roll, put on her friendliest smile and went forward.

"Good afternoon, and welcome to the Fiori Cascade. Is there some way I can be of assistance?"

Colleen's taut cheeks relaxed a bit. "Good afternoon, Ms. Ross. I was just explaining to Mr. Reilly that we've adjusted his reservation to a room on the third floor. Due to the renovations."

Mr. Reilly was not appeased. "And I was telling *her*—" he turned his back on Colleen altogether "—that arrangement is completely unacceptable."

Mari clenched her teeth. He had presented his back to Colleen, the slight deliberate and rude. But he was their guest and he had been inconvenienced. It was her job to smooth ruffled feathers. "I'm the manager here, perhaps I can be of help. You were booked in which room?"

"The Primrose," Colleen supplied over his shoulder.

Mari kept the warm smile in place. The Primrose Room was one of their best, and it was also nonexistent now. "I'm afraid the room you originally booked is now involved in extensive renovations. To compensate you, Mr. Reilly, we can accommodate you in a third floor executive suite at no additional cost. I'm sure you'll find the room more than satisfactory. Our executive suites feature a generously sized—"

"I reserved this room three months ago and it's the room I'll have," he interrupted sharply. "I don't want a suite on the third floor. I want the Primrose."

Mari breathed in measured breaths. Everything about Reilly was pushing her buttons, from his rudeness to his sense of obligation to the belligerent tone of voice.

"And I'm very sorry it's impossible, as the room is part of our upgrading." She tried a smile, hoping to appeal to his common sense. "Presently the room is full of plywood and power tools. As manager here, I do apologize on behalf of the hotel and will be more than happy to move you to the suite and also include breakfast each morning. I assure you, Mr. Reilly, our executive suites are beyond compare." Her voice came out warm and confident, but inside she was trembling, hating the confrontation.

She tried to remember the exercises her therapist had taught her. It went against everything she'd learned growing up. That to stay silent meant to stay safe. It was her job to talk to him. Yet for a moment she became the girl huddled in a corner hoping to be left alone.

She looked over his shoulder at Colleen. "You'll see to it, Colleen?"

"Yes, Ms. Ross."

Mari aimed a parting smile at him and took two steps away.

"If you think that's good enough, you're mistaken, missy. Don't you walk away from me!"

A heavy hand reached out and gripped her wrist painfully, jerking her back and she yelped and cowered before she could think better of it. Her eyes closed, waiting for what would come next, the sound of Colleen's shocked gasp vibrating through her. She stilled. It was only worse when she showed pain or fear.

"Is there a problem here?"

Mari gazed up at Luca, wanting to weep with gratitude. Luca, eyes dark with fury, glared like an avenging angel at the man holding her arm. She'd never been so glad to see someone in all her life.

"Nothing I can't handle," the man sneered, giving her wrist an extra squeeze. Mari couldn't help the wince that flickered over her face, and instantly saw a muscle in Luca's jaw twitch in response.

"I strongly suggest you release the lady's arm." He uttered the words softly but the steely threat was unmistakable. When Reilly didn't immediately comply, Luca's voice was dangerously low. "While you still can."

"We were just having a little disagreement, that's all," the man replied, looking disappointed at having to relinquish his hold on Mari. Now that her wrist was free, she rubbed it with her hand. She knew she should say something, but words refused to come. She stood dumbly, staring at Luca.

"Mari, are you all right?" He temporarily took his eyes off the man, the look of genuine concern reaching through the fear and touching her deep inside. Luca wouldn't let anything happen to her. She nodded slightly and forced calm breaths. All she wanted was for Reilly to leave. To get him out of her sight.

"Perhaps I may be of some assistance," Luca suggested tightly, his polite words laced with venom. Mari held her breath, hoping Luca didn't resort to violence. Causing a scene was clearly what the man wanted. A chill ran over her body. She knew his kind. The kind that wanted to provoke a fight. Who thought physical power solved everything.

"And who might you be?"

"Luca Fiori. Owner of this hotel."

The man smiled suddenly. "Mr. Fiori. I think perhaps you need to teach your staff the principle of the customer is always right. I booked the Primrose Room months ago, and now I'm being put in some third-rate room."

Mari spoke for the first time. She lifted her chin and willed her voice to come out without the wobble she felt inside. "I moved Mr. Reilly to the suites on the third floor."

"The Fiori Cascade is very sorry for the inconvenience, as I'm sure our manager, Ms. Ross, communicated to you." Reilly started to open his mouth but Luca cut him off. "However, we do not tolerate abuse of any kind toward our staff. She has generously booked you in one of our most exclusive suites. I'm sure you'll find it more than satisfactory."

"I assure you I won't." He turned his head and glared at Mari.

Mari dropped her gaze to the floor. She didn't want to challenge him in any way. Luca was letting him stay. It was smart businesswise, but she couldn't help being disappointed. She refused to look up. If he had to think he'd won, fine. It was better than the alternative.

* * *

Luca saw Mari's gaze drop and stay focused on the floor. She was still afraid. For the tiniest flash, he remembered her vibrancy, her laughter, on the night that they danced together. No man—client or not—had the right to frighten her, to intimidate her. To use force against her. He held his temper, but only just.

"Come to think of it, Mr. Reilly, we're terribly sorry but the Cascade has no vacancies at this time. I'm certain you'll be able to find lodging at one of Banff's other fine establishments. Please leave."

"Like hell! I intend to let head office know of this!"

His attempts to defuse the situation had failed and Luca knew that he couldn't have such a person staying at the hotel under any circumstances. This scene had to end and end now. If Reilly would do this in a public lobby, what would happen if housekeeping upset him in some way? He had a duty to protect his staff. He had a duty to Mari. Luca knew Reilly would follow through and lodge a complaint, even if it meant he would only make a fool of himself.

"Please do. I'm sure my assistant will forward your complaint to me with the utmost expediency."

"You bast…"

Luca interrupted, any pretence of amicability gone. His words were clipped and final. "I am sure the local authorities would be happy to provide transportation, if you can't leave under your own power." Luca flicked a finger by his thigh, knowing two of the hotel security would join them within seconds. He would have preferred not to get police involved, but there was a limit and Mr. Reilly had crossed it.

Reilly squared his shoulders, gathered his bags and strode out of the lobby, cursing the whole way.

Mari looked up at him, her cheeks still devoid of healthy color. "I'm sorry, Luca, I didn't mean to…"

"Don't apologize. Come with me."

She followed meekly. He didn't touch her anywhere but she felt pulled along just the same. "Where are we going?"

"To my suite, so you can get yourself together."

He opened the door with his key and she went inside ahead of him. He went to the cabinet and poured a small amount of brandy in a glass. He handed it to her. "Drink this. It will put the color back in your cheeks."

Mari sipped, opening her mouth wide and gasping as the liquor burned.

He was angry. She'd handled everything wrong and he was angry at her. At least he was going to have the grace to discuss it in private.

"Luca, I'm sorry." She took another fortifying sip of the brandy and handed him back the glass.

"Sorry for what?"

"It's my job to deal with our guests and I failed today."

"For God's sake, quit apologizing for that ape's behavior!"

She stepped back at his outburst.

He tempered his tone at her reaction. "I'm the one that's sorry, Mariella. When I saw him grab you…you looked like you were about to collapse in a heap. It made me insensible."

"You're not angry with me?"

He stepped forward and crushed her into his arms. "No, darling," he whispered into her ear. "I'm not angry."

Tears stung the backs of her eyelids as they slid closed. His wide hand cradled the back of her head as she leaned against him.

"I saw him touch you and I wanted to grab him by the neck and throw him out," Luca ground out beside her ear. "But that's not Fiori. At least that's not what the hotel stands for. Fiori is class and elegance, not brawling in the lobby. Even if he deserved it."

"I'm glad you didn't. I…I hate violence. But I was afraid, Luca. So afraid."

"It took all I had to hold my temper."

She stepped back out of his arms. "You may think you were polite, but I saw the look of thunder on your face. Oh, Luca, I was so glad to see you. I knew you wouldn't let anything happen to me."

He lifted a finger and ran it over her cheek. "I'd never let him hurt you, Mariella."

"But I know…I know what men like Reilly can do."

And then the shakes hit.

Mari felt the trembling strike deep inside and was helpless to control it. Her body went cold and suddenly it was impossible to get enough air. She stared straight ahead but could hear the gasping of her own strident breath.

"Porco mondo!" Mari barely registered Luca's exclamation as his hands gripped her arms and pushed her down on the sofa. He said something to her in fast Italian. The breaths came fast and shallow and she started to see gray spots.

"Damn it! Mari, put your head between your legs!" He bit out the command and she felt the pressure of his hand against her head, pushing it down. She closed her eyes and fought against the darkness. "Breathe, darling," his voice came, gentler now, and she concentrated simply on the in and out of respiration.

Reilly was gone. Robert was gone. No one would hurt her. If she said it over enough, perhaps she'd believe it.

After a few minutes she'd gained control again. The shakes had hit her so hard and fast she hadn't been prepared, though she should have been. She'd had them often enough before. It just hadn't happened for a very long time. She'd let her guard down since being with Luca day in and day out. She was safe here with him. He was looking after her and knowing it made her want to cry all over again. She was always alone. This time she wasn't. Luca was here.

"You… I thought you were going to hit him," she murmured, bracing her arms on her knees and holding her head.

"And I wanted to, the moment I saw him put his hand on you. But sometimes there are better ways to accomplish things than with fists. He's gone now, and he won't be back. Not to any Fiori hotel. I'll make sure of it."

At his words a tear snuck out of the corner of her eye and she blotted it. He couldn't know how much his words meant to her. How much he'd risen in her eyes, just knowing he'd preferred a calmer, more effective way to deal with a brute. Knowing he had had that urge to protect her, yet controlled his temper.

The warmth of his body disappeared for a moment and she heard him over at the bar. When he came back he pressed a glass of water into her hands. "This might work better than the brandy," he suggested quietly, his fingers cupping hers around the glass.

She took a grateful sip. Wondered what she could possibly say to make him understand. Understand both why she'd reacted the way she had and also understand how much it meant to her, having him there with her.

"Mariella, is there anything you could have done to make Reilly happy?"

She took another sip. "Short of magically making the Primrose Room appear out of our new massage facility, I doubt it. But I should have found a way. We were the ones who inconvenienced him. I should have found a better way. He was within his rights to be angry…"

"Don't you dare make excuses. Don't you dare, Mariella. There is no excuse for a man raising his hand to a woman. Ever."

In the moment when Reilly had grabbed her arm, she had forgotten everything she'd learned since that day seven years ago. She'd forgotten how to be right and instead had only known what it was to feel wrong. And Luca was right. She was making excuses. She'd been good at it. Good at blaming herself, at playing the "if only" game. If only she'd been smarter, prettier, better behaved. If only she'd said something different, or nothing at all. If she hadn't looked into his eyes, if she'd cooked the pasta a few minutes longer, if only, if only, if only.

And for a few seconds, she'd truly believed, if only she had looked away, said something differently, maybe Mr. Reilly wouldn't have grabbed her. Seven years of progress down the drain.

"Mariella." Luca knelt by her knees. "Sweetheart. I saw your face when he put his hands on you. You went so pale. That's happened to you before, hasn't it."

She would not cry. She would not.

She nodded, a tiny affirmation.

"Oh, Mariella, I am so sorry."

This kinder, gentler Luca was tearing her defenses apart bit by bit. Every place his hand touched was warmed and reassured. Every word he said healed something inside her. She didn't want his pity. All she wanted was his understanding and…and…

And his love. It was all she'd ever really wanted and she hadn't even known it.

Luca continued on. "It all makes sense now. That day in the attic, all those times you didn't want to be touched. Who was he, Mariella? An ex-husband?"

She shook her head.

"A boyfriend then."

Mari shook her head again. "No, nothing like that." She could trust Luca, she knew that in her heart. They could deny their feelings all they wanted, but the way he'd rushed to her rescue proved it. He had earned the right to the truth. To know why she'd acted the way she had all these weeks. "It was my stepfather."

Luca said a word in Italian she didn't understand but the meaning was clear enough. "He beat you?"

"Yes. Me and...and my mother."

Luca stood, went to the bar, poured himself a drink far more generous than the one he'd given her and tossed it back.

"And where is he now?"

Mari folded her hands in her lap. It helped with the trembling. She tried not to think about the beatings. About how Robert would turn to her after he'd gotten tired of pushing her mother around. "He...he was in jail, but he's out now. He made parole the day before you and I went..." She had to stop, breathe, swallow. "The day in the attic."

"Why didn't you tell me before?"

She looked up from her lap then. What she saw in Luca's eyes she knew she'd remember to her dying day. He wasn't angry with her, he was angry *for* her. Ready to stand between her and whoever would dare to hurt her.

"He's on parole, you said. Would he come after you? Damn it, Mari, I could have protected you! You should have said something, rather than go through this alone!"

"What would I have said, Luca?"

He put down his glass. "If I had known you were scared, if I'd known the reason you didn't like contact, I swear Mari, I wouldn't have pushed. I'm not cruel."

"And said what? 'Hey, Mr. New Boss! Please don't mind me, I just don't like any physical contact because my stepfather was a sadistic freak that beat me for the hell of it?' Nice ice breaker, don't you think?"

His eyes closed for the smallest of moments.

"All the times I held you, all the times I could feel you trembling. *Dio,* Mari, I'm so sorry."

He was blaming himself now and Mari was sick and tired of Robert Langston having all the power. Could she be honest with Luca? Could she tell him how she felt?

In the end she knew she couldn't reveal it all, yet she also felt he deserved a partial truth.

"I wasn't shaking with fear, Luca. Not with you. Don't you realize how much it means to me that you stood up for me today? No one's ever done that for me before. I…I…" But she stopped. She couldn't tell him how she felt, it was too new, too tenuous. "Please, don't ever think I was afraid of you. I *never* felt like I was in physical danger."

Only in danger of what I feel for you, she thought. That was the part she couldn't tell him. That was the one thing she couldn't let him know. She had known from the beginning that there would never be anything serious between them. He was Luca Fiori, based in Florence, heir to the empire. They were from two different worlds and were simply in the same place at a particular time.

He couldn't know that with each passing day, with each gesture, she was falling deeper in love with him. What was she to do with those feelings? She certainly didn't feel equipped to handle them, let alone share them. The one thing that she was sure of was that it wouldn't turn out well. And she valued him too much to let things turn bitter and angry.

"Are you afraid now? Of your stepfather? What about your mother? Where is she?"

She wasn't sure how much to tell him, how much he could handle. It wasn't a pretty story. She paused too long and he backed away.

"I apologize. I've overstepped. You don't want to talk about it, and I respect that."

"No!" Mari got up from the sofa. "I'm not trying to shut you out, Luca…you must understand. No one here knows about this. I started a new life, built it from scratch. And I thought I'd left it all behind me. I did therapy. I thought it was all okay. Only I have just realized I can't leave it behind—Reilly showed me that—and right now…"

She needed him. Luca, complicated, arrogant, and temporary—wasn't that a kick in the pants.

"Right now—" her voice shook "—you're the only one keeping me from losing it. Today brought it all back, all of it. I…I need you, Luca."

She half expected him to run screaming. What man would want an emotionally crippled woman clinging and crying all over him?

"Tell me," he said softly, holding out his hand.

She took it. "Robert Langston spent seven years in prison for the attempted murder of my mother…and of me."

LUCA sat beside her on the plush sofa, tucking one leg beneath him so that he was sitting sideways, facing her. His warm hand enclosed hers and she clung to the thought of it, a link that kept her from feeling groundless and out of control. Now that she said the words they sounded surreal. Like it couldn't have possibly happened. But it had, and she squeezed his hand in response.

She didn't talk about that day. Not ever. But perhaps now she needed to. This afternoon had taught her that it wasn't behind her as she'd thought it was. And the scary truth was Robert *was* out of prison and knowing it had chipped away at her safety barrier more than she cared to admit. Being with Luca was the only thing holding her together right now.

She looked up at him. His dark eyes were steady on hers, waiting for her to begin, giving her the time she needed. There was such a strength about him, even now when he was being gentle and nurturing. Luca was a man to be relied upon, so much more than the media's Fiori heir who liked fast cars and beautiful women. That wasn't the real Luca.

The real Luca was sitting before her now, a safe port in the storm, willing to be whatever she needed.

She stared at the sensuous curve of his lips, feeling a little wonder that a man like him had kissed a woman like her, and on more than one occasion. Things like that didn't happen. Real life wasn't like that.

They certainly didn't happen to a plain Jane from Ontario. Not one who was mediocre at best. But here he was, waiting. Not running. Not arguing. He was caring for her, and knowing it unlocked something she kept hidden deep inside. For the first time in her life, she wanted to *give* of herself to another human being.

"Mariella, you don't have to tell me if it's too difficult. It's okay."

She was brought back by the warm sound of his voice. She lifted their joined hands and kissed the top of his, holding it against her lips. She closed her eyes, grateful he was there. Even now he was being understanding and her appreciation ran long and deep. When she was with him, Robert somehow lost his power.

"When I was six, my mother married Robert Langston." She focused on Luca's face to keep the images away. "I never knew my real father. She'd brought me up on her own all that time and she said that things would get better, we'd have a new family. Only it didn't turn out that way."

"It wasn't the fairy tale you expected."

She nodded. "The abuse didn't happen right at the beginning, but that doesn't matter now. What is important is that when it did start it escalated quickly and completely, and we were essentially terrorized. He had complete control. He ruled us with fear, and it was awful. The years were…"

But she couldn't go on. Her throat closed over as memories flooded back; cowering in a corner while he yelled at her mother. The rage on his face as he used his fists on her. Mari had foolishly spent too many evenings trying to defend her mother, only to receive the same treatment.

The years of long-sleeved shirts and makeup. Being scared

to speak up and feeling guilty listening to the sound of punches on the other side of the wall, too paralyzed to do anything. Of tiptoeing around, always afraid of saying the wrong thing or doing something not quite the right way.

Years of waiting for her mother to tell her it was over, but that moment never came. She'd remained trapped in the living hell of her childhood.

For the first time, Mari forgot all the police reports, all the therapy, all the ways she'd been told she'd made progress, and she simply cried—quiet, cold, devastating tears.

Luca pulled her into his arms and held her…warm, solid, sure. She cried for the childhood she'd lost, the guilt she still felt, the fear that never quite went away, and the fact that today of all days it had finally reached the point where she could grieve for it all.

Luca had made that possible. By some miracle, he'd pushed himself into her life and had shown her what was real.

After several minutes she slid backward on the couch, wiping her eyes. Luca went to the bathroom and brought back a box of tissues, offering her two and waiting patiently.

"I'm sorry for crying all over you that way."

"Please don't apologize." He sat on the edge of the coffee table, facing her. "I just want to make sure you're all right."

At that moment the telephone rang and Luca scowled. "Answer it," Mari said, but Luca shook his head.

"It can wait."

The ringing persisted and he sighed, rising to answer. Mari watched him from her position on the couch. She was tired, so tired. Only once before had she been this drained, and it was the day she'd had to testify in court.

"It will have to wait."

Mari heard Luca speaking into the telephone. His eyes remained fixed on her and she tried tucking the hair that had come loose back behind her ears. She must look a fright. His voice came again. "I'm sorry, but I'm in the middle of something more important right now. You'll have to take care of it. I'll call you tomorrow."

He hung up the phone and came back, sitting on the table again and taking her hands in his. "I'm sorry about that."

She was still trying to absorb the fact that he'd put off whoever it was to look after her. "If you need to go, it's fine. I'll be okay."

"You're not okay. And it can wait. Right now looking after you is my priority."

Never, not once in her life had anyone said those words to her. Never had anyone put her first. But Luca—driven, workaholic Luca—had just put off whoever had been on the other end of that call. She licked her lips, unsure of where to start.

"Today I forgot all the things I learned from counseling and only felt the fear, the responsibility. If only I'd done something differently it wouldn't have happened. I…" She swallowed, having difficulty going on. "Oh, Luca, I thought I was far beyond that. I worked so hard and all of a sudden it was like no time had passed at all. And then you were there. I was so glad to see you."

"He put his hands on you. I couldn't allow that." He lifted his other hand and grazed her cheek with his fingers.

"In that moment I was trapped, back seven years ago. That day…" Her voice faded away for a moment. It was all in the police report. It was in her medical files after she'd gone through intensive counseling. But she'd never willingly offered it to someone who hadn't been paid to hear it.

"What happened that day, Mariella?"

His voice encouraged her, invited her. After all he'd done, telling him seemed the next logical, if difficult step.

"I had moved out, and felt torn because on one hand I had

left my mum behind. On the other I was away and safe. Mum had called and had said she was finally leaving him." Mari realized her eyes were bone-dry; she must have cried herself out earlier. She remembered being so relieved, so happy that her mum was getting away. Happy at the thought that maybe, just maybe, they could start building a relationship. "I said I'd come and help. But when I arrived, he'd gotten there first. Caught her packing her bags and when I found her she was bleeding, unconscious on the floor, with a broken arm and a cracked skull. Her clothes were strewn everywhere, slashed to ribbons."

"Dio Mio." Luca's low exclamation drew her out of the memory.

"It happens, Luca, far more often than it should."

She put her other hand over his. Telling him was sapping her strength but it needed to be said. Perhaps she could finally be free of it. Perhaps with Luca beside her, she'd stop blaming herself. Perhaps Robert would lose his power over her for good.

"He found me there, grabbing the phone to call the police. He ripped it from my hand and started in on me. By the time it was over, my mum was still unconscious and I had a concussion, broken ribs and internal injuries from where he—" Her voice broke a little. "From where he kicked me over and over. He left us there, Luca. Left us to die. But the postman noticed bloody handprints on the front door and the stair railing. He called the police and the rest is history."

"Only it's not history." He gently tipped up her chin with a finger. "Nothing like that can ever completely go away, can it. Oh, Mari." He lifted her hands to his lips and kissed the backs, his eyes closing. She stared at the way his lashes lay on his cheeks, the tender way he cradled her fingers. Where had he come from? How was it that he was here, exactly what she needed, at exactly the time she needed him?

"I am so sorry. No one should ever go through something like that." He whispered the words against her fingertips.

And then he leaned forward and touched his lips to hers.

She went into his embrace willingly, their knees pressed together between the sofa and table. He was strong, and somehow a barrier between her and the ugliness of her past. When she was with him she was the Mariella she'd always wanted to be, free of the hold Robert Langston had held over her for so many years.

The kiss was soft, tentative, sweet. She hadn't known he was capable of sweet.

She hadn't known she was capable of love, but here it was. She loved Luca. And being completely out of her depth, she had no idea what to do about it.

"And now he's out of prison…are you afraid he'll come after you? What about your mum?"

His voice drew her back into the present. "The authorities keep me up-to-date while he's on probation. Of course I think of it, and wonder if he hates me for my part in sending him to jail. But I can't let myself think of it too much or it becomes overwhelming. I spent too many years looking over my shoulder. And it's not one of those things you ever really get used to."

"And what about your mother?"

Mari shook her head. "I don't speak to my mum that often… there seems to be a wall between us now. I don't even know where she's living. I…" Mari cleared her throat. "A part of me still wonders how she could have let it happen. How she could have stayed with a man who beat her. Who beat me. Why didn't she try to get out?"

She looked up at Luca. "What kind of mother hurts her own child that way? What kind of mother doesn't put the welfare of her child ahead of everything? There have been times I've thought about the home I want, the children I might have someday. Could I put them through that? I know I couldn't. I've tried to understand it, but I just can't. The only thing I can come up with is that she was too afraid to do anything else."

Luca shook his head. "I don't know, either. I barely remember my mother myself."

"You said she left you and Gina. That must have been difficult."

"I only remember feeling like we never mattered." Mari's eyes widened at the loathing in his tone. "She left us when I was a boy. My dad raised Gina and me."

He stood up and walked over to the window.

"I'm sorry," she murmured, "That must have been horrible for you. Did your dad ever remarry?"

He cleared his throat. "It's not important, Mari. It was a long time ago. And it was nothing compared to what you went through. Nothing."

He spoke with such vehemence that she knew he was hiding his own hurts.

And for a moment, she forgot about herself and wondered about the boy he'd been, and how he'd suffered in his own way. Perhaps that silver spoon he'd been born with didn't gleam as brightly as she'd thought. How she wished she could help him as he'd helped her today.

How had this happened?

She'd fallen in love with Luca Fiori, and it was the one sure thing to break her heart. Luca cared for her, yes. She knew that. But love? By his own admission, Luca didn't *do* love.

She had to take a step back. This baring of souls—well hers, anyway—was all well and good, but even she wasn't fool enough to believe there was a happy ending in all of it. Luca didn't live here. He didn't belong here. He belonged at his villa in Italy with his family and the Fiori empire and what was happening between them now was a blip in their lives.

Necessary, perhaps, but still temporary. How could she tell him her true feelings?

She stared at his back, trying to puzzle it out but not getting very far. Perhaps she was just raw from everything that had happened. What if these feelings were just a byproduct of a process she should have gone through years ago? It would be foolish to make this into more than it was, and Mari was smart enough to know her perspective was skewed.

"You're categorizing."

Luca's voice reached her. He hadn't turned back around, but stared out into the growing darkness.

"I can practically hear your mind working, Mari. Please don't. Just let things be."

Mari rose and went to the window, standing behind him. She wasn't sure anything would be the right move, so she simply did what she felt like: she put her arms around his body and pressed her cheek into the warmth of his back.

Luca swallowed against the lump that had formed in his throat. Anything he'd gone through as a child was nothing, nothing compared to the hell that Mari had experienced. He tried to picture her on a floor, battered and bruised, and couldn't. It seemed too wrong, too horrific. What sort of man did that to another human being? To a woman he was supposed to love?

And yet, here she was, somehow comforting him.

"It's snowing," he murmured. Soft flakes fluttered past the balcony railing, settling on the ground in intricate patterns. He was reminded of his grandmother's lace and wondered what she'd think of this mess he'd got himself into.

Why was it that people hurt the ones they were supposed to love? He knew he couldn't let Mari do this alone, yet it brought back memories he hated, ones of comforting Gina when their mother had abandoned the family. *Nonna* had always been there to help. What would she say now, if she could be here?

He knew exactly what she'd say and he didn't like the answer. She'd tell him to stop holding a grudge and forgive.

Mari sighed against his back and he closed his eyes. What a day they'd had. He was glad now that he had handled Reilly the way he had. If this was what Mari was carrying deep inside, a physical response would have only frightened her more.

Today he'd thought only of Mari. And that wasn't good.

Mari did not need a man like him. She needed someone she could rely on. Someone who could give her stability and security and make a home with her. She'd even mentioned it, the longing for a home and children. That wasn't his life, it never had been. He'd always been the Fiori heir, the one everyone assumed would step into his father's shoes one day. And he kept fighting against it.

He looked at the reflection of the suite in the glass doors. There was nothing personal here, no pictures, no trinkets, nothing to make it a home and that was how he lived his life. It was what it was. It was the world he inhabited.

He'd forget about her, eventually.

But with her arms around him, the only thing he wanted to do was lift her in his arms and hold on.

And he'd come as close to admitting his feelings as he ever would.

"Stay tonight, Mari."

Her head lifted from his back and it felt cold where it had been warm a second ago.

"Luca, I…"

"Not in my bed." For once in his life this had nothing to do with sex. He turned, wanting her to understand how he couldn't say the words. "Just…stay. I'd only worry about you if you went home. You can have the bed. I'll sleep on the sofa."

"What you did for me today, Luca, no one's ever done anything like that for me before. I can't impose on you further."

"You're not imposing."

For a long moment their gazes clung. Words hung unspoken.

"Wait here."

He disappeared into the bedroom and returned with a T-shirt. "I don't have pyjamas to lend you."

She took the T-shirt. "Thank you."

She disappeared into his room, and he heard the bathroom door shut behind her. When he didn't hear anything after several minutes, he decided he should check on her.

She was in his bed, the duvet pulled up to her chin. Her blotchy cheeks were relaxed and her eyelashes were smudges against her cheeks. She'd fallen asleep before he could even ask if she was hungry.

He'd let her sleep. And when she woke he'd make sure she was all right.

And then, somehow, he'd find a way out of this mess.

Mari woke to sunlight filtering through the bedroom window. Pushing her hair out of her face, she realized she was in Luca's bed, the smell of his cosmetics faint in the sheets and sounds of him tinkering in the suite filtering through.

She'd spent the night. And she hadn't given a thought to going home or to Tommy…she could only hope he'd used the dog door on the porch.

Mari checked her watch: 9:00 a.m. Oh my God. She'd slept straight through, with none of the nightmares that had haunted her lately. Any lingering thoughts were crowded out by the knowledge that full-day staff were in the hotel and she only had yesterday's clothes to dress in. She should have used her head last night.

But nothing about yesterday had been about logic or sense.

"Good morning," Luca said from the doorway to the bedroom.

She scrambled up to a seated position. "Luca, I'm so sorry. I slept…"

"Here all night," he finished, a smile on his lips. His elbow leaned casually against the door frame. "Slept nearly fifteen hours."

"I must have been more tired than I realized." He was acting like this was normal, for Pete's sake! And seeing him brought back everything that had happened yesterday with a vengeance. Including kissing him, crying on him, realizing she loved him…

And in the silence she felt a blush creep up her neck and bloom in her cheeks. Somehow she had to get out of this situation with a modicum of grace. In the bright light of day it was clearer than ever that revealing her true feelings would be a mistake. She just needed time to figure out exactly what was what.

"I think that sleep might have been a long time coming," he replied lazily.

A knock sounded at the door. Mari lifted her eyebrows in his direction. He merely shrugged.

"You grew restless a while ago. I ordered up breakfast. You must be starving…you didn't have any dinner."

He opened the door while Mari hastily pulled on her clothes, jamming her hair back into the clip she'd worn yesterday. As she came out of the bedroom, one of their staff wheeled in a cart adorned with silver domed trays.

"Thank you, Geoff." Luca handed a bill to the server who nodded, then smiled in Mari's direction.

Mari frowned as the door shut with a quiet click. "I don't want this getting around the staff. What are they going to think of me up here in your suite?"

"You've been here before."

"Not looking like this. Not coming out of your bedroom."

Luca moved the cart closer to the dining table. "Don't worry, I'm used to it. It always blows over."

Mari's mouth clamped shut. Luca was used to these situations. She was not. If he was trying to put the morning in perspective, he was doing a stand-up job.

"I'm sorry about yesterday. I shouldn't have unloaded on you." She felt obligated to apologize. Suddenly there seemed to be a new awkwardness between them. Now that it was over and done with, perhaps he was feeling embarrassed at being privy to all her secrets. She couldn't say she blamed him.

A shadow crossed his features.

"It's fine. It's good that you did. I imagine it feels better to have it out. I understand, Mari, I really do."

Why was he acting so differently? Yesterday he'd held her hand and she'd told him her deepest troubles. He'd leaped to her defense and he'd held her in his arms as she'd cried. Now... God, now he was treating her like she was one of his flings. One of the women he kept on his arm.

Her mouth soured. She'd thought she'd been right to put her trust in him, but his casual treatment of her this morning was a letdown. She'd wanted to mean more to him. Which was silly because she already knew in her heart they had no future. He'd come right out and said so. He didn't do *love*.

"Come, eat. You must be starving."

"I need to go home and change." Mari stood and smoothed her slacks.

"There's no need. I had some things sent up from the boutique. You're welcome to use the shower here."

Mari gritted her teeth.

He was treating her like...like nothing monumental had ever happened between them! He was taking charge and deciding what she'd do and when. And damn it, she was done being on anyone's timetable!

He lifted the lid on a platter. The smell of French toast reached her nostrils, the tantalizing scent of vanilla and cinnamon and maple. Her stomach growled. In all the uproar, she hadn't eaten last night. It would serve him right if she sat and ate the whole serving!

"I would have thought that privilege was one reserved for your affairs," she remarked caustically, putting her hands in her pockets and clenching her fingers tightly.

She'd told him everything last night, everything about Robert and her fears and today he treated her as a polite stranger. There was only one explanation.

It had been too much. Her baggage was too much for him and it had been foolish to think that Luca could handle it. As much as she'd wanted to believe in him, she'd expected far more than he could give. She wasn't sophisticated and uncomplicated. She was a mess and he was politely backing away.

She could hardly hate him for it. Even if his cool treatment of her this morning stung. She longed to simply flee, but somehow she knew she had to handle this with some sort of dignity and composure. It would only be more awkward later if she ran out. They still had to work together for the time remaining in the renovations.

Luca ignored the voice inside that told him to knock it off. He looked at Mari and could only see her face last night as she told him about her stepfather. He'd had to help her. He'd wanted to.

But now, in the bright light of day, he needed to step back. This felt too much like a relationship and he wasn't prepared. The last time he'd been involved with a woman deeper than a dating level, he'd let it interfere with work, too. He'd fallen for Ellie, had trusted her. He'd told her that he loved her. Only that time he'd discovered it wasn't him she wanted at all, but his Fiori connection. The Fiori name almost seemed a curse to love, and he wasn't willing to put his heart out there again.

So these feelings for Mari weren't supposed to have happened at all. Their kisses shouldn't have happened. His eyes remained cool even though he knew she was right. This was exactly what he would have done for a woman the morning after, and the truth of it stung. "That's a bit low."

"I'm sorry, Luca. I think I'm still a little off balance after yesterday. I believe I will eat something," she said, going to the dining table and taking a seat. A platter glistened with raisin-studded French toast and fragrant circles of ham. She filled a plate and poured warm maple syrup over the lot of it.

He should have known better than to flirt with her like he did with other women. Mari wasn't that type and somehow he needed to extricate himself from whatever it was they shared. But he would not call it a relationship. In relationships people hurt each other. Like his father had been hurt. Like he'd been hurt when Ellie betrayed him. He'd told Ellie things and she'd used them to hurt him later, to taunt him.

Mari wouldn't do that, the voice inside argued. But this time that wasn't his worry. He was more worried *he'd* hurt *her,* and she'd been hurt enough. What an unusual position he found himself in.

A break to friendship was the best plan, wasn't it? Mari didn't need a man who would break her heart. And a man who didn't *do* relationships surely would. What she needed now was a friend.

"Juice, freshly squeezed." Solicitously he poured her a generous glass. "Enough vitamin C to last all day."

"Thank you." She sipped, then put the glass down and picked up her fork. "Aren't you going to eat anything?"

"Indeed."

He took the seat opposite and uncovered another platter containing scrambled eggs and a bowl of mixed berries.

Mari took one bite, then two, wondering how long she could be expected to survive this agony. Eating breakfast like there was nothing to be said. It was a complete farce after their intimacy of the day before.

There was nothing to fault in his behavior. Nothing. It was perfectly polite. But it was clear he was distancing himself.

It was cold as hell.

She wanted to ask him, didn't yesterday mean anything to you? Wanted to say how much she appreciated how he'd taken care of her. But she couldn't. He was acting like it had meant nothing. Like having breakfast together in his suite was an ordinary occurrence. It was no more personal than…than a business meeting.

The bite she was chewing went down with difficulty. There was only so long she could keep this up. She was still raw from yesterday's events and the insight that she'd fallen for Luca. For him to treat her so now was confusing and insulting and it hurt. Made her wonder if she'd imagined his gentle understanding all along. If he'd only been placating her because she'd been so distraught.

She put down her fork, keeping her mask carefully in place. She had misjudged him, had misplaced her trust. It just went to prove how poor her judgment still was.

"Thank you for breakfast, but I need to go now."

She pushed out her chair, avoiding his gaze.

"There's no need. You can refresh yourself here, Mariella. I'm sure the clothes I sent for will fit. You can go straight to your office from here."

Oh, he had it all planned out. He'd had lots of time to think about it, all evening last night while she'd slept, no doubt. His consideration was hardly touching. Nothing he could have said or done this morning could have made her feel worse than this politeness.

"You have it all planned out, don't you Luca?" She struggled to keep the tremble out of her voice. "I thought I was the one for planning and you were the impulsive one, but how wrong I was. You've planned it from the beginning—how to get around the difficult manager, how to handle your sister, how to handle me."

He put down the spoon of berries he was holding. "I'm sorry?"

Mari straightened her blouse and looked around to make sure she didn't leave anything behind. She spied a hairpin on the sofa and picked it up, putting it in her pocket, all the while avoiding his clear gaze. "I understand, really I do," she went on, realizing belatedly that she was echoing his earlier words. "There's no need to let me down easy with breakfast and such…genteel consideration."

He stood, his lips thinning with disapproval. "Nothing I've done this morning was out of obligation, Mariella."

"Sure it was. You could hardly wake me up and kick me out now could you? That's not very good manners, not when we're supposed to be…what is it we're supposed to be again, Luca?"

She finally looked at him, but his expression was too guarded for her to know what he was thinking.

"I will confess. I'm not sure what is appropriate to say in this situation. It's not one I've been in before."

Luca stared at her. That much was completely true. He'd never been in a situation where he cared more about a woman's feelings than his own. So why was she angry? He'd tried to do the right thing. Look after her, make her day easier, he'd even ordered breakfast for the two of them. He'd wanted to show her that what had transpired yesterday made no difference to him. If anything, it made him respect her more. Everything he'd done...including being here, instead of his office, where he normally would be found at this hour, had been to show her that he cared, that he wasn't running away. He'd wanted to start the day on an even footing.

Now she was furious with him.

Mari started to walk away, her heart sinking. This probably was a new situation for him. He probably kept his affairs nice and neat and clean. She'd needed him so much that she'd obviously imagined things that weren't real. If they had been real, this morning he would have awakened her with a smile. He would have inquired how she was feeling after yesterday and he would have told her it was all right.

And maybe he would have kissed her like she had been aching for him to.

But she'd frightened him off. And he didn't even have the decency to be honest about it.

"I'm leaving now. Thank you for the clothes, but no thank you."

"Where are you going?" Finally there was something in his tone other than perfunctory manners. Mari nearly paused, but made her feet keep going until she reached the door and opened it.

"Mari, we have a meeting with the spa people in an hour."

Mari lifted her chin. "I'm sure you can handle it, Luca. I'm taking the day off."

She went out into the hall and closed the door behind her, without allowing herself to see the expression on his face. She let out a breath she hadn't even known she was holding.

It was time Mari got back to doing what she did best—relying on herself.

CHAPTER TEN

LUCA resisted the urge to call her house for the sixth—or was it seventh—time.

He'd been here too long. And nothing had made it more clear than the call he'd had to make earlier this morning, while Mari still slept.

He hadn't known anybody could sleep that long. He kept expecting her to wake throughout the evening, but she hadn't. He'd scrounged through the snacks he kept in his bar and had thrown together what could hardly be considered a meal—bagel chips and some mix made from organic dried fruits.

And at last, around midnight, he'd lain on the sofa, listening for her, finally drifting into a vague sleep.

It was the first time a woman had ever slept in his bed and he hadn't been with her.

At a faint ringing sound, he looked down at his computer screen. Another e-mail from his father, an update on their interest in Paris, which had suffered fire damage. His father had not been pleased at being put off yesterday. And was pressing Luca to finish up and take care of their problems in France.

But it was the words at the end that had him running his fingers through his hair.

Gina's in a mess and Paris can't wait. You need to come back. The family needs you.

The words left an odd ache in him. The family was everything to him. Except…except, he acknowledged, that he'd given his whole life to the family ever since he'd been a boy. He'd been the big brother Gina needed. He'd looked after the household for his father. And he'd wanted to do it. He'd been *happy* to do it. But there were times when he longed to just be Luca. To have his own life, separate from the family. To stop being defined by the Fiori brand. He was growing tired of being at his father's beck and call. Being summoned irritated him.

He typed back: *I will speak to Gina and the manager in Paris. I will come as soon as I can. But my priority is here.*

He signed off and hit Send, then sat back in his chair, rubbing a hand over his mouth. *Dio,* there was more truth in that last line than he'd truly meant. It wasn't just the Cascade that was his priority, though he did consider it his "baby." But it was Mari. She was important.

But what did he want? He'd wanted his own place at Fiori for a very long time. But did what he want match with what Mari wanted? Hardly. Mari wanted the fairy tale, and he didn't believe in them. The best thing he could do for her was make sure she kept her feet on the ground and leave the running of the Cascade in her capable hands. It wouldn't be enough for him, but it would be enough for her. Ambition wasn't Mari's goal, he got that now. She was after something more substantial. She'd built a life; she wanted stability, not adventure. It was odd how the idea appealed to him, especially today. Normally he'd be thrilled to go to Paris; it was one of his favorite cities. Now it felt like an imposition, because he was being *ordered* to go.

And even though he'd sent his response, he knew he had

to leave. Someone from the company had to put in an appearance. He wasn't clear on what was wrong with Gina, but he knew his father would be putting her first. So it was up to Luca to take care of business.

Yet…how could he possibly say goodbye to Mari now?

"The Panorama Room is completed. Have you seen it?"

Mari stopped by his desk. Something was distracting Luca and she didn't know what it was. She fiddled with a pen on the top of his blotter. "No, I haven't made it there today."

Ever since their night together, she'd made sure she kept her distance. It was clear that Luca cared for her. He wouldn't have acted so kindly, so gently, if he hadn't cared a little. But she also knew her past was a lot to take on, and their situation wasn't conducive to deep feelings and commitments.

He looked up and smiled, but somehow his heart didn't seem to be in it. "Haven't seen it? You gave me such a difficult time over the decor, and you haven't checked it out yet?" He cleared his throat, rose and shrugged into his jacket. "It can rival any of our dining rooms in any of our facilities, I promise. I've booked the two of us a table for tonight. As a farewell."

"A farewell?"

She paused, unmoving. So soon. She hadn't expected it to be so soon. Her heart sank.

"I've been called to Paris. I leave in the morning."

Luca saw the blood rush from her face and cursed himself. He'd left it an extra day, but he couldn't put it off any longer. Yet the fragile pallor of her skin reminded him of how she'd looked: small and defenseless in his king-size bed. He couldn't shake the image of her sleeping face, the way her hair slid over her pale cheek, the color matching her long eyelashes completely. Couldn't erase the fantasy of that dark sheet of hair falling over his chest as they made love...

He turned away from her abruptly, running a hand over his hair.

"Luca, are you all right?"

He was tired of playing a charade.

This was insane. He wasn't supposed to fall for Mari. A flirtation was one thing, but he didn't intend on having serious feelings for any woman, especially a woman he worked with. And it was clear that Mariella was the *wrong* woman. She was fragile and afraid and trying to overcome something greater than he could comprehend. She deserved a man who could provide her with the stability she needed. Not a man like Luca who flitted from one place to the next.

It would never work between them. And looking at her now...he realized now how it must have seemed to her yesterday. He'd been thinking of himself and putting up walls. He'd been wrong and she'd been right. He'd treated her with no consideration at all. Like he would have a mistress. With politeness, but not genuine caring. He wanted to make it up to her. To show her she was different...because she was.

"I'm fine. I just thought...it's been an eventful few weeks. I thought we could say goodbye with a sense of occasion."

He met her gaze, though it was difficult. She was watching him with eyes wide with compassion and understanding. She only thought she understood. He knew that now.

He would ensure that nothing about his leaving caused Mari further pain. She didn't deserve that, not after all she'd been through. He'd be on his best behavior if it killed him.

He only knew that he had to talk to Mari tonight about how to end their relationship with the least hurt to anyone. He wouldn't be here to protect her, to watch over her if her stepfather decided to find her. The thought chilled his blood and his footsteps faltered. Perhaps he couldn't offer her the life she wanted, but he could damn well make sure she was looked after here.

"That would be lovely, Luca." Her voice was soft, but it cut straight to the heart of him.

"I have some calls to make, first," he said bluntly, and without another word, she left his office, shutting the door behind her.

He picked up the phone and began to put his plans in motion.

Mari studied her reflection with a frown, wondering for the umpteenth time if she should have worn the dress. But the Panorama Room was formal, and she knew the perfect dress was the one she'd bought after their gallery trip. Still heady from Luca's kisses, she'd stared at the dress in the window for only a few seconds before darting inside to try it on. Mari had been under a spell that day, she was sure of it now. The rich scarlet silk of the dress seemed so unlike her, the cut even more daring as it swept from one shoulder down to her waist, leaving the other shoulder bare, the skirt then falling negligently to the floor.

It might have been modest except for the deep slit at the side, revealing her other moment of insanity—the red, sequined slingbacks.

She didn't want to be here. She wasn't sure how to gracefully say goodbye, not when she wanted more. Even when wanting more frightened her so badly her knees were shaking.

Mari swiped a finger beneath her eyelids, wiping away any stray smudges of liner and forcing a smile to the other occupant of the public bathroom.

Her life had been devoid of affection for so long, and she wanted desperately to be romanced. Even if it was only for tonight.

She gathered her pashmina firmly around her and squared her shoulders. It was impossible, she knew that. And caring for Luca as she did and still knowing he wasn't for her gave even a simple farewell dinner a bittersweet taste.

She turned toward the marble stairs and her gaze fell on Luca, waiting for her at the top.

Her heart gave a single, satisfying thump, as if to say, "This is it."

For a few seconds her feet refused to move as their gazes locked. It was something out of a bygone movie as she climbed each of the four stairs, her hand resting on the curve of the elaborate iron railing. The night of shared secrets ceased to exist; the tense atmosphere at breakfast and in the moments since drifted from her memory as she walked to him, her shoes making tiny clicks on the Italian veined marble, her breath catching at how very splendid he looked in evening wear.

At the top he took her hands and kissed each of her cheeks and her eyes slid closed before she could think twice. Pulling back slightly, he held out his arm, and she hesitantly looped hers through his elbow, awareness and something darker skittering along her nerve endings as he placed his hand over her forearm.

"You look…*bellisima*. Beautiful, Mariella. More beautiful than I can possibly describe."

This was the Luca she remembered, not the practiced stranger from their breakfast, or the distant boss from this afternoon. Whatever had caused the change, it was gone and in its place was a man who exuded warmth and spoke to her as if she were the only woman in the world. She tried to push the hope down in her heart, yet a little of it remained. Her throat tightened as he led her to the door of the dining room. This was what he'd brought her to, then. He'd made her *hope* where before there had been nothing.

Then the door opened and her lips dropped open.

It was more than she'd dreamed, even though she'd seen the plans. Everything was gilded and regal, like stepping into a fairy tale with her prince on her arm. Chandeliers dripped with crystal and gold; pristine linens a backdrop for the cream and gold china and the distinctive tinkle of real crystal stemware. Candles flickered in clear, thick pots, covering everything with a luminous, peachy glow. Tuxedoed waitstaff darted between tables amid the hush of opulence.

It was the royal castle Luca had envisioned from the beginning and it was perfect. She knew the end was growing near, yet that little seed of hope in her heart told her it felt like a beginning. "Oh, Luca. Look at what you've done." Her feet stopped moving as she blinked rapidly.

"Not just me. You, Mariella. You inspired this the day you took me to the attic."

"Me?" She turned to him in surprise, found his eyes on her steady and completely in earnest.

"You inspire me, Mariella. Is that so hard to believe?"

"Yes," she whispered, her stomach lifting uncontrollably as his gaze dropped to her mouth. He wouldn't dare kiss her here, would he?

And the moment held, suspended.

He'd been waiting. For *her*. Tonight she wanted to live the fairy tale. To grasp the few fleeting hours and pretend she was the princess. To believe she was chosen. She knew it would end soon enough. Tonight it was hers and she would not ruin it with doubts and fears.

Mari leaned forward slightly, her lips parting, close enough to feel Luca's breath mingle with hers…

"Mr. Fiori? Your table is waiting."

Mari stepped back, her cheeks heating. Luca's arm tightened around her waist and the contact sizzled to her toes.

"Thank you."

Mariella turned around, holding her breath. She was sure now that the gossip mill was probably running overtime ever since she'd been in Luca's suite at nine in the morning. But the hostess's lips dropped open and her eyes lit. "Oh, Ms. Ross! Look at you! You look like a movie star." Realizing her impertinence, she sighed. "Oh, I'm sorry."

Mariella smiled, feeling it light from her toes. "Don't be sorry," Luca answered. "I agree with you. Shall we?"

The hostess led the way into the private dining alcove, the red velvet drapes held back by gold cord. Their table waited, champagne already chilled and ready to pour. As she sat, she beamed up at him. "Luca, this is amazing. I've never seen anything quite like it, you know. I certainly never expected it here. In what was the Bow Valley Inn."

He poured the champagne, handing each of them a glass. "To remarkable transformations," he murmured, touching his rim to hers.

Glasses clinked and Mari drank the dry, fizzy champagne, feeling more with every moment that she was in a dream…a good one this time…and that at any moment she'd awake and the spell would be broken.

First courses arrived, then second; more champagne was drunk and Mari made sure she put her glass down more frequently as things grew fuzzy and warm around the edges. Luca laughed as he recounted stories of his youth with Gina; escapades with each other and Luca's winery friend Dante who to all accounts sounded like a rebel and usually in the middle of any trouble. She alternated between feeling a beautiful sense of belonging at being privy to the memories, and an acute sadness of the sort of childhood she'd missed. She didn't have any of the sorts of memories they did, of close times and scrapes and fun. Then Luca laughed and touched her hand beneath the table and she shook off any lingering sadness. She'd learned to live in the moment a long time ago. This was no time to start having regrets or wishing for what had never been.

They were served dark chocolate terrine drizzled with raspberry coulis when Luca leaned forward and captured Mari's hand.

Mari sat up straighter, startled at the sudden, personal gesture. But Luca was completely sincere as he squeezed Mari's fingers.

"When I arrived, I only wanted to do one thing—transform the hotel into something more Fiori. But my time here has been so much more, Mari, and I have you to thank for that."

Mari couldn't reply. Her gaze darted to Luca's; his gaze was sincere. It was no protestation of love, but only a fool would expect such a thing. His statement was absolutely correct. It had been more than either of them expected. She would have to be happy with that. Luca was not in love with her. And she'd get over him in time. She would.

But she returned the handclasp with as much warmth as she had inside her. "It has been a pleasure getting to know you, Luca. And getting to know myself better. I owe you so much. I'm only sorry I don't know how to repay you."

She had fought him tooth and nail in the beginning. And then somehow he'd gotten under her skin and she'd let him see a side of her she'd never revealed to anyone before. And in trusting him, she'd fallen in love with him.

Dessert was over, and the last bit had felt like a goodbye. Mari moved to collect her handbag, but Luca put out a hand. "Where are you going?"

She looked up, confused. "Home? I thought dinner was over."

Luca tugged on her arm gently, pulling her closer. "I'm not ready for it to end yet."

With his free hand he reached out and flicked the ties on the drapes, closing them in a cocoon of velvet and candlelight.

"Luca—"

"I need to say something here," he interrupted whatever it was she was going to say. "I'm sorry about yesterday morning, Mariella. I was unbearable and I have no excuse. I can only say that I meant well and realize now how it must have seemed to you."

She would not cry. She wouldn't spoil this beautiful evening with tears, no matter how angry or hurt she'd been only hours before. The moment he had kissed her cheeks tonight she'd known that yesterday morning hadn't been real. He'd been putting on a show. A very effective one. His apology meant more than he knew.

Their bodies hovered closer together, but Mari resisted the urge to take the one step necessary to be pressed against him. "It was a lot to take in at once, Luca. I was hurt by your behavior, but only because I understood. My story isn't the stuff of polite chitchat. Your reaction made sense."

"But you don't understand, Mari, that's the thing. You don't understand anything."

It was Luca who took the step and Mari found her breasts pressed against the fabric of his suit coat. Without thinking she lifted her hand, the silky fabric of her pashmina drifting off her shoulder and hanging from her right elbow. Her finger traced the hard angle of his jaw. "Then help me understand."

He didn't answer. Instead he reached up and gripped her wrist with his hand and lowered his mouth to hers.

She opened her lips, letting his tongue sweep inside, tasting the tangy sharpness of fine champagne and the dark seduction of cool chocolate.

With his other hand he dragged her closer. The clinking sounds of the dining room echoed behind them, slightly muffled by the seclusion of the alcove. Luca's lips trailed over her cheek to her ear and down the curve of her neck, dropping featherlight kisses that made her weak in the knees and destroyed any resolve she might have had.

"Luca," she uttered, shattered, wondering what it would be like to give herself to a man for the first time since that awful day seven years before. To feel safe and protected. Cherished.

"The first time I saw you, your hair was up." He whispered against her temple and sank her fingers into her waves. "And I knew that moment that one day you'd wear it down and you'd look exactly like you do tonight. *Bellissima* Mariella."

She tilted her head back, feeling her hair slide along her shoulder blades as his mouth followed the curve of her neckline toward her collarbone. There was no reason for him to be touching her this way unless...unless...

Sensation after sensation swirled through her: touch, taste, the feel of his body holding hers and the taste of his lips as their mouths clashed again. His fingers found the zipper at the back of her dress and lowered it a few inches, sliding his fingers along the seam while Mari ached to be touched. It ceased to matter where they were.

But he stepped back.

"I can't do this Mari. It's not fair."

Her body still vibrated from his embrace. "I don't understand."

Gently he reached out, picked up the trailing end of her shawl and placed it over her naked shoulder. "I cannot be with you tonight knowing that tomorrow..."

He hesitated, the silence so terrible Mari thought she would certainly scream. Finally she broke the silence with the one question she had wanted to ask since this morning but hadn't had the courage to hear the answer.

"When will you be back?"

For the first time that evening, his gaze skittered away. "I have no plans to return. Once Paris is looked after, I am returning to Florence for the holiday with my family."

A family that didn't include her. No matter how welcome she'd felt in his arms, it came down to the resounding fact that she was an outsider.

And with that, everything went sinking to her toes.

It was clear. Despite what they'd shared, despite the attraction that clearly simmered between them—she knew that much to be true—there wasn't enough to keep him here. She stood motionless, not sure of what to say. Until she'd asked the question, there had been a tiny flicker of hope. But she'd only been fooling herself. She had *always* known he was leaving, so why was she feeling so betrayed? Why was she feeling like somehow she'd failed?

Because she wasn't ready to let him go yet. That was what he'd done to her. He'd shown her herself and he'd taught her to hope. And in the process he'd ended up breaking her heart by doing what he'd said he was going to all along. Leaving.

She should have known better. Should have thought it through more. Should have realized that in the end they couldn't just go their separate ways like nothing had happened.

"Say something, Mari."

She sat down in the chair. "There is nothing to say, Luca. We both knew this time was coming. I guess I just hoped you'd be back."

"We knew this was temporary."

She couldn't tell him how she'd grown to care for him, to rely on him. It would sound weak and clingy and that wasn't what she wanted. It was irrelevant now anyway. Tomorrow he'd be gone. There was no sense fighting what was obviously not meant to be.

"I thought you'd be around to supervise more of the refurbishing, that's all."

His jaw relaxed a little and he sat, too, turning his chair to face her. "I did, too. The plan was for me to be here several more weeks. But I'm needed more elsewhere...I know I'm leaving the Cascade in capable hands, Mari. And I'm only a phone call or e-mail away if you need help. I have full confidence in you."

The words were hollow. He was leaving the rest of the job to her. He believed in her ability to run his hotel. She supposed she should be happy about that, but instead it simply felt wrong, doing it without him.

"I also spoke to my father today and we're making you the permanent manager of the Fiori Cascade."

It was what she'd wanted, what she'd aimed for since moving to Banff and taking the administration job. Now it felt like the consolation prize. When had she started wanting more?

She looked down at her knees. She knew when. When she'd stopped giving Robert all the power and she'd started living for herself.

"Thank you, Luca. It's...it's what I wanted and I appreciate your faith in me. I won't let you down."

Luca stared at her dark head and wondered how the hell he'd screwed this up so spectacularly.

He should have kept things as he had this morning. Cool and businesslike.

Mari was important to him. Somehow he'd let her become important and that wasn't fair to either of them. And he'd tried to remind himself of that all day. Instead he'd lost his head when he'd seen her come up those stairs looking so elegant in her gown. She moved with an easy, subtle grace that spoke of a little shyness. But Mari was not coy. She did not play games. And he'd wanted her on his arm as he'd never wanted any other woman to belong to him. Not even Ellie.

And he'd kissed her and touched her and ached to make love to her so badly he'd nearly lost himself. Until he realized he didn't have the right to hurt her. And he knew her well enough now to know that to love her once and leave her behind would be the most selfish thing he could do.

The best thing he could do for her would be to give her what she'd wanted from the beginning…the running of the hotel. It didn't matter that he wasn't completely happy himself. His father's summons had irritated him from the first moment. He was tired of being at the beck and call of his father and knew now he wanted more. Yet…his first loyalty was to his family and to the Fiori empire. He'd made his choice years ago. He couldn't have both.

"You could never let me down, Mari, never." No, he was the one letting her down and it hurt like hell.

He fingered the ring on his hand, the gold one with the lily emblazoned upon it.

"That ring is important to you, isn't it." Her voice was quiet now, the soft tones burning through him like a brand. "I've never seen you without it on."

He nodded, resting his hands on his knees. Perhaps if he explained about the ring she'd understand why he had to go. "My grandmother gave it to my grandfather. It went on to become the Fiori crest—beauty, loyalty, strength."

"You have such a history, Luca, I envy that."

"Sometimes it's not all that it seems," he replied quickly, then shook his head. His issues with Fiori weren't Mari's to solve. "I just mean that with it comes responsibility. I have a duty to my family, and it's the life I was given, as well as the life I chose. It anchors me."

"But…"

He had to be very careful. He'd give anything not to hurt her yet he knew he must. He should have known better.

He got up and walked to the end of the table, stopping and closing his eyes for a moment.

When he turned back he held out his hand and she took it. He marveled again at how soft and small hers was compared to his.

"We both knew I wasn't here forever, and we both knew my job would take me away." He inhaled, bracing himself for a small truth he could spare. "We also know that what we shared is special. You are special, Mari."

"You'll forget all about me." She turned her head away. "I'll just be another one of those women you once knew."

"Don't do that. It cheapens what we've shared."

She peered back into his face. "You actually sound like you mean that."

"I do." He lifted her fingers and kissed them. "I care about you so much. And yet…the time has come as we knew it would, and I must go back to my life and you are here in yours. There really is no other choice. I simply want us to part without bitterness, but with a respect for what was between us. For you to know that it…"

He paused. He could get through this. Even if explaining it was one of the hardest things he'd ever done.

He met her gaze with his and made the decision to be as honest as he could. "To know that it meant something to me."

"You are making it very difficult to be angry with you," she choked, half a laugh and half a sob.

"If it is easier for you to be angry with me, then so be it. I only want your happiness, Mari."

And for the first time in his life, he knew it was true. He wanted her happiness ahead of his own. And a flash of fear: never did he want to become his father. Papa had dedicated his life to his wife's happiness only to have it mean nothing. Luca had seen how Papa had been destroyed when his mother left them all. He also remembered the exact moment when his own innocence, his own belief in happy endings was so cruelly broken. And he knew now that it was nothing compared to the power Mari could have over his heart.

She turned away and wiped a finger beneath her lashes, catching the tear before it could trickle down her cheek. How could she explain that somehow her happiness was now bound up in him, too? He was right about everything! How they had both known this time would come. But she remembered being held in his arms as she'd explained about Robert and feeling safe and loved. All that would go with him when he went away. She'd utterly despised him that first day in her office, and now she'd give anything to have him stay.

"And I want yours," she replied. She looked up into his eyes, wishing she were in his arms once more. It suddenly struck her that she wouldn't kiss him ever again and a surge of emptiness engulfed her. All this time she'd fought to go back to her old life. And faced with it now, it seemed cold and pointless.

"Luca?"

His fingers were gripping hers so tightly they pained.

"Will you kiss me one more time?"

She heard the plea in her voice but for once didn't care. She stood and walked into his embrace, felt his hands gently cup her neck as his lips grazed her temple.

She barely breathed, her chest rising and falling in shallow breaths as his mouth toyed with hers, treating her like precious china. Her lids drifted closed as the soft skin of his lips touched the crest of her cheek, her forehead, her lashes before tentatively settling on her mouth. The kiss there shattered her with its innocence and purity. Her wrap floated to the floor but she didn't care. Three little words hovered on her lips but she held them in. There was something tenuous and fragile between them and Mari would not break that connection by voicing protestations of love. Instead she kept the words treasured in her heart until it hurt so much she knew she had to leave before breaking down completely.

"I need to go," she gasped, pulling back and grappling for her purse. "I'm sorry. I can't do this."

She rushed out of the alcove before Luca could utter a single word.

Luca bent and picked up the wrap she'd left behind, turning it over in his fingers. Mariella, with her innocent pleas and courageous heart.

Summons be damned. He'd come here tonight to reinstate the status quo with Mari and all he'd done was stir things up more. He ran a hand over his face. He'd never had this trouble before. He was good at moving on. And he couldn't figure out why this time was different.

He'd simply let himself get too involved, that was all. He was just being a fool, thinking this was love. He folded the wrap and gripped the soft fabric in his hand. Maybe she wouldn't see it now, but his leaving was the best thing for both of them.

CHAPTER ELEVEN

THE house was dark when Mari entered. Times like this her heart always beat a little faster; no matter how much she told herself the past was over, she knew it really wasn't. She'd always have that little bit of fear lurking behind dark and closed doors. It was simple preoccupation that had caused her to forget to leave a few lights burning. As soon as she stepped inside, she flicked on the kitchen light, the instant glow alleviating some of her anxiety.

Luca was leaving. All the turmoil of the past weeks would be gone, like they'd never happened. She was getting her life back. It was what she wanted.

Aimlessly she let her fingers drift over the mail she'd brought in earlier and had thrown on the table in her distraction of getting ready for dinner. Her fingers paused over an odd white-and-red envelope that meant Express service...and opened it to find another letter-size envelope bearing an insignia and the words Toronto Police Service.

She held the letter in trembling hands. After a few minutes of staring at it, she turned it over, ripped the flap and pulled out a single sheet of paper.

It was over.

Mariella sat heavily in the kitchen chair, the paper still

open and shaking in her fingers. Tommy's nails tapped on the floor and he sat beside her, putting his head down on her knee. The warmth from it soaked into her leg, anchoring her to the present.

This was her life. Hers. And now, *hers alone*. The past was gone, melted away in a few short paragraphs.

She had to read it once more to make sure it was true.

Dear Ms Ross,

I am writing to inform you of the death of Robert Langston.

He died on November 25, when the vehicle he was driving left the road and overturned. Alcohol was determined a factor in the crash.

Mari wiped away tears. He was gone. He had no power to hurt her anymore.

She kept reading, the rest scrawled in semi-neat handwriting at the bottom of the page.

I know this isn't procedure, but I wanted to notify you myself. As the arresting officer in the original case, I have often thought of you and your mother. Some cases are like that. I can only say that I hope you are well and that perhaps this might provide some sort of resolution for you and Mrs. Langston.

Sincerely,

Cst. Pat Moore

She remembered Constable Moore. He'd been steady, firm, gentle when questioning her at the hospital and then later when he'd testified at the trial. Somehow, having him be the one to break the news brought things full circle, even through something as simple as a letter. She wondered briefly if her mother was somewhere tonight, reading an identical letter, feeling the same relief…and regret.

Her first instinct was to tell Luca.

Mari looked up, swiping a finger under her lashes. Telling Luca was the last thing she should do, though. They'd all but said goodbye tonight. And he'd dealt with her problems enough. No, it was time to stand on her own two feet. The fact that she could…and be worry free…was a heady thought.

Standing, she walked over to where the painting he'd given her hung. She skimmed her fingers over the surface, the letter dangling from her opposite hand. She knew now what she hadn't been able to put together the day she'd first seen it. She knew now not only that it had spoken to her, but what it said.

It was life; the life in her that he'd awakened. The life she'd fought for every step of the way. And it bled on the canvas and she realized that by living, by feeling, she'd also opened herself up to hurt. And the shocking, glorious realization that it had been worth it.

Tears trickled down her cheeks. She had sworn up and down that she'd moved on from the wounds Robert had inflicted on her, but that wasn't true. She'd only covered them up. And then she'd met Luca and he'd made her face them, and he'd made her fall in love with him.

Only she'd been so crippled she hadn't had the courage to fight for him. Even tonight she'd simply accepted what he'd said—that he was leaving.

She took the letter, crumpled it into a ball and threw it into the fire.

Over the past weeks she'd wondered if she'd only been attracted to Luca because of Robert and what he'd done to her. She'd asked herself if she'd felt such an attachment because he seemed to protect her from her fear. Wondered if she'd been receptive to him because she'd needed him to make her feel safe after Robert had been released.

But it wasn't true, none of it.

As the paper curled and flamed, reducing to ash, she knew without a doubt that she was free. And that freedom did absolutely nothing to release her from the longing she had for Luca.

The painting brought it all back, fresh and new. Luca's smile, his eyes, the way he challenged her and pushed her and kissed her. The way he'd gotten her to talk about her abuse and how she'd come to rely on him.

But the man who had made her life a living hell, who had beaten her mother and then her, who had put her in the hospital for weeks and who had caused years of therapy...was suddenly gone.

She no longer had to look around corners. She no longer had to deal with updates from parole officers, victim impact statements, or worry if he'd try to find her or if he'd come back to finish the job. She'd had no doubt that he was capable of it. And there was a little bit of guilt in the fact that a man had to die for her to feel free of her own personal prison.

She was rid of Robert Langston and she had the job, the life, she'd always wanted.

And somehow, she still felt completely empty.

She straightened her shoulders. As if preordained, the words of the note that had accompanied the painting rang in her ears: "When it speaks to your heart, you know it's the right one."

She'd been so very utterly wrong.

It hadn't been about Robert. It was about Luca. He was the one that spoke to her heart. He was the right one. She could either accept what he'd said tonight or she could fight for him. And she had no idea if she was brave enough to go through with it.

* * *

There had been no chance to speak privately. With Luca planning on leaving so soon, the morning was completely filled with meetings and details. Mari looked across the table at him. The sinking feeling that had begun last night widened to a gulf that threatened to swallow her up.

It wasn't about drapes and fixtures and figures anymore.

She already felt the loss of him and didn't know how she was going to manage it when he was gone. And she had no confidence at all in her ability to convince him to stay.

Something had changed. The sound of his voice as he hashed things over with the plumbing contractor both grounded her and filled her with emptiness. Never, in the seven years since she'd been attacked, had she let down her guard so completely. She'd been so used to reacting to things that she didn't know how to take control and act. And while he thought that giving her control of the Cascade was what she wanted, nothing was further from the truth. A month ago she would have taken it gladly. But now…it meant nothing, not without Luca.

But it wasn't what they agreed, and she had spent the better part of the morning desperately trying to find a time to speak to him in private to tell him that she'd changed.

Luca wound up the meeting and shook hands with the contractor. Mari smiled and offered her hand as well, knowing that from this moment on she would be the one carrying out Luca's vision. She was pleased he trusted her enough to leave her with it. No one had ever shown her that much faith before. But at what cost? She wanted them to do it together. They had thus far and it had changed her life. The last thing she wanted was to go back to her old life. It was drab and colorless now.

The door to the conference room had just closed and Mari turned, wanting to say something and not knowing what. For a few long seconds their eyes clashed and she wished she knew how to put into words what she was feeling.

Mari straightened her blouse. Should she ask him to lunch? Suggest something else? Her stomach twisted.

"That covers it, then." His voice came quietly across the room and she closed her eyes, wondering if she could take the sound of it and commit it to memory.

"Piece of cake," she replied, trying to inject some vigor into her words. They fell flat.

"Mari, I…"

"Luca, would…"

They both halted as they interrupted each other. He held out his hand, offering to let her go first.

Always the gentleman.

"I was wondering if you'd like to have some lunch before you leave for the airport."

"Do you think that's wise?"

Mari shook her head. Would she feel better or worse for it? "Probably not. But I'm tired of being wise."

The air crackled between them. She didn't look away, couldn't. She wanted to remember how he looked in his Italian suits, remember the sound of his voice, the way his cologne smelled. Wanted to imprint everything about him on her memory. She'd thought they had time, but after last night, the sand in the hourglass was slipping away much too quickly.

From the moment he'd stepped up and defended her, something had snapped, had turned around. Perhaps it was ridiculous, but she'd felt part of a unit. That with him beside her Robert couldn't hurt her anymore. She loved him for that. Loved him for giving her safety, and freedom. He was her asylum.

Now he was taking it away, and she refused to accept it. She didn't need asylum anymore. Robert was gone. He had no power over her now. And she wanted Luca more than ever before.

"Mari." He leaned back against the conference table and folded his arms. His lips were unsmiling, troubled. "Mari, if we do this it won't change anything. I'm still leaving."

"Don't."

"Don't what?" He looked confused and his arms unfolded. "Don't say goodbye? Would you rather I left without a word?"

Mari swallowed every single ounce of fear and lifted her eyes to his. "Don't go."

He sighed. "You'll be fine here. You don't need me."

She shook her head. She'd opened the door and damn it, she was going to walk through it.

"I do need you. More than you know. Robert…"

Luca's back came away from the wall. "Robert what? Did he contact you?" His hands gripped her elbows and she tried to ignore the thrill that shot through her, just having him this close. "Is he trying to find you? I swear, Mari, if he…"

Mari shook her head quickly. "No, no! Of course not… Luca, Robert is *dead*."

Luca released her arms and stared at her dumbly. She started to laugh at his confounded expression.

"I'm sorry. But you should see your face."

"How did it happen?"

"Car accident. I opened the letter when I got home last night."

Luca came forward and hugged her, surprising her with the strength of the embrace. "I'm glad. Oh that sounds awful, doesn't it? But I was worried about you. I told Vince…"

Mari pulled away. "You told Vince what?" Vince was their head of security, and she'd hired him herself two years earlier.

"I told him to keep an eye on you. To make sure you were protected."

"And why does that matter to you?"

"How can you ask that?" He nearly exploded, spinning around and going behind the table, putting it between them.

Mari smiled and leaned slightly over the polished top. "I *am* asking that very thing. Why does my protection matter to you?"

"Because I…" He faltered and then scowled. "You know why."

Oh, her Luca. He'd helped her more in a few short weeks than months of therapy ever had. She didn't know how she could ever explain how much that meant. She knew in her heart she couldn't let him go without a fight, so for the first time in her life, she stopped hiding in the shadows and came out to face her fear head-on.

She let all her love for him shine out of her eyes. "Yes, I think I know why." She straightened, folded her hands demurely and said with far more confidence than she felt: "Then stay. I love you, Luca. Stay with me and love me back."

Nothing she could have said could have affected him more. His heart pounded at her words for a brief moment of elation before reality kicked in.

And in some small corner of his mind, he heard voices from his past. Voices asking for love and having it denied. Of going through the motions until it just wasn't enough. He wasn't fool enough to believe Mari actually meant it. And even if he did love her back—which he couldn't possibly— it would be impossible for him to say the words.

"Mari, I don't know what to say." He knew he sounded cold and wished it were different. "I know what we said last night, about it meaning something, that was all true. But love…" His voice trailed away. He couldn't say the words that leaped into his brain. *I'm not ready for love.*

"You've been through a horrible ordeal, and I think if you take time to look at it rationally, you'll see your feelings are misplaced gratitude."

"I do owe you thanks," she agreed, and from the way she

worried her fingers he could tell this wasn't coming easily for her. "For showing me how to feel again, Luca. For forcing me out of my box and into the world again."

Oh, what had he done! His brilliant plans. Never had he considered they would end like this!

"I don't need your gratitude."

She drew back and he tried hard to ignore the hurt his jab had caused. It was written all over her face.

"You're turning me away."

He came around the table and took her icy hand in his. He'd give anything not to be breaking her heart right now, but he couldn't give her what she wanted. He didn't know how. He'd fought against it his whole life! He couldn't just change who he was in an instant, just because she asked him to.

He remembered how she'd cried on his chest and poured out her pain. Hated himself for how much he wanted to stay and hold her that way. She'd made him weak. That's what she'd done to him without even trying. And because he knew she hadn't meant to do it, he placed all the blame firmly on himself for becoming vulnerable to her. And for giving her hope where he shouldn't have.

He squeezed her fingers. "I meant what I said last night. We did have a connection, you and me. We just knew it wasn't forever. I will always look back on this as a fond memory."

He didn't know how to handle her tears, but to his surprise she pulled her hands away from his and straightened her shoulders.

"A fond memory. That's all." She tried a smile but he saw through it to how deeply he'd hurt her and regret had a bitter taste.

He had to get out now before he made a huge fool of himself or hurt her feelings further. There really was no choice. He was due in Paris. He'd given his word he'd be there and he'd never broken a promise to his father, even when he'd wanted to. Yet he couldn't quite bring himself to break ties with the Cascade, either. Changing it, restoring it, had meant a great deal to him and he hated having to walk away from all their hard work. It was more than a project. It was his and Mari's project. At least he knew that he was leaving it in good hands.

"I'm sorry you thought it was more. I'll be in touch anyway, about the hotel. So this isn't really goodbye."

"That's all you have to say?" Her blue eyes blazed up at him, looking for truth and he didn't have any to give.

"Yes, that's all."

"This is goodbye, then. After everything."

He nodded. Perhaps it was kinder to let her go angry. Maybe it would make it easier for her to move on. His stomach burned acidly at the thought, but he carried on. "Yes. I assured my father I'd be in Paris as soon as I could. I'm leaving with Charlie within the hour."

She held out her hand. "Goodbye, Luca. It's been a pleasure working with you."

He took her hand and felt the trembling there.

"Goodbye, Mariella."

She pulled her hand away and retrieved her purse. She walked down the hall and out the doors, through the parking garage to her car.

And once she was inside, she finally let it all go in a rash of weeping. She'd risked it all. And lost.

CHAPTER TWELVE

DAWN wasn't gray; it was pure white.

Mari looked out the window and shook her head. Last night she hadn't given a thought to a storm, but at this time of year anything could happen in the mountains. Should she go in to work, or take a day off? It was a short drive, but her road hadn't been cleared and she wasn't sure her little car could handle the curves. Not to mention the return drive, up the hill. Flakes were still falling in thick pads, obscuring the view of even the parking area above the cottage.

Tommy came back in from his trip to the yard, shaking the snow from his golden coat with great enthusiasm. Mari gave him an absent pat and went to the bathroom. Seeing her puffy eyes in the mirror, she decided that there were advantages to being the boss. She made the necessary call—they'd be running on essential staff today anyway—and decided she could work from home this once. She would log in to the server at the hotel and access all her files, and if anything was pressing Becky could phone.

She put on the coffeepot and calculated the time difference in Paris. It was afternoon there already. What was he doing?

Before long, he'd be in Italy, with his father and Gina and her children. All she'd wanted when he'd walked in that first morning was to get rid of him and retain her manager's job. And now she'd done it. And knew that the sad reality was that yesterday she'd been prepared to give it all up if only he would have said he loved her back.

She was starting on her second cup of coffee when a knock sounded at the door. She opened it to find Luca there, bundled in a heavy parka with Bow Valley Inn embroidered on the front. It was obvious he'd raided the old boutique storage for suitable outerwear.

"Luca!"

"Can I come in?"

She had been so shocked to see him that she'd been standing in the doorway like a dolt. "Of course! How did you… when are…I mean, what happened to your flight?"

He stepped inside, his already tall figure made even larger by the addition of winter boots and the jacket. "I didn't take it," he replied, pulling a black toque off his head and shoving it into a pocket. His normally precisely gelled hair was in disarray from the hat. To Mari, he'd never looked better.

And she was suddenly acutely aware that she stood before him, barefoot and braless in a pair of pink candy-striped flannel pyjamas.

"Oh Lord, excuse me a moment!" Her cheeks went hot as his gaze remained pinned to her flannel jammies.

"Mariella," he said, and her feet refused to move.

Just yesterday he'd said goodbye. He'd taken her protestation of love and had politely, but quite definitively, rejected it. Why was he here now?

"I couldn't get on that plane."

"You couldn't?"

He shook his head. And she frantically tried to beat down the hope that fluttered in her heart. There was no sense getting her hopes up. They'd said all there was to say. He'd been crystal clear.

He unzipped his coat, shrugging out of it. When he stood there with it in his hands, it came to her that she should hang it up for him.

"I'm glad you didn't go into the office today. The roads are horrid."

"Yet you came here." She turned from the closet, amazed at herself for voicing the thought so easily. A month ago she would never have done such a thing. It was more proof just how much she'd changed since Luca had come to the Cascade. She owed him more than he knew, for shaking her out of her life that had been nothing more than self-preservation.

"I have the four-wheel drive. You only have your little car."

"I called in to say I was doing paperwork from home. I should get dressed…"

"Mari wait." The urgency in those two words stopped her.

"I came here to say things. Things I should have said yesterday. But you caught me off guard."

He bent, removed his boots and padded across the hardwood to stand before her.

"My Mariella," he whispered, lifting a hand to her cheek and cupping it.

"Don't," she choked, her eyes drifting shut anyway. "Luca, I can't take it. You said all you needed to yesterday."

But he ignored her, cupped her other cheek and dropped the sweetest of kisses on her eyelids.

"That's where you're wrong. I said too much, and all the wrong things. You, Mariella Ross, made me a coward, and that's not something I like in myself."

His breath was warm on her forehead. "You're not afraid of anything," she whispered breathlessly.

"I'm afraid of you. I'm afraid of me, how I feel when I'm with you. And then on the drive to Calgary I realized how incredibly difficult it must have been for you to say what you did. And how you deserved better from me."

She leaned back, searched his eyes. "And that's why you're here?"

"That's what frightens me, Mari. You make me want to give you more. You make me want to be worthy and I'm terrified of failing. Again."

"I don't understand."

He tugged on her hand and led her to the table and chairs that covered the space between the kitchen and living room. When she was seated he pulled a chair close and sat so that their knees were pressed together, the same way he had the night she'd told him about Robert.

"Mari, you deserve so much more than what I have to give. I hadn't even given a thought to love, and everything that goes with that. You're just now stepping out of the shadow of all you've been through. I said what I did because I was too selfish to end it like I wanted to. I wanted us to stay friends, and if not that, business associates that had shared something great."

His thumbs grazed her knees. "You make me want things, things I haven't wanted for a very long time. I thought I was making the right decision by leaving. For you, for me. I thought my reasons were right. But I was wrong. I had Charlie bring me back. And I spent all of last night trying to fix it."

"You have to go to Paris."

"No, *cara*. I don't."

He took her hands in his. She wanted to believe him, even when his words of yesterday still rang in her ears. He was here and for some reason being here was important. She had to believe that was because somehow *she* was important.

She absorbed how he looked; the tanned skin, the full mouth that didn't smile, the cappuccino-colored eyes that had always been able to see into her. Somewhere along the way he'd become her ideal. She longed to cup his face in her hands and kiss him as he'd kissed her that last night in the alcove.

But he spoke, keeping her in her chair.

"You know that my mother left my father when I was very young. And though we had our father, I felt very responsible for Gina. And for my father at times as well, because I was old enough to see how our mother leaving had hurt him. Time and again I saw him ask for her love and she gave it, but the words were meaningless. He tried in every way he could but it wasn't enough for her."

"Did you think I didn't mean what I said yesterday?"

"I'm not one for words, Mari. I need to be shown…I need to show. I said the words once…remember I told you about Ellie. I gave her my heart. And it wasn't so much that I found her with someone else, you see. It wasn't even that I learned she was only with me because I was a Fiori. It was that I'd trusted her, with my heart. It was my judgment holding me back. And I vowed not to trust it again. So when I started having feelings for you, I gave myself every justification and excuse in the book."

Mari pictured a younger Luca, vibrant with being in love and having that crushed. She squeezed his fingers. "So you focused on work."

"There was never a question of me working for Fiori. It is my heritage. A heritage built by my grandparents. I would feel I had let them down if I hadn't stayed with the company. I would have felt as if I'd let myself down. I love Fiori. It is in my blood."

"I hear a 'but' in there."

He let out a little sigh. "But I spent many years focusing on my job alone, avoiding people. And I didn't know how to have both."

She raised an eyebrow. She had the magazines to prove that his nonavoidance was well documented. Yet she knew he did have it within him. The way he'd held her as she cried proved it. Luca was capable of great feeling.

"Oh," he chuckled, a smile flirting at the corners of his mouth. "I did put on a good show. But I never got close to anyone after Ellie. Never wanted to. Gina got married and started a family and I kept traveling around the world, watching out for our interests. But putting on a front takes a lot of energy, Mariella. You, of all people know that."

She rested a hand on his arm. "Yes, I do. You always seemed so self-assured, Luca. I never would have guessed you were unhappy."

"And I wasn't, not really. There was simply something missing." He put his hand over hers. "I was missing roots. Which sounds foolish considering how I just told you how my family grounds me."

"There's a big difference between coming from roots and finding your own place." Mari gazed into his eyes. "I know I'll never have the former. I never knew my real father and my childhood was a nightmare. But…but I think I've made a place for myself here."

"I know you have. I know it because I could see it from the beginning. You belong here. You fit. You fit in a way I never seemed to." He looked around the cottage. "I can see you within these walls. You've made this into a home, one that is only yours."

"It doesn't mean I'm not lonely."

"Are you lonely, Mari?"

She bit her lower lip and nodded slightly. "Yes, yes, I am. At least I was, and never knew it. You changed that for me."

"I never expected to find you, you see." He grabbed her hand, lifting it and kissing her fingers. "And when I did, I still didn't believe in it. I didn't trust in it. I had feelings for you but I pushed them away, pretended they weren't real. I told myself it was temporary and that I'd go back to Italy and I would be fine. And then you told me you loved me."

"I do love you."

He looked down then, for several seconds. When he lifted his head, he said simply, "You humble me, Mari."

He leaned forward and rested his forehead against hers.

"You, the one who had every right to be afraid…you're the one who has taught me. You're my miracle, Mariella. And I'm terrified you'll get up one day and realize I'm not good enough for you."

Tears clogged her throat. She couldn't imagine being anyone's miracle. Not after where she came from. After all she'd endured.

"I fell in love with you, and I thought you only needed me because of your stepfather."

She swiped a finger beneath her lashes. "Oh, Luca, how could you think that?"

"I wanted to be the one to make you see, but then you did and I couldn't bear the thought of you with anyone else. And I knew you deserved more than me and nothing made sense. Until you were gone yesterday and it all became very, very, clear."

"It had nothing to do with Robert and everything to do with me," she assured him. "You were the first person to see beyond what he'd done to me. The first person to make me forget and make me feel like it didn't matter. The first person to make me feel like the real Mariella. You could never disappoint me, Luca. *Never.*"

He rested his elbows on his knees, his hands on the outside of her thighs now. She smiled; when he'd arrived he'd had a penchant for touching that she couldn't stand and now she couldn't get enough.

"I've grown weary of all the travel. I have a villa, but I'm rarely there. When I was younger it was exciting. I never wanted to settle down. I thought I had life by the tail. But things change. *I* changed. I started to hate having to drop things at a moment's notice. I enjoyed building the business—being here with you and reimagining the Cascade was wonderful. And then…then my father called the morning after you told me about Robert and said I was being sent to Paris right away."

A wistful smile fluttered on her lips. "That was why you acted the way you did?"

"There was so much going on with me. I was suddenly involved with you on a much deeper level than I was prepared for, and it scared me. I wanted to show you that none of it mattered to me. And then on the other hand was my father telling me I had to leave and I resented the order. I'd put him off the day before and it didn't go over well with him. And I wanted to make a change and didn't know how, and it was all tied in with these feelings for my family and for you."

It all was starting to make sense.

"I was certain that leaving was the best thing. I didn't want to be in love. I didn't want to put myself in the position of letting someone hurt me."

Mari couldn't believe she'd ever had that kind of power. Yet here he was, clasping her hands, telling her how he felt and with every passing moment the crack he'd opened in her heart grew wider.

"I've never been in love before, either," she admitted. "But it came down to knowing I'd regret it for the rest of my life. I had to tell you. And I had to ask you to love me back."

His tongue slid out to wet his lips and Mari's pulse thudded.

"I want to kiss you right now," he murmured huskily, "but I need to tell you the rest first."

"Then hurry."

She breathed the response and again she felt the tug between them, the one she hadn't imagined all those weeks ago.

"I spoke to my father. About Fiori, about my discontent, about you. And we talked about my mother."

"You did?"

"A child's wounds take a long time to heal, don't you think? He forgave her long ago. But I never did. I always carried this bitterness with me. It made me jaded. But I need to move past it. If you can move past Robert, surely I can find a way to forgive my mother."

Tears burned on her lashes. "You're not the only one, Luca. I've been thinking about my own mother a lot lately. How can I judge her for making decisions out of fear, when I did the same thing for years?" Their hands were joined and she ran her thumbs along the base of his. "I'm going to try to find her again. I'm pretty sure the police officer that sent the letter will help me."

They sat quietly for a moment, letting it all digest. All the changes in both of them, each brought on by the love from the other. Finally Luca spoke.

"When all was said and done, by the end of the conversation I'd resigned my position and had taken a new one. As vice president and in charge of Fiori's North American resorts. I'll be managing everything on this side of the Atlantic, from one main office."

"How wonderful for you, Luca. What a fabulous job!" She smiled yet wasn't sure how to react or exactly what it meant. North America was a big continent.

He sighed, pulling away and running a hand through his hair. "*Dio,* you're tough." He regarded her with sharp eyes before finally coming out with it. "Would you be happy anywhere else, Mari? Could you leave this place behind?"

Could she do it for Luca? She looked around her little cottage, the home she'd built from nothing. Could she leave it behind her? If it meant being with him, she knew she could.

"Yes."

"But you wouldn't want to. You do love it here."

"Of course I do, but…I'm not sure what you're asking of me. Or what exactly has happened."

"My priorities changed, that's what happened. Don't you see, Mariella? It all fits now. The Cascade, that we built together. The .ew job and you. I love you. *You* give me roots. I don't want to be anywhere else. Just with you. You come first, and everything else after that."

She had no words. Never in a million years had she expected such a thing. At her prolonged silence, he spoke again.

"I love you, Mariella. I love you so much it scares the hell out of me."

"No one has ever put me first before."

"Then it's about time, don't you think?" His smile was tender-soft. "You are my center. Nothing else makes sense."

He gripped the arms of her chair. "Living without you frightens me more than risking my heart. The job is mine. Where I live as I'm doing it depends on your answer."

Tears glimmered on her lashes at his heartfelt words. "I could answer, if you asked me a question."

He let go of the chair and stood briefly, reaching into his pocket and then kneeling before her.

"Marry me. Marry me in the ballroom we recreated together, beneath the antique chandelier we found in the attic. Share your life with me. Let us make a home together here. Please say yes."

He held out the ring. There was no doubt in her mind that it was an antique. She stared at the brilliant emerald in the platinum setting, the glitter of inset diamonds on either side.

"It was my grandmother's ring. She said that the emerald was a symbol of love and hope."

She was staggered to see the sheen of moisture in his eyes.

"Don't you see, Mari? That's what you are to me. Love,

and hope. Two things I never thought I'd ever have, certainly not together."

"Oh, Luca," she whispered. "I love you so much. And I never believed in happy endings. It certainly never happened for my mother. Perhaps that's why I accepted you leaving as I did. I didn't believe in it. But I have a chance now, to believe, to have faith. And I'd be a fool to let it go."

"Is that a yes?"

"Yes. Yes, yes!"

He gripped her fingers, pulled her to her feet and into his arms.

He stamped a single possessive kiss on her lips before drawing back and sliding the ring over her knuckle.

"Mariella. It is only right that she who carries her name wears her ring. Oh, Mari, what a future we have ahead of us."

Mari touched his face. She was safe with him, body and soul.

"Starting today."

"Starting today," he confirmed, and bent to kiss her again.

THE *Balfour* LEGACY

EIGHT SISTERS, EIGHT SCANDALS

VOLUME 1 – JUNE 2010
Mia's Scandal
by Michelle Reid

VOLUME 2 – JULY 2010
Kat's Pride
by Sharon Kendrick

VOLUME 3 – AUGUST 2010
Emily's Innocence
by India Grey

VOLUME 4 – SEPTEMBER 2010
Sophie's Seduction
by Kim Lawrence

8 VOLUMES IN ALL TO COLLECT!

www.millsandboon.co.uk M&B